# Where the River Meets the Ocean

EVELYN CORMIER

Copyright © 2024 by Evelyn Cormier

All rights reserved.

No portion of this book may be reproduced in any form without written permission from the publisher or author, except as permitted by U.S. copyright law.

*To my dad, Micaiah
for being my strength when I had none*

Dear Reader,

In 2018, there was a young girl whose life became stagnant, her dreaming had ceased, her passion for living had dissipated, and the flicker of hope for her future had been snuffed out.

She decided she needed an escape, a distraction, something to pour her broken heart and soul into. So she began to write. Almost at once, a switch flipped inside her, and the words poured out. Pinebrook was built, Estella and Bodaway came to life, and once again, she had a reason to wake up in the morning, a drive to create.

Well, that girl was me. Now six years later, I am proud to present my debut novel, *Where the River Meets the Ocean*.

A couple of people over these last years have been with me each step of the way and deserve to be mentioned here.

Firstly, I want to thank my editor and friend, Taylor Clogston. Thank you for encouraging me and not destroying my will to create when I gave you my terrible first draft! Thank you for coming alongside me and helping me grow, pushing me to become a better writer.

Secondly, I would like to thank my mom for believing in me and always being my first beta reader and biggest supporter. You are the first person I call when I'm stuck in a plot hole, and you always know how to get me back on my feet. Without your persuasion, this book wouldn't even be printed and published right now. So thank you, and I love you.

Finally, I want to thank YOU, the reader! You are who I do this for. I hope you fall in love with these characters and enjoy the story that is so much a part of me, body and soul—the story that brought me back to life.

Much, much more to come.

Evelyn Cormier

# CHAPTER ONE

*Tuesday, May 23, 1854*

Estella

"Why must I marry so soon? I'm barely a day over twenty-one!" We dined in our Boston townhouse as I lamented at the table.

Father frowned at my outburst. "It's your responsibility to marry well, Estella. You should consider it a privilege, as many young women do, I'm sure."

I spread a napkin across my lap. "A privilege to marry before my time?"

Father seemed unamused. "Perhaps your immaturity does not allow you to comprehend that your actions, and the timing of those actions, affect the Wellstone name directly." A maid filled his teacup. "You are young indeed, but many marry far younger. Your mother was but eighteen when our marriage was arranged. Isn't that right?" He sipped his tea, leaving droplets behind in his dark mustache. Maids brought out dinner's main course of roasted pheasant.

Mother lifted a porcelain teacup to her lips. "Yes, Irving, dearest. And I certainly never complained about my duty to marry well." She sighed and looked off towards the young portrait of Father that hung over the dining room mantle. "I was elated to be of age, and oh..." She brought her hand to the scoop neck of her gown and closed her eyes. "What a dashing man your father was. All the eligible ladies in Boston tried to secure him, but it was *I* who prevailed, as I always knew I would. Your father simply couldn't resist me." She smirked. "And I dare say, your own Henry is very agreeable to look at."

I rested my hands in my lap and twisted them about in discomfort. "Whether or not his appearance pleases me is hardly the issue. You and Father are aware of our correspondence, and fully understand the direction we've been moving. In my opinion, it would be unnecessary to rush things along."

"Nonsense!" Father carved the pheasant. "It's perfect timing! You've known Henry since you were a child. I'd say we've allowed sufficient time for you to grow intimately acquainted with one another. I thought you would be thrilled at our approval."

"I'm glad to have your approval, but Henry and I have only been corresponding for a few months. I've grown very fond of him, but I can't say that I'm besotted with the man, let alone love him. Perhaps, granted more time, that love could develop."

"Love?" Mother retorted. "Love is unimportant so early on in a marriage, a mere trifle." She stabbed a piece of meat with her fork and brought it to her lips.

Father laughed. "You will grow in love with whomever you are equally matched with. God is the one who ordains a marriage, is He not? And does He not call wives to love and respect their husbands? Just look at your mother and me."

I shifted in my seat and corrected my posture. "You speak of love like it's a flower to be watered or just a command from the Lord, but

I'm speaking of *love*, the kind that's affectionate and endearing, something to feel secure in. Maybe it's foolishness that I've always imagined myself madly in love with my husband, but I've been a romantic for as long as I can remember."

Mother huffed and pointed her fork at me. "You've had your nose in too many romance novels. They've filled your head with stuff and nonsense."

"Is that so silly? A desire for love within marriage?" I turned my eyes to meet Mother's bewildered expression at my raised voice.

Father's nostrils flared. "Lower your voice, please."

I held back from rolling my eyes. "The thought of being confined within a loveless marriage at the ripe age of twenty-one is unsettling to me. I'm still more girl than woman."

Mother shook her head, the sandy curls arranged on either side bounced about her shoulders. "Your youth has left you with a strong will, my dear. A curse to your future husband, for certain, but a strategic marriage will only help mature you into a proper woman, the woman you were *born* to be." She raised her pointed chin and narrowed her eyes at me. "You always do cause such a fuss over the simplest things. It's quite taxing on one's nerves."

"Maybe I am strong-willed, but would it truly hurt our reputation to wait another year? I have no confusion over my duty to marry well. I only ask that you give Henry and me more time. I believe that he and I could have both love *and* an advantageous marriage."

Father threw his napkin onto his plate and stood. "That is enough, Estella." He smoothed his suit jacket and adjusted a button on the vest beneath. "We have a little less than three days before our trip to New Hampshire. I suggest you don't make things any more difficult than they need be." He stood and towered over us. His dark hair had thinned with age, but his mustache grew full and twitched about whenever he became animated.

Mother kept her gaze at her plate so as to not provoke him further. "Irving, won't you sit and finish your dinner?"

"No, Rachelle, I will not dine with an ungrateful daughter. We have given you everything, Estella. If I were you, I would be prepared for an eventful summer in Pinebrook." He left the room.

Mother stood and her green silk hoopskirt arranged itself. "I should go to him." She sighed. "Your father is right, you know. You are acting very ungrateful. All this excitement is just dreadful on his heart." She looked to the ceiling, as though silently praying for patience. "One of these days he may just give up the ghost, the poor man." She shook her head and left the dining room in pursuit of Father.

I sat alone. Empty chairs surrounded me, and three barely touched plates of food lay steaming. *Ungrateful,* I thought, tucking a loose ringlet of dark hair behind my ear. *This could very well be my last summer in Pinebrook as a girl, and even then Mother is sure to have a rigid schedule planned for me.*

Someone with such a position in society as myself had duties, obligations. I was not blind to that. Yet throughout my entire life, there had been a spark within me, the faintest flicker of a candle's flame. It gave me hope that I was meant for something more than the insignificant life of an unseen housewife in a loveless marriage.

The flame whispered to me that I didn't belong, that there was something beyond what I knew, but there was a much more dominant part of me that desired to belong right where I was. I wanted to please my family, to feel their acceptance. I wanted to snuff out the flame and merely ignore its existence. Maybe I didn't have a choice in the matter of marriage, but I could choose to be reconciled with it. Surely one does not have to sacrifice their individuality for the sake of duty, but I couldn't bring myself to marry a man that I didn't love.

If my family wished me to marry Henry Hamiton as soon as the end of the summer, then I simply needed to force myself to fall in love with him. One summer would have to be sufficient. I've read about women falling in love the very moment they saw their man. With a little time and determination, I could do the same.

# CHAPTER TWO

*Tuesday, May 23*

Bodaway

"These orders won't finish themselves!" I could barely hear the floor manager bark orders to the employees through the humming and clanking of the mill. "What's your name, boy? We don't got no room for idle hands!"

"The name's Bodaway," I shouted. "I was told I'd have work here."

The heavyset manager fingered through a sheaf of papers until he came across my reference letter. "Bodaway, eh?" His eyes met mine. "Well, says here you're a hard worker and won't be any trouble, so I reckon you'd better take on a good strong American name. We don't need no savages working for us causing problems," he said as he moved us into a quieter space. "The other working men won't take kindly to a name like that."

As much as I wanted to scalp this man, savage style, I was desperate enough for money that I agreed to everything he said.

The manager tossed me a work shirt. "You'll be called John now." He nodded to my long black hair. "And you best get that hair of yours cut."

I wasn't cutting my hair for anyone. If anything, I could tuck it into my cap.

The manager lost interest in me and returned his attention to the paperwork under his arm. "Ninety-five cents a day as long as you do your tasks right."

"Fair enough."

"Find empty machines and get to work then. Off with you!" He waved me away like I was a fly buzzing around his ear.

"Won't I need training or something?" I pulled the work shirt over my regular clothes only to find him gone after my head was free. I'd been left in the endless mill with men all around me working to take home food to their families and for the clothes on their backs. There were rows and rows of industrial equipment, looms and spinning machines. I wandered down an aisle and a young boy ran into my feet with a broom.

"Watch it!" he shouted.

I nodded to the boy and continued on.

A voice pierced through the noise. "Hey! You must be new. I can recognize that 'I have no idea what I'm doing' look a mile away!"

I turned to face a stocky, rugged-faced mill worker. "What?" I wondered how anyone could hear a thing in this place.

The man rolled his eyes and motioned for me to follow him. Everyone looked the same, so I focused on his red carrot-head of hair weaving through the crowd of sweating men and women. He led me to an empty power loom. "Welcome home," he said sarcastically, motioning to the machine in front of us.

"Thanks," I said and observed the foreign machine.

"What? Waiting for me to carry you over the threshold?" he joked with a half-smile. When he laughed, I could tell this man was young, maybe in his early twenties like me, but his tired eyes aged him quite a bit. He was definitely an immigrant from Ireland. It wasn't uncommon to see Irish men working in northern mills, especially after the devastating famine in Ireland about a decade ago.

"You'll get used to the noise eventually," he said. He moved to the machine next to me and pulled a wax pencil from behind his ear. Carefully, he scribbled something on the fabric in the power loom. "What's your name?" he asked.

"My name is Bo-" I stopped. "John. My name is John," I said and felt ridiculous.

"How do ya do John," he said in a thick accent, reaching his hand out at me. He obviously did not buy into my new name. "You can call me Art."

I shook his hand, then looked at the machine in front of me. Everyone else seemed like they knew what they were doing, while I felt completely incompetent.

Art studied my confused face for a moment. "You'd be wise to stick with me today."

"I would definitely benefit from some instruction," I agreed, staring at the machines.

He shot me a toothy grin and laughed. "You'll need all the help you can get." He slapped my back. "The big boss is coming back to town and he doesn't have tolerance for anything less than the best workmanship, but you'll adjust quickly." He walked up to the next loom and scribbled on its fabric. "I'll show you the ropes."

I wondered if the big boss was anything like the floor manager who looked like he'd never seen a day's work in his life. I guessed it didn't matter. What mattered was that I had work, which meant money to support Keme, food to eat, and a place to call home for a while.

When I walked through the mill with Art, it was obvious that I looked nothing like these men. Blending in was out of the question, but that was the least of my worries. I'd need to keep my temper under control. A bit of friction and I could be set to flame, a nasty trait that my mother begged me to grow out of as a boy. Though, she was the one who gave me a name that literally meant "fire maker." Maybe the name "John" wouldn't be such a bad change.

Art led me beside several looms. "Are you manning all of these?" I asked, unsure I could keep up.

"Sure am!" he called over the noise. "Look here." He had me come close to him. I watched as he wrote the initials "AM." "Stands for Arthur McCarthy. Whenever you come for your shift, you mark the fabric on each loom that's your responsibility. Easy as anything I've ever seen." He walked back through his line of looms. "The majority of the work here is just making sure the quality of the cloth is top-notch. Like I said earlier, nothing but the best workmanship." He reached out and gently felt the material on one of his looms. "Always check the fabric as it comes from the reed to make sure there are no picks."

"And if there are?" I questioned.

"You disable the machine immediately and find a solution in under a minute."

I pulled my cap down tighter and breathed out. "I don't know if I'm going to get the hang of this, Art."

His eyebrows crowded. "Nonsense! I know it's a lot to take in, trust me. I was you about three years ago now. Laboring in the mill is hard work, but not that difficult. If the loom needs powering down, usually all you need to do is replace the bobbin or filler thread."

"Well, I'm a hard worker and a good listener. I suppose I should pick it up within a week."

"You'd be surprised. I'm willing to bet that in two days' time, you'll be running at least ten power looms all on your own. Just stick with me today." He continued walking me beside his looms, explaining how to run them, what to do if an error occurs, and generally prying into my business.

"So, John, what do you think? Can you handle watching these machines for me while I take a smoke break? The nasty stuff is addictive, and I've been itching for it all afternoon. And besides, you wanna be independent, right?"

I'd known Art for less than one work shift, but it'd been long enough to know he was a humorous fellow who enjoyed a good laugh. I examined his face, searching for any hint of sarcasm, but he seemed serious. "What? You want me to take over, alone?"

"Sure! The only thing you've got to worry about here are the dirty looks." Art peered around us at the other men. "The townies don't care much for newcomers like us, but you look like the kinda guy who can handle himself." He let out a laugh at my worried face. "I'll be right back!"

Art disappeared through the crowded mill, and I turned to face my new reality. The men closest to me glared in my direction. I could see their lips move, saying things under their breath. I tried to ignore them and focus on the power looms. I felt the fabric as it came from the reed as Art had shown me. Maybe I could really do this.

These months had been hard, but I had promised my brother, Keme, that I would make things right again. I went to the next machine, and the next, observing the fabrics. When I reached the last loom, I felt an error in the fabric. Something was wrong. I panicked, my heart thundered in my chest.

I looked around and realized nobody else had noticed my panic. A small sharp breath escaped my lips and I pulled the lever to halt the machine's work. The threads had tangled and the weaving work was askew. I had no idea how to rectify this mistake, but my hands began to frantically untangle the mess.

"What on earth!" Art exclaimed as he approached my efforts.

"Art, I have no idea how this happened."

At this point, the men around us watched as the floor manager approached. Less than one shift and I was already done for. Art was sure to turn me in.

"No trouble? What do you call this then?" the manager shouted.

I clutched the back of my neck, about to give in and confess that I had failed at one of the most simple tasks in this place, when Art piped in.

"Sir, this was my fault. It was my mistake, but it won't happen again." He bowed his head in submission as the other men watched and snickered.

The manager pushed his sleeves up, exposing his meaty forearms, and huffed, "See to it that the problem is corrected." He glanced between me and Art.

Art nodded. "Yes, sir."

The manager noticed the lack of work happening around us. "Back to work! All of you!"

Art could have gotten himself fired, yet he still took my blame. In less than a minute after the manager walked away, Art had his machine up and running smoothly once again.

"Why did you do that?" I asked.

"What? Start the machine back up? That's one of our tasks, you know," he said with a wink.

"No, I mean why did you take the blame for my mistakes? I didn't mean to put you in that position."

Art felt the new fabric coming out of the faulty machine. "I was the one who told you to stick with me today, wasn't I? I couldn't very well throw you to the wolves on your first day." He shrugged. "It was my fault, leaving you alone so soon. Just don't screw anything else up. Next time, I'll let you take the fall." He gave a genuine smile and didn't speak of the incident anymore.

Why would he be so kind to me? I couldn't wrap my mind around it.

\*\*\*

Throughout the rest of the day, doubts whistled through my head along with the sounds of the mill until quitting time: six o'clock in the evening. The men filed out and went home to their families. Some of the younger boys were sure to be supporting their mothers and siblings. I guess when you're poor or unlucky you're forced to grow up sooner than most, but I didn't pity anybody. We all have to do what we must to survive.

Me, I wasn't going home to a wife or a family. I didn't need help from anyone else and I didn't need anyone's pity, either. I had spent most of my life with the Abenaki people on the outskirts of Kennebunk, Maine, or at least what was left of them. Those of us willing to conform to society and share the land stayed, raised families, and lived out our lives in peace, for the most part. The rest of the Abenaki sought refuge in Canada over a century ago.

My grandfather tried to raise me while he could, and he taught me the necessary survival skills to maintain independence. He always reminded me how important it was that I had the capability of living on my own, without the help of white men. I chewed the inside of my cheek thinking about his words. I was glad that he wasn't alive to see me working in a mill, making fabrics of wool and cotton. Lord knows what he would have said if he saw me working under a white man's name, slaving away for some of the richest white folk around.

Art slapped my back again as we walked out of our shift. "See! What'd I tell you?"

"What are you talking about? I followed you around all day like an idiot dog, almost caused you to lose your position here, and definitely did not make a good impression on the floor manager."

Art smirked. "But you're not an idiot dog. You're a smart dog who knows how to learn new tricks. Besides, I wouldn't worry too much about Carson's opinion of you. That old ratbag's going to be replaced the moment the big boss gets back in town."

"Thanks, Art." The sunlight burned my eyes as we left the mill along the dirt road. It seemed awfully busy for such a small town. Horses and buggies passed us by and the streets were filled with mill workers returning home. We were close to the river that powered the mills, and if it weren't for the ringing in my ears, I might have been able to hear its sound. At any rate, I could smell it.

Art took a cigarette from his pocket and lit it. "Want one?"

I put my hands up. "I actually should part ways for the night, but really, Art, thanks for everything."

"Nonsense!" he said. "Let me show you around Pinebrook. The sun's still shining, after all. You'll learn to take advantage of that soon enough." He winked, breathing out a cloud of smoke.

Maybe Art was right. If I was to work in the mills day in and day out, I might as well soak up the last of the evening's sun. "I suppose it couldn't hurt to know my way around Pinebrook."

"That's the spirit," Art said as he put out his cigarette. We walked up the road, shoulder to shoulder with working men until we turned a corner onto a narrow street. "That there is mill housing, which you'll eventually set up in if you are particularly partial to sleeping in a bed." He nodded. "Cheapest rent in town."

I observed the rundown brick buildings and their seemingly tiny apartments. "Looks a little crammed."

"It's no Wellstone palace," he agreed as we passed a filled tavern.

"Wellstone palace?"

"Aye, the big boss, Irving Wellstone. He and his family have a great big house about a mile away. A literal kingdom." He waved his hands all around us. "The kingdom of Pinebrook! Of course, they share it all with the Hamiltons."

My eyebrows crowded together.

"You'll learn of 'em all soon enough."

We continued up the road. As we left the mill housing, the streets that had been full thinned out until only a few people walked about.

"This is it?" I asked, looking around. There was a church at one end of the green, some shops, a general store, and a few unmarked buildings.

"Yep!" Art looked around with me at the whole lot of nothing. "Remind you of home much?" he asked.

"Pinebrook is bigger than where I'm from."

Art rolled his eyes. "Must I pry it out of you? Where are you from, John, and what on earth has brought you to this wretched place?"

"Maine," I said. "I'm from Maine."

"Eh! That wasn't so hard was it?" He nudged my arm.

"I'm here to make money, just like everyone else."

"Aye, of course you are," he said as we walked about downtown Pinebrook.

When we passed by the town bakery, I noticed a beautiful black horse tied out front. "You a horse man?" Art asked as we approached her.

"Sort of." I ran my hand along the horse's side.

"Did you care for horses back home?" he asked. "You've got a tender touch."

My jaw tightened, and I pulled my hand away from the beast. "I used to race horses not so long ago."

"We've got a race track here too! Not much else to do in Pinebrook, as you can see." He patted the horse's side. "You've got to come to the races with me one of these days!"

I wiped the leftover dust onto my pants. I wasn't in Pinebrook to distract myself with the past. I had to stay focused, which meant staying as far away from the race track as possible.

"I'm sure work will keep me plenty busy." I tried to muster a pleasant look, but couldn't quite manage a smile.

"And that's the truth!" He laughed. "But it's good to let yourself have a bit of fun now and again." He gave the horse's rump a playful slap, and the animal flinched.

I raised my eyebrows. "I've had enough fun for the day, Art, but thanks for showing me around Pinebrook." I held out my hand and he shook it with a firm grip.

"Alright then," he said. "I'll see you tomorrow, bright and early!"

"Bright and early."

With a nod, Art turned and began his way back to the mill housing. Maybe I would rent a bed eventually, but tonight I would search for a spot to rest my head in the place that I knew best: the forest.

# CHAPTER THREE

## Friday, May 26

### Estella

I always enjoyed my family's long trips to New Hampshire. The way the leaves changed at the end of summer, the sweet sound of the rivers and the cool breeze they brought to those hot summer days all made me nostalgic for times past. I can't remember a summer we didn't spend in the quaint town of Pinebrook.

My father, Irving Wellstone, owned several textile mills throughout the Northeast. He took it upon himself to visit each location and personally train its floor management during sporadic visits in the early months of the year. But those summer months were always set aside for Pinebrook's Wellstone Mills.

Father referred to summertime as a much-needed leave of absence intended for spending time with his family. He considered those months in New Hampshire as his *respite*—not to mention the only opportunity to get his hands around a good, stiff drink, as Massachusetts was a dry state. Despite his good intentions, no amount of time spent resting with us compared to how much time he spent at the Wellstone Mills.

Usually, I found the ride to Pinebrook exciting, and almost renewing, but now that I knew my summer's true purpose, I was neither renewed nor excited.

The town of Pinebrook, New Hampshire, was so estranged from society that a direct train from Boston simply didn't exist. The train brought us as far as Concord. From there it was necessary to take the stage for hours through no man's land, stopping to change horses at least once before arriving in Pinebrook, our long awaited destination.

If not for the collection of buildings downtown, one might not be able to recognize the property as a town at all. One main road led through Pinebrook, passing through all the most prominent establishments: Town Hall, the orphanage, the mercantile, a church doubled as a school, and of course, Father's mill. Small family-owned shopfronts lined the streets and a manicured green park stretched the whole length of town.

The handful of houses in the area, nearly all the property of farmers or wealthy businessmen from out of town, were set off the road a ways and not easily accessible by foot. The majority of Pinebrook's population lived in mill housing, though I knew some lived in rooms above shopfronts downtown.

In my opinion, Pinebrook was not a town at all, but more of a well-populated village.

The horses drew up to the front steps of our summer estate. In all of Pinebrook, we, by far, had the largest, most expensive property. The common homes were plain to look at and modest in size, but our house was a yellow-painted mansion with a grand, wrap-around porch. Floor to ceiling windows lined the front of the house, and a fragrant assortment of flowers were planted below.

I breathed the sweet country air and smiled at the squirrels chasing each other up the old oak in the front lawn. The sun was only warm, not hot, but to me its shine was the promise of a long summer.

Every time we arrived throughout my childhood, the quiet air felt almost eerie, but I never found it difficult to settle in. I couldn't wait to get unpacked and finish reading *Wuthering Heights* or maybe even start *Jane Eyre* for the tenth time. I brought an eclectic set of books whenever my family traveled to keep my mind entertained with adventure, excitement, and true love: everything my own life lacked.

Our coachman opened the door and set a small wooden crate below the stage for me to step on.

I took his proffered hand, stepped out, and stretched my legs for the first time in hours. I rested my free hand on the back of my bonnet and let the country breeze wash over me, bringing me back to life.

"Today, please," Mother huffed from behind me.

The coachman smiled with understanding eyes, and from the porch a familiar voice called out, "Welcome home!"

Hannah Miller, our housemaid, waited for us on the porch with her seasonal help. She had taken a train from Boston a few weeks earlier in order to prepare the home for our arrival and arrange the help. She had been with my family for longer than I could remember, and likely planned on staying with us until she departed in a casket.

Her long chestnut hair that had progressively peppered with gray, was parted down the middle and tied back in a low bun, and her joyful countenance had aged with graceful lines. As usual, she wore a simple black dress with a fresh linen smock tied around her waist.

It took quite a bit of self control to deny myself the satisfaction of running to Hannah and embracing her. I had missed her so, but of course it would not be fitting. Still, though she was our servant, she and I had a special bond, and I permitted myself to walk calmly with my family to where she stood on the porch. I could not resist taking her tender hands in mine and kissing her cheeks. "How glad I am to see you," I said.

She rested her hand on my face. "I've missed you, my sweet child."

Father, always in a hurry, passed by me as I dallied on the porch. Mother touched my arm. "Estella, you mustn't divert Hannah from doing her work." She nodded to our trunks and bags beside the coach. "There is plenty of work to be done."

I gave Hannah's hand one last squeeze before going inside with Mother, leaving Hannah to instruct the stable hands to water the horses and send the stage on their way.

Father, of course, was already preparing to go to the mill. "Irving," Mother asked, "must you leave us already?" She unpinned her deep purple bonnet. The color of royalty, as Father liked to say whenever he brought her a guilt present upon return from his long business trips. "We just got in," Mother protested while maids shuffled in and out of the open door with our trunks and leather bags.

"Yes, I'm afraid I must go now," Father stated firmly. He had dressed that morning for business in his black suit. He adjusted his cravat and checked his pocket watch as he spoke. "I've been away for the entire year. Frankly, Rachelle, this is my business, and it demands my attention. There will be plenty of time for repose later."

He relaxed his tone and rested his hands upon her shoulders. "You like your pretty dresses and expensive things, don't you?"

Mother gave him a look but didn't protest further as he left to visit his second family.

\*\*\*

Hannah took my things to my room and unpacked my bags. As she helped me settle in for the summer, I caught her staring at me. "I'm awfully sorry to gawk at you," she said, "but do you have any idea how beautiful you've turned out to be?"

Heat crept into my cheeks. "We've only been apart for a few weeks. Surely I haven't changed so drastically."

"Aye, something is different about you. I dare say you've gotten thinner. A wee bit taller, even." She cocked her head as though admiring me.

"And have my eyes changed shades of blue? And what of my freckles? Have they rearranged themselves as well?" I teased.

She smiled warmly. "That would be very unlikely. The freckles that crowd your nose and creep along your cheeks are a constant reminder to us all that there's still the same girl hidden away inside this proper, breathtaking young woman."

"Thank you," I responded, unsure if I should comment further. I didn't know what else to say. I've never considered myself exceptionally beautiful—and I'd certainly never go so far as to use the word breathtaking. Hannah watched me grow up, which meant she'd seen me at my unruliest stages. If she now claimed I had blossomed into a young woman, perhaps there was something to it.

"Are you planning on going to the dance hall this evening?" she continued, her voice wistful, as if she wished she could go. "I could help you choose a gown. We could even pin your hair up nicely, if you'd like! Oh, you'll be the talk of the town, I'm sure!" She clasped her hands together and looked at me expectantly.

"I'll bring it up to Mother over tea, but it's been a long day," I said, sitting on my bed. The thought of going to a stuffy function with a bunch of uptight ladies left me feeling suffocated already, but of course that's what a proper lady would enjoy. I rearranged my skirts and tried to convince myself that I *wanted* to go to the dance. It would be an opportunity to wear a beautiful summer gown... Though I could already feel the corset closing in on my ribs.

I exhaled sharply, rubbing my phantom side pains, and changed the subject. "It's so nice to be back again." I looked about the room. "We spend such little time here in the grand scheme of things, yet I always find that this place feels like home—more so than Boston does at times. Isn't that strange?" The sunlight through my window lit the cream colored walls all around me, embracing me with its rays.

"Not strange at all. It really *is* nice to be back." Hannah smoothed out the wrinkles on my bed and gave my chin a playful squeeze before leaving me to myself.

It wasn't until I was alone that I noticed Hannah had left my mahogany wardrobe doors open. The colors of my gowns clashed against each other and popped out at me as I approached them. I rubbed the fine fabrics between my fingers and wondered if Henry Hamilton would be at the dance hall that evening.

My muscles tensed. For many summers I had endured my friends' good-natured but relentless chaff about Henry Hamilton. In their eyes, it was obvious that he fancied me, but that was hardly a notion I shared. When we were all children, Henry had been terribly rude to me while seeming to consider it a lot of good fun, something I had by no means forgotten.

Of course, people mature as they grow. For that matter, Henry had grown into a handsome man. But over the many summers I'd spent in Pinebrook, I'd often overheard rumors of his haughty reputation, and observed firsthand a peculiar attitude that seemed to me to go beyond the arrogance which young people born into money often display.

Henry carried himself as though *everyone* else were below him, a trait I had noticed at times in my own parents' attitudes. I, for one, was not interested in recreating Mother's marriage. I had no desire to endure life with a husband who was married to his work first and to his wife second.

Henry was older now, of course. I never detected any air of superiority in his letters, only a gentle sweetness that lent itself at times to flirtatiousness, but never in a presumptuous or inappropriate manner. It was evidence to me of a newfound maturity of character. Nonetheless, I had no desire to rush into a marriage to someone I had only known in person as childishly cruel and arrogant even to his equals. He might be changed, but a man's words and his actions can be very different. Why commit to marriage now?

Against my better judgment, my romantic flame flared in my chest. I wanted a marriage that I could be valued in. I desired to feel heard. I wanted a love to consume me like in a fictional novel, full of adventure and freedom.

I closed the wooden doors of my wardrobe, locking those uncomfortable, sinful thoughts inside with the dresses.

***

That evening, before I could make up my mind about the dance, Mother made it for me. In the brief moments of our hasty teatime she informed me that I was not going to the dance later that evening, nor any other evening. She would require all my attention for the planning of a ridiculous party for my birthday. We celebrated it in New Hampshire every year with an intense evening at our home, filled with Pinebrook's finest. This was the first year she had asked me to help with the preparations, claiming that all my other birthdays paled in significance compared to this one.

"What about visiting Lillian? Please let me go to her tonight!" I pleaded as we sat on the chaise lounge in our parlor. The crystalline, candle-filled sconces shone all around us as our grandfather clock ticked just past seven.

Mother took one last sip of her tea. "At this hour? Absolutely not."

"But Lillian is practically family! It's not as though I were barging in on a stranger, uninvited."

"I don't care who it is, you're not going anywhere tonight. Goodness." Her eyelids fluttered. "It's been a long day, Estella, and you and I both have another full one tomorrow."

I sighed and leaned back in the most unladylike fashion onto the velvet upholstery. In a small way I felt a prick of relief that I didn't have to attend any events, at least for the time being, but I longed to confide in Lillian about Henry.

"Do sit up straight, Estella." Mother barely had the energy to pester me as she let out a small yawn.

As I sat up, I felt exhaustion overcome me as well. After a full day of traveling and settling in for the summer, I could retire to my room without any protest from Mother. I excused myself and retreated to my room as my mind drifted to the duck feather pillows and down comforters that Hannah had turned down for me.

Thinking back to her comments about my appearance made me dread the idea of an evening full of similar comments from my parents' guests, each one of them with their wide eyes fixed on me. Mother and Father would insist on something new to wear that night. Something simply *eye-catching*, shipped from a far away city, costing a small fortune. Everyone at the party would know it, exactly as Mother desired.

I had no particular reservations about feeling beautiful, but the attention that my party would bring plagued me with anxiety. I sat at my vanity and looked at my reflection for a moment, trying to see myself as someone else might. I gathered my dark curls into a bunch on the top of my head and tilted my chin down. *I did look older,* I thought. *Maybe even pretty.*

\*\*\*

Early the next morning, before even Hannah had stirred, I slipped out of the house undetected to wander our estate grounds like I used to as a child. Those few moments in the beginning of daylight might be the only time I would have to myself the entire day.

I looked up at the early gray sky, blending with shades of soft pinks and golds, great cotton-like clouds floated above effortlessly. I walked with long, slow strides through our property, heading for its edge. The quietness of the early morning settled around me.

I passed the place where our horses would later graze in the lush greenery and climbed the grassy bank where our house was just out of sight. The maintained part of our estate turned into an unkempt field, and I bunched my skirts as I continued. When I reached the crest of the bank the sweet scent of lilacs filled me completely, a smell with the power to send me back through time in an instant. Just ahead, at least fifty lilac bushes lining the forest were in full bloom. I took a great breath of air and held it in my lungs.

Approaching the forest's edge, I noticed that the mouth of my usual trail appeared overgrown and untouched since the last time I'd walked it. Various trails led from our property all the way down the Sugar River and even as far as the mills. They had been here since Creation, I was sure, and I liked to believe that they held mysterious stories of the past. It pleased me to think that my dearest Lillian and I were the only humans to know of this sweet escape now. We alone shared it with the wild.

My path was just wide enough for one person. I took to it and let the woods instill in me the calmness and carefree spirit of a child, as though I *belonged* amongst the trees and the river. I remembered a time when I roamed this place with Lillian, running, climbing up trees, and splashing in the shallow parts of the river. Time passes, but nostalgia remains forever.

I wasn't a mile into the trail before my troubles didn't seem so daunting anymore. It was amazing how insignificant one could feel surrounded by God's creation. Tall pines and hemlocks swayed slightly above me, while loose needles fell to the ground. No scent compared to pine mingled with the sweet decay of the Sugar River.

Just when I had become comfortable, a frantic rustling off the trail to my left shook me to my senses. I turned abruptly and faced the direction of the rustling. Nothing caught my eye, but the sound of heavy movement continued, too heavy to be that of another person. Whatever it was, it was not concerned with being quiet. It wanted me to know its presence.

I had never been scared of anything before, and I wasn't going to start today. Father used to brag about me as a child, how fearless I was, how even as a babe I was abnormally curious.

I snuck towards the noise and left the familiar dirt trail behind me. The brush had grown in for the summer, making it difficult to navigate. A few prickers lanced the skin of my hand, drawing blood. "Oh for goodness' sake!" I whispered and brought the tiny cut to my mouth.

I heard the movement again and refocused, pushing back a few branches to get a better view. All at once, my breathing stopped. Before my eyes stood a horse, a wild-looking mare, dusty white, though very disheveled. Yet even her unruly appearance couldn't take away from her majesty.

It didn't make any sense at all for a wild horse to be roaming the small town of Pinebrook. Everyone kept great care of their horses. If one broke loose, it wouldn't look as unkempt as this one, and upon its disappearance someone would surely go looking for it.

The sound of light footsteps through dried leaves and twigs broke only a few feet from the horse, and quickly grew louder. A tall silhouette appeared, about the height of a man. Hoping not to be seen, I dropped to the ground, not thinking of all the insects that could be crawling up my legs or how the dirt could ruin my dress.

Without warning, the horse darted past me with surprising speed—so frantic, she nearly trampled me. I didn't move. For the first time in my life, I was truly frightened.

I could see the man from my place on the pine-needled ground. He had long black hair, golden bronze skin, and the most striking face. I'd never seen one like it. I let out a sharp breath, not realizing I'd been holding it in for so long. Seemingly in response, he turned in my direction, catching me off guard. His black eyes searched beyond the brush that hid me, never meeting my intrusive gaze. What was this man doing here in these woods so close to Pinebrook? My fingers tightened into a fist, but I kept still.

He looked around, clearly knowing that *something* close by had spooked the horse, but did not approach my hiding place.

I swallowed hard and closed my eyes, wishing the action could make me invisible. When I opened them again, he was gone. *Who was that man,* I thought, *and why was he here?* I rose and violently brushed my skirts free of pine needles before starting back home with greater speed than before.

I could never tell Mother about what happened. Most assuredly she would forbid me ever to leave the house again. I looked down at my dress, covered as it was with dirt and pine pitch. What was I going to say?

# CHAPTER FOUR

## Saturday, May 27

### Bodaway

I woke before light to cold feet and the sound of robins. The fire I had built the night before was nothing but embers, but with some dried leaves and kindling it would catch flame once more. I sat up and brushed dirt from my elbows and forearms. Nausea nagged at my stomach, reminding me that I was starving. Over the last day I hadn't eaten much more than a few berries and a trout I caught in the river, but I had set some rabbit traps the night before.

The forest around me was still dim, but the hot coals left in the fire cast an orange glow around my camp. I retrieved my sap-stained work boots, and tied them snugly.

The forest air, damp and fresh, filled my lungs with its coolness. I tried to savor these fleeting moments of clean air as I set off to check my rabbit traps. I couldn't help but shoot a prayer up to the heavens asking for a good meal this morning.

I had set them close to camp, so close that if it had been broad daylight I might have been able to see my traps from the place where I'd slept. I pushed through some brush and thicket. To my great relief I saw a rabbit's figure wriggling around at the sound of my approach, trying to break loose from the twine noose before I could snatch it.

Silently and respectfully, I knelt and took the frightened creature into my hands. My grandfather taught me how to make this part quick and painless, but that never made it easy. I laid the poor rabbit on the forest floor and set a sturdy branch across its neck. Then I placed my feet firmly on either end of the branch and gave the rabbit a swift tug upward until I felt its neck give, signaling death.

I slung the limp rabbit over my shoulder and retraced my few steps to camp, gathering firewood and dried leaves as I went.

Moments later I crouched by the fire and tucked the kindling around the embers. I blew across the outer edges and watched the embers grow into a spreading flame. My grandfather had given me a pocket knife many years ago, *a useful tool*, he told me. I used it to cut, bleed, and dress the rabbit, then roasted the meat over my small fire.

I picked every last bit of cooked meat from the bones with eager fingers, for once eating until I was satisfied. By the time I had finished my tough, gamey breakfast, the fire had burned down again to ash and coals. I stomped out the lingering flames, took up the rabbit carcass, and began for the mills with a single hour left for myself.

The light just started to peek through the pines. I was amazed at how peaceful it was here, while just miles away was a hectic mill and hundreds of men ready to begin the day's labor. Pinebrook was no city, but there was work, and work meant money to a lot of people.

It was a long trek to the mills on foot, but easy enough. All I had to do was find and follow the river. A good mile away from camp, I discarded the rabbit bones for some coyote to ravage later and continued along a dirt footpath for another quarter mile.

Finally I heard the rush of water and caught the glint of sunlight reflecting off the river through the trees. I left the path to take a better look. Great trees grew on the bank over the river, their roots stretching in all directions.

I navigated down the bank using trees to steady me. The rocky shore was narrow and damp, it shifted beneath my steps. *The Sugar River*, I thought as the water lapped my boots. I cupped the icy river water in my hands and rinsed away the dried rabbit blood and dirt that caked my skin.

The shallow water ran over pebbles and stones, making them smooth enough for skipping. Some sparkled like treasures in the sun, and I picked one up. Flecks of minerals shone on its surface as I turned it over in my hands.

When I was a boy, my brother Keme would sit on the river's bank while I tried my luck at fishing with handmade nets. He would ask me to gather any rocks I found interesting or unique for his collection, and of course I complied. I called to mind one summer in particular when I was fourteen and Keme was only eleven.

*Keme threw his head back in laughter as a fish fell right through my handmade net. I turned to his seat on the bank behind me. "Really? Why don't you come give it a try." I refocused on the river and my net. "It's not as easy as it seems." I concentrated on how the fish moved, how cautiously they swam over my net. I held my breath, and kept still. In an instant I would pull up a net filled with trapped fish, but it had to be the right moment.*

*Just then a stone splashed the river next to me, scaring the fish away. "Keme!" I turned and threw my net to the ground, but my* brother only giggled more. "That's it! Get down here and pick up the net."

Keme stood and wiped off his gray trousers, the pair that used to be mine. His frame, similar to my own, resembled that of our father, but unlike mine, his sweet face held a strong resemblance to our mother's. They even had the same dimple on their right cheek. When I looked at Keme, I couldn't help but remember our mother and what she would say to me if she saw me yelling at my brother. Taking a deep breath, I continued in a more gentle voice. "Keme, you don't have to try if you don't want to. Just let me focus."

Keme waltzed down the bank, snatched my net, and stood where the water came up to his knees. I crossed my arms and watched him carefully lay down the net at the bottom of the river. Then, with a sly hand, he dropped something into the water. He waited a moment, squinting at the river below him, and then in one fluid motion pulled the net up.

Keme looked at me with the biggest grin and a net full of fish. "You're right, brother, it is harder than it seems," he said, walking out of the river with his dinner.

"How did you do it?" I asked him, dumbfounded.

He smirked. "You have to learn to be patient... and smart!" he laughed, pulling out the inside of his pocket, revealing a handful of bread crumbs. "Grandfather taught me that trick. If you spent more time with him, and less time trying things your own stubborn way, you might learn a thing or two."

I shook my head and ruffled his hair, unable to stay mad at him for long.

Keme craved the love and approval of our grandfather, always following him around, always willing to listen to and obey him. For his part, my grandfather admired Keme's desire to learn the old ways. I could admit, looking back, that I had been a bit jealous of their relationship, but now I couldn't wish for anything more than Keme's happiness. I owed him my life, and he deserved a much better brother than me.

I slipped the stone into my pocket.

A sudden noise broke in the forest, piercing through the roar of the river. It was a noise I would recognize anywhere. A horse was loose.

I lifted myself slowly and climbed back up the bank to the trail. The bank was muddy, giving me a firm grip and strong footing as I moved upward. A lone birch, just wide enough to get my hand around, sat at the top of the bank, and I used it to pull my weight to level ground once more.

I stood silently, my heartbeat quickening, my ears straining for the familiar sound. The rustling started again. Without hesitation, I pushed my way through branches and stomped through dried leaves and tree roots, completely forgetting to be quiet. The next sound I heard was the horse's heavy breath. The great beast's form appeared through the dense and seemingly endless thicket.

I gently clicked my tongue the way I'd seen my grandfather do once when he tried drawing a spooked horse near to him. Sure enough, the horse showed its head, its big beautiful head. That was one thing I took away from my time with him, at least. I smiled. I had done *something* successfully.

It was a massive white horse. *There's no chance this horse could be wild, could it?* I wondered. The horse looked at me with tender, wild eyes. Its mane was tangled and covered in burdocks. One step at a time, I approached it. The twigs that cracked beneath my feet prompted it to take one slow step back.

The early morning sun rose higher. Its soft light settled on the horse, revealing that it was a mare. She had what looked like a gash on her hind leg, likely from a trap of some sort.

I could treat her if she'd let me. I could even find her owner. But at that moment, she needed attention. I raised one hand towards her, as if to let her know my intentions were honest, and I swore she understood me. I moved closer and closer until my hand barely brushed her soft nose. Her eyes cried for help.

I glanced at the sun again. I needed to be at the mills by six, and didn't have much time left. My fingers traced the horse's white, dirt stained face. I couldn't leave her there, injured, alone.

As I pondered what to do with this mystery horse, a new noise broke in the woods. I sensed the light, consistent rustling of leaves underfoot to be the movement of another person, but before I could breathe, the horse was gone. She limped as fast as she could manage away from me. I almost chased after her, but what good would that do? I looked in the direction the noise had come from, but could see no other person after all. I shook my head in disbelief. Keme was right. I should've spent more time with our grandfather. Now look at me. I couldn't even approach a horse without spooking it.

\*\*\*

## Estella

The door at the kitchen entrance groaned as I shut it behind me. My heart still raced and my breathing was ragged from the excitement in the forest. I thought for sure the pots and pans hanging from the ceiling would rattle, feeding off my adrenaline, but they hung silently in their respective places.

Thankfully, I didn't have to wonder about Mother's whereabouts. She was sure to be in bed, fast asleep for another hour or so before waking at 7:15 as she did every morning.

Just as I breathed a sigh of relief, Hannah walked into the kitchen carrying a tray of tarnished silver. After one look at me, she seemed about to explode with questions. With a quieting finger to my lips, I took the tray from her and set it on an empty counter top. "Not here," I whispered. I took her hand in mine and led her through the kitchen and up the narrow servants' staircase.

The hall at the top of the stairs was too open and vulnerable, too risky for me to share the details of my morning. Though the other help did not live in our home, they often began their shifts as early as six, and might easily overhear us.

I guided her down the hall into my bedroom and quickly shut the door. "What on earth happened to you?" Hannah finally blurted out, looking at me with concern, but also curiosity.

I've always been closer to Hannah than to my own mother, and I've felt I could tell her things that my parents wouldn't understand, yet I was still hesitant to bring up the Indian man. "I was walking in the woods, and… well… I came across a couple of wild animals. To shorten a long story," I said. I tried to avoid the truth of the matter, but guilt jabbed at my stomach for referring to the Indian man as a wild animal. "Somehow, I managed to find myself on the ground." I revealed my scrapped hands from the thicket. "After that, I ran home with all my might, hence the filthy clothes and glistening brow." I sighed, as though I'd just told her my whole life's story.

Hannah looked at me for a moment, then laughed. Her always-pink cheeks flushed brighter, and the pleasant wrinkles that stretched over her face from years of contagious laughter grew deeper.

I tried to keep the smile from my lips. "Mother must never find out I've ruined another dress by running off into the woods like an unruly child. She'd have quite the fit." I caught a glimpse of myself in a mirror across the room. My disheveled reflection made me jump a little.

"I'm not even going to ask how often you sneak out before the dawn." Hannah rolled her eyes. "It's better that I don't know. But I'd say the first thing you need is a good old bath and a set of fresh linens if you still plan on joining your family for breakfast in a presentable way!" She smiled, shook her head, and left to prepare the bath for me. I could still hear her softly chuckling as she moved down the hall.

\*\*\*

Later that morning, before Father left for the mills, we were to eat our traditional first and last breakfast as a family. Every year, Hannah prepared a breakfast of fresh eggs, sausages, blueberry muffins, coffee, and a variety of fruits. I suppose we had this breakfast to maintain the idea that we were focused on family while summering in New Hampshire. Every morning after the first, Father was usually off to the mills or paying attention to his champion racehorse, Black Magic, before Mother and I even sat at the table.

Father already had his nose in the paper, and Mother salted her eggs. "Good morning," I said.

"Good morning, darling," said Mother. "Have some breakfast! We have a lot to talk about." Father peered over the paper and scratched his mustache as he cleared his throat. "Estella, don't you look elegant today," he said, sounding as though he didn't know how to broach the real topic at hand.

"Thank you." I couldn't help a smile from spreading across my lips when I thought back to my appearance just an hour earlier. Hannah appeared with fresh coffee and gave me a wink.

Upon Father's request, Hannah had saved Pinebrook's weekly papers leading up to our arrival. He retrieved a new fold of papers from the stack at his side. "How terrible!" he exclaimed, squinting at the paper's front page. "There was a nasty fire just fifteen miles north about two weeks ago." He shook his head. "Practically nothing survived the fire's clutches, not even the farmer. One lucky horse broke free, but nobody's seen the blasted thing."

"How sad." Mother stuffed her mouth with a muffin.

"The poor thing," I said, looking at the scraped hands in my lap, my mystery horse suddenly much less mysterious. I shook my head slowly. "And to think of the animal just wandering about, starving all these days. Makes me lose my appetite."

Mother shot me a disapproving glare and changed the subject back to me. "Estella, we really must plan your party as soon as possible. It's not something that should be put off any longer." She looked to Father, urging him to continue as another maid took away his plate.

"Yes, my dear. Shall we pick a date now?"

I shifted in my seat to face him, leaning in closely, hoping to appear exceptionally attentive. "Please, Father, tell me more about whatever is in that paper of yours, or anything at all, really."

He took a sip of coffee. "Must you really act like a spoiled child?"

My silver spoon made a loud clunk as I set it on the table, and Mother jumped back into the conversation. "The sooner your party, the sooner we can secure the engagement!" Her eyes were wide with excitement. It was obnoxious how she used "we," as though we were all in this together.

"I suppose you mean to say, the sooner everyone knows I am of age, the sooner we all benefit from the loveless fortune I will marry into?"

Father set his paper down in his lap. "Have we really coddled you so, that you have become such an ungrateful brat?"

"I am no such thing!" My palms began to perspire. "I'm just a girl, transitioning into a woman, with essentially no time to adjust from one day to the next."

"Well," Mother reprimanded, "it is high time you took on your responsibility and duty *as* a woman, without all this fretting and moping about."

"How about we strike a deal?" Father asked, crossing his arms over his chest—a true business man. Mother appeared unamused.

Father sighed. "I know how you've longed to see Lillian. Though you may not believe it, I do wish for your happiness." He actually sounded genuine. "I know this has been hard on you, Estella, I do. So, I propose we set a date for your birthday celebration, and in return for this, I will have Hannah bring you to see Lillian as soon as this afternoon."

I twisted my napkin in my hands beneath the table. My party was inescapable. In fact, if I persisted in pushing against the idea, Mother would no doubt plan an even grander party to spite me, and I would not be allowed to visit my sweet Lillian today.

"That seems reasonable enough," I said softly, without looking up from my plate.

"Oh chin up, darling," said Mother cheerfully. "How about a week from today? That will give me plenty of time to arrange everything. The front rooms will need to be completely rearranged!" She produced a pencil and a piece of paper and jotted down all her grand ideas.

"I have no objections to that."

"Good girl." Father smiled, then added, almost reluctantly, "Another matter I'd like to discuss with you. Your mother and I think it appropriate for Henry Hamilton to be your escort for this event."

I felt my face flush.

Mother babbled, "Oh, I can't wait to see the look on everyone's face when they see you and Henry together. The two of you will make the most divine match." My whole future was planned out for me before I had time to finish my sausage and coffee.

Father joined in. "He's a fine young man, very fine, and intelligent too. I've even decided to make him the new floor manager at the mills while I'm away." He said this to Mother, as though to impress her. To his apparent delight, her face brightened.

"Irving, how splendid! He is in very capable hands now." She nodded to me and added, "A fine, upright, godly man for our beautiful child." She sighed in absolute bliss.

I shook my head in disbelief. "I might not go as far as to call him a man of God. Haven't you noticed his arrogance? It's been plainly obvious since childhood, and I know for a fact that pride isn't something that one grows out of so easily."

Father stood from the table and wiped the crumbs from his suit. "Though I am aware that you speak from a place of ignorance, others may not regard your opinion so kindly. A proper Christian woman would never dream of slandering a well-respected man like Henry. You'd do well to remember that. Besides, I thought you were fond of the boy?"

He was right, I couldn't prove that Henry had carried his arrogant ways into adulthood, but my stomach still knotted and my lips tightened. "I am fond of him, but I don't know him intimately enough to know his character for certain, that's all."

Father rolled his eyes and checked his watch. Clicking it shut, he tucked it away. "Then I'd advise you not to speak of it so freely. I should think you owe him the benefit of the doubt." He walked around the table to Mother and kissed her cheek. "Ladies, I'm off."

"Yes, yes, we know." Mother's emerald earrings dangled about as she fiddled with them.

He nodded to me. "See to it that Hannah takes you to call on Lillian this afternoon." He left for the mills.

With this happy news still lingering inside me, I released my fingers from the unintentional clenching that I had adopted over the course of breakfast. I rubbed them back to life while Mother whispered to herself, intently drawing a map of the front rooms as she planned to arrange them for my party.

I sat back in my chair and drank the last of my coffee. For all I knew, Henry could be just as unnerved as I at the accelerated rate of an engagement. Aside from silly childhood antics, he really hadn't done anything to deserve my hostility.

His family was almost identical to mine: a wealthy, passive father and an overbearing mother. Even as a child I recall feeling uncomfortable and almost frightened around Alice Hamilton. I could only pray that Henry and I might never recreate our families' picture of marriage. My mother was in no position to quell my anxieties. I knew it wouldn't matter to her what kind of man Henry turned out to be, as long as he turned out rich.

I didn't want good fortune and name to dictate my social standing in society. What made Alice Hamilton, or my own mother any better than our housekeeper, Hannah? Their money? Their charities? Their prestigious names? Frankly, I had more respect and admiration for Hannah than for anyone else. She treated each person with the same amount of respect, kindness, and love, whether or not they were born into a family in high standing. That's how I wanted to be, how I wanted Henry and me to be. As long as I remained optimistic and determined that such a future was possible, there was hope for us.

\*\*\*

"Thank you." I smiled at the coachman. He gave me his hand and helped me into our coach parked at the front of the house. He nodded to me as Hannah followed. She adjusted her black skirts as she sat, then proceeded to tighten my bonnet.

The coach moved along the road to town and the sun shone brightly as I leaned out of the window in the most improper way and let the wind brush my cheeks. Hannah tugged on my skirts. "Estella!" she laughed in surprise. "Sit, my dear. You could fall right out into the streets and be trampled by horses, or break your neck." She shook her head. "Quite the handful you are."

I flashed her an adventurous smile. "Oh stuff and nonsense! Let me live."

"I'm trying to help you live long enough to see twenty-two."

I wrapped my arm around hers and rested my head on her shoulder. "You always do look out for me, don't you?"

"Yes, my child." She sighed and rubbed my gloved hand with hers.

The town of Pinebrook was only a few miles from our estate. The coach pulled us along the familiar road, oak trees lining the edges and lush farmland on either side. It wasn't long before the Pinebrook church steeple peeked through the trees, then showed itself completely as we rounded the bend.

There was a great strip of green around which all the shops and establishments were crowded. The church at one end, and the orphanage at another. Pinebrook Town Hall was a brick building with white columns along the front, set adjacent to the church. We turned on a small dirt road just past Town Hall, at the end of which Lillian's home lay.

Our coach came to a stop before the Sterlings' plain center-hall house, a small home with black shutters and a blue-gray slate roof. Though it was simple, it was much nicer than any home they would have lived in if it weren't for Father's kindness.

About ten years earlier, Thomas Sterling, who had been a loyal employee to Father for over twenty years, died suddenly in an accident at the mills, leaving his wife a widow and his young daughter fatherless. Generously, Father vowed to look after the wellbeing of Sarah Sterling and her daughter Lillian, providing them with this house and a modest stipend. Lillian and I became fast friends until we were nearly inseparable. Given the circumstances, despite our differences in social standing, Father allowed the friendship to continue.

Hannah and I climbed from the coach, our shoes shuffling in the gravel.

"I promised your mother I'd have you home within an hour," Hannah said as we approached the front door. I didn't mind that the visit would be brief. I was glad to see Lillian at all. Hannah knocked and we stood, waiting.

A young maid opened the door, but before she could speak, a familiar small, but lively figure pushed past her excitedly. Lillian's doe-like eyes lit up at the sight of me, her braided mahogany brown hair hanging over her shoulder. She dressed comfortably in a loose-fitting gown without her usual crinoline petticoat, and her sleeves fell effortlessly to her elbows as she reached her arms out for me. "Oh Estella! It's really you, isn't it?" Her embrace was warm and welcoming.

"How I've longed to see you, and tell you so many things," I murmured with a sigh of relief.

She drew back, resting her hands on my shoulders and simply looked at me as we stood in the doorway. "Nellie, if you would, bring us some tea outside in the garden."

The timid maid nodded and Hannah followed her into the house. "One hour," Hannah reminded me, and then disappeared.

Lillian's smile grew even larger and her brown eyes sparkled. She clutched my gloved hand. "I'm so glad that you and your family are back. It's been such a bore these past weeks, just waiting for you to arrive. I've tried to keep myself busy at the orphanage, but it seems all I've done lately is write in my journal! Without you in town, I've had no one to share my gossip—my mother never took a liking to it, the sensitive thing. The talk of the town is wasted on her, and it does me little good in the pages of my journal, either!"

"Oh," I laughed, "I'm sure it hasn't been all *that* dull. Though," I added, "perhaps if I were left with only my mother to confide in, I might go mad with boredom as well."

A mysterious smirk spread across her lips, as though she had something secret to add. "Come, shall we enjoy the gardens?" She closed the door behind us.

"Nothing sounds more perfect." We linked arms, and practically skipped through her property.

The gardens were lavish this summer, filled with flowers of every color and scent. Even the grass was vibrant and soft beneath our steps. "Lillian, I've never seen your gardens quite so beautiful." I looked around in wonder.

"Yes, I know! Mother says it was because of the Indian summer last year, but I think it's just a sweet gift from God. Why must there be a scientific explanation for simple beauty?" She smiled as she sat at a granite bench, and I stood at her side.

Lillian always held a hidden innocence behind her eyes. When you were in her presence, you couldn't help but be warmed and at ease. I sat with her and removed my white gloves, setting them in the lap of my pale, rose-colored skirts. It was an effort to rid myself of any visible vexation. I leaned back in my seat and focused my attention on Lillian and her gardens, willing myself to be swept away in the beautiful, fleeting moment.

The name Henry Hamilton echoed in my mind, distracting me, then I thought of the Indian man and the horse I had seen earlier. I had not spoken a word of it, and part of me wanted to keep it to myself. "I know that face." Lillian studied me with care. "Something's troubling you."

Lillian would be sure to disapprove of me wandering about unchaperoned, putting myself in danger, but the story was much too interesting not to share with my closest friend. "You know me well," I sighed. "I hardly know where to begin."

"Do start somewhere!" Lillian leaned in closer. "Though I'm surprised your mother's allowed you to do anything worth chattering about at all."

"Well," I started slowly, "I'm twenty-one now. It's about time I became a woman, and, well, married."

Lillian's hands clasped together. "Oh, how wonderful! Why on earth should this be troubling? I've never heard you speak of wanting to join a convent." She laughed and seized my hand.

"No, I have no wish to join a convent, you're right." I smiled. "Mother and Father have their hearts set on this particular arrangement, but I can hardly say I love the man."

"Love and a happy marriage go hand in hand." She looked away from me and hesitated a moment before whispering, "It may be silly of me to speak so boldly and so soon, but I believe that I, too, may marry before the year is out."

"But you're a whole year younger than me!" My hand flew to my lips.

"Don't be angry with me for betraying my girlhood so soon, but I've found the love you speak of."

"Angry? I'm more astonished than anything!" My brow puckered. "Well, who is it? Who's the man to have won your affections so fully? Someone I know?"

Lillian bit her lip. "There is something else."

"Lillian!" a woman's voice called frantically. Lillian's mother, Sarah, a woman who looked almost identical to her daughter, approached our seat in the gardens.

Lillian shifted in her seat and stretched a hand towards Sarah. "Mother, isn't it wonderful? Estella's come back to us!"

Sarah was clearly out of breath. "What are you doing outdoors? You were given specific instructions to rest." She removed a glove and rested the back of her hand on Lillian's forehead.

Lillian crossed her arms. "I am resting, am I not?"

"Estella, I'm sorry, but Lillian is unwell, and is not to be excited."

"But Mother! We haven't even been served tea yet!"

"You can have tea another day." Sarah turned towards me. "I do apologize, Estella. If I'd been home when you sent word of your intention to visit, I never would have let you drive all the way here only to be sent away."

I tried to read Lillian's expression, but couldn't bring myself to pry with her mother around. "Forgive me for springing myself on you both." I offered an apologetic smile to Sarah, who looked frazzled and strange. Lillian slipped her hand into mine and I squeezed it. "Expect an invitation to my party. I'll pray for a swift recovery."

"Thank you, sweet Estella." Lillian's eyes shifted to her mother, then back to me. "I can hardly wait to see you again."

"And I you. Good day to you both."

I believe Lillian would've told me of her sickness herself if I'd had but one more minute alone with her. Instead, I was left with worry and many unanswered questions.

When I reached the coach, Hannah was already waiting for me. The coachman helped me into my seat and closed me in. Hannah eyed the tension in my shoulders and could surely tell that I was troubled, but decided not to pry.

I glanced out the coach window as the horses pulled us down the drive. Sarah held onto Lillian's arm closely, escorting her across the grass and back indoors where she belonged.

\*\*\*

That night, I could hardly sleep. I repositioned myself more times than I could count, and when I did manage to fall asleep, I was plagued by nightmares. I woke in a cold sweat, my heart pounding in my temples, my ears ringing. Why was I so completely restless?

I lay there in the silence of night, looking up at my ceiling. I clutched my comforter up to my chin as I thought about Lillian's health and how her mother sent me home.

But I also thought about the Indian man, his eyes so piercing it was as though they looked right through me. My mind traced the way his black hair, blacker than onyx, fell past his shoulders, how his golden-bronze skin looked as though the sun had kissed him. This striking memory was still so clear in my head. I could replay it over and over, until I absorbed every detail, leaving me helplessly, utterly intrigued with no way of getting answers.

# CHAPTER FIVE

## Saturday, June 3

### Estella

It was the night of my party. Over the past week, Mother had kept me occupied day in and day out with planning the most tedious details of this dreadful event, and I hadn't had a single moment to revisit Lillian. My mind burned with questions since my first visit, though I was relieved to at least receive a letter from her mid-week informing me that her health was improving and that she was eager to attend my party.

Upstairs, Hannah helped me prepare the night's ensemble. My stomach turned when I heard the chatter of guests waiting for me below. *Is Henry already here?* I wondered. *Does he still look as boyish as ever? Will he think I'm beautiful?* Hannah laced my corset, and I pretended I wasn't dying of asphyxiation. *Dear Lord,* I thought, *how am I ever supposed to breathe, let alone* enjoy *myself wearing this contraption?*

Finally, Hannah pulled the pink gown over my head and tied the back just as tight. My dark hair was set in a mature arrangement, parted at the center and pinned back in a mass of curls. My gown was the perfect combination of elegance and grace, at least in

Mother's opinion. The sleeves rested at my shoulders, leaving them practically bare, while my neckline revealed much more of my chest than I preferred to show. The pink material poured over my hoop skirt into a silk waterfall with cream-colored rosettes at the hem.

I sat at my vanity in hopes that being still might calm my nerves, but it only emphasized the shallowness of my breathing.

Movement in the doorway reflected in my vanity mirror. I turned, startled, to find Mother watching me. I wondered how long her hovering had gone unnoticed.

"My goodness, you look quite the lady." Her eyes swept over me, while her thoughts clearly filled with my future with Henry and all of his money. It was easy to tell what Mother was really thinking. She wore her feelings on her face—that is, on the rarest of occasions when she hadn't already expressed her opinions to great extent.

Hannah left us alone as Mother approached me. She rested her hands on my shoulders and looked at our reflection in the vanity mirror. "You're simply stunning. I can't wait to see Henry's face when he lays his eyes on you!"

I raised an eyebrow, but she didn't notice.

Mother produced a silk bag. "Here." She opened it and removed a piece of jewelry, a string of perfectly clear-cut amethyst stones with soft pink pearls that tapered off the sides. "Your great-grandmother gave this to your grandmother on her twenty-first birthday, and she gave it to me on mine. I want you to have this necklace as a remembrance of this night and how special you felt wearing it." She laid the cold jewels on my neck and fastened them with deft fingers.

"Thank you, Mother." I touched my neck. It was an exquisite piece and it *did* make me feel that much more beautiful.

She smiled at me with, as far as I could tell, genuine pride, and gave my shoulders a soft squeeze. Before leaving me alone, she reminded me that Henry was waiting for me.

I took a last look in the mirror and decided I felt like a woman. I certainly looked like one. The jewels ornamenting my chest accentuated my slender, yet womanly frame, and paired well with my rose-colored gown. My cheeks held a warm, youthful glow, yet their familiar plumpness had seemingly vanished overnight.

I added a touch of translucent powder to the freckles on my nose. It wasn't becoming of a woman who was out in the sun too much. I had to look perfect. This party was much more than a birthday celebration. It was one step closer to my engagement. This was my duty that ran deep in my blood, and I was ready. I sighed, pulling on my stainless white gloves and wrapped myself in a shawl made of cream-colored lace.

The door cracked open. It was Hannah again. "There's something I wanted to give you," she said, rustling through her apron pocket. "You don't have to wear it if you don't take a liking to it, but it's for you to keep." She opened her hand, and a golden hairpin decorated with a white stone glistened in my candlelit room.

"Hannah, it's beautiful," I whispered as my fingers traced the golden piece in her hand. "What's that stone set in the middle?"

"Moonstone." She smiled at me. "I had it made when you were a babe, and I've been saving it for a special occasion. Your twenty-first birthday seemed appropriate enough."

"Would you put it in my hair?" I turned my head to the side.

Hannah set it in place, and it shone beautifully against my dark hair.

She rested her hand on my face. "You're perfect."

I touched the pin in my hair. It felt like it was a part of me somehow. "Thank you," I whispered.

Hannah's calm blue eyes welled with pride. "Go on now," she prompted. "Don't keep them waiting any longer, and go lightly with the wine. It can tamper with your senses when you aren't accustomed." New Hampshire hadn't outlawed alcohol as Massachusetts had. I'd only sipped Father's wine once, and didn't care much for the taste.

"I will take care." I gave Hannah a quick kiss on the cheek and left the room.

My dress rustled with every step I took down the hall. At the top of the staircase, there stood a tall silhouette: Henry Hamilton's. My heart began palpitating so intensely that I feared he might be able to hear it.

Henry turned and laid eyes on me for the first time in a year.

He wore an expensive-looking black suit, and his hair had gotten lighter since the last time I saw him. He looked like a completely different person. To be precise, Henry no longer looked like a boy. His face was sculpted and defined, his jawline squared and sharp. All his features were alarmingly symmetrical, and his fair complexion shone even in the dim light.

Henry flashed me an inviting smile. His full lips curled back, revealing a set of crooked teeth that in no way detracted from his allure. It brought to mind a time many years back when Henry had lost two teeth and could hardly form proper words. I resisted the urge to laugh, but couldn't stop the smile at my lips.

I noticed Henry's own smile never reached his eyes, the deep blue orbs that always appeared sad. *That's one thing that hasn't changed,* I thought. Still, Henry was handsome; I couldn't deny it. Twenty-three suited him well.

We met, and Henry offered me his arm to escort me down the steps. His face turned red at our touch. "Happy birthday, Estella. You look beautiful this evening. I almost didn't recognize you." His gaze moved from my face down my body, prompting me to adjust my lace shawl over my chest.

I cleared my throat. "Thank you for escorting me this evening. My parents have spoken very highly of you," I said, wondering if I truly had to *remind* Henry that he was a gentleman.

Henry looked at the floor, seeming embarrassed. "Of course they have." He lifted his gaze to meet mine again, then began leading us down the stairwell, arm in arm. "I've given them no reason to doubt me."

I raised an eyebrow. "Yes, it seems as though my father already has great plans for you. He informed me of your new position at Wellstone Mills."

Henry pushed his shoulders back. "Yes, your father's been kind enough to put his trust in me and my abilities, I believe. Of course, none of those laymen at the mills have ever been as capable or as prepared for the task as I am. I've received quite the extensive education, as I'm sure you know."

"I see," I said flatly, but he didn't seem to take notice.

Before he could say anything else off-putting, the chatter of mingling men and women caught our attention. Henry held his head high as we came into view of the crowd. His arm tightened, while his free hand rested lightly over mine as though I were a dazzling possession that he wanted everyone to gape at.

I instantly felt a prick of guilt for assuming the worst in him. Why did I read his firm hold on me as an act of possession? Perhaps he was simply delighted to be with me. I so wanted Henry to be the man in the letters we'd exchanged. He'd been so sweet, so thoughtful, and maybe even a touch romantic.

Everyone stopped what they were doing to catch a glimpse of us descending the final steps that led into the warm, candlelit front rooms. Their attentions must have lasted only moments, but an eternity seemed to pass before they returned to their conversations as though nothing had happened. The nonchalance of it all relieved me, and an inaudible sigh escaped my lips. I glanced up at Henry and found him smiling and nodding to my guests, completely and utterly comfortable.

I scanned the crowd for a familiar face. Ladies with tight dresses, huge skirts, and silk gloves filled our summer home as far as I could see, while an accomplished harpist played at the end of one room.

With amusement, I watched as the gentlemen guests began picking their way out of the house. They were sure to find themselves in the stables before long. It never ceased to amaze me just how fast men disappeared from any party, as restless as antsy children during a long-winded sermon. I knew from years of eavesdropping experience that once the men were alone, they would be free to survey topics such as politics, racehorses, and affairs of their estates while the ladies stayed behind to enjoy the food and drink.

My gaze finally discovered a sweet face in the back of the room, a face that instantly set my heart at ease. I excused myself from Henry and maneuvered through the crowd, nodding and smiling at guests as I passed. Lillian had just arrived and stood elegantly in a pale yellow silk gown with a modest shawl wrapped around her waist and an ornamented straw bonnet pinned into her hair. The moment our eyes met, I returned to the summers we'd spent riding horses, running about the woods, and trading books. It was hard to believe that we were both ladies now, soon to wed.

I reached her spot on the floor. "Lillian!" I breathed out. "I'm so glad to see you. I've longed to finish our conversation this whole week, but couldn't find a single moment to escape."

She embraced me. "Well, we are together now, and I must say, you look beautiful!"

I withdrew, but held both her hands in mine. I craved a moment alone with her. I'd thought of a thousand questions since our last conversation, and I'd resolved to tell her about the Indian man and the horse I'd found roaming the woods.

"I really do apologize for my late arrival this evening," Lillian continued, seemingly disappointed. "I missed your grand entrance and everything!"

There was something off about her now, but I couldn't place it. Was my friend still unwell? She appeared physically fine, but there was urgency in her tone.

"When can we see each other again, in private?" she asked, looking around at all the people in the room as if they didn't belong.

Before I could answer, a voice spoke from behind me. "There you are. I wondered where you had run off to." Henry appeared closely at my side holding two glasses of birch wine. Lillian's face grew pale, her brown doe eyes confused.

Henry nodded to her. "Drinks, ladies?"

Lillian took the crystal glass mindlessly, her chest sinking deeper with each breath.

I took hold of her arm. "Are you feeling alright?"

Her eyes fluttered wearily, and she thrust her glass into my hands. "I shouldn't have come here." She shook her head, and before

I could question her further, Lillian departed through the front door through which she had only just entered.

"What was that about?" I looked to Henry, who had somehow linked his arm in mine. "Why was Lillian so disturbed?"

His face reddened and seemed strained, perhaps an attempt to mask his true feelings on the matter. "I suppose she's still a bit upset with me." He opened his mouth as though he wanted to say more, but instead finished the glass of wine in his hand and discarded the empty vessel on a passing tray.

"She seemed more than a bit upset," I snapped. "You wouldn't have any idea as to why?"

He touched his lips and hesitated again. "This is neither the time or place for such a discussion, but I promise to explain myself another time, Estella."

I pulled my arm from his. "Tell me you are not the mystery man whom Lillian is in love with!"

The look of shame on Henry's face did not quell my fears. He adjusted his coat and averted his gaze before answering. "Look, I don't think this is a proper conversation to be having at present, but to avoid a scene, I'll indulge you."

I crossed my arms. "You'll know me to be most improper soon enough."

He took my arm again, more firmly this time, and led me across the room to a less occupied corner, while everyone else mingled in the middle of the room. His eyes shifted from side to side, observing the room before speaking rapidly. "I swore to my mother that I wouldn't share this with anyone, but you might as well know that the Sterlings wanted to arrange a courtship with me. I suppose Lillian really fancied me and thought she had a great opportunity at my fortune, but you, most sensible of all people, understand the absurdity of that notion."

He let out a smooth laugh, as though to reinforce the absurdity of the idea, as though I could clearly see how he was superior to Lillian. "I swear to you," he continued, "that I dismissed the idea quite gently, but one can only do so much to soften a blow like that."

Something happened when he said that. Holding my tongue, as I had been becoming so skilled at, seemed impossible. My cheeks flushed hot and my hands balled into fists. When I opened my mouth, all my brimming thoughts spilled forth like vomit. "The man standing before me now is not the same man who has been writing me letters these past months. *That* man would never speak of my friends in this manner. *That* man would act like a gentleman. But you? You carry yourself as though you're God's gift. You... You... "

The floor began to sway beneath my feet, my head as weightless as air. My corset closed in on my ribs, tighter and tighter. I tried to steady myself with a hand on the wall behind us. Henry's expression shifted from shock to worry. Then everything went dark.

I awoke in bed with Hannah and Mother sitting at my side. Hannah was clearly worried, but Mother's face bore a different expression. She was angry. No, that would be an understatement. She was *furious*. I considered closing my eyes again and pretending to sleep to avoid our inevitable argument.

But Hannah leaned forward, offering me a cup. "Here you go, dear. Drink this." The cup contained Hannah's homemade tonic to help headaches, and oh, did mine ache. I must have fallen right on the back of my head. *Leave it to Henry not to catch me*, I thought. I took the cup and choked down the nasty liquid, leaving a bitter taste on my tongue.

Hannah took a cool cloth to my damp forehead. "You took quite a fall," Hannah started, but cut off her speech at Mother's glare.

"Please leave us," she said in a hard voice.

*Here it comes,* I thought.

Hannah left the room. The door clicked shut, followed by a moment of complete silence. Mother rose and turned her back towards me, her hands clasped tightly behind her. "I do not know exactly what happened tonight, but you may have single-handedly ruined the best chance this family had at the Hamiltons' name and fortune. You had better hope that the situation can be repaired."

She breathed out, then in deeply, as I piped up. "Mother…" I hesitated. "You should have heard the way he spoke of Lillian."

"Under no circumstances should a lady insult her escort and future husband." She turned towards me, her brown eyes ablaze. "Can you imagine if you said those things loud enough for our guests to hear?" She rested her hand on my head carefully, but not quite lovingly, and sighed. "I just want the best for you, my darling. It is difficult when I have given you everything you've needed to be a sensible adult, and you still insist on acting like a child. Now, get some rest and we won't speak of this again." Her hand slid limply from my hair to my cheek.

I stared up at her, observing her arched eyebrows and her thin, twitching lips. Surely if she'd heard Henry's words, Mother would have been more understanding. Well… perhaps not. Some conversations are simply meant to be had privately. The knot in my stomach and the ache in my head both served as my punishment for letting impulse outweigh discernment.

"How will I fix things with Henry?"

"I have faith that you will be creative." She looked pleased with herself as she walked to my wardrobe. "Tomorrow you will send word to Henry expressing your apologies, and then on Monday you will bring your father lunch at the mills. Henry happens to work there as well, of course." She pawed through the arrayment of gowns before retrieving a new and slightly ridiculous dress, which she then threw onto my bed. "Men cannot resist a beautiful woman. I saw how Henry looked at you tonight."

"So, to be clear, Monday, you want me to bring lunch for Henry and apologize in that gown?"

She smiled. "What a marvelous idea, Estella. I couldn't have thought of something more fitting myself."

I rolled my eyes, but it made the back of my head ache. "Me, at the mills, alone? You can imagine how that will play out."

"Goodness, no. Hannah will accompany you, naturally, and ensure that you are not in harm's way." She patted me on the arm. "All is not lost. Now get some rest and be thinking of all the sweet nothings you will write out tomorrow."

Before turning to leave, she paused for a moment. "And Estella, I do *not* want to hear of you sneaking off to see Lillian tomorrow, not until you've fixed this horrid mess you've created."

With that, Mother left me to my own thoughts. I had completely forgotten how Lillian reacted tonight. Why hadn't I run after her? I needed to speak with her now more than ever. She was my only true friend in this place. All the other girls here in Pinebrook were too uptight for my liking, and in my opinion cared much more for young men than they ought to.

I lay in bed and counted the cracks on my plaster ceiling until my headache dulled and I drifted off to sleep.

***

## Bodaway

"Make yourself at home!" Art tossed me a wool blanket. He had finally helped set me up in mill housing, and now, I was one of his four roommates. The room already felt tight with just the two of us occupying it, but Art claimed he hardly ever saw the other men he roomed with. Whenever they had free time, they were either at the tavern or at the races, just doing something with whatever money burned holes in their pockets.

Night had fallen and the only light in the room came from two candles, one in the window and one on Art's nightstand. As we sat at the table and picked at some bread crusts, I took a moment to observe my new home. There were five beds, a wood stove, the table we sat at, and not much else.

Art gave me one of the silly grins he always had on his face. "John, I'm glad you decided to room with me. You're a good man. Hate to see you all alone."

"I don't mind being alone." After all, it's what I deserved. "But thanks for everything."

"You bet." He dusted the breadcrumbs from his lips and leaned back in his chair. "It isn't the King's chambers, but I'm sure you'll find this bed much more comfortable than the outdoors."

I doubted that I'd find the confines of this room to be more comforting than the wild, but Art really seemed to like my company, and I sure wouldn't mind a shorter walk to work.

A woman's voice came from the doorway. "I'd say any room would look like a king's chambers compared to a dirt bed." A red-headed beauty entered the room, carrying a basket. I could tell with one look that this girl was Art's sister. Both of their faces were covered in freckles, but her face looked like it lived in the sun. They both had the same tired blue eyes and hair the color of carrots, though hers was long and tied in a braid that trailed down the back of her brown work dress.

Art peered up, arms crossed over his chest. "Look who decided to stop by. I hope there's food in that basket."

"I swear all you think about is your stomach," she replied.

Art turned to me as the girl set her basket on the table and sat between the two of us. "John, this is my sister Mary. Mary, this is John."

"Pleased to meet you." She smiled and shook my hand excitedly. There was something simple and sweet about her. "And why haven't I seen you around these parts? I would remember a face like yours."

"That's because John here is new to Pinebrook," Art answered. "All the way from Maine." He rifled through Mary's basket and, with apparent delight, pulled out a hunk of cheese.

I shifted uncomfortably in the chair, its spindly legs creaking and groaning beneath my weight. "Your brother's been kinder to me than I deserve."

"I remember when *we* were new to town." Mary's eyes softened as she looked at her brother, whose mouth was filled to the brim.

Art licked his lips and used the sleeve of his shirt to wipe his mouth. "This isn't our home either, so trust me when I say we both know what that feels like. Might as well have a couple kind folks looking out for you."

I rubbed the back of my neck and stood from the table. "And I appreciate it." I cleared my throat. "I'll leave you two to visit then. Figured I'd get some air while I still can."

Mary reached up and clutched my arm before I could escape. "Nonsense! Stay if you like. No need for you to rush off on my account." She released her grip and motioned to my empty chair.

Reluctantly, I set myself back down. Mary began again. "Art and I are more than happy to have the company. And you *must* join us for supper one night, you must! It's the neighborly thing to do."

Art shook his head. "My sister has a tendency of being a tad forceful, if you can't tell."

Mary thrust her hands onto her hips, and her Irish accent grew thicker. "Forceful? Is that what you call me now? Well, maybe I should *force* you to make your own supper then! You'd like that."

I couldn't help but laugh at the two of them. Their relationship reminded me of Keme. I missed him already, but I was in Pinebrook for his sake. "I just got to town and I'm already getting others into trouble."

Art nudged Mary in the ribs. "In all honesty, you'd be smart to take her up on the offer. Mary makes an amazing beef stew." He kicked up his feet and crossed his legs on the edge of the table. "What do you say, John? Tomorrow night? Sundays only come around once a week."

"It's a kind offer, but I've already planned to spend Sunday in the woods to clear my head." Not to mention my lungs. I turned to Mary. "I'm learning to savor my time in fresh air and daylight."

"I can't say I blame you, but a man's still gotta eat!" she persisted, nonchalantly shoving Art's feet from the table. Mary clutched my hands. "Promise me you'll let me make you dinner one of these nights."

If I didn't agree, I had a feeling that she would never return my hands. "Alright, you have my word."

Mary released me and clasped her hands together. "Oh, how wonderful!" She stood and kissed Art on the cheek. "See you boys soon. I won't forget about dinner, John."

I threw my hands up in defeat. "A promise is a promise."

She gave me a playful wink, then left.

"Please forgive my sister," said Art with a chuckle. "Once she gets something in her head, there is nothing stopping her." He took an apple from the basket his sister left behind and headed for his bed.

My chair creaked across the wood floor as I stood and retreated to my own bed. "I don't mind it. I can't remember the last time I had a good, home-cooked meal," I confessed. I pulled the stone from my pocket that I'd picked from the river and set it on my nightstand. I kept it close to me, as it was my only tangible reminder of Keme.

When I looked at it, it gave me hope that I would return to him one day soon.

# CHAPTER SIX

*Monday, June 5*

Estella

By the time Monday morning came around, I was much recovered from the incident at my party. Sunlight filtered through my window brighter and much warmer than usual. I slowly propped myself up in bed with my elbows and rubbed the back of my head where only a tiny bump was left behind.

I had spent the day before mostly resting and drafting letters to Henry, but no amount of eloquent, apologetic writing seemed genuine enough. Of course, Mother wouldn't hear any excuse that might keep me from smoothing things over. I penned a simple message, informing Henry of my intention to bring lunch to the mills, and expressed my desire to speak privately. Whatever words I had for Henry would be better spoken in person.

*How was I to fix this?* I thought, hugging my knees to my chest. Why was it *my* responsibility to fix the situation, anyway? *He* should be the one apologizing.

I thought of Lillian, and how urgently I needed to speak with her. I could only imagine what she might be thinking now, how embarrassed she must have felt seeing me with Henry. I was determined to pay a short visit to the Sterlings on my way into town. Surely Hannah would allow it.

Hannah entered my room and laid my dress, with all its lacing and contraptions, out on my bed. "Come on now! It's nearly eleven, and you've barely stirred."

I groaned and pulled the covers more tightly around me.

"I know you don't want to do this." She sat on my bed and caressed my shoulder.

I shot up and shook my head. "Can you believe what Mother wants me to do? Parading around the mills in *that!*" I pointed at the anything-but-inconspicuous yellow gown waiting to be filled by me. "I've seen canaries duller than that fabric!"

"I'm sure she has her reasons. Remember that she's managed your father, a very successful man, for many years. Credit where credit is due." She pinched my chin. "Besides, I'll be with you. It might even be fun."

"Hmm," I huffed, and maneuvered out of bed. The wood floor was cold on my bare feet as I slipped out of my white linen nightgown.

Hannah helped me dress and was sure not to lace my corset so tight this time. "We don't want anyone fainting again, my sweets," she said, prompting me to flutter my eyelashes in tolerant annoyance.

I smoothed my gown and examined myself in the full length mirror next to my wardrobe. The fabric, from its fitted sleeves to its full and voluptuous skirt, was outrageously yellow. Its neckline showed just the right amount of skin to be considered modest, while not concealing so much as to be prudish in Mother's eyes. The whole ensemble was so far beyond anything I'd have chosen for myself that I hardly recognized the woman watching me in the mirror.

"We should be going now," said Hannah. "Heaven forbid we be late for lunch at the mills and ruin your mother's big plans!" She winked at me.

I leaned over and kissed her rosy cheeks. "Shall we, then?" I lifted my hem and walked down the hall, careful not to trip as I descended the stairwell. Hannah left me briefly to fetch a basket filled with lunches from the kitchen.

"Estella, is that you?" Mother called from another room. She came into view around the corner, holding a Spanish fan.

"I'm off to carry out your plan," I said, giving her a sarcastic twirl to show off the dress she had chosen for me.

She smirked. "You mean *your* plan?" she corrected. "Let us pray you haven't bungled things beyond reparation."

"Thank you for the well wishes, Mother."

"Change your tone, miss. Go on now, the carriage is waiting for you out front. Please, for the love of God, do *not* wander around on foot. You must break yourself of this tendency to creep through the forest like some woodland creature."

"What on earth would lead you to believe I'd do such a thing?"

She crossed her arms, unamused. "Go."

I left through the front door. The carriage waited for me, just as she had said. It was true that under different circumstances I would've been tempted to cut onto the wooded trail to town. The forest was much more scenic than the dull, dusty drive.

But only a dimwitted ninny would stomp through the forest in a corset and gown. Besides, being a lady meant riding into town like a civilized woman, and I was determined to make my family proud.

Pushing my shoulders back and holding my head high, I took the footman's hand and climbed into the carriage.

Hannah waited for me within. "Have you practiced your lines?" she teased as I settled in beside her. I gave her a playful nudge and the horses pulled us on our way.

\*\*\*

For such a small place, downtown Pinebrook seemed to be busier than usual. Horse-drawn buggies passed by, newsboys waved papers at pedestrians, and dogs outside shopfronts patiently awaited their masters.

Ladies with wide bonnets nodded to each other as they passed by in the streets, and one little boy dressed in a worn, ill-fitting tunic suit waved up at me from the side of the road.

I smiled and waved in return. "I've missed this place," I sighed, and leaned back in the leather seat. "Hannah..." I hesitated. "Perhaps we could call on Lillian?"

Hannah was about to say no, I could sense it, so the next words practically fell out of my mouth in a jumble. "Please, please, oh please let me!" I took her hands. "It will be the briefest of visits! As though it never happened!"

Hannah closed her eyes and a sigh of defeat escaped her lips. "Driver," she shouted through the carriage window, "turn right after we pass Town Hall." She then looked at me. "As though it never happened."

I sprung from my seat and kissed her cheeks. "Thank you, Hannah! Lord only knows the next time Mother will allow me to call on Lillian," I added as the carriage turned past Town Hall and pulled us along the Sterlings' drive.

The gray home came into focus, and my palms grew sweaty beneath my gloves. An orange cat scampered across the lawn as our carriage came to a stop.

Hannah, noticing my nerves, handed me her handkerchief. "Are you sure everything is alright?" She asked.

I nodded, dabbing at my glistening brow. "It will be soon." I forced the smallest of smiles to my lips, and we both climbed from the carriage.

Hannah knocked at Lillian's door and we waited silently. Moments later, the door cracked open to reveal Nellie, the Sterlings' maid. She was such a tiny creature that it was astounding she was any help at all. Nellie stared up at Hannah and me, blinking stupidly. Her lips parted as though she weren't quite sure how to react or what to say.

Though she was a finicky thing, I had never known her to act so anxious. "Is Lillian in?" I prompted. "Can I see her?"

Nellie glanced nervously over her shoulder and cleared her throat, not lending any power to her sheepish voice. "Umm… Miss Lillian is… out."

I sighed. "Well, might I leave her my calling card?"

Nellie nodded. "Of course." She held out her hand.

"I'd like to leave a note as well," I added.

Reluctantly, she opened the door wide enough for Hannah and I to enter the foyer where the silver tray meant for calling cards would lie.

Hannah always carried my family card with her, so she reached into her apron pocket and retrieved one for me.

The small table was just to the right of the doorway, hardly inside the house, yet Nellie stood like a soldier, watching me intently.

I took hold of the fountain pen on the table and scribbled a note on the back of my calling card, asking Lillian to meet me at our special meeting place that night, as we had done every year since we were both young. Carefully, I set my card in the empty tray. "All finished," I said with a smile. "Thank you, Nellie."

She nodded, and ushered us to our carriage.

Neither Hannah nor I spoke as we began down the Sterlings' drive. It wasn't until we had returned to town, passing the orphanage that Hannah spoke up. "That was quite strange, don't you think?"

I turned to face her. "Very strange! But you were so quiet, I thought maybe I had been reading too much into things."

Hannah shook her head. "No, Nellie has always been very friendly to me. I've never seen her act so... so..."

"Nervous," I finished.

"Exactly."

"Lillian was very disturbed the other day. This all seems odd. Not only Lillian's behavior, but *everything* since we've come back to Pinebrook. Henry's attitude, this whole sudden engagement. It just hasn't felt the same this summer as it always did before."

Hannah rested her hand on my arm. "You're not a child anymore. Nothing is as simple as it used to be, but it's not all that bad. Everything is new, and it just takes a little time to adapt. And I wouldn't fret so very much about this. I'm certain you'll work things out with Lillian. Nothing could ever break the bond that the two of you share, not even your mother." She gave me a warm smile.

I cocked my head, wanting to believe her. "I suppose if Mother had her way Lillian and I would never have become so close. Though I don't fault Mother on account of her disapproval. She follows a very rigid set of rules, so completely devoted to propriety—

perhaps as I should be. But at times I hardly understand her at all." I paused in thought. "Do you believe me to be ungrateful?"

Hannah sighed and brought her hands to her lap. "I may not agree with all of your family's priorities, but it is not my place to say anything."

"But am I unreasonable for desiring love?"

Hannah hesitated a moment before answering. "No, I don't blame you for that, but you ought to give Henry a chance. He seems like a handsome fellow."

I raised my eyebrows and let out a deep breath. "Handsome indeed."

The smell of homemade breads and baked goods filled my senses as we drove down Main Street. I was reminded of Boston for an instant. Of course, in Boston, you could find a bakery on every corner. Not so in Pinebrook with its small, singular bakery. The thoughts of Boston and the smell of bread brought Henry and his lunch to mind, and I tried to remember my premeditated apology as we drove on.

After turning down a few side streets and passing through the mill housing, I could finally see and hear Wellstone Mills. The rumble of the mills overtook the roar of the river, as well as every other noise of the surrounding town.

As we approached, I noticed some men already taking their lunch break outside. "Here is perfectly fine," Hannah called to the driver, a man whom I did not recognize. We had different summer help every year and it was difficult to remember every new name.

The driver seemed nice enough as he helped me down first, then Hannah. "I will wait here for you, miss." He nodded to us as we left.

Several men sat on the stone wall that hung over the river. They whispered with silly grins and shamelessly eyed Hannah and me.

Heat spread across my face and traveled down my neck. "I thought we'd avoid the men on break by coming in a little earlier. They've always had the most disagreeable habit of staring."

"Don't pay any mind to them," Hannah advised. "Your mother sent me to keep you away from mischief, and she can trust that I will do so." Hannah linked arms with me as we approached the entrance of the Wellstone Mills. I had forgotten how unsettling it was to stand before its endless brick walls and massive double doors. The air carried its familiar smells of angst, hard labor, and the river.

Though the looming brick building intimidated me, I found a new strength in Hannah's presence. My chest rose with the deepest breath my corset would allow, then with a confident stride, I entered the mills.

# CHAPTER SEVEN

*Monday, June 5*

Bodaway

The hours at the mills passed quickly if you focused on your work, and fortunately for the work room, the new floor manager didn't take pleasure in harassing its workers.

It was almost noon when Art walked past me at one of my looms and tossed me a plum. "Meet me outside for a smoke in ten," he invited. He'd been right before when he told me that the humming of the machines wouldn't bother me once I was used to them, and I heard his words perfectly.

"Alright, I'll be taking lunch here soon," I said. He walked into the sea of workers and out of sight.

Like the other men, I spent most of my time in the weaving room, but there were so many moving parts, aside from weaving, that kept the mill running on a daily basis. There was a whole spinning room filled with just women, and even young boys had their place in sweeping and keeping the mill in order.

I walked an aisle of looms under my command and touched each piece of fabric, feeling for picks and imperfections, but there were none. After a short while, a tall, gangly white man came to take my place at the looms so that I could break for lunch, and I headed for the exit.

It was all fairly mindless work once you got the hang of it, and I really *had* gotten good at it. Itching heat creeped up my neck at this thought. Part of me was embarrassed at how well I had adjusted. My grandfather would've been furious that I had resorted to what he would've called women's work, but he wasn't here anymore.

I knew I wasn't abandoning my culture. I wished my grandfather was here. Then I could explain myself, justify why I was doing what I must for Keme.

As I rounded a corner towards the exit, I stumbled over someone's leg and almost crashed right into machinery. Instead, I caught myself on the hardwood floor, scraping my hands open.

"Savage," the man scoffed under his breath. I recognized him from previous comments he'd made, though I tried not to let him get to my head. He worked the looms across from me, and I would catch him multiple times a day, glaring at me with his beady, sunken, eyes.

I clenched my jaw, hoping it would help contain the murderous wrath that every part of my body longed to unleash. But I controlled myself, wiped the debris off my knees and tried to ignore the man.

He turned and rolled his sleeves up, waiting for me to move. I stood without meeting the eyes of anyone around me and walked past him.

"A coward, huh? You think I'm about to let you walk?" the man yelled, coming up from behind me and shoving me into the nearest wall.

I felt my face grow hot with rage. "Stop causing problems and let me go on my merry way, unless you've got something to say to my face." Other workers gathered around to see the commotion.

The man stepped real close to me and put one of his grimy clubs on my shoulder. He knocked the cap from my head, letting my black hair fall past my shoulders. "Take a good look at him, boys." He tugged a strand of my hair and I shoved his hand away. Instead of relenting, the man laughed deep in his throat. "You're a good for nothing savage who best stay out of my way. I'm tired of seeing you around these parts where you don't belong." His putrid spit sprayed my face with each harsh word. The wild darkness behind his eyes and the crude angle of his mouth taunted me to react.

The workers crowded us, restless and animated. I swear I saw them making bets on who'd be left standing. Some commented on my rugged build and apparent sobriety, but others doubted my ability to go up against this man's sheer mass, a clear disadvantage that even I noted.

"Fight!" they yelled. "Rip him to shreds!" Their predictable comments made it nearly impossible to judge who they were meant for, but I didn't need any man's backing. I'd held my own for as long as I could remember, a feat any man would be proud of.

My opponent, still pinning my shoulder against the wall, seemed tired of waiting for me to throw the first punch. He took his huge, fat fist, and swung, hitting me dead in the jaw.

I'd had it.

The men around us spat at me and screamed "Fight!" I heard one man yell, "Dirty savage, he'd better fight like one! Hit 'em!"

Then another. "The boy can take 'em! I've wanted to pop the old drunk myself." A handful of workers roared with laughter.

My drunkard released me and turned around. He smiled at his divided supporters, so pleased with himself, so ready to claim victory.

What he didn't know was that I was wild with anger. It'd been pent up for two weeks, and I was ready to blow.

That anger got the best of me in the form of my fist ramming into the man's face.

He staggered, almost done for. He grasped at my shirt, but I shot an uppercut to his chin that threw him back further.

He stopped fighting and tried only to protect his head.

I couldn't stop my fists from plowing into him over and over again until he was well off into dreamland. He laid flat out on the floor, covered in his own blood and drool.

The crowd fell silent. The workers stared in shock and confusion as I stood over the man's unconscious body like David when he slayed Goliath. I fixated on my bloody fists and stained clothes. I looked like a monster.

Art's face appeared in the back of the crowd. He pushed his way up front, clearly trying to get to me before I could destroy myself any further.

"What in God's name is going on here?" rang a bellowing voice through the crowd. The infuriated boss and a younger man hovered in the stairwell that hung over the workroom. "Who's responsible for this?" the boss called out in fury.

I stood there, speechless, with a blood-stained shirt and guilty hands. The men who'd been watching couldn't rat me out fast enough, even my few supporters had fled the scene. The boss turned and spoke sternly to the younger man. "This is exactly why I need a floor manager like you while I'm not around. I want you to take care of this. It will be excellent training for you."

The young man squinted at me. "You there! You may leave at once. Don't expect any compensation for the work you've done today." He scratched something on the sheaf of papers he carried, and the boss nodded to the young man, seeming pleased. That was it?

All the men who'd stayed behind chattered amongst themselves. I wanted to beat the lights out of every smirking and whispering man around me. Not one of them would mourn my absence. If *that* man had just minded his own business, I'd still have work. And if the floor manager had only used common sense, I'd still have work.

I plunged my hands in my pockets and felt Keme's stone. I wouldn't grovel, and I wouldn't beg. Instead I shook my head and turned to walk away. *If I weren't Christian*, I thought.

But at that moment, something else seemed to distract the whole room of workers. Even the boss's gaze drifted beyond me. A young woman dashed through the crowd of dirty men. "Wait!" she cried. "Henry, wait!" The boss rubbed his eyes gingerly with his thumb and index finger, while the young man's face paled.

The woman stood in a yellow dress, as fancy as if she were attending a party. Her eyes locked with mine for what seemed longer than a moment. I was astounded by her boldness, but my chest burned with humiliation. I didn't need her help.

"Estella!" the boss shouted. "This is not a safe place for you."

She pulled her gaze away from mine to address the boss and Henry. "I was coming to bring you both some lunch," she said, lifting a small picnic basket. "When I got here, I stopped in the doorway with Hannah." She pointed to me. "I overheard the unconscious employee calling this man here a savage. I witnessed enough of this unfortunate situation to believe that *this* unconscious man took the first swing." She had spoken with so much conviction that she was now out of breath. She directed her next plea to the boss. "Father, he was relentlessly provoked, that much is evident, and it wouldn't be fair to let him leave." She looked back at me. It was hard to imagine that this balding man had created such a beautiful creature.

Her father and Henry looked at each other as if holding an inaudible conversation, then shifted their backs to me.

At this point all the workers cleared out. Work paid for their booze and their horse bets, they wouldn't risk any of it.

The boss patted Henry on the shoulder. "This is your call. I trust you can make a wise decision." Then he disappeared up the stairs once more.

Henry swallowed hard as he watched the boss leave him to fend for himself. He looked at me. "Is that true?"

I squared my shoulders. "Yes, sir."

Henry sighed as he descended the stairwell towards me and the girl, Estella. "Then get back to work and stay out of trouble. This is your one, final chance."

Estella's gaze was still fixed on me, but it wasn't the normal stare I got from people noticing my Indian blood. This seemed like a look of recognition, but of course that was impossible. I knew for a fact that I'd never seen her before in my life. I wouldn't forget eyes like hers, blue, as clear as crystal pools.

I suppose she could've mistaken me for another Indian man, but even that would be strange. I'd been here long enough to notice only a handful of others like me, and all of us worked here at the mills, a place where no girl of her upbringing would have any business socializing. And while I couldn't make sense of it, the tender throbbing in my jaw quickly distracted my thoughts.

After another long moment, she tore her eyes away from me and let the younger man escort her off. His arm wrapped tightly around hers and his eyebrows crowded together in obvious frustration. The woman's maid followed closely behind, nodding to me as she passed.

*Why?* I rubbed the bruising side of my face and winced. Why would this Estella girl help the likes of me? I hated the fact that I was indebted greatly to her, and that there was no way to repay her or to break even. I was sure she didn't mean to make me feel indebted. It was brave of her to jump into the lion's den for a stranger like she did.

But really, I didn't need a woman on my mind for any reason.

Just then, Art snatched my arm and dragged me outside. "What the hell was that?" His eyes looked more tired than usual. "You're going to need to keep that temper under control or I won't be able to help you."

"Who's that girl who came to the mill?" I asked, ignoring his comment.

Art rolled his eyes. "That's Estella, the boss's daughter. And yes, she's beautiful, but off limits to you for many reasons."

"I'm not interested in her at all," I snapped. "I'm not delusional just because she spoke up for my position, Art. I know my place, and I didn't even notice if she was pretty or not. Not that it would matter."

Art smirked. "Mmmhmm. Well, she's as good as engaged to Henry Hamilton, the man with her father today."

"Him? You saw the way he was so quick to let me go. Any other man here knows me to be the better worker than that old drunk. Clearly a testament to his inexperience." I shook my head. "And Estella seems too kind for an arrogant prick like Henry, kinder than he deserves. She's a different sort of person than him, I can just tell."

Art chuckled. "Yeah, and you know her so well."

I scoffed, but it was true. I couldn't stop thinking about this girl, Estella, and what she'd done for me.

"Why don't you head on home and get cleaned up?" Art motioned to my blood-stained shirt.

"I'll be back in fifteen minutes," I said, rubbing my newly bruised jaw.

\*\*\*

I walked to my room as a knot in the pit of my stomach twisted and contorted each time I relived the fight in my mind. But eventually, the simple pleasure of sun on my skin was enough to lift my spirits. Working in the mills all day with filthy air, loud noises, and the lack of anything resembling sunlight really helps one appreciate everything outdoors.

Only a few paces from my door I came across Art's sister in the street headed towards the mills. Mary clutched a pail, probably packed with lunch for her brother, but I didn't bother breaking my stride. I only nodded to her in acknowledgment, hoping she'd continue on her way and leave me be. Instead, she called out to me. "John!"

Begrudgingly, I lingered in my doorway and waited for Mary to reach me.

"What happened to you?" she asked, catching her breath.

"Oh," I said, "it's nothing." I didn't want to talk about this with her. "Just a little bruise."

She stared at my bloodied shirt. "Come on now, you're going to let me help you." She pushed past me into my empty room. "Sit down here," she said, and pulled out a chair at the table.

If there was one thing I'd learned about Mary, it's that she's quite stubborn. She knew exactly what she wanted, and she always got it. Art liked to blame it on her working on a farm. That lifestyle might condition you to act a certain way, but I had a feeling the stubborn streak ran in the family.

"Here." She took a cool cloth to my face. "Have some of this food before I give it all to Art." She smiled. "You know as well as I that there won't be any leftovers."

Why was she so persistent? I didn't take kindly to handouts, but it seemed people in Pinebrook didn't understand that.

I took a small piece of mystery meat and bread. "Thanks," I said, trying not to seem bothered. I just wanted to be alone.

As if she could read my mind, she said, "Well, alright, if you really don't want to talk, I'll head on out and leave you be." She put the pail of food back together and headed towards the door. "I'll be taking a look at that wound tomorrow," she said, and left out the door.

Finally alone, I moved to my night table, where I kept a wash bowl. I cupped some water in my hands and splashed it carelessly over my face. My shirt needed a good washing, too. I didn't have many, and I needed a decent one for work.

*Work,* I thought. I was lucky to even still *have* work to go back to.

I unbuttoned my soiled work shirt and set it in the wash bowl to soak until I could deal with it. Impatient to get back to the mills, I retrieved a fresh shirt and slipped my arms through its sleeves. My fingers fumbled over the buttons, fastening them down the front. As I tucked the shirt's loose ends into my trousers, my hand grazed a familiar object.

I removed the stone from my pocket, carefully clamping my fist around it. I'd made a promise to Keme. Then, in a moment of stupidity, my hot head almost cost me that very promise. Fighting the urge to hurl the stone across the room, I loosened my grip and slipped it into my pocket where it belonged. My mind went back to Estella and what she had done for me. *Why?* I wondered. *Why help someone like me, someone who can barely honor a simple promise to his brother?*

\*\*\*

## Estella

I couldn't pull my gaze from the mystery man I had seen in the woods. His expression was confused with his jaw turning all shades of red and purple. After explaining to Father and Henry what I had seen, of course, they had no choice but to believe me and let the Indian man go back to work. Had he seen me that day in the woods? Was he angry at me for helping him now?

Before I could find any answers, Henry locked his arm around mine and led me away.

He brought me to the upper level of the mills where he and my father kept office space. Henry opened the door and stood aside, presenting a finely furnished room, organized and spacious, with built-in bookshelves lining an entire wall. The balcony's open French doors allowed a cool breeze to come in off the river, leaving the room with only the faintest scent of tobacco.

"Hannah," Henry said evenly, "Make yourself at home. I won't be keeping Estella long."

We stepped into the room, and Hannah nodded to Henry. "Thank you, Mr. Hamilton. And what a fine office you keep. Very orderly." She moved to the center of the room and traced a gloved finger along the large mahogany desk that was strewn with stacks of paperwork, as well as bottles of fine liquor for entertaining business associates.

"You are too kind," Henry said respectfully. "Mother has done well in teaching me the importance of order in one's life. Without it the whole world would crumble to bits. Though, despite Mother's wisdom, you'll still find my desk in utter chaos." He glanced towards a disturbing portrait of his mother, Alice Hamilton, that hung behind his desk, positioned so that no one walking into his office could miss it. Her eyes were cold and her posture rigid, even in the portrait.

"A handsome woman she is," Hannah remarked.

"And I've always believed your mother to be a very sensible woman," I said hastily, shocking myself with how much I'd just sounded like my mother.

Henry's lips twitched. "A very admirable trait in a woman, to be sure."

Hannah smirked as though she wished to add something. Instead, she remained quiet and seated herself on a small sofa to the side of the room.

"Shall we, then?" Henry asked before I could respond to his last remark. He offered me his arm and led me out to the balcony overlooking the river.

For the first time in days, we were alone. Hannah was one room away, but with the roar of the river we had privacy to speak freely.

We sat at a small table set with crystal glasses sparkling in the sunlight with a mystery drink within. Henry's newfound silence was unsettling. He had yet to blatantly speak of the incident that had transpired downstairs, but I believed his comment of sensibility to be a subtle jab at my indiscretion. I set the basket of food beside me and folded my hands in my lap, prepared for the inevitable confrontation.

I wondered if perhaps I was expected to speak first, but to my relief, Henry broke the silence. "That was quite the show you put on downstairs," he said, offering me a glass. "I know you feel compelled to do the right thing, but you can *never* put me or your father in a public situation like that again. Your zealous whims simply can't come at the expense of my worker's respect for me. Understand this, Estella, half of these men are more than twice my age and refuse to look to me as their head."

My cheeks grew hot again. Yes, my speech should've been made privately, but I'd been overcome with passion. "Your employees will respect you more for doing what's right. I spared you from looking foolish."

"*Foolish?* Goodness, Estella, the only one looking foolish these days is you!" His voice grew more perturbed with each word. "It seems as if you go out of your way to humiliate me publically." Henry tapped his fingers along the side of his untouched glass, as though resisting the urge to toss the vessel across the balcony.

I raised my chin slightly. "I do no such thing!" I stood, and set my glass down hard.

Henry glanced nervously at the French doors, perhaps expecting Hannah to rush out at the commotion. His face relaxed when nothing happened, then stretched out his arm like he was offering an olive branch. "Forgive my frustration, just please take a seat. You wouldn't leave me on such a discordant note, would you?"

Reluctantly, I sat back down. "Nonsense, but I don't wish to argue with you, Henry. I can assure you that today's indiscretion will not happen again. It's in my best interest to practice prudence—a virtue I'm sure to be reminded of now and again."

I transitioned into my premeditated speech as the river bubbled on below us. "...And about the other night at my party," I stammered, looking into his eyes in hopes of softening his heart towards mine. "I'm terribly sorry for the way I conducted myself, and I hope that you can forgive me. I truly don't intend to embarass you, or to act foolishly." I prayed that first half *sounded* sincere, because it wasn't.

Henry reached across the table and clutched my hand. "Let's not speak of it anymore. Same for today's events. We can forget them." He smiled at me and moved his chair closer to mine. Mother would be very pleased.

I took a sip from my glass. Tart lemon made my lips tingle.

He continued. "How is your head?" He touched my hair gingerly and without hesitation. I stiffened beneath his touch and he took his hand away slowly. "You took quite the fall the other night, so I must say that I was relieved to receive your letter upon my return from church yesterday afternoon."

"I'm much better, thank you. I hope you'll find lunch to your liking. It would be ill-mannered of me to keep you much longer. I'm certain your day's work keeps you plenty occupied without me lingering about and distracting you." I tried to stand again, but he stopped me.

"Wait one moment. I was wondering if tomorrow night you'd like to join me and my family for dinner?" He smiled. "We could go for a ride through town as well. I know how you've missed Pinebrook."

Thinking of Mother, I said, "Yes, I'd love to join you."

Henry ran his fingers along his chin. "Splendid." He stood and reached for my hand. The sun burst through the clouds and shone in Henry's hair, turning it golden. When I gave him my hand, he kissed it lightly. "Until tomorrow."

\*\*\*

When Hannah and I returned to the ground floor, I tried to catch a glimpse of the Indian man again. Though men worked all around us, I couldn't see him anywhere.

Father was occupied with another employee, so I didn't bother disturbing him as we left through the front doors.

I kicked around some pebbles in the dirt as we stood outside.

Hannah shook her head at me. "You did the right thing."

"Then why do I feel so wretched?" I asked, adjusting my bonnet.

"Sometimes the right thing to do is the hardest thing to do," she said. "You spoke up for someone today, and saved their position." The carriage rode up to meet us. "For that, I am proud of you, Estella."

"Thank you," I said softly.

The footman helped us into the carriage, and we drove home.

# CHAPTER EIGHT

### Estella

Mother made it her mission to fill every moment of my days with social calls, and dinner guests. That night, the mayor and his wife dined with us at our home. Mother expected me to play the dutiful daughter, and I had no choice but to oblige. My countenance, posture, and conversation were flawless all evening, simply exemplary.

Mother and Father, thoroughly impressed at my performance, stood at my side on our front porch and waved off our dinner guests at their departure. As their coach disappeared over the drive, Mother smiled down at me and rubbed my arm almost tenderly. "Well done, really," she hummed before returning indoors, leaving me with Father.

We leaned on the white railing together and breathed in the silence of the evening. "It seems as though your night is freed up," he said to me with a nod. "Your mother has a tight rope on you these days. I know how you miss your walks and your little freedoms."

"I do." And if I didn't find a way to leave soon, I would miss my meeting with Lillian.

He nodded to the fields. "Well, go on then. What are you waiting for?"

My brows crowded together. "Are you giving me permission to run wild?" I almost laughed, but a tight smile spread over my lips instead.

"Of course not. If your mother finds out that you've disappeared for the evening, there might be consequences. In my infinite wisdom, I would have to deny this very conversation." He glanced at the front door. "Of course, once she opens a book for the night, hardly anything can disturb her." He wrapped his arm around my shoulders and kissed my head. "Go on. Go, but don't be too long, Estella."

"Thank you, Father!" My cheeks flushed with joy, and Lillian's face was all I could think of. "I shall be as stealthy as Darcy." I referred to Mother's beloved cat with a note of sarcasm, for the horrid ball of fluff was known for its destructive clumsiness, yet still had a way of sneaking underfoot.

"Blasted cat," my father muttered, waving me off.

I started down the porch steps, towards our fields. When I looked back to wave at Father, he was gone. I saw an empty porch with summer flowers blooming around it.

It was almost sundown, the time of night when the sun shone gold over the trees and the fields. After receiving my note, Lillian would know to meet as we had so many times before.

My deep blue skirts caught in the brush as I started up the hill by our barn. We kept a large property, complete with lush land, livestock, and beautiful horses. As I passed the fenced-in fields where they grazed, I heard the horses whinny as though they were mocking me. They must have known that Father preferred them to me, but I shot them a fiery stare. Father had fenced them in, while he had given me permission-of-sorts to roam freely.

It was true though, that if Father was not at the mills, he was with his race horses. Every Saturday afternoon, he'd go to the track and enter his favorite horse, Black Magic, who won more often than not. She was the fastest, strongest horse around this end of the Northeast, and all the other men with horses in the race would groan whenever they saw him coming.

I guess I couldn't blame Father for liking this particular horse more than me. *It* complied with everything he asked of it. *A real winner,* I thought to myself as I approached my trail's entrance at the treeline, leaving my family's property behind me.

Lillian and I had a special meeting spot in the woods that we had stumbled upon as children. Each summer night we'd sneak away to this abandoned cabin and play house or cowboys and Indians.

I thought of the Indian man I saw today, then of my uncomfortable encounter with Henry. I didn't want to feel uncomfortable around the man I was to marry.

I often heard bits of gossip about him on my occasional visits to town. The townsfolk feared that Henry's shortcomings, paired with his charm and social status, might hinder him from choosing a bride. They'd say, "A gentleman like Henry has the whole world at his hands and simply no incentive whatsoever to settle down."

But I tried to keep my judgment to a minimum. Ladies have a way of prattling on over tea—the criteria of "interesting enough to whisper about " is easily attainable. Not a soul is immune, not even the most eligible bachelor in town. A rumor started a few years back when Henry left for boarding school. According to recent whispers, Henry's mother and father realized how their son's habits with alcohol and his shameless flirtation with the ladies could prove destructive to the Hamilton name. They sent Henry to boarding school, hoping it would straighten him out, clean him up.

The boarding school, in fact, sent him back home. It'd been kept quiet as to why exactly he was sent home, but the story his family consistently told was that Henry had been a studious, model pupil, and had finished his schooling early.

The rumors went a step further by saying Henry couldn't bear being away from home, and was ready to settle down and start a family. I laughed a little to myself thinking of Henry, the man with the world at his hands, wanting a simple life, married and a bunch of children running about his feet.

I feared if he was anything like the rumors spread about his reputation, our marriage would prove horribly and utterly disastrous. Could I hold his interest—if not his interest, then his loyalty? Had the Henry in our letters been so misleading?

I worried these things to myself, while carefully maneuvering the narrow trail riddled with tree roots growing at will.

Decomposing leaves crunched beneath my every step. Golden light filtered through the pines above, but faded as I wound the trail deeper into the woods.

The shadowy outline of the abandoned cabin was just visible through the thicket and trees ahead. The sight of it made my steps quicken and my heart light with anticipation. I couldn't keep the smile from my lips as I ran like a child, stumbling over roots and loose pine needles until I stood before the cabin. My breathing was heavy, the air fresh and cool as I scanned the premise for an eyeful of Lillian's brown mop of hair or her doe-like eyes waiting for me.

It was quiet. Only the sound of birds calling to one another distantly lingered in the golden light. The cabin sat with a silent grace about it. The glass in the windows remained intact since last summer, and though the wooden frame had begun to rot over the years, the structure still stood tall. It was as though I'd never left this place, as though I could still see a young Lillian running out that front door with braids flying, calling for me to catch her. We had made so many memories here, in simpler times.

But now Lillian was not in sight. I thought surely she would be waiting for me inside, as she had done in the past often enough.

I could already sense emptiness as I approached the moss-covered door, but I refused to accept it. Putting both hands lightly on the door, I pushed it open.

The stone fireplace still held twigs and branches from summers past. The broken rocking-chair sat, lopsided, in the corner where we'd left it, and the air smelled faintly of mildew and dead leaves.

Had Lillian not received my message? Had her mother prevented her from leaving? She would have come if she knew and was able, I was sure of it. Maybe Nellie had kept the note from her? She'd acted quite strange.

The distance from Lillian's house to our meeting spot was a great deal further than the distance I had traveled. And, of course, she had been unwell two days before, but whatever the reason, it was unlike her to not send word to me.

I dragged my feet, circling the cabin when something caught my eye in a window pane. It was only my reflection, but it looked much older than I felt. The harsh way the light caught in the glass contorted my face, aging me into something horrid. My features had been elongated and my skin appeared worn and transparent— the radiance of youth eluding me completely.

I *wasn't* a child anymore, and neither was Lillian, and we were no longer playing games. Maybe she had come to the same conclusion and left me to my devices.

The sun was setting. I knew I had better start back home.

I took one last look around the cabin to see if I could find her walking to meet me. Nothing. In a last-ditch effort, I called out her name. "Lillian!"

Nothing but birds answered me, flying out of the bushes and into higher branches. A small chipmunk watched me, amused, from a pile of rotted firewood, while I tried to keep my tears from falling as abruptly as my wishful thinking.

\*\*\*

## Bodaway

A short window of light lingered at the end of my work day, but it was closing in on me faster than I liked. Taking full advantage of it, I walked through the woods to clear my head and hoped for another glimpse of the horse. I'd been tracking her over the last few days, even leaving bits of food behind. She always seemed to end up around a mile from the mills.

Though I tried to keep my mind busy with tracking the horse, my thoughts kept returning to my fight. The duty to provide for my brother weighed so heavily on me, and I could've lost my position at the mills in just a moment. I'd have been out of work with nothing to show for it except proof that I couldn't control my temper.

I supposed the day hadn't been all that bad. It *did* feel good to punch that man unconscious. I smirked as I remembered him falling, pleased that he wouldn't be an issue anymore. In fact, I'd like to see him try and come at me again.

Though I felt smug, I knew in my heart that my mother would be disappointed with me, and this cooled my mood. Keme would tell me that Estella's intervention was a blessing, but I still felt disgusted that I was even in a position to need her help. My hands clamped into fists. I couldn't believe that the only person to do the right thing was some silly rich girl. She had to force her father and the floor manager to acknowledge my innocence.

I sat on a tree stump and watched the setting sun light the sky on fire with shades of orange and pink. Though a room close to the mills was convenient, it could never compare to the peaceful stillness I found amongst the trees.

The wind rustled the leaves a short ways away, commanding my attention. Standing before me was my mystery horse. She limped away with purpose, as if she had a destination in mind.

I decided to follow close by. If I could stay far enough behind her, she might lead me to her usual resting place. Maybe Keme has always been better at these things, but how could I fail at tracking a slow, injured animal?

She led me around white birch trees and great red oaks without noticing my short distance to her. The trickling sound of a brook met my ears and then shortly came into sight. Water flowed gently through a bridge of stones and fallen branches.

The horse navigated through the stream, while I kept on her trail, stepping from one dry stone to the next. We were only about half a mile into the woods from Pinebrook, but the trees grew thicker and thicker until I felt completely surrounded, enclosed in dusk's golden evergreen.

Finally, the horse stepped out of the trees and into a clearing where what looked like a cabin hid behind brush and branches. It was overgrown, like no one had lived there for many years.

With a few more cautious steps, I moved through the branches, but halted when I heard the unmistakable sound of feet in the leaves.

th caught in my throat when Estella appeared from behind ...n's overgrowth and walked towards my horse.

I quickly regained my composure, and focused on being still, undetected, hoping she'd decide to leave before the horse inevitably ran off.

What could possibly bring *her* to these parts of Pinebrook?

Estella hadn't left my thoughts since that morning, but she looked different here, very out of place and yet somehow natural. Her nose was red and her eyes were glassy as if she had been previously disturbed, but they had shifted by now to a state of wonder at the horse. Her hand rested lightly along the groove of the horse's chin.

Yes, I was right, she had been crying. Tear stains on her cheeks caught the light as she moved. The sight of her in the forest with this white horse made me think of a princess and an enchanted creature.

I considered turning on my heels and leaving right then.

Instead, I took another conscious step, making my presence known.

Her eyes met mine in a new burst of wonder, and a gasp escaped her lips.

"I didn't mean to startle you," I said, raising my hands in peace.

"You didn't," she said. "I was just expecting someone else, is all." She wiped away the moisture from her cheeks, clearly embarrassed. "You're the man from the mills."

"That would be me." I didn't know what else to say. It was a foreign feeling that I didn't enjoy one bit.

She spoke again. "I've seen you with this horse before, is she yours?"

What? I moved closer to Estella and the horse, my brain almost exploding. Her eyes widened and she swallowed hard.

"You've seen me here?" I asked in a strained voice. How many others had seen me? What if someone were to see me here now, with Estella?

"Yes, I figured maybe she had been your horse and broken loose. Her leg needs attention badly, and she's limping far worse than the time I saw her with you." She stared at me, clearly awaiting my response.

Thankfully, I stopped myself from going down a winding trail of what-if's before I drove myself mad. I only knew that I had to be much more careful. I would stay away from Estella and this horse before I found myself out of work, or worse. "She's not mine," I said at last, "but I've been looking for her. I'm glad she's been found by someone with the means to help her. She'll be in good hands with you." I tried to smile, but felt stupid.

"I don't know how I could possibly help this horse. I've been around the creatures long enough to know a fatal wound when I see one." Her crystal eyes sparkled, and I could tell she was unnerved by my presence, like a fawn in the deep wood sensing a hunter.

"May I?" I asked, motioning to the horse's leg.

She cleared her throat and crossed her arms. "Please, by all means."

I approached the wild-looking horse and reached out slowly, touching her for the first time. Her side was dusty and warm beneath my fingers. The horse flinched, but didn't step away from me. I dragged my hand along her coat until I stood at the back of her. *What a magnificent beast,* I thought. With one touch, we were already connected.

Estella rested her hand on the horse. "Do you know much about horses?"

"I guess you could say that." I looked at Estella. Her concern for this horse was so genuine and pure. I wanted to trust her. I knelt beside the injured leg and found that the wound was much worse and much larger than I'd expected. It had crusted over around the edges, but still oozed at the center. I cleared my throat at the sight and looked up.

"It's bad?" Estella asked.

I nodded. "It's worse than I thought."

She shook her head as if unwilling to accept reality. "Are you telling me that she's a lost cause?"

I stood and ran my hands along the horse's neck. "No, not completely lost, but in my best judgment, I'd say things aren't looking hopeful."

"So there really is nothing to be done for her?"

I cocked my head, uncertain. "I might know a thing or two that could ease her pain, but I couldn't guarantee her healing. I grew up north of here with my grandfather. He knew a lot about these things, and taught me the art of medicinal plants."

Estella took the horse's nose into her hands and looked at me. "If you have any faith in her healing at all, even the smallest shred, it's only right that we help her. My father has owned racehorses for as long as I can remember, so I know enough of their upkeep and well-being to be of assistance. Of course, your knowledge will be the most useful."

She looked back to the horse as if it were a child. "We won't let anything happen to you," she cooed.

*We?* I thought. That implied Estella and I would be spending a dangerous amount of time together.

I looked up at her, not knowing how to back away from this situation without smothering her desire to heal the horse. She could do it without me. She had money, and plenty of land and resources. "Where do you reckon she came from?" I asked at last. "There aren't wild horses around these parts."

She pushed a loose curl behind her ear and replied, "I know of a farm in Pinebrook that burned down just a few weeks ago. Devastated the entire estate—apart from a runaway horse, that is. The poor thing must have been living off the land when you found her, and not a day too soon." She smiled with hope in her wide eyes.

"That's a shame," I said. "At least that explains her wild appearance. She's been wandering about these woods for weeks."

"Yes, I suppose it does." Her smile seemed innocent. It disarmed me, diverting my normally sensible judgment onto a path of momentary insanity. It made me think that maybe I *could* heal this horse. At least, I could most likely *help* this horse in some way. It had been years since I'd even thought of medicinal plants, but I hoped my grandfather's teachings would stand the test of time.

I was consumed by thoughts and self-doubt that when Estella spoke up again it half-startled me.

"You never told me your name." she blurted out, tilting her head sideways, blocking the golden sunlight from her eyes.

Without hesitating, I said, "Bodaway." Why did I tell her my real name? It came out so easily when, frankly, I'd gotten used to saying that my name was John.

Uneasy with myself, I walked around the horse, examining her some more to make sure there was only the one wound. "I already know your name," I said, and then looked up to meet her eyes. "Well, it seems as though everyone knows your name in these parts."

Her face reddened. "My family is well known around here, which isn't surprising since my father owns the largest textile mill within fifty miles." She looked away. "I don't mean to sound so self-absorbed. It's just—"

"I know what you mean," I said. "Your family's well known around here; it's a small mill town. Nothing to be ashamed of." I quickly shifted the subject away from unimportant conversation and back to reality. "So what are you going to do with your horse?"

"My horse?" She looked surprised. "You were the one searching for her."

"I don't have anywhere to keep her. You know, mill housing." As I spoke, I felt down each of the horse's legs. The muscle mass was incredible in itself. It would be such a waste if this horse didn't pull through. It made me wonder about her speed and agility, but I could still feel the small tug in my pocket from Keme's stone, and I didn't let my mind wander any further.

"Oh, yes, naturally, but we can't just leave her here to die. You've confirmed that her wound is worse than you thought, and could even be grave. She needs help." Estella stepped closer, her voice full of pleading. "What can we do about it? You said you know your way around medicinal plants."

"We?" I laughed and shook my head. "What do you have in mind?" I made certain to put emphasis on the "you." "I'm sure there are much more efficient ways for people like you to fix up the horse's leg. She might even have a fighting chance with the kind of help you can buy."

Estella seemed uncertain. "Most people wouldn't give such a wound any chance at recovery. I couldn't risk bringing her to my father. I've seen him put down horses for much less a reason, and *those* were prized racehorses. This might sound a bit mad, but... what if we healed this horse together? I can provide her with shelter, and you possess the know-how." Her face glowed as if this were the most incredible plan.

How could I explain that this was ridiculous? Night was creeping in on us faster than a solution, and I simply didn't have the time or the words.

Yet, my bruise still throbbed, reminding me of my debt to her.

"It's the only way!" She rested her face carefully on the horse's nose.

Even if it were, *I* would be the one risking everything. The second someone saw a well-to-do richy like Estella with someone like me, I'd be left running around with my head cut off, trying to nurse this horse along with no work.

Suddenly, I was no longer under the spell of Estella's naivety or beauty. "No way, this isn't a good idea at all."

"What other options do we have? We can't just leave her here. My family owns a sizable estate, and with that comes acres of land. There's an old stable that we haven't used in years at the mouth of the forest. You can't even see my house from there. This plan will work! She could stay there in peace, I just know it... You said it yourself! All hope is not lost! If we don't at least *try* to help her, she will die." Estella traced her fingers along the horse's dusty-white coat as if to comfort her.

"You know how this would look if we were found out. I can't risk my position at the mills again."

"So you're more worried about what people think than about the fate of this horse?"

I stared at her in disbelief. "Some of us have responsibilities to other people. I'm the one taking all the risks by helping you." Heat crept up my neck. Did she think I was one of her little servants to do her bidding? "And, you know, I could be risking more than my position by helping you."

"I can make sure you and your position at the mills are safe. If anything were to go wrong, I would take all the blame."

As if I wanted to be more indebted to her than I already was. "Are you that naive? You've already done enough. Stop trying to help me and focus more on helping the horse."

This obviously annoyed her, and she put her hands on her hips. "Well, please forgive me then! I didn't realize you were so puffed up with pride that you would reject the help God brings to you."

"Pride?" I spat, my eyebrows crowding together. My hands clenched into fists, but I consciously released them, then forced myself to speak in a more rational tone. "Listen, I'm sorry, but this isn't something I can help you with. Simple as that. You're going to have to do this on your own." I looked at the horse. I wanted to help her so much, but this was too dangerous for me, and I knew I had to leave before I changed my mind.

"I can't do this without you!" Estella cried. She stood there in her dirt-stained dress, looking helpless, almost as helpless as the horse. "Look at her! Come feel her." She slid her hand down the horse's dusty, coarse, white side. "Look," she said as the horse's ribs expanded softly with each breath. "She's alive. As long as this creature is upright and breathing, I say we try to make her as comfortable as possible. I can't heal her on my own! She came to us for help, and you're just going to abandon her?"

No, I've never abandoned anyone. I've always done what needs to be done. I tried to justify the scenario where I'd leave Estella to fend for herself, where I'd forget about this suffering horse and get back to my monotonous life working my days away at the mills. But I couldn't do that now, not even if I wanted to. Settling my debt with

Estella was a matter of great importance—a matter I hoped to resolve swiftly.

I hated myself for what I said next. "I'm only doing this to repay you for getting my position back at the mills. After this, successful or not, we're even." I rubbed my bruised jaw again. "But this *is* a mistake."

Estella looked surprised. "You are not indebted to me in any way. I spoke up for you at the mills because it was the right thing to do, not so you would owe me any favors."

"I guess it's only natural that we should see things differently," I said, resolving to not argue the point.

She left it at that, her gaze moving slowly over the horse. "So, what do we do now?"

"Just take her home with you. We can meet here tomorrow night to collect what we need to help her. The cabin can be our meeting spot; it's private enough."

She clasped her hands together and sighed. "Oh, thank you!" Then she whispered to the horse, "I think you're going to be just fine."

I patted the horse's neck. "I suppose if she isn't dead in a few days, she may just have a chance. We can at least try and make her comfortable."

Estella's eyes met mine. I saw sincerity in them, and maybe some admiration. "Tomorrow night before sundown then? I'll bring her to my stables tonight, and let her rest."

I grabbed an old rope lying around and I fashioned a makeshift lead, which I gave to Estella. "*After* sundown," I clarified, observing the cool cover of darkness settling over the forest. Our odds of getting caught were much lower after nightfall. She nodded in triumph before leading our wild project towards her family's estate.

After they disappeared down the wooded path, I kicked a moss-covered stone and watched it roll away, annoyed with myself. Whether she accepted it or not, I owed Estella this much. Running both my hands through my hair, I started home through the dark wood with the opposite of a clear head.

# CHAPTER NINE

*Tuesday, June 6*

Estella

Upon waking the next day, the first things in my mind were Bodaway and our horse. For once, my life wasn't solely dictated by Mother and her rigorous schedules. I was focusing my energy on something bigger than myself. It was invigorating to have something completely my own, something that had nothing to do with my family. Mother would be mortified should she discover my new project, but there was no reason that she should know about any of it.

I sat up in bed and placed my cold feet on the hardwood floor. I wondered if Bodaway had spent his night on the forest floor. My cheeks burned and flushed red when I remembered he'd mentioned mill housing.

Moments later, Hannah came in to lay out a dress for me while I readied myself for the day's events. I hummed a mindless tune as I brushed through my hair. "Someone's happy today," Hannah said. She noticed a mess of garments on my floor and bent to pick them up.

I smirked. "I suppose I am."

"Could it be that you are actually *looking forward* to your outing with Henry and his family this evening?" Hannah folded the garments and placed them at the end of my bed.

All at once, a knot grew in my stomach. Somehow I had completely forgotten that Henry even existed. The knot twisted once more as thinking of Henry brought to mind Lillian, and how she never did show up.

All the warm feelings left me at once, and I couldn't help returning to my bed.

Hannah stared at me, probably regretting that she'd even brought him up. "I didn't mean to upset you," she said. "Henry left a lovely bouquet of flowers with his calling card this morning to remind you of your plans together. I thought you knew." She came to my bed, leaned in, and hugged me close. Her embrace was as comforting as I imagined a mother's embrace might feel. Mother had never been one for outward displays of affection. In fact, I couldn't recall a time when she'd held me—nor could I recall a time when I'd longed for her particularly foreign embrace.

"I must have forgotten," I said slowly. "Actually, I've accepted two separate invitations scheduled for the same day." I hesitated. "Do you think Mother and Father would let me live to see another day if I canceled my evening with the Hamiltons?"

Hannah sighed. "I know you are in a tight place. When I was a young girl—"

"A long, long time ago?" I teased.

"Eh! Mind your manners, you!" she laughed and poked me in the ribs. "Yes, ages ago. When I was a young girl, I loved school and learning and such. I even wanted to become a school teacher. But when my father died, I had to leave school to take care of my mother and sister. I left home and found work as a housemaid in Concord, all so I could send home my wages to put food in their mouths."

Hannah gazed into the distance. "You know, sometimes I wonder what would have happened if my father had lived, but I don't regret doing what I did one bit. If I had become a teacher, I never would've met the love of my life, God rest his soul. And I never would have met you kind folks all those years ago." She touched her heart and smiled up at me with pure joy in her eyes. "I love you, Estella, like my own, and it pains me to see you give up anything, no matter how small, for the duty you owe to your family.

"I want you to have everything you desire in this life, but us ladies don't often get to have things the way we want them. Most of our life is set for us, my sweets." Hannah rubbed my shoulders briefly before putting her hands on her knees, standing. She crossed the room. "That's just how this world works. What we want and what we must do are almost always two different things."

Then, as though we hadn't just been speaking about anything important, Hannah opened my wardrobe, removed a gown the color of seafoam, and asked "Is green alright?"

I nodded, and she laid it out on my bed.

I debated whether or not to lay bare my heart and tell her about Bodaway.

No, now was not the time to share. I looked to Hannah's aged face and smiled with sincere gratitude. I was very thankful to have someone who loved me and wanted the best for me. Sometimes it felt like my own parents only looked to their own interests. "Thank you, Hannah," I said. I reached over and squeezed her hand. "You mean the world to me."

"And you to me." She smiled and left me with my own thoughts and the sound of birds outside my window. I slipped out of my night garments and pulled the soft green gown over my petticoats. Smoothing the skirts, I took one last look in the mirror. I touched my favorite perfume and dabbed it behind my neck and my wrists before leaving my room.

The stairs creaked beneath my steps as I made my way down to the dining room.

Mother sat at the captain's chair, eating a soft-boiled egg and drinking her morning tea. "There's my beautiful daughter." She raised her eyebrows and smirked. "Henry's flowers are simply perfect, are they not?" She motioned to a bouquet of lilacs set in a simple vase at the center of the table.

"Indeed they are," I said, pulling out my chair and sitting. A maid rushed in and set a soft-boiled egg before me. I smiled at her as she filled my teacup.

"I knew that my advice would work," Mother continued, "but I had no idea to what extent!" She laughed and placed a napkin over her violet skirt. "Of course, I cannot claim all the praise for such success. Your lovely show clearly held some sort of effect. That yellow gown is purely *irresistible*. Credit where credit is due."

"A small victory for the both of us." I said, laying my napkin over my lap. I brought the china teacup to my lips.

"A victory for our family." She corrected me then tapped a silver spoon over her soft-boiled egg.

"Yes, perhaps," I said, hoping to put an end to any further discussion on the matter.

The moment I had returned from visiting Henry, Mother had gouged me for every detail. She simply couldn't get enough information to satisfy her, even though she exhausted my every answer. She could talk about the Hamiltons and our blissful arrangement all day with hardly a breath in between, but I didn't share her enthusiasm.

"Whatever you did," she said, "it worked. You managed to procure a dinner invitation and a beautiful bouquet of flowers. I dare say any trouble between the two of you is forgotten." She nodded and took a sip of tea, her emerald earrings bobbing about. "Oh, another thing, Alice Hamilton has invited us to join her at the orphanage this afternoon! So don't run off too far. You know, Estella, I really am impressed with you." She seemed hardly able to contain her excitement.

But I was no longer thinking about Henry or his family. My head felt light as I recalled Lillian telling me of her time spent in charitable work at that orphanage. I longed to hear the truth from her and to explain myself. Lord knew when I might have another opportunity to see her. Why had she ignored my note? She couldn't possibly blame me for Henry and his actions. I simply had to speak with her.

"I should like that very much," I said at last then broke apart my eggshell.

Mother smacked her lips together. "Excellent. We will leave for town at half past one."

I then realized Father had not been present for the conversation.

Mother shook her head when she noticed me staring at the empty seat and rolled her eyes. "Your father sends his apologies for missing breakfast, but you know him well enough. Already off to the mills, no doubt."

"Yes, I imagined as much." I took another sip of my tea, then returned the cup to its saucer with a clink. If I planned to venture to the stables before our trip to town, I'd need to leave immediately.

I finished my egg, then glanced at Mother. She seemed in such high spirits that I couldn't imagine having any trouble going about my own business.

I mustered some courage and stood from my seat. "I'd like to be excused."

Mother's gaze met mine, her teacup hovering in front of her lips. "Yes, by all means, prepare yourself for this afternoon." She studied me a moment, her lips pressed tightly into a smile. "And wear something blue. That green dress makes you look quite gaunt. You always look so nice in blue."

I nodded and left the room with haste, careful to keep my steps even and quiet as I passed through the few rooms leading to the kitchen. I stopped in the doorway before entering, taking note of my surroundings. Only one maid occupied the room, cleaning dishes. The rest were sure to be busy around the house. I acknowledged her with a smile, then went about my business. I imagined she found it odd, me tinkering about the kitchen, but I hoped she wouldn't speak a word of it.

I filled a pail of water and then approached the pantry, scanning the shelving until I found several apples. I bunched my skirt into a makeshift pocket and placed as many of the apples inside as I could manage. One rogue apple fell from my skirts and rolled across the floor, but I didn't dare bend to retrieve it lest I lose the whole lot.

I began for the back door with my skirt full of apples while my free arm lugged a sloshing pail of water. It would be a miracle if I made it to the stables without losing all my supplies. Whatever might be left would simply have to suffice until Bodaway arrived tonight.

Finally outside, I started off towards the old stable close to the forest's tree line, making sure to lift the hems of my dress, securing the apples. Though the sky was bright and full of cotton-like clouds, the grass still held onto the morning dew—my shoes were surely done for. Of course, ruined shoes were the least of my worries. I had a wounded, suffering horse hiding in my family's stables.

A scary thought nagged my mind: *What if our horse died? What if I killed it by not giving it proper attention right away?*

But as I stood before the stables, I was quickly greeted with a loud whinny from the open window. The horse's eyes smiled at me as she caught sight of the great red apples I brought her. I set the half-filled pail on the ground and let the apples fall from my skirt, but retrieved and shined one on my dress.

"Here you go, lovely." I offered her the apple in my hand, which she eagerly accepted from the window.

I opened the stable door, letting in more sunlight, then approached the horse. Cautiously, I walked around her, dragging my hand along her back.

Her mane was quite knotted, it would take hours to brush through it all. I looked to her leg and cringed. It was bad. My heart ached at the mere idea of losing her, but I managed to convince myself that Bodaway would know what to do.

I emptied the sorry remains of my pail of water into the feeding trough set against the stable wall, then fed her a few more apples.

When she seemed satisfied, I sat on an old stool. How was I supposed to see Bodaway tonight if I was going to be with Henry? If I canceled with Henry, my family would be furious. They might also become suspicious of my time spent in the stables. Mother's face appeared in my mind, and I remembered how proud she had looked of me to have smoothed things over with Henry.

*Maybe I could talk to Bodaway at the mills while I'm in town,* I thought, but that might embarrass him, and there was no way Mother would let me out of her sight for that long.

In the end, I resolved to simply make both appointments. I could be with Henry and his family for a few hours in the early evening, and then find my way to Bodaway by sundown. It all made sense, at least in my head.

\*\*\*

"Estella... and your mother... I am so glad that you could join me on such short notice." Alice Hamilton welcomed us into the orphanage, clearly surprised to see my mother. Her hair was pinned in a tight knot, and her slender figure appeared skeletal in her black silk gown.

"Oh, nonsense," Mother said. "It was no trouble at all, really."

Alice ushered us inside the grand entryway and let out an almost inaudible sigh. "Follow me, ladies; we can take tea in the parlor."

We walked its long corridors in a quiet that seemed strange for a building supposedly filled with children. "This is quite a building," I commented, looking around at the craftsmanship and dark woodwork. It must have dated back nearly a hundred years.

"Yes," she answered, "it really is. The building was once a mansion that belonged to my husband's grandfather, you know. After his passing, we decided to donate the building for the children's use."

"How generous of you," Mother added.

Alice produced a skeleton key from a hidden pocket in her skirts and unlocked the door at the end of the hall, revealing a private parlor.

The room was small but full of light. Floor-to-ceiling windows surrounded us, and the original crystal chandelier above us cast rainbow light all around. A lovely, antique sofa had been arranged along with a short table for our tea. Alice, seeming to realize there was not enough room for the three of us on the sofa, pulled the chair from a desk that sat at the back of the room, overlooking what little garden they had. She also fetched a third teacup, further confirming that she had not expected my mother to come along. Setting the chair down in front of the sofa, she motioned for us to take our seats. "Please."

Mother sat to my right and Alice sat directly in front of me, making it nearly impossible for my attention to wander. The only thing stopping our knees from touching was the short-legged table holding the tea.

"Where are all the children?" I craned my neck to peer out the windows, though in truth I was searching for Lillian.

Alice took the steaming pot of tea and poured us each a cup. "Isn't it quiet?" She smiled and looked around the room as though it were the most serene thing she had ever experienced. Bringing the cup to her lips, she continued, "During the day, most of the children have taken up work. Some of the young boys have even found work at the mills." She nodded to Mother. "Thanks, of course, to your wonderful husband. And the girls have taken up work in some of the houses in the area as maids in training. As I have always told my son, you are never too young to learn what hard labor is."

Mother gave a flattering smile. "I must agree with you, Alice, as well as commend you and your charitable work here."

Alice bowed her head. "I am but a humble servant of God."

"Amen," Mother whispered.

"Now, ladies, you might be wondering why I've invited you here. As you know, my husband and I are very pleased by this arrangement." She reached a hand out and took mine for the briefest squeeze. It made my skin itch.

"As are we." Mother added, and began rambling nonsense about wedding arrangements and how divinely suited Henry and I were for one another.

It was hard to say how long Alice permitted Mother to babble on, but it must have been minutes of mind-numbing chatter before she interrupted with careful smoothness.

"Simply divine," she agreed. "Yes, a match formed by God Himself! Now, returning to *why* I've invited you here." Her lips tightened into what I think was supposed to be a smile, and her eyes narrowed in on me. "I would be most grateful if Estella would consider spending Sunday mornings here, at the orphanage. We could use the extra hands these days. I thought perhaps if you saw the place, you might feel the same connection to it that I myself do."

"Oh, what an honor!" Mother gushed. "You do so much, really." She rested her hand at her bosom and lowered her eyes. "To think my Estella could take part in such distinctive, charitable acts of service. What do you say to that?" she asked, turning to me with the unflinching, unnerving eyes of a wildcat.

If I hadn't been so anxious to know Lillian's whereabouts, I might have laughed at Mother's flowery praises, but I also saw in them my opportunity for answers.

"Yes," I said, breaking away from Mother's gaze. "Mrs. Hamilton, you give so much to these children. I would love to be a part of your work here. I so admire my friend, Lillian Sterling, for everything she has done these past months for the children."

Alice's face turned hard. "She is no longer with us... I am afraid Lillian has turned out to be quite troublesome."

"Surely we're not speaking of the same Lillian? The Lillian *I* know is quite the opposite of troublesome." I kept my voice firm but calm. Mother's foot rammed silently into my ankle, but I kept my composure.

Alice set her teacup on the table next to the steaming pot. "Are you accusing me of slander?"

My lips tightened. "You misunderstand me. I am only surprised to hear of Lillian's sudden change in character."

Mother cleared her throat. "Do forgive my daughter's imprudence." She glared at me and rested her hand over mine.

Alice smirked. "I wish it *were* only slander, but I must advise you not to associate yourself with Lillian Sterling. It's sad, really." She shook her head. "And we wouldn't want you catching her malady."

"She's unwell again?" I asked impatiently.

"Apparently she's out of town for, well... I'm not sure how long. She's visiting a more experienced doctor in Concord with her mother. The poor girl is too weak—a tragedy to see health fail at such a young age. It makes one wonder what she has done to grow so susceptible to illness."

My teeth ground together, and my hands trembled. For fear of crushing the porcelain cup in my hands, I set it down.

"Strange she didn't tell you, since you know her so well." Alice arched one thin eyebrow, studying my confusion.

Mother leaned forward. "I am so glad that you had the courage to share this with us, Alice, though I've suspected as much for some time now. I will be sure to keep Estella from Lillian's corruption, and sickness, of course. Estella must be in excellent health for the wedding."

Mother's words shocked me. How could she turn against my friend so easily? Lillian surely had an explanation, and I would trust Lillian's story over Alice Hamilton's any day. If Lillian had truly been so ill, she would have told me.

Mother took her first sip of tea, which by now must have been cold. "Alice, this tea is simply splendid, you must tell me where you get it!" She swirled the liquid in the cup and brought it just under her nose, smelling it like she was some wine connoisseur.

Alice's eyelids fluttered with clear impatience. "I'll send you a box."

For the next fifteen minutes, Mother hardly took a breath. She talked on and on about God knows what—a miracle if even *she* knew. I, for one, stopped listening many "Henrys" in, and let my mind wander to Lillian and her sickness.

Was Alice listening to a word Mother said? Her eyes shifted between Mother and the clock over the mantle every few sentences or so.

When it finally chimed half-past four, she clapped her hands together and exclaimed, "My goodness! Look at the time! I really must be left alone to prepare for the children's return from work. Dinner preparations begin early." She stood, evidently trying to push us out.

I tried my best to hide the fact that I was still fuming over the comments made about Lillian.

"Thank you for having us for tea, Alice," Mother said, but what she should have said was, *thank you for pouring tea in cups that we hardly touched because I was quite occupied tickling your ears with puffery.*

"Yes, thank you," I forced out. Mother and I stood in unison.

Alice smiled, but that only made me more uneasy. "I do apologize for the shortness of our meeting, though I look forward to receiving you at my home this evening. We shall have so much to talk about." She glided across the room and opened the door. "Allow me to show you out."

Mother and I nodded to her as we passed through the doorway. Alice shut the door, careful to lock it behind her, and returned us to the front entrance. "Until tonight, then." She ushered us outside, the same odd smile still preserved on her thin lips.

"Yes, good day to you, Alice!" Mother managed before our hostess left us on the orphanage steps alone.

One thing troubled me—Why had Alice invited me to the orphanage to begin with? What had she expected to accomplish, outside of nurturing my distaste for her? If Alice had gotten me alone, as she planned, what might she really have said?

And *Lillian*? So sick that she needed a city doctor? Why would she not tell me she'd been so poorly? There was nothing I could do about it but pray, wait for her return, and go to her the moment she set foot back in Pinebrook.

\*\*\*

Whether I liked it or not, the time eventually arrived for my outing with Henry. Mother *and* Father were both home and ready to see me off.

Father scratched his mustache before putting a cigar to his lips, puffing out a heavy, strong smelling cloud of smoke.

Instantly, Mother's hands flew to her hips. "Irving, is that really necessary right now? Henry will be arriving any moment to take our daughter, and you're sitting on our front porch smoking a cigar—look! You're not even wearing a cravat! Lord help us."

Mother turned towards the house. "Hannah!" she yelled, "Bring Irving a cravat as soon as humanly possible." She blotted her glistening brow ever so daintily with a handkerchief.

I moved to sit beside Father.

"Sit still, young lady!" Mother waved cigar smoke away with the same handkerchief. "I feel like the only one taking the weight of this evening seriously."

Father and I looked at each other, and then he motioned for Mother to sit. "Darling, please. Take a seat." She sighed and collapsed into a wicker chair near us.

"I *am* taking this seriously," Father continued. "I want this marriage to happen as much as you do, Rachelle."

"Then please, just be more useful. You know how I work myself up running about, trying to make sure nothing is left to fate! Oh, the burden that rests on my shoulders, and mine alone!" She let out a dramatic sigh, tilting her head back. "All I want is for you to look presentable in front of our future son-in-law."

Just then Hannah burst through the door with a burgundy cravat, prompting Mother to jump back into her frenzy.

Just as Father finished adjusting his cravat, Henry's carriage pulled up the drive. Father walked to meet him and his horses.

That's another thing that Father had in common with Henry: Henry enjoyed taking part in horse racing. My observation over the years was that Henry had less interest in the horses themselves and much more in betting large sums of his family's money—not to mention overindulging in ale—but it was all the same to Father.

I watched the two of them shake hands while Mother watched *me* as though making sure each hair on my head was finely in its place. She smiled. "Have a wonderful time, Estella. You look so beautiful in that blue satin gown, so you mustn't get anything on it! And make sure you don't say anything to offend his family—by all means, avoid any conversation about Lillian." She looked up to the heavens as if to say, *God have mercy on you if you put this family's future in jeopardy.* "And goodness, please keep your bonnet on well. An open carriage could do something fierce to that hair of yours." She stepped close to me and tightened my bonnet's ribbons a bit too tight.

"I shall hold on for dear life, and that of my hair." I dug my finger in between the ribbon and my chin, loosening its suffocating grip.

Henry and Father approached the front porch as they conversed about next week's big race. "Old Black Magic here," Father was saying, "is ready to run again. First race of the season for her, but now that she's back in town, she's ready to win it all."

Henry smiled. "Oh, she will do well, as usual, but you can never be sure there won't be a dark horse that sneaks by right under our noses."

Father laughed. "Black Magic *is* the dark horse, my boy."

They shook hands one last time and Henry helped me into his carriage. "What a sight you are, just radiant," he said as the driver took the reins and kissed at the horses to move.

I forced a smile. Henry's mother had only made it more difficult to love him, but I tried not to let her ruin our chance at happiness. I needed to keep an open heart, a difficult task given the circumstances surrounding Lillian.

We drove past a field that we used to play in as children. I laughed to myself as I remembered a time we had been running about, chasing each other with friends from church, when Henry's trousers fell to his ankles. I could still picture his face turning bright red, his eyes wide, just before hauling up his trousers and running away faster than any of us had ever seen anyone run.

Henry nodded to the field. "You don't recall anything in particular that happened over there, I'm sure?"

I smiled, and for the first time I didn't need to force it. "Nope, not one memory at all." We both laughed. Henry was very handsome when he wasn't being completely full of himself.

"We spent a lot of time together during those long summers," he said, "but perhaps you don't remember. You always cried that I was mean to you, but everyone knew it was because I was sweet on you."

I raised my eyebrows. "Yes I *do* remember those summers though I never pictured us as anything more than friends." Even that term was generous.

He looked me nervously in the eyes. "Well, what do you think about us now?" He swallowed. "I know our families are pushing things along much sooner than we had planned, but how do you really feel about all of this?"

My thoughts immediately went to Lillian and how she had reacted to Henry at my party. That, and the horrible things Alice had said about her. "I believe there could be a future for us if we get to know one another a bit better." I thought for a moment, and then spoke carefully. "You know that Lillian is my best friend. Whatever history there is between you, I'll need to know that it's over and that you'll make things right with her."

Henry pulled back. "Estella, does your hesitation towards me concern Lillian? Let me assure you that she is nothing more to me than an acquaintance, a woman I nod to cordially in church each Sunday. You of all people know I've stumbled into a rough patch! The whispers on the streets are unforgiving, but I'm trying to become a better man. I can feel you holding back from me, I've felt it for some time now." He raked a fast hand through disheveled blond hair. "So, please tell me why you've set your heart on resisting my advances. Nothing has changed for me since our correspondence."

I didn't know how to respond.

Birds flew overhead. Warm breeze rustled through the fields at our side and pushed its way beneath my bonnet, blowing a few strands of hair loose.

"You aren't wrong," I said at last. "Your reputation *is* troublesome, you know, but shame on me for letting whispers infiltrate my feelings towards you. We may have gotten to know one another through our letters, and I do hold a sort of fondness towards you…" I turned away. "But I feel as though I don't know you as a gentleman, nor you, myself as a woman."

"Well, most ladies around here wouldn't care about my reputation." He sighed in frustration. "Nevertheless, I'm trying to be better. I want to be someone that my family doesn't have to be ashamed of. I'm home from school now, and I'm working at the mills with your father. I know what I want, Estella. I'm not the one holding us back." He grabbed my gloved hand and his forwardness caused me to stiffen. "There you go again," he said, "pulling away when all I want to do is get close to you."

I pulled away, clasping my hands together in my lap, ensuring they wouldn't be taken again.

Henry continued. "I'm trying to show you that I am interested in pursuing this whole ordeal, that it's not just our families pushing for this. I started writing you of my own accord, and no one forced you to return my letters. I want something more for us than just an arrangement, and I know you do too."

"Love," I said softly. Could Henry truly want the same things I desired? I shook my head. "Henry, the other night at my party, when we were around other folks, you seemed different. You were distant, and refused to talk straight to me when I asked you specific questions. I want to know *you*. That is, if you can be honest with me, I think we can learn to trust each other. Trust comes *before* affection. You say you want to be a good man. If we're to pursue something more than friendship, it's in our mutual interest for you to truly become that good and respectable man that you say you aspire to be."

He looked off into the sky. "Alright," he said, scratching his chin, and that was it for the ten silent, dusty minutes which passed before we reached his family's home.

\*\*\*

Dinner was exactly how I expected it to be: friendly, stuffy, uncomfortable, and forced.

Alice, strangely, seemed to be pretending this was the first time we had seen each other that day. She and her husband both were kind enough, making casual conversation about my time in Pinebrook so far.

Now and again, Henry looked up from his plate and smiled at me. Even if one could not stand Henry, one could not deny his contagious smile. He was too charming for his own good, which was no doubt the cause of so much of his trouble and scandal.

He seemed relaxed after our conversation in the carriage, and there was something which seemed *genuine* in his countenance. That was the only redeeming quality of the evening, what made all the small talk bearable. For the first time, it felt like I was seeing the Henry from our letters.

"Shall we retire to the parlor?" his father, Richard, invited. He stood, stocky and plump, and adjusted his coat.

In contrast, his wife stood inches above him, slender, her frame petite but in no way frail.

Henry and I rose in unison, our chairs gliding silently across the carpeted floor, and followed.

The Hamilton's house was almost as large as our own summer home, and much more extravagant. Each piece of furniture had been delicately arranged, leaving plenty of room to walk about. Red velvet tapestries hung from a tall picture window, and a handwoven carpet ornamented the wide-planked floor beside a chaise lounge. A great portrait of Alice hung prominently over the fireplace, her eyes cold and hollow, strikingly similar to the portrait hanging in Henry's office at the mills.

A crystal cart topped with bottles sat beside a large cushioned chair, which I could only assume belonged to Richard. "Brandy?" he asked Henry as he began filling glasses.

"No thank you, Father," Henry said, waving away the glass. Maybe he really *was* trying to change.

Alice offered me some wine, but I only wet my lips with it—I'd never taken a liking to the bitter taste it left behind. For a while the four of us discussed the plaque recently hung in the Hamiltons' honor at the Church of Pinebrook.

At last Alice took a final sip and said, "Come with me." She motioned for me to follow. "Let the men have their talk. Louisa, bring in my tea, please."

I threw an anxious look to Henry as she led me down the hall and into her husband's study, where she made herself at home. It seemed backwards that we women would retire to the study while the men remained in the parlor.

"Please, Estella, make yourself comfortable." Alice sat at her husband's desk in a way that said it was not the first time she had done so.

I sat in the chair in front of her desk. As though things were not uncomfortable enough, it now felt like I had been called into the headmaster's office, about to receive a harsh reprimand. I shivered.

"Now Estella, I really didn't intend to corner you in my home and talk business when I invited you here. That was the purpose of our meeting earlier, but what can I say? We know how that turned out. You've forced my hand." She squinted at me, her lips pursed into a smile.

I looked back at the door.

"Oh, no reason to be frightened. I only wanted an atmosphere where one can speak freely." She folded her hands and laid them on the desk. Why the intimidation?

I cleared my throat. "Won't the gentleman be missing us?"

She waved her finger, tsking at me. "Come now, Estella, you have much to learn about men. Have you any idea of the work cut out for you? My goodness."

"I don't quite understand what you mean," I said slowly.

To my great relief, Louisa appeared with the tea, serving it in small, elegant cups with watercolor roses painted along the edges.

Once we were alone again, Alice produced a tiny silk pouch containing some sort of herb, which she pinched into her steaming cup. She caught me staring as she stirred her tea gently, the silver spoon clinking against china. "It's rue. Small amounts work wonders for lingering coughs like mine." She smirked. "I always carry some with me. One can never predict the time or place one might require a tonic… or a fast way to poison someone." She gave an eerie laugh. I swallowed hard.

"Oh, don't be daft," she said. "I see the fear in your eyes. I would never poison *you*, my dear. Why would I ever dispose of someone so compliant? Someone, simply put, in my good graces? The Hamilton name has smiled upon you."

My stomach fluttered, but I laughed with her nervously.

"We—my husband and myself—are inclined to believe you are the perfect match for our son." She arched an eyebrow. "He has taken a liking to you, and you do come from a generous family and from high society. In every respect, you seem the equal match of our little Henry."

I tried to clear my throat. I felt like a young man approaching a lady's father to ask some sort of permission. "My family believes the same of Henry, I'm sure."

"Yes, of course they do." She hesitated. "I just wanted to make sure you held the proper amount of respect for this family's name, the same you hold for your own. We have a very small circle, we Hamiltons, and we keep our business to ourselves. I am sure you know by now that Henry has been a… spirited young man."

Is that what they call whoring around these days? Nevertheless, I felt compelled to agree. "Yes, I understand that discretion is very important." I had heard before that Alice had a way of making you agree to anything she wanted. I never fully understood what that meant until this moment.

"And another thing." She took a sip of her tea and then set the cup back onto the desk. "Look around you."

I observed the study awkwardly. At least there were no imposing portraits of Alice, but then the real thing was already sitting across from me.

"This house, this marriage, Estella... I know you may think the life of a housewife has to be dull and quiet, but just look at me! A wife has the power to control and lead from the background." She tapped the desk with both hands. "This is really more my office than Richard's. The key is they never know that. Let them believe they make all the decisions."

Could she have poisoned my tea? I held my teacup, staring at its steaming liquid, and tried to grasp Alice's words. "That puts quite the burden on our backs, wouldn't you agree?"

She folded her hands again and stared me in the eyes. "That's exactly what I am saying. In your youth, you had certain duties. In your marriage, you will adopt a set of new and very different responsibilities. The honor of the Hamilton family name rests in your hands, Estella. If that is not a burden you can take on, then there is no reason to continue this conversation."

I thought of my family, and how furious they'd be if I were to return with a broken arrangement.

And I raised my full, untouched teacup to my lips.

Alice watched me intensely.

I emptied its contents into my mouth in one confident gulp, as though it were hard liquor, and set my cup back on the desk with a delicate clink. "Then let us continue."

"Wonderful! Then we are of one mind." Her almost transparent skin stretched across her face into a smile as she stood up from her husband's desk. "I knew this would be a fruitful conversation."

We joined the men once more, and it was as though we had never left.

Henry rose from his seat at our return. "Mother, I hope you didn't scare Estella off."

"Oh, I am far too strong to be swayed so easily," I said, looking to Alice. I wondered if I would die in my sleep later that night.

Alice smiled oddly. "Let us hope so." Richard finished his glass. "Estella, don't pay too much attention to Alice and her ways. Can I get you another drink?" He hastily wiped the leftover droplets of liquor from his mustache.

"I am sure Estella would prefer to get back to her family before sundown," Henry said, stopping his father from entertaining me further.

I was more than glad to be leaving at such an early hour. "Yes, thank you all for such a lovely evening," I said.

\*\*\*

The sun was just starting to set as we approached the carriage waiting for us on the Hamiltons' U-shaped drive.

"I hope you don't mind if I drive you home alone," Henry said as he helped me into my seat.

"How scandalous!" I exclaimed in a theatrical tone. "You know, I actually had a really nice time tonight."

"You sound surprised." He laughed and seated himself snugly next to me.

"No!" I shook my head, laughing. "I meant I didn't really know what to expect tonight. I had a nice evening, that's all."

"I'm glad you were able to tolerate my family. My parents adore you, and if I heard my mother correctly over dinner, she said you agreed to help her Sunday mornings, before church, at the orphanage?" He ran his hand through his hair. "Is there anything this girl doesn't do?" He laughed with his crooked smile.

*I'm nursing a horse back to health tonight with an Indian man,* I thought.

The horses pulled us along through gold-tinted scenery, the summer air a bit cooler than a June night should feel. I wrapped my satin shawl tightly around my shoulders.

"What did you two talk about in my father's study?" Henry asked. "I hope she didn't frighten you. You looked a little pale afterwards."

"Oh, not too much. Just something about trust, and secrets, and respecting the family name." I raised an eyebrow.

"I would be lying if I told you I was surprised."

I looked over at him. Henry had dressed finely for our evening in a sleek black suit, a long tailcoat, and a matching hat and cravat. "Aren't you cold at all?" I asked, and linked arms with him.

"No, I quite like these cooler summer nights." He tipped his hat at me. "Why? Shall I wear your shawl?"

"I fear this color would not suit you."

Henry shook his head with a hint of a smile that lingered on his lips in between our silly remarks and comfortable silence for the rest of the drive.

By the time our carriage approached the front of my house, the evening's golden light was nearly gone. With the long night ahead of me, I'd be grateful for any light at all.

Henry pulled us to a stop then helped me down from his carriage.

"I suppose this is where our evening meets its end." The remaining daylight made his blond hair sparkle. It was easy to allow his appearance to distract me.

"Good night Henry," I said. "Thank you again for a lovely evening."

He looked at me for a moment, and then reached for my hand. I didn't resist him this time. I couldn't; he had been so *different* tonight. It gave me hope for the future, if this was truly what our life had to be.

Realizing that I wouldn't turn away this time, Henry pulled me gently towards him until I was so close to his face that I could see every detail, even the little scar just above his left eyebrow.

Was I going to let him kiss me? Was I ready for this?

He leaned in and whispered, "Good night, Estella," smirking as though he could read my thoughts. His cheek just barely brushed mine as he pulled away, and without another word, he was off, leaving me with nothing except the mystery of why he hadn't decided to kiss me after all.

I made my way into the house, accurately anticipating the questions upon questions my mother immediately heaped upon me.

"How did it go?" she asked eagerly. "Did you make a great impression? Please tell me you did."

I needed to get to Bodaway, and every moment spent talking was a moment wasted. "It was a wonderful evening. You'd be proud to see me socializing with his family the way you taught me."

Mother put her hands on her hips and gave a dramatic sigh of relief. "Praise be to God. Estella, we were so nervous about tonight."

"And did you take a look at my gown?" I asked. "Spotless."

Mother turned and called into the parlor. "Did you hear that, Irving? Our daughter is a real lady after all!" She laughed to herself, sounding very pleased.

Restlessness stirred within me. "Mother," I began, "If you don't mind, I believe something I ate didn't agree with my stomach, and I'd like to retire early."

"Oh alright," she said, "I supposed you've earned it. Should I send Hannah up with some tea and tonic? You do look a bit pale."

I swallowed hard. That was exactly what I *didn't* want. "No, Mother. I need my rest and a quiet space."

"Alright." She planted a moist, unpracticed kiss on my forehead. "Go on now, off to bed."

"Good night," I said, forcing a smile.

After moving around the stairwell and out of sight, I wiped away her kiss with the back of my hand. Once I was in my bedroom, I closed the heavy door behind me.

There was no way I could go into the woods in this dress. I found and changed into an old calico dress, a garment that no one would notice getting stained or torn. Then I removed the pins from my hair and shook my head to loosen everything.

Far trickier than changing clothes would be sneaking out of the back door. I decided that if I carried my shoes, it would keep my steps quiet.

Slowly, I creaked down the servants' stairwell. I was a million times less likely to be caught this way, as all the kitchen help would have been dismissed by this hour. So long as I could make it to the kitchen, I was almost sure to be safe.

As I crept, I could hear the chatter of Mother and Father from the front rooms. No doubt they would forget all about my accomplishments with Henry if they saw me right now. Anxiety and annoyance burned at the base of my skull as I thought about the way things worked for proper ladies of society. Alice and her stupid conversation about the power and responsibilities of a wife still nagged at me.

Upon finally reaching the kitchen, I rubbed my scalp and tried to push my obligations and duties to the back of my mind for the rest of the evening.

As I reached for the door knob, a long meow nearly made me jump out of my skin. It was Mother's cat, Mr. Darcy.

"Darcy? Is that you, my little angel?" Mother called.

For the briefest moment, I considered turning on my heels and returning to my room. Instead, I left the kitchen behind me. The door shut louder than I'd expected. Hopefully Mother would think it was Darcy alone making noise and getting into mischief.

But I was on my way, undetected, barefoot, as I trod the cool grass beneath my feet.

# CHAPTER TEN

## Friday, June 9

### Bodaway

It was almost sundown before I reached the meeting point. Twigs on the forest floor snapped in quiet submission to the weight of my steps, and the abandoned cabin grew closer and closer into view. A couple of blackbirds landed in my path, chasing each other, pecking and squawking playfully, then took off into the sky where they came from as freely as they had arrived.

Would I ever find my way back to where *I* came from? I was a mockery to my Abenaki blood, and an outcast everywhere else I went. Did I belong *anywhere?* I tried not to focus too long on that. What good would it do to acknowledge these things when my soul already knew them full well?

Just being outside the mill walls was usually enough to lift my spirits, but today was different. I was anxious. Anxious at the thought of getting caught, anxious to help this horse, and anxious to get this whole thing over with.

Once I reached the cabin, I searched my surroundings for a place to rest my weary bones. I sat on a stack of rotted wood. The moon rose steadily in the evening sky, waiting out the sun for its turn to shine. A cool breeze stirred up the damp smell of earth and pine until it was all I could focus on.

The scents took me back to the days I had spent with my brother and grandfather, hunting, trapping, and studying medicinal plants. I held my breath, trying to keep the evening air inside me. I hoped it would change me somehow, that it would cleanse me and give me peace.

It didn't.

I blew out the air I'd trapped in my lungs, then removed a scrap of paper from my pocket.

Squinting in the dim light, I double-checked my list of medicinal plants I knew we'd need to heal the horse. I'd learned to read and write from the missionary family that my father left me and Keme with, but my handwriting wasn't so neat.

Before I left for work this morning, I drew pictures of the plants I would need with abbreviated names I could remember. Nothing fancy. I wondered if Estella would look down on me for not having such a common skill.

But it didn't matter if Estella could make out a single word of it or not. I could do this without her help. I could do it all on my own.

Remembering the weight of what I was doing, I quickly looked around me, making sure I was completely alone. If anyone ever learned that I'd been seeing Estella, I was in for some trouble. I couldn't stand either to lose my job or to have Estella save it again. *I'm my own man,* I thought. *That's why I'm here, isn't it?* I didn't need to prove anything to anyone. My responsibility was to make money for Keme, nothing more.

It was the least I could do for him, given the circumstances. I hadn't heard a word from either him or the missionary family these past weeks, but in Keme's case, no news was probably good news.

Because I had so much resting on my shoulders, I reminded myself to thank God every day that I was healthy and able-bodied. *Keme* would.

*God, if you're real, and out there listening, this is for Keme.* I looked to the sky. The evening wind blew the tree branches, spreading them across the sky like black cobwebs. *Please help me find the plants needed to heal the horse.* I dug my heel into the dirt. *And help me keep my temper at bay. I get frustrated and lose myself, then end up in ridiculous situations like this one.*

I frowned, knowing I had no one to blame but myself. *I was the imbecile who had agreed to help Estella.*

A rustling in the trees just beyond the cabin lifted my eyes from the ground.

There she was. I stood immediately and walked to meet her on the path, knowing that I had to heal this horse. I owed it to her to try, whether she viewed it that way or not, but after that, I would be done. Done with Estella, done risking my job, and done being indebted to anyone.

"I'm glad you showed up," Estella said with a smile that only annoyed me further.

"Showed up!?" I exclaimed. She really doubted me after I gave her my word? "Of course I came. I told you I would, and I'm a man of my word." I had *just* prayed for a cool head, but was already losing it.

She seemed taken aback. "I'm sorry," she said. "Being here is a risk for both of us. You could've changed your mind once you had time to think things through, and I was glad to see you hadn't."

I shook my head, catching my frustration in its early stages. "No, I'm sorry." I closed my eyes and tried to mean it. "It's been a long day, but I'm here. Let's just get started."

She stood in her worn-looking dress and pushed a loose strand of dark hair behind her ear. "Thank you," she said softly.

I rubbed my face and continued in a deliberately calm tone. "We should try to find everything we need within the hour, while the moonlight is at its brightest. Then we can find our way to your stables, where I assume the horse is resting. I brought a list of medicinal plants that could be useful." I handed her the list of drawings and waited for her to be surprised at my sloppy handwriting.

After thoroughly examining the list, she handed it back to me. "Alright, so you tell me where to start."

I met her eyes, silver in the moonlight. "A plant known as white man's foot can cleanse the infection. We also need yarrow to stop the bleeding and clot the wound."

"I think I know where we can find yarrow. There's a grassy area on the trail back to the stables not fifteen minute's walk from here. I've seen some there in years past."

"OK, and we're more likely to find white man's foot in dry, grassy areas as well. We may be better off heading in the general direction of the stables to begin with."

A brief gust of wind prompted Estella to wrap her arms tightly around herself. "That's a good plan."

We started off together in search of the plants we needed. I knew the exact type of places to look for white man's foot, but worried that the lack of sunlight might prove to make our task difficult. Our feet crunched through the dead leaves on the path, and a nearby owl began its evening call.

Estella looked at me sideways as we walked, then looked away. "Did you really learn all of this from your grandfather?" she asked. "The knowledge of medicinal plants, that is."

"My grandfather taught me in the old ways of the Abenaki Indians. Of course, that includes how to use medicinal plants and the natural resources at hand." I tucked my silly drawings and scribbled words into my pocket.

"He sounds like a very wise man," she continued awkwardly.

"He *was* a very wise man." I held back some branches as we passed through them, then let them snap back into place. "I will always be grateful for the knowledge he passed down."

Estella twisted her hands around in clear discomfort. "I'm sorry," she said quietly.

That man had been more of a father figure to me than my own father could ever be. He took so much pride in teaching me the old ways, showing me how to weave baskets and fishing nets. I was only nine years old, but he never treated me like a child.

*"Here, hold the splint nice and steady." My grandfather put his firm hands over mine to correct me. "Now, carefully weave the sweet grass around the splint." My grandfather was patient, never willing to give up on me. Keme was too young to learn with us, but he looked up to our grandfather as if he were the greatest man who walked this side of the earth.*

*We sat outside our small cabin in Maine on an old tree stump. I took the sweet grass and furrowed my eyebrows. "I can't get it right! The grass keeps falling out of place."*

*"Bodaway," he said, resting his hand on my shoulder. "You become frustrated too quickly. You must learn to have patience."*

*I kicked at the dirt, knowing he was right, but protested once more. "But it's too hard!"*

*My grandfather stood up. "Nothing in life worth having comes easily. Sometimes you have to walk further than your feet wish to take you. Perseverance and determination are virtues."* He looked at me in seriousness, but his eyes were kind.

I loved him so much and respected every word he spoke. I took the mess of a basket into my hands and stared at it.

My grandfather nodded to me and said gently, "I believe you can do whatever you put your mind to. Perseverance." Then he left me on my own to finish what I had started.

What would my grandfather have to say about me now? I could hardly remember my native tongue, let alone everything else he had taught me. Perhaps I could honor him and his memory by healing this horse in the ways that he taught me.

Seeming to sense my uneasiness, Estella pointed to the tree line in front of us. "We're almost there," she said.

Suddenly a noise broke ahead. I paused in my tracks and stretched my arm out to stop Estella from walking further.

A squirrel ran past and climbed up the tree next to us, nearly giving me a heart attack.

"What are you doing?" asked Estella.

"I thought I heard someone else in the woods." I raked a hand anxiously through my hair.

"We won't be caught, so you have nothing to worry about. Nobody else lives within two miles of this place." She sounded amused.

"Nothing to worry about?" I tried to keep my voice from rising. "I'm risking my life for a stupid horse, all because you had to go and save the day by convincing your father to let me stay and work for him."

"You don't owe me anything. I've already told you this, I did what I thought was right, and I don't expect anything from you in return." Even the night couldn't hide the way her face hardened towards me.

"And *I'm* doing the right thing by repaying my debt to you. Some of us have responsibilities, Estella. Who else is going to send my brother the money he needs? Not you, and certainly not the horse!"

Estella's face softened once more, but this time her elegant features were tainted with something worse than stone: Pity. I hated pity.

"I didn't know that you sent money to your brother," she said softly." I can't imagine the weight of that."

My stomach turned to a lump of steel. "I don't want your pity. I'm just telling you how it is. The only reason I'm here is to provide money for my brother. I didn't just abandon him, if that's what you're thinking." I looked straight at her. "I'm doing what I must."

"I never said you abandoned him, or even thought about it. You need to stop assuming the worst in people... including yourself."

I was silent for a second. "You know what," I finally said, "We've wasted so much time standing here arguing that hopefully the horse is still alive when we get to her." I didn't wait for a reaction as I pushed by her and walked to the edge of the woods.

I took my first step onto the Wellstones' property. The stables were set off to my left. Out of sight from peering eyes, just as Estella had said.

Even through the darkness, I could sense the property's vastness. How could so much land belong to one man? I had no doubt I'd be able to find the plants I needed here. I walked out further into the field and crouched low, picking at the grass.

*Dry.*

I remembered when my grandfather taught me about white man's foot. He said to always look for it in the dryer places. They grow in small clusters and their leaves have a sheen about them.

I picked for a while in the dry grass, but to no avail. When I finally stood up, Estella walked towards me.

"Is this what you're looking for?" she asked, lifting leaf-filled palms.

I held her hands still, then examined the leaves that shined in the moonlight. "Yeah." I shook my head. "Where did you find it?"

"In the dry grass, like you said." She smirked, obviously pleased with herself. "What's next?"

"Yarrow."

"And that's it?"

"Yes, well, it would be amazing if we could get our hands on some lavender, but that's highly unlikely."

A smug smile spread across her lips, and she dumped the white man's foot into my hands. "You find the yarrow. There's a patch with white blossoms that tends to grow along the treeline by the trail. I'll be back." She turned away.

"Wait, where are you going?"

"I'm going to get us some lavender." She sounded as if she believed herself an angel of salvation sent from God Himself.

I shook my head at her impulsiveness, but she had already disappeared over a grassy bank, headed in the direction of their estate. "Yarrow..." I muttered, and began for the treeline.

\*\*\*

The stable was small and contained only two stalls. The poor animal, certainly in pain, stood in the cleaner one, favoring her infected leg as she hovered it over fresh hay on the dirt floor. Still, she seemed to be in fairly good spirits for a horse standing at death's door.

Natural light probably illuminated the room well enough during the day, but the night time called for something more. I searched the stable's uneven shelving for anything useful to light the room but only found a candle stick nearly burned to the wick, a rusted knife, and a holey woolen blanket. "We'll manage," I said to the horse.

She craned her neck out of the stall into a shaft of moonlight and I took her face in my hands. "I'm going to try my best to make you better, OK? I'll try."

I set the yarrow blossoms on the dirt floor and held onto the white man's foot.

Estella had been right again. I'd found yarrow fairly quickly, following along the treeline.

Come to think of it, she'd now been gone for about fifteen minutes. I began to wonder if she'd gotten caught, or worse, if she was spilling all the details, particularly the detail of my involvement.

With a deep breath, I grabbed a nearby feeding trough and rested on a bench that was set against the stable wall. Carefully, I set the trough between my knees and began sorting out the leaves of white man's foot, shaking out any remaining dirt, then depositing each leaf into the trough.

My grandfather had taught me that the most efficient way to make a paste out of white man's foot is to chew the leaves until they thicken, and so I did. The leaves were bitter and grassy on my tongue. They left a peppery taste behind as I spat the thick paste into the trough.

Sitting alone in the stables gave me time to think. I had been unnecessarily short with Estella since the moment I saw her earlier. She really didn't mean any harm to me, and she had the purest intention to heal this horse. She needed to understand the position she'd put me in, but I was going to try and be pleasant for the rest of the night.

Finally, Estella walked in through the open stable doors with a lantern and an armload of fresh lavender.

I jumped up, leaving my work, and helped her set the plants down.

"You think this will be enough? I can always go back to my gardens and pick some more." She looked over at the horse, her brow knitted.

"This will be plenty," I said, staring at the mound of lavender. The stable already smelled strongly of it. "Once I prepare it properly, I'll be able to use it to bring down the swelling and soothe her pain."

"I hate that she's in pain," Estella said as she leaned against the stall door.

I sat back down at the bench and began working again, chewing the white man's foot into a paste. I paused briefly after spitting, then wiped my lips. "Uh... Listen, I just wanted to apologize for being so short-tempered with you this evening."

She glanced down at the pile of plants at my feet. "Yes, you were quite ornery." Then she met my eyes. "If there's one thing I've learned about you tonight, it's that you're selfless. You're here, working to send money to your brother. That's very honorable."

"We all have responsibilities. Even you, I'm sure."

I began chewing the leaves again.

"The difference is," she said, "your responsibilities come from love. You meet them for your brother, but my responsibilities come from obligation." She set her lantern on the ground, then seated herself against the wooden door of the stall.

I resisted the urge to shake my head.

Estella let out a sigh. "My family has decided that I'm to marry... Well of course, you know him already. Henry Hamilton, that new manager who almost put you out of work. It's my responsibility to comply, even if it means a loveless marriage."

Ah yes. Henry Hamilton, floor manager at the mills. The man who had so easily dismissed me from his employment with a wave of his clean, soft-looking, work-free hand. I wanted to feel some sort of empathy for her, some kind of understanding.

But I couldn't. So long as Estella's problems were about tea parties and suitors, I just couldn't muster it up. Not when my problems were long, hard days spent rectifying my greatest mistake.

"I know you must think that I am some silly girl, who doesn't truly understand the concepts of sacrifice and obligation, but you're wrong."

I spat out my mouthful. "Like I said, we all have responsibilities. Even if they're simple ones."

She crossed her arms and laughed. "Agreed."

"I hope that things work out for you in the end," I added. I didn't feel like sharing any more. I'd already said too much earlier. The horse even looked like she was saying, *"Alright, Bodaway, that's enough."*

"Thank you." Estella cocked her head at me, looking as if she might pry further.

"All done." I wiped my lips clean again, but I was sure the earthy taste would linger through the night. "The paste is ready."

Estella jumped up and hovered over the trough. "How will we know if the paste is working?" she asked in an anxious tone.

"Well, it's not going to do anything in the trough. I planned on spending the night here with the horse to make sure she gets what she needs, if that is alright with you. I still have to prepare the yarrow and lavender."

She seemed surprised. "I couldn't let you spend the whole night on the dirt floor. It gets cold in the stables, and there are insects and... well... spiders! You'll be exhausted for work in the morning."

"You do know that I've spent more than one night sleeping in the woods, right?" I flashed her a brief smile, then ran my tongue across my teeth self-consciously. "I've got this handled. She could really use the attention."

"If you're sure I can't convince you to rest."

I stood up and walked into the horse's stall. "I said I was going to heal the horse, and that's what I'm going to do." I leaned down by the horse's wound. "Would you hand me some paste?"

Without hesitation, Estella scooped a large glob with her fingers and lifted her hand to me.

Our eyes met, equally anxious, as I took the paste from her and pressed it into the wound. The horse made a deep sound of pain and backed herself into a corner. "Estella, you try and put the paste in the wound while I hold the horse's neck so she won't move as much. This is really going to hurt her, but she'll feel so much better if this works."

Estella took another glob of paste and came into the stall with me. She crouched by the horse's leg and rubbed the clumpy paste around in her hand, as if to make sure it was properly mixed.

I was surprised that she didn't seem faint at the idea of touching the infection—let alone the paste I made in my mouth—but I supposed that I should stop assuming things about Estella. "Ready?

I've got her tight, so go ahead and push the paste all the way into the wound."

"OK," she said, and raised her hand.

The moment Estella touched the wound, the horse went mad. I clutched her neck and I tried with all my might to hold her steady. Estella didn't flinch. She put the paste on and rubbed the horse's leg. "Shhh," she soothed. "Hush now, you'll feel better." The horse seemed to understand her and calmed down immediately.

I shook my head in silent amazement. The girl afraid of insects and spiders wasn't afraid of a dangerous, unruly beast. "Now we need to let that dry. I'll apply the two other plants before the night is through." I paused. "You should be getting home. It's late, and I'm assuming your parents expect you to be in your bed this very moment, dreaming of high tea and Henry Hamilton."

She put her hands on her hips, unamused. "But what about the horse?"

"She'll be fine here with me."

"Alright then, until tomorrow." She looked at the horse with tired eyes. "I'll leave my lantern. If you need anything, my house is just over the bank." I could tell by her facial expression that even she knew that was a ridiculous offer.

"She's in good hands," I said.

When Estella reached the doorway, she turned back for a moment. "Good night."

"Good night." I watched her move out of sight. The moon illuminated her slender frame and her skin shone in the blue light like a goddess of the night. *Do you have a mental ailment?* I asked myself in disbelief. I could not let myself notice her—or her beauty—any more than necessary.

I let out a huge sigh and ran both hands through my hair. I could really reflect on everything we'd talked about. Thinking about my grandfather and everything he'd done for me and my brother made me realize how angry I was at my father for leaving us to our own devices. Our grandfather had taught us everything worth knowing, all while my father roamed God's Earth doing whatever he pleased, never even bothering to send word to his sons. I wouldn't be surprised if he never sent for us at all. For all we knew, he could be long dead.

But something inside me told me he wasn't. I could feel it in my bones. He was out there, alive and well, while Keme continued to rot away in a bed.

Anger burned away at my insides as the tension in my fingers forced my hand into a fist. I didn't even know how long I'd been harboring the bitterness that had caused me to lash out today.

Right then, I swore that I'd never do what my father did to my own family. I would always be there. That was the promise I made to myself.

The horse stomped in the dirt and hay.

"I'm not going anywhere," I said. "You need a name, don't you?" I supposed I should wait for Estella's help in naming the beast. If I'd taken anything from our conversation, it was that Estella was the kind of person to want a say in the matter.

I checked the paste on the horse's leg. It was almost dry and ready for the next coating. "How are you feeling, girl?" I petted her soft nose and slid my hand down her neck. A small lump formed in my throat. I didn't really know for certain that anything I'd done would heal this horse. *Is this all for nothing? Is the infection too far gone to be reversed? God, just give me a sign that I'm doing something right.*

The horse interrupted my plea with a sharp whinny. She still seemed strangely good-natured, given her condition. It struck me that she really could be a beautiful horse with some brushing and grooming. If it weren't for her injured leg, she'd probably give those racehorses a run for their money. I'd only seen legs like those one other time, and they'd belonged to a wild mustang captured out West and auctioned off in upstate Maine. Fastest creature I'd ever seen.

I touched her leg with the leftover paste made of white man's foot, and she stiffened. "There, there, stay still. That's the last of it for now."

Within a few hours I could apply the lavender to bring down the swelling, and then the final paste made out of yarrow to clot the wound. I took the worn wool blanket from the stable shelf and balled it up beneath my head as I lay out on the cool hay.

Crickets sang their summer song while the rest of the world slept through it. I rested my hands behind my head and let out a tired sigh.

Estella's lantern burned on, its soft glow warm and calming. She really wasn't at all what I'd expected her to be. Sure, she liked to pry into my business, but I didn't think she meant any harm.

Why was I thinking about her again? The last thing I needed was an unavailable woman on my mind. I knew it was important to focus on the task at hand and not let my mind wander to her beautiful eyes. I'd never seen eyes as clear as hers, and everything about her face just seemed so graceful and perfect.

*What is wrong with me?*

The horse huffed, as though saying, "Idiot." And I couldn't argue with that.

I rubbed my face roughly with both hands, turned over, and shut my eyes. "Get some rest, horse."

## CHAPTER ELEVEN

*Saturday, June 10*

Bodaway

The next morning, I was startled awake by a quick shake to my shoulders. My eyes shot open, only to see Estella hovering over me in a hooded cloak.

"What time is it?" I rubbed my eyes, feeling exceptionally tired. I could see the night sky through the open stable doors, with hardly a trace of morning light showing over the trees.

Estella lit the lantern on the wall once more. "It's nearly four in the morning! I might not have another chance to slip away, so I saw an opportunity and I took it." She rushed over to the horse and let herself into its stall.

"I brought you some breakfast." She pointed to a small basket of apples and day-old cornbread muffins set on the bench where I'd made the paste.

Still sitting in my makeshift dirt bed, I rubbed my face awake. "Thanks."

"We have less than two hours before you're to leave for the mills and I'm to be at the breakfast table, but I need to know that what we did worked."

I joined her beside the horse. Estella's face was full of optimism and anticipation, and I tried not to roll my eyes. Did she really believe that we could have healed this horse overnight?

"I can't promise you anything. Even if the plants are working properly, it'll be days before we see results, and weeks before the wound heals up nicely. Even then, she might never run the same as she used to." Rationally and silently, I mourned the loss of her incredibly muscular legs and ran my hand along her dusty white coat.

Estella's cloak hood fell to her back, her brown curls tumbled over her shoulders. "Well, I have some faith." She nodded. "Now, let's take a look at that leg."

I swallowed hard and shook my head. "Alright then." I crouched low to the ground, smelling the scent of lavender leaves mixed with hay. It all made my stomach turn. "It would help keep her calm if you talked to her softly and stroked her. I'm going to unwrap her leg... God knows why." I muttered the last part under my breath, then raised my voice again. "It may cause her some pain once the wound is exposed to the elements again. I hope you don't mind that I ripped up that old blanket I found on the shelf. I needed something to keep pressure on the wound and hold in the medicine."

"I'm glad you were able to find something to be of use." She took the horse's face in her hands carefully and whispered something inaudible.

I loosened the two woolen knots I had made, and slowly, I was able to remove the bandaging completely. The sight before me practically made me fall backward.

Estella frowned at my behavior. "Bodaway? What is it?" she asked, trying to remain calm for the sake of the horse.

145

"The wound!" I could hardly breathe. "How could this be?" I stood up and backed away, trying to make sense of it all.

Estella hurried to the horse's leg. "Bodaway, it's scabbing over, and the swelling is only half as bad as it was last night!"

"This just doesn't make sense. You saw the wound last night, the infection, and the pain she was in." I propped myself up against the stable wall, trying and failing to hide my utter shock.

"See, we did a fine job! Oh, would you just look at how nicely it's closing up!" Her face was as bright as the lantern on the wall.

I remembered my prayer to God the night before. I'd asked for a sign. "But I don't think you understand. The rate of her healing is unnatural, and frankly unheard of. This doesn't just happen." I waved my arm at the horse in disbelief.

"Then praise God for His grace!" She ran her hand along the horse's neck. "That would be the perfect name for her, don't you think? Grace."

"Call her what you want," I said, trying to sound indifferent, but could feel myself growing more irritable with each passing second.

God had heard me. It couldn't be any more clear if it hit me across the face. But instead of feeling overjoyed, a bitterness filled my chest. It soured my tongue. Looking at this horse, I couldn't help but wonder how God could miraculously heal a mere animal, but let my brother suffer.

"Aren't you pleased?" She sat on the bench and frowned, clearly sensing that something was off.

"Of course I am." My tone wasn't convincing. I took a cornbread muffin from the basket, then leaned in the doorway. God was responsible for this, that much was evident. But I couldn't shake this new, sudden feeling in my chest that flared each time I looked at the horse.

The sun was just starting to rise, the dew of the field glistened like tiny crystals.

"She was lucky," I said at last.

"You should be proud." Estella said, sounding as if she were picking her words carefully. "Grace would have died if it wasn't for you."

I popped the rest of the cornbread muffin in my mouth and huffed as Estella approached me.

She leaned against its frame so that she was directly in front of me. "So, what can we do for Grace now?"

"Well," I said, trying to keep my inner turmoil from her. I pulled out a tied-shut cloth from my trouser pocket. "We have to apply the lavender leaves each night to make sure she doesn't swell up again. This is just the beginning of the healing process, but I'll admit that she has a fighting chance at full recovery." I tossed her the cloth. "I can come by once a day, but it'll be harder to rely on an exact time when I work all day, six days a week."

"Well, what can *I* do? I'll be around to help with anything useful."

What *could* Estella really do to help? Rubbing my jaw a little, I said, "She definitely needs to take a short walk once a day, but under no circumstances is she to be ridden. It would cause unnecessary pressure on her leg, and could slow down the healing process quite a bit."

We returned to Grace's stall and looked at her wound for a second time. This time I had my bearings about me, and was able to really examine it. It seemed clean and clotted, both very good signs. "A little exercise will be good for her, just... nothing straining." I caught my fingers in her knotted mane. "Maybe you could give her a good grooming."

Estella rested her hands on Grace's side, across from me. "I can make sure that happens."

Grace flicked her tail in protest.

Estella sighed and looked to the sun that had almost risen over the hill. "I really should go home."

I nodded in agreement. Any longer and someone would notice she was missing. Estella lifted her cloak hood once more and turned to leave. Pausing, she said, "I really wish I could stay. You know, to be with Grace if she needs anything."

"It's alright. What she needs now is rest." I still stood by the horse. "We've all had a long night. I don't want you in any sort of trouble. Go on home and I'll stay with her for a little longer."

"OK," she said slowly. "I'll be back as soon as I can."

As she turned to walk away, I noticed her basket of food still sitting on the bench.

"Here," I called out, "don't forget this," I met her in the doorway and handed her the basket, then felt compelled to say something kind. "I never got a chance to thank you for what you did at the mill the other day."

I brushed my hand across the faded bruise on my jaw. "On the other hand, I've had plenty of time to be ungrateful, and I apologize for that."

Her eyes softened. "I don't normally speak up like that. I even surprised myself." She laughed nervously, but still held my gaze. "You're welcome," she said, then rifled through the basket and, with a small smile, handed me an apple. "For Grace." Then she returned home through the fields.

Grace and I were alone again.

I rubbed the dull apple's waxy film onto my work shirt, making it shine.

None of this was Estella's fault, and it wasn't Grace's fault, either, that God had decided to heal her instead of Keme.

*God, I know that I asked for a sign. I can't ignore this miracle, but I can't pretend that I know what it means. Maybe this is a punishment for losing myself, my Abenaki blood—or maybe this is what I get for losing my temper and almost breaking my word to Keme. Whatever it is, I guess it's working.*

I sighed, releasing the tension in my jaw, and patted Grace's nose. Her eyes seemed thankful as I fed her the apple from my hand.

Before long, I was off to work. I was functioning on a few hours of sleep and a head filled with questions and possible explanations about Grace's miraculous healing. I tried my hardest not to acknowledge the only explanation that made any sense: Somehow, Estella and I were meant to heal this horse together.

## Estella

That morning, I had breakfast with Mother in the dining room and tried to pretend as though I hadn't spent the morning with a stranger in the old stables.

Sunlight lit the room and brightened the already-white walls. Mother sat at the head of the table, while I sat at her side. She was talking about the Hamiltons, as usual, about how Henry and I were destined to have beautiful, intelligent children. Her earrings bounced all around with every word.

"We have much to do today! I think that we had better send word to our relatives out of state and let them know of your wedding plans."

"Mother, I don't *have* any wedding plans. What would we tell them?" I pulled apart a doughy biscuit on my plate.

"Oh, it couldn't hurt to give them advance notice of your impending wedding in September."

I almost choked on my tea. "September? Since when did you decide on September? Does everyone know but me?" My breathing came in long, painful gulps as I realized that my wedding's timeline was much shorter than I had anticipated.

"Oh, calm down! We haven't set an official date yet, but I can assure you, it *will* be set soon."

"September is more than *soon!* That's less than three months away!"

Mother raised an eyebrow at me and popped a grape into her mouth. "Precisely why we must inform our relatives at once."

She continued on about some nonsense, but the whole conversation eerily reminded me of my meeting with Alice. Despite having occurred only the previous evening, it felt as though it had happened long ago.

My mind drifted towards Bodaway and Grace, and eventually Mother noticed I had ceased paying attention to her.

"Estella!" She said it firmly, but did not raise her voice. "It is exceedingly rude of you to look as though you've not a care in the world as to what I'm saying." She straightened her back and folded her hands in her skirt, which was, as it almost always was, a deep shade of violet. "So unbecoming of a lady."

This was one of those times when I found it nearly impossible to hold my tongue. It was truly exhausting, the act of trying to be the perfect daughter, and my mother was not an easy woman to please. "If you'll excuse me, Mother. I believe breakfast is finished." I said it in a matter-of-fact tone and set my tea cup on its saucer beside my plate.

"You are excused," she said crossly, "but you are excused to your room, Estella."

"Thank you. I will gladly retire to my bedroom while it is still *my* bedroom. God knows when my whole life will be pulled from under me. September, I suppose."

"That is enough from you!" Mother stood, face red. "This wedding is happening with or without your consent, and that is the final word."

My knuckles were white, and my cheeks sore from biting down on them. I turned and left without another word.

I was close to tears by the time I escaped to my bedroom. Falling in love within such a short time frame was not as easy as I had tried to convince myself it would be. I closed the door behind me, then opened a window to let in the summer breeze.

Our property was stunning. I couldn't deny it, even if I was upset with my family. A new barn stood atop a flower-covered hill. Down in our fields, Father worked with Black Magic, preparing her for the races next week. He'd be damned to see any other horse take the prize.

The other, less-valuable horses grazed along the edge of the fenced-in field. I crossed my arms as I stared at them.

*I'm fenced-in too. Even when I'm not trapped in my room, then I'm trapped in this house. Even when I'm not trapped in this house, I still can't escape family obligation. I'm always fenced in by something or other. The fence merely goes by different names.*

Bodaway seemed to think that whatever my troubles were, they were no match for his, that his burden was so much greater than mine. Perhaps he was even right. However, at the end of the day, he was free to come and go as he pleased.

I watched Father from my window. He held Black Magic close to the bit as he attached a lunge line, then led her in a perfect trot around him.

She swung her neck about, causing her mane to flow beautifully, and her sleek black coat caught the sun's light with every movement.

Grace's white coat could be just as majestic as Black Magic's if properly groomed, but I couldn't say the same about her speed. Black Magic moved about as though in a smooth, effortless dance.

It made me wonder if Grace would ever trot again, or even walk painlessly. I wanted to believe it. After seeing how miraculously her wound had clotted overnight, how could I not have hope?

I thought Bodaway also shared that hope.

He was so obviously surprised to see how quickly Grace had yielded results, but I could tell he didn't want to get my hopes up by reacting too soon.

Or maybe it was fear of failure. Maybe Bodaway didn't want to get his *own* hopes up.

# CHAPTER TWELVE

### Sunday, June 11

#### Estella

It was Sunday. More importantly, it was the Sunday when I was to help Alice Hamilton at the orphanage before church.

Hannah tied my hair back in a white silk ribbon and pinned my bonnet on securely, then sent me on my way to wait for the Hamiltons' carriage. I had no choice but to take the road into town, of course. It wouldn't exactly reflect respect onto either one of our families if I were seen gallivanting through the woods like a wild beast.

Before long, the horse and buggy pulled up before our estate. A footman offered me his gloved hand and helped me into the enclosed carriage. The door clicked as he shut me inside.

I sat back in the leather interior and watched through my window as the footman ordered the horse to move. The birds were chirping, but clouds blocked the sun. It appeared as though it might rain.

\*\*\*

As I entered town, I noticed the quietness around me. During the week, women bustled about, buying what was needed to prepare supper, while dogs ran alongside children playing in the streets. Today was Sunday, and there was none of that. All the stores were closed.

I arrived at the orphanage, stepped down from the carriage, and made my way to the entrance.

Alice waited for me in the doorway. "Estella, how kind of you to give your time to the orphans here." She showed me into the dining hall where I'd help serve the food. It was nothing as spectacular as her parlor room had been. These walls were painted a dull gray but were otherwise plain and empty. Worn-looking tables and chairs were set up for the children.

"You will be in charge of handing out the bread," said Alice, "and Henry will ration the porridge."

The kitchen doors creaked behind us. Alice and I turned in time to see Henry appear in the doorway with a steaming pot.

"I'll leave you to it then." She nodded once to her son, then shifted her gaze to me. "Rest assured, you are in excellent hands." Her tight lips turned up into a smirk as she left us.

Henry set the pot on the long oakwood table and chuckled to himself. "I promise serving the food requires much less expertise than my mother makes it sound."

I laughed, unpinning my bonnet. "Don't tell me you can cook, too?"

He smiled. "No, I can't take credit for this here." He lifted the pot's lid and the pleasant aroma of porridge and honey filled the room. "I'm just delivering."

I set my bonnet aside. "I would've thought you'd prefer sleeping the morning away until it was time to make your appearance at church." That may have been a bit too mocking.

"Lazy and self-centered? Is that how little you think of me?" He shook his head.

"I'm sorry," I said. "I didn't mean to offend you."

He laughed. "I've actually come here every Sunday since returning from school."

Just then, children piled into the dining hall. They quickly formed a line, greeting Henry with toothy smiles as they moved along. Child after child passed us by, each more excited for their portion of bland food than the last. One last young girl lifted an empty plate, her eyes wide and focused on the steaming rolls in front of me. Instead of tearing the bread in two, I placed the entire roll discreetly on her plate. Though it wasn't much, her thin lips flashed into a brief smile before she moved along without a word.

"It was my understanding," I said, cautiously, "that Lillian Sterling volunteered here as well. Did you know she's unwell?"

The ladle slipped from Henry's grip and splashed messily into the pot of porridge. "I had heard rumors of her... well-being. And yes, she gave of her time generously to these children." He removed a handkerchief from his pocket and wiped up the mess on the table.

"And is that how you two became... better acquainted?" I pried further.

"In light of pledging my transparency, yes. We became good friends. Then she had the notion that we could have more than just friendship. But you know my parents and what they value most." He chose his words carefully. "She just... wasn't the right fit."

I supposed that made sense, but it didn't quite explain why she refused to see me nor had she written to me. Nonetheless, I was impressed that Henry explained this to me in such a respectful manner. Surely it was a sign of some kind of integrity? *Maybe he's not the man the rumors have painted him out to be.*

"Can you tell me the real reason she left the orphanage?" I finally asked.

Henry looked behind him at the empty doorway where his mother had recently stood, and cleared his throat. "I really shouldn't talk about such things. For the sake of integrity and honor."

I shook my head. "Whose honor are you preserving? Lillian's?"

"Listen." He looked at me with what seemed for all the world to be sincerity. "I care about Lillian. She is a wonderful person, and a fine match for *someone*, but I'm trying to be a man that my father and mother can be proud of. My whole life, I've watched my father do his duty as husband, as a leader, and my mother does so much to ensure he is respected. She loves her family, even if she isn't the warmest woman.

"I've disgraced the Hamilton name more times than I'd like to admit, but now I have the opportunity to rectify the past. There's nothing more important to me now than doing just that. So, whatever may have transpired between Ms. Sterling and my family, trust that it is of no concern to you. Our families did not separate amicably and the details are better left unspoken—not only for the sake of Ms. Sterling, but for the sake of the Hamilton reputation."

He paused, then met my gaze with his sad blue eyes. "And I tell you all of this with utmost earnestness. I don't wish to keep things from you, Estella, but I'm simply not at liberty to discuss these particular matters any further. We all have a duty to someone or something."

I nodded my head, as though in agreement, but still felt vastly unsatisfied. I longed to prod further, but resisted the childish urge.

My stomach twisted as my thoughts ran wild, sifting through the possibilities.

Perhaps this was Henry's way of showing restraint and prudence. Maybe things were truly better left unsaid, left within the family. "You don't need to explain family obligations to me." I managed to respond without further questioning, though it wasn't without difficulty. I now understood that whatever information I was to acquire would have to come directly from Lillian.

We made some lighter conversation as we worked, and it wasn't a miserable time at all. It was, in fact, enjoyable. Henry's eyes were soft and sweet towards the orphan children as he served them. In some small way, Henry was proving that he wanted to be a good man, or at least someone to respect and be proud of.

Just like the kind, sweet-tempered man his letters had led me to hope for.

After the last child came through our line, we returned the leftovers to the kitchen and washed the tables with damp rags. "We should leave now," said Henry, "if we want to beat the rain on our way to church." He tossed his rag aside.

I set my bonnet back in its place. "Shall we?" I asked.

Henry offered me his arm, and I took it as we passed through the front door.

It was already raining, but the clouds looked as though they were just passing through. Henry glanced up. "Looks like we were a little bit too late." He removed his overcoat. "Here, take this so you don't get rained on before church." His eyes had that soft look again.

I took the coat. "Thank you, Henry."

"Alright," he said, "I'd say church is a good five-minute walk, but a three-minute run."

"Are you suggesting we run through the town like mad men?" I laughed.

"Are you suggesting we take our sweet time and ruin our Sunday best?" he retorted.

"I am most definitely *not* suggesting that," I said, then took off running with Henry's coat. I heard him laugh behind me, his footsteps gaining on me. A few wide-eyed bystanders, no doubt shocked by our misconduct, looked on wordlessly.

In less than three minutes, we arrived at the church steps and found that it had already stopped raining.

"Where... did you learn to run so fast?" Henry asked, out of breath.

"Don't pretend like you've never chased after me before." I sat on the church steps and tossed Henry his coat, taking the chance to catch my own breath. Neither of us had gotten wet, but my bonnet had fallen to my back and my hair was sure to look wild and out of sorts.

Henry stood up and unwrinkled his coat before putting it back on.

I ran my hands through the ends of my hair and tried to look presentable for church.

My gown had once been the pure color of a spring rose, but was now stained with mud on the hem—and I could only imagine where my hair ribbon had wandered off to.

We were the first ones to arrive at church, aside from a few old folks who made it their life's mission to be early to everything. Lord help me if my mother were to hear of my running through the streets as she arrived.

I looked to Henry and saw that his cheeks were flushed pink from running, that he was still out of breath. I smiled at him.

It seemed that Henry wasn't as boring as I'd thought. Perhaps he was even a romantic of sorts after all.

## Sunday, June 18

### Bodaway

"Wow, she doesn't look half bad." I stood back, admiring Grace's brushed coat and mane. Estella had done a great job grooming her. We stood together in the old stables on the outskirts of the Wellstone estate.

"Almost as pretty as a show pony." Estella smiled and patted Grace's groomed—but dirt stained—neck. The room smelled of damp hay and horse dung.

I'd been working with Grace for over a week, and her wound was healing nicely. We'd been walking her each day, helping her regain strength and confidence.

The grooming done, Estella fastened a harness on a resistant Grace.

"Do I want to know where that came from?" I pointed to the expensive-looking leather lead hanging on the stable wall, clearly pulled from her father's supply.

"Absolutely not." She smiled. "Just hand it to me, why don't you?"

I grabbed it and felt the smooth material beneath my fingers. "Where are you going with her?"

"Well, I know you still have to take her for a walk, but I thought that perhaps we might wash her in the river? I tried my best to clean her before trimming the matted parts, but she looks far more dirty now than she ever has." Estella rubbed her hands along Grace's filthy coat, and a dust cloud appeared above them.

I rolled my eyes as I took the lead and brought Grace outside. "Don't you have something better to do, like high tea or needlepoint?" I teased.

Estella took up an empty pail and leaned on the stable's bare wooden frame. "I actually *do* have tea time later, but I've plenty of time now to wash this horse, thank you for your concern. Taking her to the river is a two-man job."

"Fine with me." I repressed a smirk.

She squared her shoulders and narrowed her eyes at me. "And I'll have you know that I am the *last* person you'd want wielding a needle."

"Good to know," I laughed.

Estella's dark hair fell over her shoulders and down her back, the shorter strands curled around her high cheekbones. I began to realize that maybe she wasn't at all the way I'd assumed, a happy, rich girl living a carefree life. She spent every moment she could manage caring for Grace, waking up early each morning to bring her fresh food and water.

She'd even taken it upon herself to muck out the stables, a very unpleasant task for someone who'd hardly gotten her hands dirty a day in her life.

From what she'd told me about her family, I couldn't help but think her dedication to Grace was a distraction she welcomed, a challenge that kept her thoughts far from reality—something I could relate to more than I'd like to admit.

"You know," said Estella, "Grace has healed up nicely, and… well… I thought that perhaps you should try *riding* her to the river."

"That's not a good idea," I replied. "Her leg might not be able to support my weight without experiencing pain."

I chewed the inside of my cheek. That was the best excuse I could come up with on the spot. I hadn't let my mind linger on the idea of riding Grace. Though I imagined her speed and strength must be incredible. Though there was a part of me that wanted to find out for sure, I just couldn't bring myself to relive Keme's accident.

Estella's eyebrows crowded, but she didn't protest. "It was just an idea."

The early evening sun felt good on the skin as it crept over us. We walked Grace down her usual path through the woods, then switched to the longer trail that led to the river.

Birds flew overhead as we walked in silence, nature filled the emptiness.

When we first began the task of healing Grace a week earlier, Estella would fidget and become ridged looking if any hint of uncomfortable silence appeared, if conversation wasn't moving along seamlessly. She'd attempt to fill most quiet moments with idle conversation. But now she was different.

As Estella grew accustomed to my quiet manner throughout the week, I noticed her words had more intention behind them. Even today, her demeanor appeared more and more relaxed the longer we walked.

Grace knew these woods so well, it was almost like she was leading the way.

After winding along the seemingly endless trail for some time, the once-distant sound of the river became more prominent.

"Just through these trees." Estella moved in front of us and held back thicker branches so that Grace could walk through unscathed.

The river sparkled, and stones shone from its bed under. A haven of pine trees enclosed us, the river running through its middle.

I led Grace to the edge of the water, then removed my boots. The icy river rushed over my feet, then my legs as I waded further with Grace. It was shallow enough that I could keep my footing, and didn't seem to bother the horse at all.

I looked back to the rocky bank. To my surprise, Estella was taking her shoes off. Her brown dress looked like something borrowed from a servant, and the hem of her skirt was covered in filth and pine pitch. Even if someone *did* see us together, I liked to think that nobody would recognize Estella, looking like she did now.

She started towards Grace and me, carefully lifting her pail and skirt from the clutches of the river. She looked around us in awe and closed her eyes a moment. "Do you think this is what Heaven sounds like?" she asked.

I listened to the hum of the forest around us, the sound of chickadees, and the sweet lull of the river flowing southward.

"My grandfather used to think so." I carefully led Grace deeper, attempting to let the water run over her wound and coat. Reluctantly, Estella let the hem of her dress fall, allowing the current to have its way with its skirts.

She followed closely behind until we were waist-deep in the river. "Here," I said, "let's trade." I handed her the lead and took the pail from her.

I soaked Grace's body with bucket after bucket of water, washing away the layers of filth. I smiled to myself, remembering how Keme and I would take our horses to the river for a good washing before each race. By the end of the trip, one of us would always start an argument—usually me—and Keme would end up going for an involuntary swim. I'd jump in after him and we'd laugh about it until we'd forgotten what the argument had even been about.

I wiped an arm across my forehead. "Do you ever wish that things didn't have to change?"

Estella stared at me intently as she stood with the lead in hand. "I think I know what you mean. Does this have to do with… well… are you referring to your brother?"

"Yeah, I suppose so. I haven't heard from him in weeks, and it's getting under my skin. The smell of the river reminds me of him."

"Some things don't have to change," she said. "You and your brother, you're family."

I scooped a bucket full of water then let it run over Grace's head. She squinted as she flicked the droplets from her ears. "Well, some things can never be the same. I've come to accept that."

"Whatever's going on between you, I'm sure it can be amended." She hesitated. "He blames you for something, doesn't he? You'd be surprised how much can be resolved by simply talking."

I clenched my jaw, feeling my face grow hot. "You can't fix everything, Estella." I splashed icy water onto my face and over my head.

Estella seemed startled by my outburst, but her eyes softened. "Then tell me. What happened between you two?"

I took the lead from her hands, then waded out of the river with Grace. My chest was tight and my head was spinning. I didn't have to share my problems with Estella. She would never be able to understand my guilt, nor was it in any way her business.

Once ashore, I tossed the rusty pail to the ground and sat on the sun-baked rocks.

Estella waded back towards the rocky shore as Grace whinnied next to me.

I looked to the cloudless sky, basking in the evening sun. The sunlight was sure to dry Grace and me in no time.

A sharp scream prompted Grace to jump. I looked up and couldn't see Estella.

I sprang to my feet and plunged back into the water. Estella surfaced again.

"I'm fine!" she yelled. "I'm fine." She caught her footing and stood, wiping water from her eyes, soaked from head to toe.

I waded to Estella and helped her to shore. She looked like a beautiful, drowned, embarrassed rat.

She sat beside Grace on the river rocks and coughed up water.

I sat beside her, letting the sun start its work over. "You sure you're alright?" I asked.

"Yes," she said, wringing her hair out. "I slipped into a hole too deep to stand, and before I knew it, I was underwater."

Pine needles stuck to both of us all over. Someone might have mistaken us for trees.

"Thank you for coming back for me," she added softly, not looking me in the eyes.

I sat quietly for a moment. I *wasn't* going to tell her the details of Keme's accident. It didn't pertain to the healing of this horse whatsoever.

Sometimes I got carried away with Estella. Even during the first night we'd spent together trying to heal Grace, she'd gotten me to open up about Keme—sharing much, much more than I would have shared in my right mind. But lately, I found myself wanting to talk about the past with her, wanting to explain how my grandfather was the strongest, most honorable man I'd ever known—and how my father was a ratbag.

Though, even in my weakness, I still couldn't bring myself to speak of Keme. At least, not about what I'd done to him.

The strongest of men could fall victim to Estella's wishes if he looked into her eyes. Maybe I had become too fond of her company, had forgotten the seriousness of our situation. If we were found out, it would be Keme who yet again dealt with the aftermath of my mistakes.

Estella hesitated at my lack of engagement, but eventually spoke again. "Why don't you ever want to talk when I ask about your brother? You mention him quite *often* for someone who doesn't want to talk about him."

"Is my life just some form of entertainment to you?" I was tired of Estella thinking she was entitled to anything she wanted, even the private lives of others. My eyebrows furrowed together, and the back of my neck tensed.

"No, not at all! Please don't think that. It's just… I've never had a sibling before, and I'm curious. I know you send your brother money, and that your relationship is strained, and that's all. I've been trying to put the pieces together, and thought maybe there was some way I could help."

I rose, my blood boiling. "I've told you before, I don't want any more of your help! What would you do? Ask your rich father for *money?* Money isn't some magic potion that can solve all of life's problems. No amount of money can make Keme walk again!" It just fell out of my mouth in my anger. There it was.

Estella stood slowly, wiping the pine needles from her skirts. "I wasn't talking about money," she said in a tone much calmer than I deserved. "I just thought… perhaps I could help somehow…" She stared at me, her face flushed.

I knew that Estella meant well, that she was genuine, but even *she'd* begun to realize that there was nothing she could do to help.

I nodded at her, my anger fading slowly at her innocence. Those eyes of hers had a strangely calming effect. When she met my gaze, it was like she looked into my soul. Every part of me that had become angry just melted away.

I had let my temper get the best of me, and yet there she was, still standing in front of me, hair wet, skin sunned, and freckles sprouting about her nose.

I let my jaw relax and my fists hang loose. "I shouldn't have lost my temper," I sighed.

"Sometimes you must," said Estella. She held my gaze, looking completely serious. "Though," she added, "I don't particularly enjoy being the object of your anger."

The world around us fell silent until the only sound was my heart beating in my eardrums. Estella had a drive to help, to fix. I, on the other hand, strived for independence, and had a tendency of self-destruction.

There was inevitable friction between us, but I could stand to be more level-headed.

The sun flared through the trees behind Estella, revealing the pine-needles sticking in her wet hair. I squinted at the brightness. "I've treated you unfairly," I said. "For that, I apologize." I reached my hand out and pulled a pine needle from her hair.

She swallowed hard and looked away. "I really should be getting back home."

I stepped back, feeling my face flush. "I'll take Grace back later," I said. "Best to let her dry out some more here."

Estella glanced back at me once more. "Thank you." She clasped her hands awkwardly in front of her.

I nodded, feeling equally as awkward, as Estella gave a small smile and left Grace and me alone.

## Estella

I sat in a rare moment of solitude on our front porch that evening, thumbing through the fragile pages of *Pride and Prejudice*. I had read it many times before, and knew its contents well. The exciting twists and turns, the wit and good humor, the miscommunications and slander. All of it enticed me, and never failed to draw me in completely. That is, under normal circumstances.

But I couldn't stop thinking of Bodaway, of what he had revealed to me that day. His brother had lost the ability to walk somehow, but I couldn't guess how. The more I pressed, the more agitated Bodaway became.

I felt as I imagined Elizabeth Bennet to have felt when she misjudged Mr. Darcy, to have taken a moral high ground, believing that she knew the truth of his character, when in reality, she had spoken unfairly and out of place.

I shouldn't have stuck my nose into Bodaway's business, business that I knew nothing about. The way his demeanor changed, the way his eyes darkened when speaking of his brother, it all made my heart break for him. Clearly he was suffering, as clearly as Grace when she bucked in pain. Though his wound was emotional, it might as well have been gaping wide and festering.

But I feared that Bodaway's remedy would prove elusive. His wounds couldn't be healed simply with a few sprigs of lavender or a paste made from medicinal plants. He needed something much more difficult to obtain: Vulnerability. Trust.

I needed to show Bodaway that he could *trust* me, that I wasn't simply using him to fill my life with diversion.

To that end, I decided against pressing him further. I closed my book and sat back in my seat, taking in the fleeting light of the evening. I wouldn't utter another word of Bodaway's brother until he felt comfortable—no, *vulnerable*—enough to bring it up himself.

## Bodaway

"You boys can eat as much as you want. I made plenty, because I know *this one*." Mary poked Art in the ribs, then scooped some stew into a wooden bowl.

The mill housing was close quarters, but with our three other roommates out, there was just enough room for the lot of us to have dinner—the dinner that I'd promised Mary three weeks ago.

"Hey!" Art protested. "I'm a growing boy, Mary. What's *your* excuse?" He let out a hearty laugh as Mary gave him a light smack to the back of his head.

"Respect your elders," Mary teased, then pulled a chair out and sat in it. "John, can I get you anything else?" she asked sweetly as she reached across the table and set a candle at its center. Her fiery braid hung over her shoulder and the candlelight lit her freckled face.

"I'm all set, thanks Mary."

Mary placed her napkin in her lap and bowed her head. "Thank you, Lord, for this food, and for good friends to share it with. In Jesus' holy name, amen."

"Amen!" Art added with enthusiasm before digging into dinner.

The three of us sat there in our tiny room, and for the first time, it felt like a home. I had food to eat, a warm place to stay, and friends. "What kind of stew is this?" I scooped a heaping spoonful into my mouth.

Mary dabbed her lips with a napkin. "It's beef stew."

Art raised an eyebrow. "I thought beef stew was supposed to have beef in it."

Mary slammed her hands on the table, shaking it. "Art, would you just eat it? Beef is expensive."

"Then why call it beef stew? What's *in* this?" He lifted his spoon and dropped its contents back into the bowl. It made a gooey sound as it fell.

"Vegetables." She shot him a death stare, her face turning red.

"Mary," I interjected, "it tastes great." I smiled at her and took a bite. It was nothing special, but she sure didn't have to make us anything at all.

She smiled at me.

Art and I finished eating our dinner, each of us scraping our bowl clean.

Art leaned back in his chair and rested his hands on his stomach. "So, Mary, anything exciting happening on the farm?"

She stood up, taking our bowls. "Well, one of their horses gave birth this week. I never did see a prettier foal. It has this sleek brown coat with a white patch on its head in the shape of a heart." She placed our bowls in a bucket of sudsy water by the wood stove and left them to soak. She poured a few cups of steaming water through tea leaves, then brought them back to us at the table.

"How fascinating," Art said sarcastically as he took a mug from her.

"Well, what do you want me to say?" Mary laughed. "I work on a farm." She sat with us again.

Art took a big gulp of tea. "No I mean, anything *exciting!* You mentioned something about a barn dance a while back."

Mary rested her elbows on the table and pulled her mug close. "Yes, I did, didn't I." She smiled smugly. "I didn't think you would want to come to such a silly party."

Art's eyes grew wide. "You know I've had my cap set on your gal Lydia for months now. I was the one to suggest a way to introduce us in the first place!"

"Hold onto your hat, Art. I haven't forgotten. I might've even mentioned you to her already." She suddenly turned to me. "What about you John, will you come too?"

I felt cornered. "Ugh, well… No, I don't dance."

"Oh you *must!* It'll be so much fun, and you'll get to watch Art act like an idiot in front of Lydia." She reached over and grabbed my arm. "Say you will!"

Art downed the last of his tea. "You might as well, John. Keep your mind occupied and your body out of this tiny prison." He looked around the room with contempt.

Mary was still waiting for my response. "I suppose so," I finally sighed.

Mary clasped her hands together. "Oh, splendid! It's settled, then! Art will attempt to convince Lydia to make him her escort, and you'll be mine. The dance will be held at the old barn on the McNerry's farm in two weeks." She stood and took Art's empty cup to the wash bucket, then turned back around. "Art, you'd best buy a new shirt before then. And comb your hair, for goodness sake!" She returned to the dishes.

I shot a look to Art. "Escort?" I whispered. "Dancing?"

"You said it, not me." He chuckled. "This could be good for you. Meet some folks, some *lady* folks." He winked.

"Well, boys," said Mary, drying her hands on her skirt, "I should be getting on home to bed. I'll see you both soon!" She sounded excited, like she'd accomplished some important mission.

Art stood, clearly to walk her out, but to my surprise, Mary came to me first and wrapped her arms around my neck in a tight embrace. "Good night, John."

I didn't return the gesture, but it didn't seem to bother her. She kissed Art on the cheek and then scurried out the door, as if she had never been here at all.

I made a face at Art as the door shut behind her.

He shook his head. "That girl. She always seems to get what she wants." He leaned over the table and blew out the candle.

I should have just said no. It was a silly thing to do, and what if Estella needed me to help with Grace that night? But it was only right that I should be able to have a night off every now and then, too. If Estella had a fancy party with Henry Hamilton on that night, she wouldn't think twice before leaving me on my own. Maybe this party would be a good thing after all, and Mary was good enough company.

I couldn't remember the last time I'd done something for myself—all the more reason not to feel guilty about taking a night off. I'd go to Mary's party, and I'd enjoy myself.

# CHAPTER THIRTEEN

## *Monday, June 26*

### Estella

Another week or so had passed, and Grace was just about as good as new. Henry found himself busier than ever with his new responsibilities at the mills, leaving me with more available time to spend with Bodaway. He and I spent hours each week together, exercising Grace and keeping an eye on her quickly improving leg.

The more time I spent with Bodaway, the more I found myself craving his presence, but now that Grace had improved greatly, my reasons for spending time with him were fading fast. Mother's schedule for me had grown over this week to occupy more and more of my time, though the past few days had been different. She'd taken to her room with a terrible headache, leaving me with an unusual amount of time to myself. Perhaps a month ago I might have been glad of it, might have been able to contain my wandering thoughts by simply losing myself in a novel. But not today.

I closed the book in my hands and set it on my vanity. My thoughts were with Bodaway.

I had promised myself that I wouldn't bring up his brother anymore, and Bodaway hadn't offered me any more information. When he was ready to share that with me, I'd be ready to listen—and not make any more silly assumptions.

I knew he *would* be ready, eventually. I recalled the first few times we had worked together with Grace, the tension in his posture, the anxiety in his demeanor. Now I recognized a slow shift in him as he relaxed and began to trust. Well, to an extent.

I'd also spent another evening with Henry and his family. The Hamilton's had been exceptionally kind to me these last weeks—especially Henry. He was consistent, and that was the truth.

Even Alice, Henry's mother, had been unnaturally pleasant, no more calling me to strange conversations in dimly lit rooms. My lips still fell into a tight, flat line at the thought of her. My previous apprehension had begun to feel unjustified, but even still, the uneasiness lingered.

I still sat at my vanity when Hannah burst through my bedroom door without warning. I swung around to see her face erupting with excitement.

"Lillian is back!" she cried.

"She's home? This very moment?" I leapt to my feet, forgetting my troubled thoughts at once.

Hannah came to me and took my hands. "She and her mother arrived only last night. One of the kitchen maids just told me."

"Oh, this is splendid news! You mustn't tell Mother, or she'll put a stop to it." I glanced towards my window. "I know what I need to do. Thank you for sharing this wonderful news in such a timely manner." I wrapped my arms around Hannah's neck in a quick embrace.

"I'll leave you to your scheming," she said, then winked at me. She took up my garments to be washed from the floor, and left me.

I sat back at my vanity and opened a delicate glass box that held little treasures and trinkets. I pulled out an old locket and opened it, a dried flower petal tumbled out. Lillian had given the petal to me at the end of one of our first summers together, a piece of Pinebrook for me to remember her by as I returned to my Boston life.

All at once, I returned to the moment I set the petal in the necklace. Lillian and I had sat on this very floor, by the fireplace. I could recall her rosy cheeks and huge brown eyes promising me we would always be the best of friends.

"Always," she had said. Those days seemed so long ago.

The day was warm. The breeze that blew in through my open window made for ideal summer weather and reminded me even more of years past. It only made my heart burdened for Lillian and her failing health. Even if Lillian herself didn't wish to see me, I was determined to speak with her today.

Father held a fondness for me that Mother simply did not share. If I was to obtain permission to pay an unexpected call to Lillian, Father would be the one to ask.

I moved to my window and took in the sight below me.

It was early evening, and Father was back at it with Black Magic. She'd already won her first races of the summer, and Father was only getting started. I supposed that's why he had trained Henry to maintain the mills so early in his career. "Priorities," I said to myself, and pulled the curtains shut.

I made my way outside. Father was barely visible through the tall grass by the clearing. He was dressed like one of the farm hands and working hard beside his newer, larger, and much more efficient stables.

"Father!"

He didn't respond. Father always had a hard time hearing when he was concentrating—or perhaps it was all that time he spent in the noisy mills.

"Father!" I yelled again.

He turned around as though he had only now heard me. "Is this urgent, Estella? You know how I feel about being interrupted while I'm working." He motioned to Black Magic.

I clenched my teeth and put on a smile. "Sorry, Father. I was wondering if I could go into town this afternoon? I would like to call on Lillian."

"Well," he said, wiping the sweat from his brow, "I've just dismissed the staff for the afternoon, but I suppose I could take you there myself in thirty minutes. I've been needing to stop by the mills anyway. You'd have about an hour's time to visit before I'd come back to get you." He pushed his glasses up his nose and tugged at his dirty linen shirt. "I'm going to change my clothes and clean up. Wagon leaves in thirty minutes sharp."

"Alright," I said with a smile. "I'll be ready."

\*\*\*

Father and I started off to town precisely on time. We passed the park by the orphanage, its grass a bright summer green. Ladies picnicked with their little ones, rocking the sleeping babies in their arms.

I felt that familiar knot in my stomach again as I thought about my future. Was that all I was to expect from life? Marry, have babies, and socialize with other women leading the exact life as myself?

Lillian's family lived a short distance from the center of town, so it wasn't long before we pulled up her drive and stopped at her doorsteps.

"Here we are," said Father, pulling back on the reins. "I'll see you in one hour. If you're done early, just walk on down to the mills and meet me." He chuckled. "Your mother would have a fit if she knew I was letting you walk through the mill housing alone. God forbid you interact with the town folk. Frankly, I don't see why you shouldn't have a little walk and take some fresh air. It would do you some good."

"Well, what mother doesn't know won't bother her." I leaned in to kiss him on the cheek as he held back a laugh. He gave me his hand to help me down from the carriage, then pulled away, leaving me standing in front of Lillian's door by myself.

The entryway loomed over me. I'd been there countless times before, but even still, it was intimidating knowing she might send me away. I took one last breath and knocked on the door.

Almost instantaneously, their maid opened.

"I'm here to see Lillian," I said.

The maid had mouse-like features, and looked as nervous as she had the last time I had called on the Sterlings. She fidgeted about and refused to look me in the eyes. "Miss Lillian is not well, and doesn't wish for company."

"Is she recovering, at least?" I prodded. "What's wrong?"

The maid tried to close the door on me, but I wasn't going to be shut out any longer. "I'm sorry, but I have to see her." I pushed my way past the much-smaller maid and moved as quickly as I could up the staircase to Lillian's room. The maid, alarmed and distressed, could do nothing more than follow behind me. "Miss, you can't go in there!"

Running through the dark hallway, I finally came upon the door to the room I knew so well.

I swung the door wide open, revealing Lillian seated at her vanity.

She turned and stared at me, wordless. The maid pushed past me, apologizing profusely, until Lillian raised her hand to silence her. "You may leave, Nellie."

The maid scurried away.

Lillian and I were alone now, and in an instant, I transformed from the proper lady my mother had trained me to be, back to the girl I'd been just one summer earlier.

"Lillian, what on earth is wrong?" I blurted out. "You won't answer my notes, and you refuse to see me! Worse, I learn through Alice Hamilton that you've been terribly ill and have sought help from a doctor in the city!" I shook my head, then hesitated. "I've… missed you more than I can express."

I sat on her bed, pushing back the loose strands that had fallen from my upswept hair with palms slightly damp after my outburst.

Lillian fixed her eyes on the floor for a long moment, as though gathering her thoughts, then met my gaze with a look of pure distress. "Estella, you know I've always been loyal to you. I wanted to tell you… but under these delicate circumstances, it just didn't seem right."

"What are you talking about?"

"Summer after summer I've watched you get everything you've ever wanted: the finest clothes, more books than you could ever read, the luxury of a family—I've never begrudged you any of this. I *want* you to have the things in life that fulfill you.

"But now you're getting the one thing that *I* want, the one thing I *deserve!* I won't just sit around and pretend that I'm not desperately hurt." Lillian wore a navy blue woolen robe. She pulled it more tightly around herself as she crossed her arms. Her big brown eyes welled with tears.

My worry shifted seamlessly to irritation. "*Me?!* Getting everything I want?" I stood. "How is an arranged marriage 'getting everything I want?' You *should* be happy for me that I'm at least fond of Henry, that I don't find myself completely miserable in his presence, that there's hope for love.

"You know my heart, Lillian. You know that I've never desired a loveless marriage like my parents! I have a chance here at real happiness." I breathed out, studying her look of shock. I approached her slowly and sat at her feet, taking her limp hands in mine. "You know me."

Lillian's tears spilled over her cheeks. She pulled away her hands. "An arranged marriage," she said, wiping away the tears. "It's much more complicated than you could imagine. I can't bear to be around you any longer."

"I just don't understand you, Lillian." I shook my head. "What happened to forever?"

She closed her eyes. "*I* love him," she whispered. Lillian took a deep breath in, and then released it slowly. "I love him, Estella. And he loves me. Or at least, he told me he did. Henry is the one I was telling you about all those weeks ago."

I was baffled. Henry had started writing letters to *me*. *He* had been the instigator. *He* had led Lillian on to believe they could be something more, then promptly forgot her in order to pursue me. This whole time, Henry has been working at Father's mills and courting me while Lillian suffered in silence.

"When?" I mumbled, almost too quietly. I repeated myself in a stronger voice. "When did he tell you that he loved you?"

"I can assure you it was not recent. Henry's love for me has endured for many months, and it can't be broken so easily." She held her chin high, but her voice wavered.

"Henry said that your family wanted you to marry into his fortune and that was the extent of it."

Lillian winced. "Oh, that's what he's saying now?" She shook her head, and her cheeks showed the briefest sign of color. "Well," she continued, the small quiver still in her throat, "I don't wish to talk any more of this." She crossed her arms even more tightly.

My friend's skin was a dull yellow and her hair hung over her shoulder in a brittle braid, like she was about to take to bed midday. She looked quite the sight, truly sick. This was not the same girl I had once known.

"Lillian," I spoke softly, trying to break through to her, "I would've never stolen Henry from you had I known your true feelings. Hearing of the way he's treated you only reveals his true nature and character…"

Her face grew pale and her eyes rolled back in her head.

"Lillian!" I hastened to my feet and caught her in my arms just as she fainted. "Help!" I called desperately, "Help, Nellie, anybody, help!"

Lillian's mother and Nellie came rushing in. "What is it?" Mrs. Sterling cried. "Mother's here." She threw herself at Lillian's side and rubbed her head, acting as though this had been a common occurrence.

I stood clasping my hands until they turned white as Nellie left to fetch some hot tea for Lillian. "What's going on?" I asked her mother.

She took a breath as to speak, but then tightened her lips, seeming unsure. "Estella, I really think it's best that you're not here when she wakes."

My heart dropped. Had *I* caused this? "Let me stay," I pleaded softly. "I'll sit in the corner—you'll hardly know I was here—but I'll assist you in any way possible."

"Please, Estella, don't make this more difficult than it has to be."

A huge lump rose in my throat and tears welled in my eyes as I backed away. I felt my way out of the room and down the empty hallway, biting my cheek so hard to stop myself from crying that I tasted blood.

I rested a hand on the front door before leaving and turned to look back into the parlor. The portrait of Lillian still hung over the hearth, as it had before, but her eyes now appeared strained.

How could that be? It was only a painting.

The whole house felt empty and cool. I forced my eyes away and left the Sterlings' home.

The sun outside shone as though it hadn't an idea about anything wrong in the world. The air still smelled like their flourishing gardens, and butterflies fluttered about as though I weren't falling apart inside.

I started mindlessly down the Sterlings' drive. I had no idea what to think about Lillian. Perhaps we were never to be the same as we once were. I tried holding back my feelings of frustration, at least enough to keep the tears at bay. I couldn't imagine explaining myself to Father, and I feared if I spoke a single word, I would lose my careful composure completely.

Entering town, I began thinking of Henry, about how I had really begun to care for him. But all of our progress, all of the hope that my heart had held for the pair of us, vanished after seeing Lillian in shambles, so completely convinced that Henry loved her.

How could I, in good conscience, marry her love? How could Henry profess love to Lilllian, then leave her, then tell *me* how insignificant their situation had been? I was now convinced that he was a master manipulator, a liar, and, evidently, a skilled actor. In a matter of only a few minutes with Lillian, everything, all my feelings, my good opinions, had changed for the worst.

As I wound through the busy streets of Pinebrook, heat crept up my neck and tingled down my spine. An emptiness formed in my mind, making room for these new, bitter feelings towards Henry Hamilton. Children ran past me, laughing as they enjoyed the day. Horses trotted by, pulling carriages, and the gentlemen who passed tipped their hats at me and exchanged pleasantries. It seemed as though everyone else in all of Pinebrook was having a better day than me. Nobody took notice of my cheeks, so flushed I feared they glowed as two hot coals.

"Estella?" a voice called out from the front of the general store.

It was Bodaway.

He and another man had been sitting on the store steps, eating apples and taking in the evening air.

"Bodaway!" The tightness in my chest released in a way I couldn't understand. Everyone else's smile had only deepened my bitterness, but his smile had a different effect.

Somehow his smile promised that everything was going to be just fine, and I almost believed him.

He briefly observed his surroundings before walking to meet me. "It's actually John, here." He laughed. "It's supposed to help me fit in, so my "savage" name doesn't cause problems."

I smiled a little at the realization that he had never offered up this new name to me. I'd only ever known him as Bodaway.

He studied my distraught look, clearly seeing that something wasn't right. Stepping in a little closer to me so the other man wouldn't hear, he lowered his voice. "Are you alright?" His dark eyes were so serious.

I didn't want to cry in front of Bodaway. He would think me weak or silly. So I bit my lip. "I'm alright." But that cursed quiver in my throat persisted. I turned away from Bodaway's gaze and tucked a loose strand of hair behind my ear.

I could tell that a part of Bodaway wanted to comfort me, but he hadn't forgotten his place. Instead, he said, "Let's get out of here." He said it in such a certain tone, as though he were completely unbothered by the idea of wandering off with me. His manner was so exposed, so vulnerable, that I simply couldn't refuse him.

My encounter with Lillian had shaken me to my core, and the only thing I wanted now was to be near someone I trusted. Even if Bodaway hadn't let himself trust me completely, the fact that he had been the one to suggest an escape was proof enough for me to believe that some form of trust had finally stirred up inside his hard shell.

I simply looked at him and nodded in agreement, not speaking for fear of crying.

Bodaway looked towards his red-headed friend who still sat on the steps and tossed him his extra apple. "Not a word of this, Art."

Art caught the fruit. "You have my word," he said, resting a hand over his heart.

Bodaway led me down the road a ways until we passed the tavern, which, to my surprise, seemed to be already full. Laughter, broken glass, and piano music spilled out the doors and into the streets. I caught Bodaway's gaze as he smirked and shook his head a little. I could only imagine him to be judging the men in the tavern, who were content to spend their evenings wasting away their hard earnings.

"Over here." Bodaway crossed the street towards the opening of a trail into the tree line.

"This is the trail I used to take when I first moved to town. I'd made camp a couple miles north of here. " He pointed to a mass of rocks which forked the trail within sight. "The other path leads to where we're going." He smiled mysteriously.

"How do you know your way around these woods so well?" I asked, looking up at him.

"I spend a lot of my free time here," he said as he pushed back a branch for me to get by. "I guess I just like to have a clear head, and this is one of the only places I feel completely free."

We walked along the trail together for a couple of miles. We wound across ledges, holding onto trees for support, and even scaled rocks at times. I looked around me and tried to find even one thing that I could recognize, but for a long while nothing was familiar.

Finally, just ahead of us was a twin birch tree with a great divot in the trunk where the two trees had grown as one. I smiled and then turned to Bodaway. "For a moment, I had no idea where we were. I used to play in these woods so often when I was a child, and that tree over there was a sign that I was almost home. Be aware that I know where each trail around these parts leads. In fact, I might have even made some of them." I laughed, feeling proud.

"You know where we're going, then?" Bodaway pointed through the trees and I saw the old stable on my family's estate in the distance.

"Certainly."

"Well, this is only our first stop," he said. We approached Grace. She stomped excitedly and flicked her tail.

"Hello, girl," Bodaway said as he touched her soft nose. "You ready to go out?" He smiled and handed me the lead.

"Where are we going?" I smiled through the intrigue.

"You'll see." He led us down another small path in the woods, another that I was unfamiliar with. I bit the inside of my cheek. My bragging had come back to haunt me so quickly. I hoped Bodaway didn't notice the brief flush in my cheeks.

It was therapeutic to hear the twigs snap under Grace's hooves and to breathe in the scent of pine as we marched through the forest.

"Alright," he said at last, "now left."

"Left?" I peered through the brush. "There is no left, just trees."

"Go left," he repeated, and we broke off of the path. Bodaway held back heavy pine boughs, allowing Grace and I to pass through. When I turned around, I could hardly see him through the dense green. The branches and brush rustled and parted as he pushed through them, reappearing.

Bodaway continued to give directions as we made our way through the thick of the woods. We scaled moss-covered rock and passed by narrow streams. He was making us work for our progress.

He didn't need to announce when we arrived. The trees thinned out until we stood on the outskirts of a grassy clearing. I heard running water, but it didn't sound as strong as a river; it was much gentler.

Bodaway took Grace's reins. He led her out of the woods and into the field, I followed close behind.

It was beautiful, and I'd definitely never been there before. A small brook ran along the tree line, and wildflowers lay scattered everywhere. It was a little Heaven on Earth, or maybe a Garden of Eden.

Bodaway had led Grace to the brook's edge to allow her to drink. He looked up as I followed behind. "You seem surprised," he said smugly.

"As a matter of fact, I am." I looked around in amazement. "I've never been here in all my life. I would have remembered a place like this."

Bodaway tied our horse to a sturdy branch that hung over the brook, and I sat in the shade under some pines. "It's like she's singing."

He bent down by the water and cupped some in his hands. "This is the freshest water in Pinebrook." He drank some and then shook the water off his hands before sitting next to me.

I looked at him seriously. "Why did you bring me here?"

He returned my gaze. "Close your eyes. Listen."

I did as he asked.

"Listen," he said again softly.

The wind pushed its way through the grass and into our hair, the brook bubbled on, and the birds sang their sweet songs—much sweeter than I'd heard them sing before. "Do you hear it?"

I opened my eyes slowly and met Bodaway's gaze. "Yes," I said. "It's beautiful." I lay back on my elbows to take in the moment.

"Whenever I was upset as a boy, I'd always find my peace in the woods." He picked at the grass underneath his fingers. "I could tell something's troubling you and hoped this would help."

It was fascinating that though Bodaway was strong-willed, and occasionally hot headed, he was also thoughtful and selfless. I couldn't help but admire him for it. "And here I thought I was excellent at concealing my feelings. I... went to see my dearest friend Lillian today." I rearranged my skirt and shook my head, trying to keep myself from crying again. "She's not the same person she once was. Something happened between her and my—" I stopped myself from uttering the word *fiancé*. "Between her and Henry Hamilton. I don't know all the details. And to make this horrible situation worse, she's been sick. Very sick, apparently, and I haven't the slightest idea of what it is that plagues her."

I looked at him. "She doesn't want to see me. She's furious. All because Henry's been courting me for the sake of both our families. Her mother, who's known me for years, practically threw me from her home."

Bodaway looked off, but I held my eyes to him. "All of this makes me question everything I thought I knew about Henry. My feelings have changed, that I know for certain."

"I'm sorry." His eyebrows crowded together, the sun lighting up his bronzed skin.

"Don't be sorry." I cleared my throat. "You were the one who told me that everyone has responsibilities, even small ones. My mother would agree with you, I'm sure. She'd add how *feelings* are fickle and foolish, and simply not substantial enough grounds to break an engagement."

He shrugged. "If you put your mind to it, I'm sure you could stomach the marriage. I mean, you didn't flinch once at Grace's festering wound."

I gave a small smile. "I wanted to believe that Henry was a good man. If I must marry him, how could I *not* desire that?" My smile faded. "But something *happened* between him and Lillian, something neither of them wish to speak of, and I intend to find out what it is."

I couldn't tell if Bodaway's expression was one of confusion, intrigue, or just plain indifference. "So you aren't officially engaged yet?" he asked, tilting his head.

"That depends on whom you ask. My mother would tell you yes. In reality, no, I'm not engaged to anyone, and if I had it my way now, I'd never be. To Henry, that is."

"It seems odd that your so-called friend faults you because of this. I'd assume that anyone in your inner circle would understand that you have to do everything your family tells you to." His voice was tinged with sarcasm.

"It's not like that. I don't do everything they tell me." I flushed. "Please, let's talk about something else. I don't want to think about Lillian anymore."

Bodaway raised his eyebrows as though he wanted to say more, but then let it go. He looked deep in thought for a moment, then asked, "What are you doing on Sunday?"

"I'll be at church for most of the afternoon. You know that red-haired man you were with at the mill housing? He goes to church."

Bodaway nodded. "He and his sister both go, don't they? I'm surprised Mary hasn't invited me to come along…"

"You should come," I invited with a smile. "The church is having a picnic after the service. Everyone always has such a nice time."

Bodaway grunted. "I can barely go to work without a name change or starting a fist fight." He rubbed his knuckles. "It's just best if I stay away. The less people I've got to deal with the better. And Sunday is my only day off. I've got plenty to keep me occupied. Also, it's best for me to stay away from Mary. I can tell she likes me, even though I haven't given her much to go off of yet."

"Yet?" I asked, feeling a little silly. "So you think you might be interested in your friend's sister?" The tightness in my chest returned. Anytime that Bodaway had ever mentioned this girl, Mary, he always spoke of her in the fondest way, of her sweetness and forcefully hospitable nature.

"Like I said, I'm here to do my part and provide for my brother, not to find a distraction."

I bit my cheek, a little embarrassed. "Well then," I said lightly, "you have to do what you believe you must." That sounded jealous even to me, and Bodaway looked pleased.

"So then what?" he asked, smiling playfully. "You spend your Sundays leisurely taking tea and crumpets with your rich parents?"

I laughed. "Oh, is that all you think of me?" I sat up. "Actually, before church, I've agreed to help Henry's mother at the orphanage. Afterwards, though, you're not wrong. There's certainly tea involved."

His response was hot and instantaneous. "If you're as skeptical of this courtship as you say you are, why are you getting so friendly with his family? I mean, I'm just curious. To me, that sounds like you're trying to move beyond your doubts." He said these last words with what seemed a forced indifference.

"I'm still trying to please my mother and father, as demented and pointless as that sounds. It's my responsibility. As my parents always say, the duty to marry well is in my blood."

"See, you've got your reasons." We sat there quietly, though the finality of his last words hung in the air, disrupting the stillness. I rose and shook the grass from my skirts and the uneasiness from my thoughts before approaching Grace. The weight that had settled on my chest seemed to lighten again as I took her reins and pressed my palm to her nose.

"She really is much better, isn't she?" I asked, leading her in an effortless walk.

Bodaway stood and joined us. "Practically perfect."

I hesitated for a moment. "Maybe I'm not so different from my father after all."

"How's that?"

"Well, I spend so much of my free time with Grace." I dragged my hand along her neck. "And my father spends *his* time with Black Magic, though I suppose his reasons are different."

"The races." Bodaway nodded. He looked almost unnerved. "It cost much money to enter in these parts?"

"Only a dollar or so. The track is very simple. It's nothing like the track my father races at in Long Island. It just gives the men something to do here in Pinebrook, an entertaining way to make a few dollars." I smiled.

Bodaway's face turned hard for a moment, and then relaxed. "I know all about the money you can win racing."

"My father wins very often," I added, "and he's always so proud of his prize and title. It's not about the money to him, though. I think he just really enjoys the feeling of being superior."

"Yeah, maybe that's it." His dark brows crowded, creating shadows over his eyes.

After a brief silence, I added, "I really should be finding my way home. No doubt my father is wondering where I am." A small smile tugged at my lips. "But it was very kind of you to bring me here. It's exactly what I needed." I looked around us, as if to absorb the last of its sweetness.

Bodaway grabbed the back of his neck. "Don't worry about it. Grace needed exercise anyway." He said it nonchalantly and moved closer until he stood right in front of me. "This is for you." He reached up and set a small yellow wildflower in my hair.

I reached up and touched it, feeling my cheeks flush. "Thank you for all of this," I repeated, truly grateful.

***

I finally made it to the front of the house, fully aware that I had lost track of time. Mother waited on the porch for me in a rocking chair with Darcy on her lap. I tried to think of an adequate excuse as to where I'd been, but none of them excused the fact that I had visited Lillian. There was going to be trouble waiting for me, but I was willing to give myself over to that fact. I had to face Mother one way or another.

The moment she saw me approaching, she stood from her watchful seat. "Estella Coraline Wellstone, where have you been? And don't give me any nonsense at all."

I carefully lifted the hem of my dress—my poor, grass stained, and absolutely filthy dress—as I walked up the porch stairway to meet her. "I went to visit Lillian."

Mother pursed her lips. "Yes, so I've heard. When your father came to get you, Sarah Sterling informed him that you had left more than forty-five minutes earlier." She put her hands on her hips. "So, why don't you start with the reason you were visiting Lillian, whom I *very* clearly instructed you not to see? Lord, and would you just look at that dress."

"I simply *had* to see her, Mother, she's my dearest friend. Though you'll be happy to know that she does not wish to see me any longer." I sighed and pulled at my sleeve. "After I left Lillian's house, I took a path through the woods home…" I bit my bottom lip. It was *partly* true. "I was quite upset after our meeting and didn't wish to speak of it with Father."

Mother beckoned to a servant passing by the open doorway and handed Darcy off to be brought inside. Then she turned back to me, massaging her temples. "How many Godforsaken times do I need to remind you that you are *not* to be roaming the woods like some wild beast, or some savage?!"

Her words held a particularly wretched sting to them, a sting that caused my venomous thoughts to build up until I had no choice but to send them flying out of my mouth. "Mother!" I raised my voice. "I am exhausted of trying to be the daughter you really wanted. I'm not the perfection you've always longed for. And yes, I *know* a lady should never raise her voice, or go into the woods with her nice gowns on, or question her parents, but I'm not that lady! I may never be.

"Lately it feels as though my life's purpose is to please your every whim while you plan away my future." I tried to push my way through the front door, but Mother crossed in front of me, blocking the way.

A tight smile formed on her lips and she growled her words at me through clenched teeth. "Well, you'd better *start* trying to be as close to perfection as you can, because if you ruin our chances of marriage with the Hamiltons, you'll be sorry, Estella. You can be sure of that."

"You don't even care to know what kind of man Henry really is," I retorted. "You're willing to marry me off to the man with the best fortune, while character and happiness are things of little importance to you!"

She moved aside to let me burst through the door, but followed after me. "Estella, do *not* run away from me. I want to hear about what kind of man Henry supposedly is." Her mocking tone awaited my response.

I had no proof of anything, so I remained silent.

"That's what I thought. You'll do well to remember that *I* always have the last word. You have a duty to obey, and it runs in your blood." She squared her shoulders and lifted her chin. "As I've said before, your father and I have given you everything. I mean that. Everything you have is owed to me and your father. It is our right to marry you off to whomever we think is best, and it is your job to comply, young lady. It's not as though I'm requiring something of you that I have not already done myself. I've done it, your grandmother has done it—every respectable woman on God's earth has done it, and, Lord help us, you will too."

It turned my stomach to hear the things that I'd already assumed to be true. "Good night," I said with tight fists and retreated to my room.

It was only 7 p.m., but I wasn't planning to leave my room until the next day. I sat at my vanity, my chest heaving with each hot breath. There were tear stains on my cheeks. Had I been crying? I hadn't even noticed.

My whole life seemed to be all wrong. I was angry at everything, not just at Mother. As I sat there, looking at myself blankly in the mirror, a cluster of yellow among my dark curls caught my eye. I had forgotten about Bodaway's flower. It was so pretty with its delicate petals.

I removed it from my hair and held it in the palm of my hand for a moment, then placed it on my vanity next to Mother's heirloom necklace. I laughed when I thought about how little the necklace meant to me. Though its tangible worth was much greater than that of the little wildflower, I held much fonder sentiments for the simpler gift. The thought of Bodaway dulled my ache for just a moment, washing me with a gentle warmth.

# CHAPTER FOURTEEN

*Saturday, July 1st*

Bodaway

After I returned Grace to her stables, I made my way into town. The evening sun made my shadow appear ten feet tall, perhaps a reflection of my inward optimism. My lips curled into what wasn't exactly a smile, but a pleasant expression all the same.

Maybe my spirits were high because I wasn't expected at the mills the next morning, or maybe I was just bursting at my very seams with hope that I might have received word from Keme. It'd been over five weeks since my move to Pinebrook. I hadn't heard a word from him yet, but I still sent a letter each week, along with all the money I could manage.

The walk wasn't more than ten minutes from the mill housing if I stayed on the dirt road that cut through town. Pinebrook was small, but a lot of people populated the area. Downtown was always bustling with ladies shopping and children playing in the streets. Horses waited patiently for their masters, tied up in front of the shops.

I walked into the general store and was greeted with a smile from the old woman behind the counter. The whole store smelled strongly of her cologne making it hard to breathe. "Can I get you anything?" she asked me, moving her spectacles up her crooked nose.

"Just a stamped envelope, please." I gave a nod to the stack behind the cluttered counter. The store wasn't the most organized establishment I'd ever seen, but they always had what I needed.

She retrieved an envelope from the top of the stack, pressed a stamp onto it, and held it out to me in twisted fingers that quivered with age.

"There wouldn't happen to be a letter for me?" I asked. "For Bodaway."

"Let me check." She tilted her head and looked through the mail shelf. After a few seconds she retrieved a letter and handed it to me. "Looks like you do have a letter." She smiled.

I held my breath as my hands smoothed out the envelope addressed to me from Maine. "Thanks," I said, before walking to a small table placed in the corner of the store for customers to address letters and prepare packages. My fingers fumbled as I struggled to open the letter. Finally, I pulled it from its envelope. I closed my eyes tightly for a second, begging for good news, then began to read.

*Dear Bodaway,*

*I pray this finds you well. Your brother asks for you every day, and although he is very grateful that you send money for his medical expenses, there is nothing he wants more than for you to come home. He regrets not sending word sooner, but over the past weeks, he has been unable to sit upright, let alone pen a letter in his own hand. He implored me not to write to you of his worsened condition, believing* if he sent word that you might return to Maine, and he recalls just how insistent you were on the matter of leaving. He anxiously awaits your return, but his anticipation in no way lessens his gratitude for the money you have been kind enough to send. He seems especially pleased to learn of your newfound friends and work.

Margaret and I understand that you accept all of the blame for what happened to Keme, but it is not your fault. I know you believe staying away is the best thing you can do for him, but he needs you now more than ever. Our intention is not to alarm you, but over the past month, Keme's condition has weakened greatly. It seems that the only hope of recovery, in any form, is an operation. Your brother shows no signs of getting better on his own, and the doctors here believe it to be pointless to continue treating him as they have.

There is good news to this letter. We have been in contact with a unique doctor in Canada who experiments with modern medicine and techniques. He has brought patients similar to Keme back to health by performing a special operation on their spines. Of course, there are many risks that come with this procedure, but we are grasping here at any shred of hope. Though he still has no feeling in his legs, Keme is in good spirits and wishes to try this new means of recovery.

Bodaway, this operation will be very expensive. We do not want money to stand in the way of Keme getting better, but the reality is we need twenty dollars. We are doing everything in our power to raise that money, and are sure you will too. Ultimately, Keme is in the good Lord's hands, and sometimes we simply cannot understand His ways. Come home if you can, and we will make do.

God Bless,
William and Margaret

My breathing was shallow, and my mouth felt dry and tasted like the postwoman's cologne. It would take me well over a month to save that kind of money, and I didn't have that much time on my hands.

I cleared my throat and shook my head. There was no way I could go home now. Keme needed money for an operation, and I would make that money even if it broke me. He'd just have to understand that I did this all for him.

I grabbed a small, dull-tipped pencil resting on the table and addressed the envelope to Keme. I didn't know what to say. Should I tell Keme about Estella and Grace, or would he feel like I was rubbing salt in his wounds? I didn't have the heart to tell him how God had miraculously healed Grace, either. I tried writing about how I carried around the stone I'd found for him in the Sugar River, but I scratched that out. In the end, I just opted to fold the money inside the envelope and keep my message brief.

*Dear Keme,*

*I pray for your recovery every day, and wish I could go back in time and trade places with you. I'm going to get that money for your operation by any means possible. Take care of yourself, Brother.*

*Bodaway*

After paying rent each week, I was left with a grand $4.70 in banknotes to send to Keme. I lifted the envelope and felt its lightness in my hands. Just knowing how much Keme really needed made the envelope look sparse and pathetic. My brother needed this money now more than ever, and all I could offer was a few dollars?

I handed the old woman my letter and stormed out of the post office, angry and defeated. Where was I going to get twenty dollars?

\*\*\*

## Sunday, July 16th

Sunday mornings were quiet at the mill housing. Most of the men were at church, only to return to the tavern on Monday. Upon waking, I sat up in my bed and looked around the empty room. I hadn't slept well, still very much troubled by the responsibility I had to my brother. After dressing, I picked up his stone from my nightstand and watched the specks of different minerals reflect the sunlight coming into the room before tucking into my pocket.

I still needed to make twenty dollars appear out of thin air. I'd asked around about extra work in town. Where there's land, there's sure to be work, and farms can almost always use an extra set of hands to plow fields or keep up the stables, at least that's what Mary told me. She tried to set me up with some work at the McNerry farm, but the work hours conflicted heavily with my work at the mills.

Even Art tried helping me, but his advice only set me back. He brought me to the tavern late after work one evening and introduced me to Pinebrook's underbelly: A group of men who arranged fights. "There's money to be had in these bare knuckled fist fights," Art assured me. "I'm even betting myself. I have it on good authority that a great Polock, Merik, he's called, is going to take the next fight."

Merik did not. I gambled and lost. After that, I kept a tighter hold on the few dollars I did have, and decided against future betting with Art.

Defeat slowly crept over me. It amazed me how easy it was to become consumed by money, even if you had none of it.

Art's bed had been made neatly, and there was a plate of biscuits on the table. All signs pointed to Mary having been here.

I leaned over the side of my bed and tied my boots on my feet. Sure enough, lying on the table by the plate of biscuits was a note:

*Enjoy the biscuits, and if you feel like joining us at church, you're always welcome. -Mary*

Taking a biscuit, I asked God, *Is this what you want from me? To go to church? To rely on You to provide the money for my brother?* I sighed, and felt the weight of Keme's stone in my pocket. *Fine, but I'm doing this for Keme.* Reluctantly, I grabbed my cap and walked out the door. I was going to church.

\*\*\*

Songs of praise came from the double doors of the Church of Pinebrook, its steeple reaching for the heavens. The sun was shining, the sky was summer blue, and a warm breeze almost made the oppressive heat bearable. I lingered outside for a short while, my neck growing tense. The last time I had been inside a church had been with Keme in Maine. He loved church, and would sit right up front to best take in everything the preacher said. Even after his accident, my brother's faith never wavered.

Maybe everything going wrong in my life was God's judgment for what I did to Keme. At this point, I wasn't in a position to dismiss the thought. Either way, Keme needed all the prayer he could get.

I began to anticipate the moment when I'd step into the church, the townspeople's turning heads and their whispering lips. If anyone had a problem with me being in church, they could leave. If they wanted to fight me? Let them try. I swallowed hard and hastily tucked my shirt in before stepping up to the small entry stairwell. *They can call me savage one time before I rip their heads off.*

I had to move past this habit of working myself up all the time when I really wanted to become a better man. I tried my hardest to convince myself that I did this for Keme. Nobody else mattered. I took some air into my chest and prepared myself for whatever was to happen.

Before entering, I noticed a wide golden plaque bolted to the church wall.

*In honor of the Hamiltons' great generosity in helping further the Lord's kingdom.*

This whole church had been financially provided for by the Hamiltons. Struggling not to become further heated, I walked through the church doors and paused, expecting to cause a scene...

But nothing happened.

The people kept singing, and hardly anyone stared at me, with the exception of a child or two who were promptly poked in the ribs by their mothers.

The room was split in half, each side filled with rows of pews. Stained glass windows lined the walls, and an elderly preacher stood at the front of the church, Bible in hand, singing with the congregation.

I looked around the room, paralyzed, until I saw two familiar redheads.

Mary and Art sat a few pews from the back. They waved me over to sit with them.

"I'm so glad you decided to come." Mary whispered as I approached. The singing stopped and we all sat.

"I never thought he would," Art added.

I raised my eyebrows. "Well, I didn't think I would either, but things change." I turned my attention to the preacher at the front as he began his sermon.

I looked down at my clenched fists, my knuckles white. When I looked back up, I noticed a pair of crystal eyes burning into mine from the front pew.

Estella's face was a mix of confusion and surprise, but then her lips formed the slightest of smiles. That smile. She sat there so beautifully in a plain, plum-colored dress while her bonnet hung loosely at her back.

When Estella didn't provoke frustration in me, she made me feel calm and rational. I couldn't explain it. Quickly I remembered that anyone could be watching me, so I refocused my attention on the preacher. At least, my eyes focused on him while my mind remained distant and distracted.

For the next forty-five minutes or so, my mind wandered, searching for answers to my problems when I should have been listening to the sermon.

Eventually the preacher finished his sermon with some Bible verse. "'Let your conversation be without covetousness; and be content with such things as ye have: for he hath said, I will never leave thee, nor forsake thee.' Hebrews 13:5."

*No worries about loving money. I don't have any to love.* The people around me loved *their* money. Of course the sermon would be about money. But what was that part about God never leaving me? What else do you call it when your earthly father abandons you, your mother is dead, your brother is a shell of a boy, and you're the only one left to provide for him?

*God sure is watching out for me, making sure I get the short end of the stick.* I pictured Keme being sent away because the missionaries couldn't afford to provide for him. I pictured him never being able to get the operation that he needed, living a dormant life, or worse. I clenched my jaw, and knew what I was feeling was wrong. But when everyone in my life had left, it was hard to imagine the God of the universe would stick around for someone like me.

We sang one last hymn. I stood uncomfortably with Art and Mary until the music stopped and the preacher said a few words in parting. "Please remember that there will be a church picnic held in the green following the service. God be with you all this week." He raised his hand and dismissed us.

With that, the congregation exited the church in bunches. Art began conversing with a friend of his, and Mary and I decided to wait for him outside by the oak tree in front of the church.

Mary fanned herself, flushing from the heat. "It was getting so warm in there I thought I'd faint dead away."

"Not much better out here," I replied, watching people exit the church, hoping to catch a glimpse of Estella again.

Sure enough, she soon came through the church door, her eyes scanning the people lingering outside. Was she looking for me? I almost waved to her, but before I had time to act like an idiot, Henry Hamilton joined her at the top of the stairs. He took her hand tenderly in his, and led her down the steps. *What a flapdoodle.*

"At least there's a lovely breeze." Mary closed her eyes and let the summer air brush past the fiery wisps along her forehead.

I made some sort of grunt in response to Mary, but I was having a difficult time focusing on her when Estella was being paraded around by her elegant suitor. My neck grew tight and I clenched my jaw.

Estella made quick eye contact with me as she passed by, moving towards the green for the church picnic. *She doesn't want him, and she knows it.* I was astounded at how she could disregard all the concerning things she had told me and hang off his arm as if nothing bothered her. She was so stubborn I could easily see her follow through with this stupid marriage.

"Are you alright?" Mary rested her hand on my arm.

"Fine. Why?"

"You've been staring at Henry Hamilton with this brooding look in your eyes, and you don't seem to be listening to a word I'm saying."

Had Mary been talking more? I hadn't realized it. "I've just got a lot on my mind."

Just then, Art stepped up beside me. "What's on your mind, John? I could think of two possible answers off the top of my head."

I shot him a look and he changed the subject. "Well, anyway, I don't know about you, but I'm starved." Art gave my shoulder a squeeze.

Mary smiled up at me. "John, come sit with us at the picnic! It's always such good fun. Maybe it'll cheer you up."

"Thanks for the offer, but I've got things to do." I rubbed the back of my neck. "Maybe next time."

"Well, if you change your mind, come find us." Art linked arms with his sister.

"Yes, please do, John," Mary added before Art led her across the street.

I stood back and watched the people preparing for lunch, but looked away before I risked spotting Estella again. I turned on my heels and headed blindly in the opposite direction. Where I ended up would be better than staying at the picnic.

\*\*\*

I shouldn't have mixed myself up with Estella back on that first day. I'd known full well that it would be a mistake. With great strides, I entered the mouth of the trail by the mill housing and found my way to Grace's stables to clear my head. I needed to stay away from Estella as much as I could. I needed my space. And I still needed money, immediately.

Grace stood in her stable as if she were waiting for me. "Hey there," I said softly as I led her out. "Should we go for a ride?" I had a habit of talking to her like she could answer me. I suppose she did answer with her eyes, the way they didn't shy away, the way they shone with readiness.

I led Grace into the daylight and circled her, examining her legs. My hands trembled as I felt the flesh along her healed wound. She'd been better than new for a while now, but I hadn't been able to ride her. She could have taken it, but I hadn't been able to let myself go there. It was as if it would wrong Keme in some way, but now I had to do this *for* Keme.

I took a fistful of her mane and with one good jump mounted her for the first time ever. She stood so tall, and I felt no hesitation in her body at my weight. I clicked my tongue and signaled her to move.

She went from a slow trot to an untamed sprint before I could count to three. "Whoa there, girl! Whoa!" I tried to make her stop, but she was too fast and too focused, dashing of her own accord for the mouth of the trail.

Grace was a wild one for sure, and as agile a horse as I ever saw. Pine trees passed us in blurs, and her skilled gait avoided the rocks and holes in the ground like she knew these parts well.

For the first time in months, I felt alive. I was laughing, a huge grin spread across my face. Grace was so fast that I imagined her running across the whole country overnight... or at least to Maine.

I grabbed her firmly by the mane and pulled back. "Woah!" Grace slowed her pace to a trot. "Whoa," I said again, pulling a little harder until she stopped. I hopped down and stood in awe at her speed. She hardly looked tired. "You could beat any of those race horses, couldn't you, girl?" My throat felt sore from breathing so intensely and my eyes burned, welling up from the wind that whipped past me while riding.

God's provision? I was going to race Grace at the Pinebrook track. She'd need some training, but it was nothing I couldn't handle. I'd get this money on my own, as I'd done many times before.

# CHAPTER FIFTEEN

*Friday, July 21st*

Estella

I had seen Bodaway at church last Sunday, and knew he saw me with Henry. I hadn't seen him since, but wondered about him more than I should.

A few days later, Father received word that one of his oldest business associates had passed away. He was obligated to attend the man's funeral services in Boston, and brought Mother along with him. He also brought Henry along to introduce him to his other associates.

I'm ashamed to admit that I took advantage of a man's death and induced a swift but fleeting illness, using a page out of Alice Hamilton's book of tricks. One evening, while walking Grace, Bodaway had pointed out a small cluster of rue growing in a sunny patch of dried grass along our trail. When Father announced his trip, I gathered some of the herb and made a simple concoction of tea, only taking a small sip every hour or so until I was sufficiently unwell.

The rue induced symptoms of illness, but it was nothing severe enough to cause actual damage to my well-being. Though it was dishonest of me, the violent vomiting convinced Mother that I was unfit to travel. The sudden severity of it all surprised even me—the pain surely a swift punishment for my sin of deception.

Much to my dismay, Mother left a pile of envelopes, filled with news of my unofficial engagement, for me to address from my bed as I rested.

My family left a few days previous, and wouldn't be back until next week. With Bodaway nowhere to be found, Henry out of town, and not being on speaking terms with Lillian, this left me with no one to talk to and nothing but frustration and paper cuts to keep me occupied.

To escape the confines of my room, I sat in the window seat of our parlor. It was a cloudy evening and the wind bent the tall grass of our field in a funny way. At a certain point, Hannah entered. "Estella, dear, you look a bit pale. Are you feeling worse again? Should I send for the doctor?"

I leaned back in distress. "That won't be necessary. I'm in good health, Hannah, don't worry yourself on that account. This day has simply proved to be more dull than I can bear."

"Why don't you take a good book outside? You've always loved doing that." She approached and sat beside me, touching my forehead to check for a fever. "It seems I don't find the same satisfaction in reading as I once did." I leaned further into the window and wondered what Bodaway was doing right now. He was probably just leaving the mills.

"That's a shame, dear, but I'll leave this here with you, just in case." She smiled, pulling a book from her smock pocket. *Sense and Sensibility*, a title Henry and I had discussed in great admiration over our many letters.

"Henry had it sent here to you from his personal collection, in case you found yourself feeling drab."

I reached up and took the book. "How thoughtful." I traced its binding and then opened it. Inside, written on the first page, was a note.

*Estella,*

*I hope this book will captivate you as much now as it did the first few times you read it. I know you've grown distant from me this past week, though I am unsure of the reason. I truly pray that when I return home to you, that we can work through whatever it is that's troubling you.*

*Sincerely yours,*
*Henry*

"Thoughtful indeed," Hannah said with a smirk.

Though it was a gray evening, there was no reason I couldn't find my way outdoors. I thought of the place Bodaway had taken me after my visit with Lillian. It had been so beautiful and peaceful. "I do think I'll take a walk after all, Hannah. You won't mind if I'm out later than I ought to be, will you?" I rose and headed towards the front door.

"Please don't be out too long, my sweets, and mind you, be safe out there!" She pulled me into a warm embrace, and tied a cloak around my neck, before sending me on my way.

\*\*\*

It wasn't difficult to find Bodaway's secret haven again. Without Grace and Bodaway, I expected to find it sad and empty. Much to my surprise, I heard voices and laughter coming from within. *Who else would be out this far?* I wondered, and slowly walked into the clearing.

It was Bodaway and the friend I'd seen him with at the mill housing.

They had Grace. Bodaway was *riding* Grace.

Why would he bring a stranger into *our* special place, and why was he sharing Grace with other people? How many others know about her? My throat went dry, and I couldn't fight this strange feeling that sat like a brick in my stomach.

It was silly, really. Bodaway had as much a right to Grace as I did. Yet, he should know the dangers of the wrong person learning of our horse. I wouldn't know what to do with myself if Grace was taken from us.

I attempted to push past my own feelings, and waved my arm at them as I approached, book still in hand. "Bodaway!" I called.

Bodaway didn't seem any happier to see me than I was to see him. It reminded me of our early interaction, and it took me by surprise.

He dismounted Grace and held her by the bit. "Estella."

I put my free hand on my hip. "I see you've brought company."

The mill worker seemed amused. "Where are your manners, John?" He turned to me. "You can call me Art, Miss Wellstone." He removed his cap, revealing his head of red hair, and curtseyed.

I turned back to Bodaway. "What are you two doing with Grace? And when did you start riding her? I thought you said she wasn't ready."

He patted her neck. "I've only been riding her a few days. She's stronger than I thought, and Art and I planned on timing her speed."

"Whatever for?" I was thoroughly confused.

Bodaway looked at Art, clearly deliberating whether or not he should share his plans, but Art beat him to it. "Johnny here thinks Grace has a fighting chance at winning the races."

Bodaway rubbed his face. "She's fast, Estella. I was going to tell you."

"When?" I asked, annoyed. "When were you going to tell me you planned to race our horse—who's just barely healed, might I add? She could injure herself again if she's not careful."

Bodaway lifted his hands. "Don't lecture me on what's best for this horse. I didn't tell you anything because it seems you've been occupied with your fiancé or whoever." He crossed his arms.

Art stood there awkwardly in the middle of our disagreement. Grace tried to graze the fresh grass beneath us.

"Why would you want to race her?" I asked. "Money?"

Bodaway said nothing.

I shook my head. "I thought you didn't care about money, that it couldn't fix all of your problems."

"You know, Estella, Grace is healed up. You should be glad to know that she doesn't need you anymore. It frees you to do the things you care most about and to be the lady you were *born to be*." His words were cold and coarse against my ears.

My composure began to waver, but my words came out smooth as velvet. "How could you say something so insensitive? I spent weeks of my life helping you heal this horse. I practically had to *beg* you to help me in the first place, so you have no right to suggest that I don't care about Grace! You know that I do."

For a flicker of a second, it seemed as though Bodaway realized he was mistreating me, but then his face was overcome with frustration once more. "That's not what this is about at all, Estella! Just do yourself a favor and go home."

"No! You're being completely unfair! I've earned the right to have a say in what we do with Grace."

Bodaway dropped Grace's lead. "Unfair?" He raised his voice almost to a shout. "What do *you* know about unfair?"

When I spoke again, I did so in a harsh but level tone. "My time is running out. I'm being forced into a marriage that I don't want, to a man that I don't love. Now, to make things worse, you're trying to take away the one thing that's brought me true joy and happiness this summer. Does that sound fair to you?"

Bodaway's body, tense and agitated only a moment before, now quivered with what seemed closer to rage. He took another step closer to me, directly in front of my face.

Art's eyes had gone wide with shock at Bodaway's behavior. He tried to place himself between Bodaway and myself, but was unsuccessful. "Whoa there, John, why don't you take a moment to cool off?"

Bodaway ignored his friend, clenching his jaw. His eyes were the most intense I'd ever seen them. I swallowed hard, and remained still as he responded in a whisper that was anything but gentle. "My brother lies in a bed, somewhere, wasting away because of one stupid mistake that I'm responsible for. He may never walk again because of me!"

He spat his words. "I spend my life estranged from my own culture and the people who raised me, unwanted and not welcome in yours, all the while trying to tolerate people like you so I can manage to send a few measly dollars for my brother to have a second chance at life. Does *that* seem fair to you?" His furrowed brows cast dark shadows over his eyes.

Bodaway had been carrying around such guilt and responsibility, a burden too great to share alone. I could tell by Art's expression that this was his first time hearing it as well. Bodaway had kept this to himself, and slowly but surely it had eaten away at the core of his being. This angry frame of a man standing in front of me was just a broken boy in need of someone to put him back together.

I dropped my book to the ground, then stepped forward until the short distance separating us was nonexistent. I wrapped my arms around him, his body was stiff beneath mine. Then all at once I felt him let go and accept my embrace. Surely the reason God brought us together to heal Grace had a much larger purpose. Bodaway had been put in my life so that he could heal and release the inner anguish that he had clearly not come to terms with yet. As I held Bodaway in my arms, I prayed silently, *God, please help heal Bodaway the way that you healed Grace. Mend his broken heart.*

# CHAPTER SIXTEEN

## Bodaway

*M*y heart raced faster than any of the horses at the race as I ran to Keme, who lay on the ground surrounded by people. Their incessant shouting made it hard to concentrate. I frantically pushed through the crowd, steamrolling over anything in my path. Finally, I saw it all.

Our racehorse stood to the side as Keme lay in the dirt, moaning in a pool of his own blood. The dust of the accident hung heavily in the air, making it hard to breathe. When Keme fell, it seemed the entire audience had run to his side. I dropped to my knees and grabbed his shoulders. "Keme! Keme, can you hear me? Listen, I'm going to get help."

I used all my might to pull him into my lap. His hair that had been tied back so neatly now hung over my legs in disarray. Keme cried out in pain, his whole body mercilessly scraped. He managed to look up at me with dirt and tears staining his cheeks. "Bodaway... I can't feel my legs."

I shook my head, unable to comprehend what he was saying. "What do you mean you can't?"

Keme's eyes rolled back into his head. I slapped his face in desperation, his skin feeling hot to the touch. "Keme!" I looked up at the people surrounding us. "What are you standing around for? Somebody get help!" I screamed, angrier with every passing moment. I took my brother more tightly into my arms and bit down on my cheek until it bled.

I never should have pushed him to race. He didn't even want it. "I'm so sorry, brother." I rested my face in his hair and cradled his head as I tried to hold back sobs. I didn't even know if he could hear me. "I'm sorry. This is all my fault, and I'm going to do whatever it takes to fix this. I promise this to you."

\*\*\*

Art took Grace for a short walk through the field to give us privacy while Estella and I sat in the grass by the brook.

"That's pretty much the whole story," I said. "My brother's racing accident happened because of me. He's paralyzed because of *me*. The fact that he needs money for an operation that he can't afford is my fault. I made him race. It should be me who can't walk. I *have* to get that money to him."

I looked at my hands. They trembled with adrenaline.

Estella's eyes were soft as she reached her hand over to mine and grabbed it. "Bodaway, it's not your fault. What happened to Keme was terrible and tragic, but you can't blame yourself."

"You don't understand, I pressured him into racing one last time. He never liked gambling. He said God had entrusted us with a small amount of money and that we needed to spend every penny wisely. Eventually he quit racing altogether.

"But I wouldn't hear of it, not when there was money to be had. Not when I thought I could make our lives that much better.

I smiled faintly. "Keme was the superior rider, the most incredible rider I'd ever seen. Without him, I began losing." I cleared my throat. "Small amounts at first. But then I had the chance to win more than triple the amount I gambled.

"I put down the money without telling Keme. I told him that I couldn't risk this kind of loss, not with that much money at stake. 'We'll give it up for good after this,' I told him. 'Just do this one more race and I'll never ask you again.'"

I stood and paced, the tension in my neck growing until it felt as if a boulder rested at the base of my shoulders. "And he did race that one last time, because I asked him to. I think about that every day. I ruined him."

Estella stood and quietly took my hand. "You should go to him. You say Grace is fast, so take her. You could ride through the night and be with him by tomorrow."

"I have to do this before I can show my face there again." I pulled my hand away and clenched it into a fist, determined. "I'll get that money."

She cast her eyes to the ground, her dark lashes almost brushing her cheeks. "I know you believe you have to do this on your own, and I won't get in your way. Grace is *your* horse, and always has been. If you do decide to leave Pinebrook to be with your brother, you have to take Grace with you." Her eyes lifted to mine. "I mean it." She was so sincere, though I could tell that even talking about Grace's absence made her heart heavy.

I relaxed my clenched hand and slipped it into my pocket where I kept Keme's stone. When my fingers traced along the stone's smooth edges the tension in my neck released, just a little. "I'm sorry for the things I said earlier. I don't really want to take Grace away from you." I watched the brook in the dull light that filtered through the clouds. "But thanks."

"Are you two about done?" Art called from the middle of the field. "We're losing daylight!"

Estella nodded in their direction. "Can I at least see her run?"

I brushed the remaining grass from my trousers, "I suppose you are entitled to that." I tilted my head to her with a smirk, then the two of us rejoined Art and Grace.

"Let me get my watch ready," said Art, fishing around in his pockets.

Estella looked at me. "You'll be the one to ride her if you race?"

"That's the plan," I grabbed Grace's mane and mounted her bareback.

Estella backed away to stand beside Art.

He clicked open the watch. "Alright, John, get ready…"

I guided Grace to a good starting spot.

"Get set… Go!"

Then Grace and I were off running along the edge of the clearing. It was a fairly accurate representation of the town track's size, according to Art.

Grace moved like an experienced racer. We must have looked like a streak of white among the greenery. I kept a firm grip on the reins and leaned in closer to Grace's neck, narrowing my focus as we approached the makeshift finish line ahead.

"And… finished!" Art called out, flinging up both hands.

"How long was that?" I turned Grace around and walked her back towards Art and Estella.

"One minute and seven seconds. That's three seconds faster than you predicted!"

I looked to Estella, hoping for any form of approval. Grace was fast, and she couldn't deny the facts.

"She was incredible." Estella walked over and patted Grace's nose. "Really something."

"I think so too. I haven't seen many like her."

Art, still messing with his watch, called out, "I think you should try it again a few more times."

Estella nodded to Grace's healed leg. "Are you sure she'll be alright?"

I met her unsure but earnest gaze. "She'll be fine. I wouldn't race her if I didn't believe that, I promise."

Art's face beamed at me with hope that we could actually pull this whole thing off.

"I've never been so sure of a horse before."

"I trust you," she said, running her hand along Grace's side. "Alright," Art barged in, walking towards us. "She trusts you, I trust you, we all trust each other, so are we done with the shenanigans? We need to time her some more before the daylight's completely gone!" He put both hands on his head in impatience.

"He's right," said Estella. "My father's horse, Black Magic, still has a good ten seconds on you. You'll need to work with Grace as much as you can. And you'd do well to remember that Grace has never been on the track before, while Black Magic knows every inch of it." She smiled at Art. "I'll let you boys get to work. I should be getting home before dark anyways." Estella sighed, but her usual look of optimism was back.

"No, Estella, stay!" Art exclaimed. "Actually, John and I are about to head to a barn dance, and you should tag along!"

I shot a look at him. "Art, I don't think that's a good idea."

"Nonsense, people would barely recognize her looking like this." He motioned to Estella's dirty dress and wild hair.

I rubbed my neck. "Still, I mean, I doubt she'd even want to come."

"Yes I would!" she piped in. "A barn dance sounds exciting!"

"Well, it's not the normal sorts of parties that you're used to."

"Why? Don't you want me to come?" Her eyebrows furrowed together.

"Yeah, John?" Art seemed amused, acting like he knew some secret. I shot him another quick glare.

"That's not it…" I thought uncomfortably of Mary and Estella together at the dance. "She's free to speak for herself." Art crossed his arms. "Then it's settled, she's coming with us."

When I didn't respond, Art added, "Don't mind him, Estella." He laughed. "I'm sure we can all have a wonderful time under one barn roof."

\*\*\*

For lack of time, we brought Grace with us and tied her among the other horses a ways from the party.

The barn doors were swung open wide, and lights, laughter, and music poured out into the night. Art, Estella and I were dirty from training Grace all evening, and Mary would surely have something to say about that. *Mary.* I still hadn't shared with Estella that I was technically accompanying Mary to the dance.

The night was crisp, and the stars were incredible.

"I am going to head in alone," said Art. "I'd rather the ladies not see John here first, if you don't mind." He nudged me in the ribs. "If Lydia gets an eyeful of you, she might forget about me completely.

How do I look?" He took his hat off, tousled his hair, and smoothed his wrinkled shirt.

"Like an absolute gentleman," Estella said with a smile.

He returned his hat and nodded before leaving us alone.

"He's hopeless," I said, shaking my head.

Estella's wild hair fell about her shoulders as we walked. Though she didn't look as elegant as she normally did, there was something even more attractive about her simple beauty emphasized by a plain blue dress. She carried a book tucked under one arm, and a wool cloak hung over her shoulders.

Estella stayed close to my side as we walked towards the barn, and our hands brushed. Her skin was as smooth as a skipping stone. The warmth of her skin passed through me, and I rubbed my neck in discomfort. I felt like I had to say something, anything. "It's not that I didn't want you to come here tonight." Should I mention Mary?

Her innocent blue eyes looked up at me. "Then what is it? Are you worried that someone might see us together? I know what work at the mills means to you, especially now."

"No, I'm not worried about that."

"Really?" She crossed her arms, clearly not believing a word.

"Well, maybe a little." I tried to continue, determined to say something about Mary after all, when Estella interrupted.

"I hardly think one dance would do any harm." She smiled at me, stopping directly in the open doorway.

"No, maybe not, but there's one more thing, actually."

"I'm sure it's just another excuse. Besides, we might just enjoy ourselves."

"I don't know if I'd go that far." I gave her a teasing smirk, but before either of us could say anything further, another woman's voice reached us.

"John! You made it!" Mary called, pushing her way through the rowdy crowd of dancers. She wore a simple mustard-colored dress, and her long, red hair had been combed back to fall loosely down her back. I had to admit that she looked beautiful. Her warm spirit could brighten a room.

My palms grew sweaty. I looked over at Estella, whose face had turned deep red as she looked Mary up and down. I should've warned Estella. She would think I'd given in to Mary's advances. "Nice party," I said to Mary as she reached us. "Did you do all this alone?" I forced myself to smile as she linked her arm through mine.

"Can't take all the credit; I had plenty of help." The musicians started their fiddles up once more. "Oh, John, we *must* dance to this song!" I looked back at Estella, intending to explain myself, but she was gone. I allowed Mary to drag me onto the floor.

Couples danced and twirled around us, clapping and laughing as the music carried on. Mary held onto my hand tightly as we moved in circles. I scanned the room as we spun, trying to find Estella again. Art danced nearby with Lydia, his face as red as his hair, but no Estella to be found. I began to worry about her.

Suddenly I realized that I was dancing with a beautiful, available woman while obsessing over another. Had I gone mad?

The fiddles stopped and everyone clapped. I let go of Mary's hand and she stood there giggling. "You're no dancer, but then, neither am I." She finally caught sight of my wardrobe and frowned. "What on earth?" she asked, pulling at the dirt stains on my white shirt.

"I'm sorry!" I apologized. "I was training my horse with your brother later than I anticipated."

The music started up again and Mary lost focus on me. "Oh! My friend Martha just walked in. I'll find you in a bit." She pulled me in faster than I could react and planted a kiss on my cheek. "Go find yourself a drink and enjoy the party!" she exclaimed, evidently having indulged in some drinks herself already. She turned and left into the crowd while the party went on around us.

I pushed my way off the dance floor. Lanterns hung all around the room, and the air smelled of cider and spit-roasted chicken. I recognized a few men from the mills, while the rest looked to be farm hands and household help. The drunken ones nodded as I passed by, lifting their glasses to me. A few empty chairs sat against the far wall, one of which held Estella's few belongings.

Just then, Estella whirled by me with a man I recognized from the mills, both of them laughing and smiling. I felt heat creep up my neck as I watched this man doting over her every move. He took her soft hand in his and pulled her close, their bodies almost touching. I clenched my jaw and tried not to care, but it was all I could think about. *She shouldn't be here. This is unfitting for a girl like her. Doesn't she have a fiancé?*

Estella's eyes met mine and her face lit up as she smiled at me. The lanterns cast an orange glow on everything in the barn, making Estella radiant like an angel. For a second, I forgot my jealousy. The music stopped, and I was still holding her gaze like an idiot. In a barn full of people, all I could see was her.

Someone stumbled into me. "Oh, I'm *so* sorry!" It was a drunken man, and he'd spilled two full ales down the front of my already-dirty shirt.

"Watch where you're going!" I shouted, glaring at the mess. I tried to wring out my shirt, but to no avail.

"I said I'm sorry," the clumsy ratbag muttered.

"Just get out of here." I waved him off, then sought out the exit. I now smelled of cheap alcohol and grass.

The night air cooled me as I exited the party. It was much quieter outside, and with the barn doors now shut, the whole party seemed like a distant memory. I sat on a wooden bench set against the barn and sighed.

The barn door cracked and Estella walked out, holding a lantern. "Bodaway?" she called.

I didn't really wish to talk, but instinctively muttered, "Over here."

She walked over and sat beside me. After a moment of silence, she said, "I'd offer you a drink, but it seems you've soaked up half the supply." She burst out giggling. Her cheeks were rosy and her eyes seemed relaxed.

I couldn't help but smile at her. "You really think you're clever, don't you?"

She pushed some hair behind her ears. "Why are you outside all alone?"

"I'm not much fun to be around tonight." I crossed my arms over my wet shirt.

Estella raised an eyebrow. "You seemed to be having fun with that girl. Interesting how you forgot to mention you were accompanying a girl, and a very pretty one, at that."

"It didn't concern you. You didn't seem too bothered by that stranger putting his hands all over you." I said it maybe too quickly, and Estella's face gained a smug expression.

"I believe what you are referring to is called dancing, and it's quite appropriate. Do I sense a streak of jealousy, when *you* were the one who let me believe that maybe we'd be the one's dancing this evening?" Her blue eyes burned into me.

"No, I'm not jealous!" I spat, realizing I sounded more jealous with each word. "I just... The way that man was holding you... I mean, aren't you engaged or something?"

She leaned back on the bench, her lips curling into a mischievous smile. "Since it's obvious that you are, indeed, not jealous, perhaps you'd fancy a dance with me after all?" She stood and rested one hand on her heart. "I'd be terribly upset if you were to refuse me."

I rolled my eyes and pulled at my soaked shirt. "You don't want to dance with me, Estella." The music was muffled, but it still came through well enough.

She reached down and grabbed both of my hands in her soft ones. "Come on! This song is beautiful." She closed her eyes and hummed along to its familiar melodies.

Finally, giving in to her wishes, I stood. "You mean right here?"

"Yes, here. If your lady friend sees you dancing with me, she'll steal you away." Estella placed one of my hands around her waist and kept the other in her own hand as she pulled me closer.

My heart raced. I felt her breathing beneath my hand as we swayed slowly to the music. Her lantern, resting on the bench, lit a halo of light around us, and the crickets sang along to the music as we danced in the grass.

For once, we weren't together because of Grace, or because of any other excuse. It was just the two of us alone of our own accord. Nothing else mattered.

Estella reached up and hung both her arms around my neck. My eyes traced her perfect lips. I tried not to imagine what it would be like to feel them against mine.

The pull I felt towards Estella was undeniable. I could hardly keep my emotions under control around her, and it frustrated me to no end. I knew how stupid it was to let myself feel anything for her, but all my feelings, notoriously, lacked logic.

I reached up softly in my moment of weakness and rested my hand on Estella's face. She seemed unsure, but not frightened. Her hand moved up to meet mine, her touch like flames across my skin. The music stopped, but we still stood in the grass.

Just then, the barn door swung open and Estella and I broke apart. A couple of men stumbled out, singing along to the new song that started up. Mary peeked her head out the door. "There you are! I've been looking for you."

I glanced at Estella, who still was taken by the previous moment. She rested her hand on the cheek where my hand had been.

Mary looked at her. "Am I interrupting?"

"No!" I exclaimed, rubbing the back of my neck.

"Alright, then! Come on inside, you two! We can't miss the next song. It's a slow waltz." Mary took my hand and dragged me in.

Estella followed close behind, but lingered against one wall instead of joining. Colorful dresses whirled by as the fiddlers played a romantic tune. Mary rested her head on my shoulder, too far gone to notice my wet shirt. I could see Estella watching us carefully, but whenever I caught her gaze, she looked away.

Whether I liked it or not, I had feelings for Estella Wellstone, and I believed those feelings, in some way, were reciprocal.

# CHAPTER SEVENTEEN

*Tuesday, July 25th*

Estella

It had been four days since the barn dance and all I could think about was the way Bodaway's arms had wrapped around me and how I longed to feel them again. The only arm which I had the pleasure of feeling since then was Henry's, wrapped around mine like a cuff. Then again, all I could think about now was the redhead wrapping *her* arms around Bodaway whenever she pleased.

Mary with Bodaway. She didn't have to concern herself with who saw them together, and could visit him any time she liked. I hated her in a way. Her hair was striking, and she had such fair skin. I didn't look anything like her, and there was nothing I could do about it. My family had finally returned from their trip just yesterday, making it almost impossible for me to slip away again.

As Henry and his family were coming over for dinner tonight, Hannah laid out a new dress for me. Henry had made it known that this evening was to be special, and my parents wanted to oblige. My dress was light green, bunched in the back with sleeves that fell from my shoulders, leaving my neck and arms bare. The bodice was made of French lace, embroidered with hundreds of tiny pearls. How decadent a dress for one mere dinner in my own home.

I sat at my vanity and set my family necklace around my neck. Somehow its deep amethyst and pink pearls appeared plain when set against my gown. As I carefully adjusted its golden clasp, I noticed Bodaway's flower still sitting where I had laid it. Weathered and dried, but still so beautiful. *Where is he tonight? Is he training Grace, or crammed in his housing with Art?*

Hannah appeared in my doorway as I pulled on a pair of long gloves. "Estella, it's time. They're here."

I took a deep breath, "Alright." I moved through the hall and down the stairs, careful not to trip on my hem.

As I descended the stairs, Henry entered our center hall and met me at the bottom. "Estella, you look like a masterpiece." He offered a gloved hand to me, the other held behind his back.

"Welcome back." I gave him my hand and let him lead me to the porch. Henry wore an expensive-looking suit and his hair was slicked back, combed into a curl that just barely touched his forehead.

"Tonight's a very special night," he said.

"Why," I replied, "what am I missing?"

My family, and his, already sat at our outdoor table with a bottle of wine between them, clearly waiting for us.

Henry sat me next to my mother. *Oh no*, I thought, *it's happening.* Henry stayed standing, and before I could think anymore, he cleared his throat and began to speak.

"Estella Coraline Wellstone..." He produced a small velvet bag that just fit within his palm. "I know our families have been eagerly awaiting this moment for quite some time. You must know of my affections for you, and you alone hold my deepest admiration. Would you do me the greatest honor of becoming my wife?" He opened the bag and poured out a golden chain with an obnoxious medallion that bore an inscription I couldn't quite make out. Did he really expect me to wear that?

"The Hamilton family crest," he said with a smile. "It's been passed down for many generations. I'd be glad for it to now grace *your* neck."

My mouth suddenly felt dry and my heart palpitated in my chest. All I could think of was Bodaway and what he'd say if he saw me now. I looked to the Hamiltons, seeing how they smiled and waited, then to Mother and Father who watched me so intensely that I swore I could feel their eyes searing into my flesh.

"Yes," I said, thinking of my duty. "I will."

Still holding the necklace, Henry took my hand and lifted me from my seat. His arms wrapped around me like winding ropes and his quick fingers unlatched my family's necklace. He passed it off to my mother for safe keeping, then set his family crest around my neck, the gold piece weighing on my chest like a ball and chain.

"How wonderful!" Mother exclaimed, her hands clasped.

Henry's father, who was dressed almost identically to Henry, though a few suit sizes heftier, lifted his glass of wine. "To the happy couple."

Everyone raised their glasses, including me. I felt like a puppet as Henry and I sat together in unison. Why was I so sad? I never imagined my engagement would feel so empty. I had truly wanted to get to know Henry over the past months, but the secrets surrounding him and Lillian had indeed shaken me to my senses. After that chilling incident at the Sterlings' home, I realized that Henry's pledge of transparency had been broken the very moment it left his lips.

I'd been too cowardly to confront him back then. Instead, I became distant and unfeeling. Henry should have known it would take a whole lot more than a good book to win me over. He couldn't compare to Bodaway in any way.

Why was I comparing him to Bodaway? I'd told Bodaway things that I'd never shared with anyone else, nor *could* I share them with anyone else. I couldn't make sense of it, but I was connected to him, drawn to him. I was drawn to him more than a woman should be to another mere friend.

"Estella!" called Alice, interrupting my thoughts. "We must begin wedding preparations at once!" She spoke with Mother while the men excused themselves to the stables to pay a visit to Black Magic. I wished I could excuse myself to go see Grace, but Henry sat next to me, his hand resting over mine.

He flashed me a wink and a crooked smile. He really was charming. For a moment, I could almost bring myself to go along with this whole ordeal.

A comment from Mother caught my attention. "I've never considered a simple ceremony; the whole town will want to be there!"

"Well…" Alice raised a thin eyebrow. "Not *everyone* in town will be invited. Not to mention any specifics, but it *must* be a highly exclusive event."

"Very true, and I cannot forget all our friends in Boston. This will be an occasion they won't want to miss. All eyes on Estella and her beautiful gown. With a face like Henry's, I have no doubt people will say they are the most beautiful couple ever to grace Pinebrook. I can already see it in print."

Henry laughed smoothly at this.

I suddenly realized how uncomfortable these wicker chairs were, and how they were going to leave an oddly-shaped pattern on my skin. I realized that the thought of marrying Henry made me want to run. I realized that I was trapped in the endless cycle of ladies in high society.

I emptied the last of my wine into my mouth. Was that glass number two, or three? I'd lost count.

I pulled my hand from Henry's and sat in somber thought, fiddling with the awful necklaces dripping from my bosom as the mothers planned our future. They did so for another hour before making plans to meet again later in the week for more in-depth preparation, then parted ways.

\*\*\*

After everyone left, I sat alone in my room again. I couldn't tear my eyes away from the Hamilton family crest with its great golden "H" looming over my chest. My head felt light as I twirled the chain around my fingers, unable to keep my focus on anyone or anything other than Bodaway. I needed to see him.

Mother and Father, quite tipsy, were tucked into bed for the night, surely intoxicated enough not to stir till morning.

I changed into the usual brown calico I'd worn many days this summer helping Bodaway with Grace. Before slipping from my room, I removed Henry's necklace and placed it on my vanity. My hair was down, free from pins, and my heart stuttered at the thought of seeing Bodaway. I crept down the servants' stairwell and, to my surprise, didn't make a sound. The kitchen was still lit up with the dim glow of the day's embers, guiding my way to the back door where I knew Hannah kept a lantern. My fingers fumbled in adjusting the wick as I set a flame to it, then I left the kitchen and the whole sleeping house behind me.

Just as easily as that, I snuck away. I didn't know what I would say to Bodaway, but I needed to see him.

The sky was black with no hint of moonlight, but my tin lantern shone enough for me to know my surroundings. I kept closely to the path that led to the part of town near the mills. I was on a mission, and nothing could stop me. The blood that pounded in my ears syncopated with my breathing as my sure strides quickened. I welcomed the call of the owl, the rustling of the leaves. They made me feel alive.

My feet moved along the familiar path with confidence, covering over a mile of land with a speed fueled by my unshakable feeling of invincibility. Eventually the lights of town and the shadows of buildings appeared at the end of my trail.

I lowered the lantern's wick and concealed it behind a rock wall at the forest's edge. Then I left the woods behind me and walked along the town road a ways, soon passing by the tavern's open door. The scent of cigar smoke and whiskey wafted out into the streets along with drunken laughter and piano music. I knew better than to linger, so I kept on my way a few streets further until I could make out door after door of identical mill housing rooms. I had never actually seen where Bodaway was housed, and all the wine from earlier in the evening caused my head to spin as I searched for any sign of him.

Two men sat outside the rooms on a couple of crates, smoking and talking amongst themselves quietly, though neither seemed approachable. I moved along and saw another man leave his room, but he turned and called to me from across the street. "You shouldn't be here, miss. Not safe for a lady to be out alone in these parts."

I cleared my throat, startled. "I was only looking for a friend."

"If you know what's good for you, you'll go on home to your folks." He shook his head at me as though I were the most daft girl he'd ever met, then continued towards the tavern I had passed down the street. I could still hear its distant piano music.

I swallowed hard, embarrassed. The man was right. It was a bad idea for me to be out here, alone, at this hour. I should be home, asleep in my own bed.

I couldn't very well ask another stranger where I might find Bodaway. I already felt silly enough. I clutched my head and tried to concentrate on one thought at a time. The street was quiet around me, and my breathing echoed heavily in the emptiness. Just then, a door swung open a few rooms down.

Light spilled into the street, and a girl lingered for a moment in its frame as she spoke with someone inside. I recognized her immediately by the way she laughed, and the red braid that hung down her back.

Mary turned and got a good eyeful of me. She put a hand to her lips, clearly confused by my presence, perhaps even as confused as *I* was to see *her*.

Bodaway joined her in the doorway. "Estella?" he asked, his eyes wide. "Is everything alright?"

I stood a couple doors away from the pair, looking from Mary to Bodaway. I tried my best to gather rational thoughts, but nothing came to mind.

Bodaway had told me that he didn't have time for women right now, especially not for *this* girl. Clearly he had changed his mind.

An overwhelming ache clawed at my chest. "Everything's fine," I said, smoothing the damp hair from my forehead. I backed away from the pair, then turned and started back down the street at a pace faster than when I'd arrived.

Bodaway stepped outside. "Estella!" he called. "Come back here."

I didn't stop, even when I heard his footsteps in the dirt as he ran up behind me. Bodaway caught up and grabbed my arm, saying, "Hey, stop!" He turned me around and stared into my eyes. "Why did you come here? Is Grace alright?"

I shook my head, "Grace is perfectly well."

Bodaway's shoulders visibly relaxed. "Then what is it?"

"It doesn't matter anymore, obviously." I motioned to his room, where that red-headed girl still stood watching us.

"Oh…It's not what it looked like," he said, his voice sounding nervous.

"Really? The girl from the barn dance is in your room at this hour and it's not what it looks like?" I put my hands on my hips.

"What's wrong with you?" he asked. "What possible reason could you have to be angry with me?"

"Henry's asked me to marry him tonight," I said, "and I've accepted." I touched the empty place on my neck where his necklace had lain.

Bodaway took a step back and clenched his jaw. "Well, then there you go. Everything's worked out the way your family always wanted it to. I hope you'll be very happy."

"You know I'm not happy," I said in disbelief. "I never wanted any of this!"

"This was *your* choice, Estella. It looks like we really don't have anything to talk about. If you were expecting my congratulations, you've wasted a trip." He practically spat his words.

"I just needed to see you," I whispered, and looked away. "This was a mistake."

He looked me over as we stood in the street like a pair of idiots. "You know, I really believed you wouldn't go through with this. I believed you were stronger than this, and that you had a mind of your own. Mary is Art's sister. You *know* that! She was in my room to see him." His cheeks burned red hot.

"Well, it's none of my business who visits you, is it, now? You don't understand how people like me live. I'm doing what I need to do for my family!" I cleared my throat. "You know what that means."

"Actually, no. You're doing this to *please* your family, who you claim don't really have your best interest in mind. I'm telling you that Henry gives me a bad feeling. He's not a good man."

"You don't have any facts to prove that…"

"Estella, you have all the proof you need." He raised his hands in confusion. "*I know you don't want this, you know you don't want this, and frankly I'm getting tired of you bringing your problems to me, then ignoring the truth you already know! What do you want me to say?*" He stood right in front of me, staring into my soul. "When it's all said and done, when you're married to that pompous meater, you'll remember all the chances you had to back out, to think for yourself, but by then it'll be too late."

I shook my head. "I can't accept that."

"Well, *do* you have feelings for Henry?" His voice was frank. "Do you?"

I dropped my eyes to the ground. "I… that doesn't matter."

"Now tell me this, Estella. Tell me you didn't feel anything when we danced."

"I can't let myself go there, Bodaway."

He shook his head and waved his hands in utter frustration. "Then why did you even come here? If you're so hell-bent on disregarding anything I say to you, why keep coming back? Why not leave me be?"

I bit the inside of my lip as the truth of Bodaway's situation dawned on me. Everyone in his life had left him, and he had carried around these feelings of abandonment for years. I would soon be just another person to leave him behind.

I wanted to speak, but couldn't think of anything that wouldn't start a fire between us. I wanted to tell Bodaway how I felt reckless around him, how he made me feel like my own person, how it seemed I saw his face wherever I went.

But allowing him false hope would be incredibly selfish of me. I simply couldn't share any of my feelings for him aloud, not when it would ruin everything. Our friendship would never recover, and my feelings for him could never stop my wedding to Henry. "I don't know what else to say to you."

He stared at me with blank black eyes.

I turned and fled down the street towards the trail, and Bodaway let me go. Part of me wanted him to come back for me, or to make me stay with him, but he did nothing. I didn't know what I expected from this trip.

"Estella, is that you?" said a slurred voice in the distance, from the direction of the tavern.

This was exactly what I had read about in my books.

The man walked over to me in slow, uneven strides. "My beautiful fiancée," he said, his hot breath blowing on my face as he came closer.

*Henry.* He stunk of alcohol and cheap perfume. "What are you doing all the way out here?" he asked, cornering me until I'd backed myself against the stone wall of the tavern. "Why are you here?" His eyebrows crowded in fury as he wiped his lips with his sleeve.

"Stop it, Henry, you're drunk!" My heart quaked in my chest and a horrid lump rose in my throat.

"I'm celebrating! I've been so very good lately. I can handle a drink or two."

"Let me go home, Henry!"

He laughed, his eyes suddenly hard. "No woman of mine should be caught in this part of town alone!" he shouted, like a child throwing a tantrum, then grabbed me by the shoulders. "How *dare* you treat my name with disrespect!"

"Stop it!" I tried to push him away, but his grip became tighter. "Help!" I yelled.

"Stop your screaming! Stop it!" He shook me. "I never, ever want to see you in these parts again, Estella!" He pinned me harder against the wall.

Just then, someone ripped Henry from my body.

It was Bodaway.

I sank to the ground, my stomach lurching. I realized I was crying when I noticed the small convulsions shaking my body.

Bodaway held Henry by the neck with one hand and plowed his fist into Henry's perfect face with the other. "You'll never touch her again! Do you hear me? You ratbag!" He must have heard my screams from down the street.

Blood ran down Henry's face, flowing from his nose and staining Bodaway's clothes. Bodaway had this look in his eyes that I'd never seen before; it was feral, barbaric. Bodaway raised his fist, clearly ready to strike again, but Henry was barely conscious.

"Bodaway, stop it!" I shouted. "You're going to kill him!"

He lifted Henry against the wall, and put his hand firmly around Henry's neck.

"Bodaway!" I yelled.

He finally dropped Henry, who crawled to his knees and then fell, unconscious and pathetic, to the ground again. A few other drunk men stumbled out of the tavern, but didn't seem to notice the commotion.

Bodaway turned to me, eyes crazed. "Are you alright?" He reached down and picked me up. I collapsed into his arms crying, and he caressed my hair to comfort me.

My calico dress was ruined, Henry's blood staining its skirt, but that didn't matter. I was safe in Bodaway's arms as he carried me to his room. I was still so dizzy that each time I tried to open my eyes, the world seemed to whirl around me. Eventually I kept my eyes shut and waited for my stomach to settle.

"Quick, Art, grab some water. Mary, find some clean linen. Everything's alright, Estella, you're safe here." Bodaway squeezed my hand gently.

When I finally opened my eyes, he was sitting me in a chair. Mary and Art hurried about the small room, gathering what he'd asked for.

Mary gasped as she handed him a damp cloth. "John, you're bleeding!"

He flexed his swollen, bloodied hand, as though realizing his injury for the first time. "It's nothing, Mary. I'll take care of it." He tore the bottom of his shirt and wrapped the fabric tightly around his knuckles.

I couldn't find it in me to speak yet. I could still feel Henry's grip around my shoulders, and it made me cringe. With trembling fingers, I pulled my dress just away from my shoulder. Sure enough, there were already small bruises forming, and I quickly returned my dress to its place before Bodaway could see.

Bodaway sat down next to me and wouldn't leave my side. I didn't want to be touched, and he seemed to understand that, but I felt safe being beside him.

Finally coming back to reality, I observed the closeness of my surroundings. The little room was hardly big enough for all its occupants. Five beds took up most of the room: one for Bodaway, one for Art, and three more for the other absent tenants, most likely drinking at the tavern. There were a few wooden stools, and an old table with someone's book on it. *Oliver Twist*.

I'd long forgotten about all the books I'd brought from Boston to fill my summer with adventure. I scoffed now at the notion that this summer could have been dull. These had been the most eventful months of my entire life.

"Here, drink this." Mary handed me a hot cup of tea. She had a kind face and a pleasant, naturally flush complexion. Even though her eyes presently appeared troubled, how could Bodaway not find her charming?

Bodaway's brow furrowed, his shoulders were rigid. He hardly took his eyes off me.

I mustered the will to speak again. "Please don't be upset with me." My voice went hoarse, and I cleared my throat. "I already know your opinion on the matter. You've made yourself very clear. I'll be fine."

Art and Mary exchanged glances before going outside, permitting us some privacy.

Bodaway stood and walked away from me until he stood before the room's one small window. He raked his good hand through his hair before turning and speaking "I don't know, Estella, *are* you fine?"

I rubbed my bruised shoulder self-consciously.

"I mean, you're going to marry this man. What would've happened tonight if I hadn't been there, if I hadn't heard you scream?"

I cleared my throat. "But you *were* there, and that's what matters."

"No, Estella, you don't understand. If you marry Henry, you'll be alone with him forever. You'll be his responsibility."

"You're right," I said quietly. "Thank you for being in the right place at the right time. I need to rest before I can make rational decisions." I drank the last of my tea and set the cup on the table beside me.

Bodaway's face hardened as he shook his head. He said nothing, but I knew he was still angry with me. I could tell by the strained look in his eyes.

He sighed and lit a lantern. "Let's get you home, then."

I stood and followed him outside, where Art and Mary were waiting. "Thank you both for everything," I said, trying to smile.

We retrieved my lantern at the forest's edge and walked to my house in silence, but it wasn't one of our comfortable silences. It hurt, like pins and needles pricking at my throat, but neither of us said a word to break it.

By the time we reached the end of the trail by the stables, I couldn't bear it any more. "I can take it from here." Our lanterns' flames were fading and cast an orange halo around us, revealing Bodaway's crowded, foreboding brow.

I raised my lantern's wick mindlessly. "Good night," I said, then turned to leave.

Bodaway grabbed my hand and held it in his bandaged one for a moment.

The gesture was unexpected, but I didn't pull away. He gave me one last glance, then, without a single word, he gently dropped my hand and left me alone.

When I returned home, the house was quiet, and nobody was stirring. I made my way to my bedroom and rushed to the porcelain basin where a pitcher of cool water waited for me.

I raised the pitcher and hastily dumped its contents into the basin. My fingers worked frantically to peel the stained calico dress from my body until it fell to the floor. I plunged a dry cloth into the water, soaking it, then washed my face and bloodstained hands with rough, harsh movements as though I could somehow wash away the entire evening.

I threw the cloth back into the basin, then stood completely still. My cold, wet arms wrapped around my body. The feeling of being alone was more oppressive than I could bear. It hung heavily in my room, weighing more and more upon me until I was unable to keep myself from crying any longer.

Great release came to me as I let myself cry freely, and it soothed the dull aching in my chest. So many things happened tonight. I knew, after what he did, that I could never love Henry Hamilton. Had Henry done something similar to Lillian? Or even worse?

I retrieved his necklace from my vanity, clutched the gold piece in my fist, and threw it violently across the room.

# CHAPTER EIGHTEEN

### Bodaway

After I brought Estella home, I returned to my room. Henry was a scoundrel, and if he ever tried to put his hands on her again, I wouldn't show mercy.

Mary waited for me at the door. "How is she?" she asked.

"She was pretty shaken up, but she'll be fine," I sighed, leaning in the doorway.

Mary offered me a puff of her cigarette. I didn't normally smoke, but I took a drag anyway. The smoke soothed my body like a warm embrace.

"How are you?" Mary watched me carefully.

"I'm fine. Why wouldn't I be?"

"I see the way you look at her." Mary turned away. "The way your whole body changes when she's in the room, the way you were so tender with her." She looked back at me, the hint of a tear in her eye. "I see the difference between the way you treat us."

"I didn't want to get mixed up with anyone."

"Except her, huh?" She took another puff of her cigarette.

"You're a kind soul, Mary. The way you cared for Estella tonight…" My neck tensed. "Maybe if I'd never met Estella, things could be different. Better, even. You deserve someone who only sees you."

Mary wiped a tear from her cheek. "Don't worry. I won't be playing the fool around you anymore." She reached up, looking into my eyes, and pressed her gentle lips upon my cheek. "Good night, John."

What was wrong with me? Mary was a perfectly fine girl, and I was outright rejecting her for a girl who I knew I could never fully have. *I* was the fool. Estella had turned me into a fool. I was in love with her, and I hated her for it.

\*\*\*

## Wednesday, July 26th

"Mr. Hamilton needs to speak to you immediately." A mill worker I didn't recognize motioned towards the stairwell a ways down the aisle.

I observed my row of looms, all working perfectly. "I'll need someone to take over for me."

The messenger nodded. "Will do."

I knew exactly why Henry wanted to see me, and I was ready to fight him all over again if need be.

*I can't live my life in this state of mind.*

When I removed my cap, my hair fell around my shoulders at will. I twisted the cap in my hands as I made my way to the stairs. I'd wished that Henry's drunkenness would've blurred his memory of the night before, but wishful thinking was for saps.

I took a few steps up the rickety stairwell, then stopped and looked over the mill floor. Art craned his neck to watch me, awaiting my impending doom with a look of helplessness on his face. I raised my shoulders at him in defeat, and continued to the second floor.

The door at the top of the stairs had been shut, and muffled voices floated over the clanking and humming of the mill. He had someone else in the room, a girl, and she sounded frantic. I carefully stepped in closer to the door, thinking it might be Estella. Unfortunately, I could only make out a few words here and there.

"...don't take responsibility ... engagement falls apart," the girl's voice threatened.

"...Lillian, nobody ... believe..." Henry answered.

My forehead wrinkled in concentration. *Lillian? Where have I heard that name before?*

"...ruined me ... honest woman!" Her voice grew more shrill and desperate. "...whole life ... over."

Was this the friend Estella had been worried about?

The voices grew louder as footsteps sounded towards the door. I clearly heard Henry speak, his voice barely muffled now. "You should have thought of that before. You know that I want to do the right thing. I'm giving you exactly one hundred silver dollars. It should help pay for you to get out of town, and live comfortably until I can figure something else out. It's a much kinder offer than what my mother would suggest you do with the money."

The girl said nothing—and then the door knob rattled.

I jumped back and pressed against the wall just as the door swung open.

The girl ran out, distraught. She passed me without a notice, then hurried down the stairwell.

There was no more wondering what had been discussed in that room. Clearly, Henry had fathered an illegitimate child and wanted the girl out of the way.

Recomposing myself, I knocked on the open door frame.

"Come in," he called.

The office was much nicer than he deserved, complete with a small plaque on his desk that read, "Henry Hamilton: Floor Manager."

He noticed me. "Oh yes, please sit. What is it again? John?"

"Yeah." I shot an unamused look in his general direction, unable to hide my disgust. I didn't sit.

Henry studied me, hands together on his desk, blinking far too quickly for comfort.

I crossed my arms over my chest, waiting out the silence.

"OK then," he sighed at last. "I believe you already know why I've asked you to come. After what you did last night, I planned to dismiss you from the premises... but one might say I'm feeling generous today." His smile seemed calculated. "So, how about this—it's simple, really." Henry reached across his desk, lifting a crystal bottle of liquor and pouring a glass. The smell of it hung in the air.

He took a mouthful, and swallowed hard. "I like to think I know my fiancée better than most. I know that she has a good heart, and that she's impulsive and imprudent at times. In fact, she may very well ask after you, or worse, she may want to come down here and thank you personally." He paused. "You can see how that presents a little problem for me? If she were to come searching for you, only to discover that you've been dismissed, she would recognize my hand in it. So long as you don't tell anyone what transpired between the two of us, I won't dismiss you for taking a swing at me last night.

Though, to be fair, I suppose I did deserve to be hit—and I feel terribly about slipping up like that. You see, I'm a completely different man when mixed with spirits, as many a good man." He waited a moment before jabbing, "Are you mute? I've just shown you a great act of kindness. The least you can do is show some gratitude." He leaned back in his chair, awaiting a response.

Given this new information, I chose to keep my response agreeable. "Thank you, sir. I appreciate your generosity."

"That's much better." He emptied his glass.

"Do I have your permission to take my leave?" I asked, clenching my jaw.

With a pleased look on his face, he replied, "Yes, you may go." He waved his hand at me, and without lingering another moment in his stuffy office, I left.

\*\*\*

That evening after my shift, I made my way to the stables to continue preparing Grace. She grew stronger and stronger each time we trained, and I longed to show Estella the progress we'd made. I needed to share this new information about Henry with her too. She deserved the truth, but the rules of society were not on my side. Maybe I couldn't see Estella, but I could see Grace.

The trees bent over one another like an inviting archway as I hiked the trail to the stables, the air smelled of damp earth. The birds called to each other sweetly. I must have walked these trails a hundred times, but it never tired. A small brook ran along next to me and squirrels chased each other up trees. This was true healing. Here, walking through this trail, I wasn't a brother working to provide. I was just a man.

The stables came into view at the end of the trail. For a moment, I half-hoped Estella would be there, but when I saw the doors stood shut, I knew she wasn't.

I approached the stables and propped the doors open. Grace stood by the stall window, soaking in the sun.

"Shall we take a ride to our little haven?" I asked Grace, dragging my hand along her dusty white body. I attached her lead and led her outside. Her perky ears flicked the pestering flies away, and with one good jump, I mounted her. "Take us away," I said, and clicked my tongue at her.

She knew exactly where to take us. She started a slow, controlled trot from the grassy stables and into the forest. She, too, seemed at ease among nature.

As we rode the winding trail to our special clearing, I reflected more on the things I'd heard in Henry's office. How could Estella marry such a ratbag? The kind of man with the nerve to take things that didn't belong to him, then refuse to assume responsibility for his actions, could only get worse over time. Selfish, entitled, and arrogant, all attributes that eerily reminded me of how my father had walked out on his two sons and never looked back. For what? Adventure? Soul searching?

Grace rode into our clearing. It was unchanged since our last visit. The grass still popped with greenery and scattered wildflowers in purples, oranges, and blues. The brook sang just as sweetly as it had before, and though the warm night was well past seven, the sky was still summer blue.

Dismounting Grace, I led her to the brook while I sat on the bank, watching the stones glimmer beneath the water.

How was I going to convince Estella that she should run from this arranged marriage? And then what? Be with me? I didn't have a penny to my name or a house of my own. I barely had the clothes on my back. I tossed some stones into the water and watched them splash.

"Bodaway?" Estella walked into view from around the brook's bend.

I sat up. "How did you know I was here?"

"I didn't. I come here now and then to collect my thoughts, or to read." She tilted her head, then came and sat by me. "I've been here for the past hour. Sitting, thinking… praying. There's a lot on my mind these days." She sighed and rubbed her shoulder.

"I need to talk to you," I cut in. "About last night."

She looked intrigued, though her soft skin turned pale as she recalled the horrible events of the night before.

"Listen," I continued, "I don't want anything like that to happen to you ever again. Henry's a sorry excuse for a man."

"It's not as though I will be the first woman in history to marry a drunkard. You know, Henry called on me early this morning and apologized profusely. He knows he made a mistake, and he's trying to make things right, though I don't think I'll be able to trust him again." Her last words caught in her throat and the look in her eyes made her seem miles away.

"That's what I wanted to talk to you about." I hesitated. "Something happened today. I overheard a conversation between Henry and… well… a girl."

Estella seemed to pull herself back from wherever she'd gone to and refocused on me. "A girl? Who?"

"The one you told me about. Lillian."

"And what were they talking about?" she prodded.

"Lillian is carrying Henry's child."

Estella put her hand to her lips, looking as if she was calculating some sort of equation. "Are you sure?"

"I'm certain. Today at the mills, I heard Henry offer to pay Lillian off to leave town and have the baby far from here. I thought you needed to know."

She rested her head on her knees. "I don't know how much more I can take. Maybe you misheard them? Maybe it's all one big misunderstanding!"

What about Henry was so appealing to women? He seemed like a scoundrel and dead weight to me, and whenever I thought of Estella marrying that man, it felt like a brick dropped in my stomach.

"I couldn't tell you word for word what they said, but it didn't sound good or honorable." I sighed and picked at the grass. "But I heard enough to speak on this confidently."

"I just can't believe that Lillian would be that naive. She wouldn't do that! I *know* her, Bodaway." She sounded even more troubled than before. "And Henry, I mean… not even *he* could be so cruel."

I sprung up, enraged. "Are you seriously doubting the lengths of wrongdoing that Henry is capable of? Do you remember what he did to you just last night?"

Estella stood to face me. "Henry was drunk. He's not normally so disagreeable."

"Why are you defending him?" I stared at her in frustration and tried reading her face. The sun shone down on Estella's dark hair and lit up her skin. She was as beautiful as what I imagined an angel must look like.

After several heavy breaths, she brought her hands to her face. "You're right, I know. I just want to see the good in people, especially in the man I'm to marry."

No one could frustrate me or defuse my fire faster than like Estella. I felt complete when I was around her, like all my problems were so small I couldn't even see them anymore. On the contrary, her problems and solutions filled the forefront of my mind.

"Not everyone is worthy of your respect," I told her. "Some people are just bad, Estella. *Henry* is bad." I shook my head, wishing I could bring her to common sense.

Estella sighed. Noticing Grace grazing beside us, she wrapped her arms around the horse's neck. "Things must be so much simpler for a horse. She doesn't have to worry about anything, not even her next meal." She flashed me a soft smile, clearly wanting to change the subject.

I scoffed. "No concerns except winning the races she's worked so hard for." I joined Estella beside Grace, catching my fingers in our horse's knotted mane. She needed a good brushing again before the races. Her tail flicked as she stood there by the brook, grazing at the clovers.

"Is she really concerned, or are *you* the one who's concerned?" Estella tilted her head at me.

"Both, I guess. My heart will be at ease once I get the money I need."

"What's going to happen when you've paid for your brother's operation?"

"You mean, will I stay here in Pinebrook?"

"I suppose." Her eyes seemed sad. She stepped next to me, then dragged her hand along Grace's neck, wiping the dirt and debris from her coat. "You could shake off this town's dust if you wanted." She hesitated. "Will you?"

"I suppose, eventually." I moved closer to Estella. For once, I didn't ache to leave Pinebrook, but I wouldn't hesitate to leave the second she married Henry. I hadn't thought through that scenario completely.

She continued to caress Grace, and our hands touched.

My heart stuttered as our eyes locked, retracing the feelings we felt at the barn dance. I didn't move away. Instead, I took Estella's other hand in mine and pulled her in close to me.

She didn't say a word, her eyes still focused intently on mine.

"Do you have a reason for me to stay?" I asked, staring at every detail on her perfect face. I looked at her pink lips as they parted slightly, so innocent and inviting. I'd never felt anything stronger than the magnetic pull I felt towards Estella.

I pressed my lips against hers.

My whole life felt worth living in that one moment. Estella's hands went to my face as she kissed me back with suprising sureness. Her lips were gentle and warm on mine, that same fire I felt at the barn dance spreading through my whole body. But when I touched her shoulders, she winced in pain.

"Are you alright?" I spoke in a whisper as I searched her face.

She pulled the side of her dress off her shoulder to show me the dark bruises shaped like finger prints on her skin.

My hands turned to fists. "I'll kill him." I ground my teeth.

"No Bodaway, I'm OK." Estella grabbed my hands in hers. "I'll be OK, I'm just a little sore."

I shook my head, the words falling out of my mouth with destructive passion. "This can't go on. If you can still go through with this, even now, you're weaker than I thought."

Estella's clear blue eyes clouded over and her hands dropped limply from mine. She parted her lips as she looked away. "I should get back home." She whispered.

"Fine," I said. "Go."

She looked as if she wanted to say something more, but instead left me standing in our field.

I quickly forgot about our kiss.

# CHAPTER NINETEEN

## *Thursday, July 27th*

### Estella

The next morning, as I sat reading in bed, Hannah came into my room and lay my dress on the chair by my vanity. "Here you go," she said, moving to my bed and fluffing my pillows. "You know, I can't help but notice your change in spirits." She sat beside me and rested a hand on my back.

Had my traumatic experience with Henry been so noticeable? "There have been so many changes in my life, with the wedding… with Henry." Hannah sighed. "I know he's not exactly what you would have chosen for yourself, but I'm proud of you for doing what you must." She caressed my hair before leaving me to change.

If Hannah had seen my bruises, she might have had something different to say, but I couldn't tell anyone how I really felt. Besides, even if I did say something about Henry, it might not make a difference.

I put my feet on the cold floor and let my nightgown fall from my body. Mindlessly, I slipped on the cream-colored gown and tied its black laces at my bosom.

A beautiful sun hat matched my attire ever so sweetly, and Henry's family crest hung around my neck as the finishing touch. I looked into the mirror and saw an elegant, proper woman, full of grace and propriety. I tried to force a smile on my lips.

Then I thought of Bodaway, and no longer had to force my warmth. I longed to see him, to talk about the other day. I brought a hand to my lips, remembering Bodaway's kiss. Had his beautiful lips been on mine just yesterday? I closed my eyes, trying to remember how it felt, but my memory of it had already begun to fade.

I feared my resolve to stand by my obligations had turned him against me, and perhaps damaged our friendship beyond repair. The idea twisted a knot in my stomach that only worsened as I thought of everything I'd learned about Henry.

I smoothed my dress one last time before joining my parents for breakfast outside.

The gleaming white porch was almost blinding in the sunlight. Darcy sat smugly on Mother's lap.

"Good morning, my dear. Sit." Father motioned to the empty wicker chair beside him. A few maids scurried about with plates of fresh eggs, ham and muffins.

"Yes," said Mother, "join us for the calm before the storm." Her words hinted at the scheduled tea with Alice later that afternoon. Mother seemed barely able to contain her satisfaction about my impending wedding. Her blue satin dress reflected a glow on Darcy's coat as she caressed him.

Father waved away rogue cat hairs with the newspaper in his hands. "Rachelle, *dearest*, must you have the cat at the table?"

"Irving, *dearest*, he isn't causing any problems." Mother rolled her eyes and beckoned a maid to carry Darcy inside. Then, sighing heavily, she refocused her attention on me. "You look beautiful in the new gown your father bought you!"

"Thank you." I managed to sound grateful. It was a fine gown—costly to be sure, but its expense would dull in comparison to the expense of my wedding gown.

Mother had set up an appointment later that evening with a well-known Northeastern designer. He would come to our home to take my measurements and to show us his designs. I tried to put all these thoughts behind me as I poked at my breakfast with my fork.

The wind was cool like an autumn breeze as it blew through the porch, though it was still July. How quickly the summer had gone by, and how much had changed. I lost my appetite when I realized my summer's purpose had already been completed. I was equally matched, engaged to the most eligible suitor in town.

\*\*\*

When afternoon came around, my family and I waited in our grand parlor for Alice to arrive. Mother frantically rearranged knickknacks and pushed small pieces of furniture around. Though, by the end, she had moved everything exactly as it was before.

"Rachelle, everything looks fine." Father scratched his mustache. "It's only Alice Hamilton. Estella, tell your mother the room looks fine."

"The room is fine," I said mechanically.

"Well, we aren't aiming for fine," she muttered under her breath, finally sitting in one of our green velvet chairs.

I observed the room. It really did look fine.

The walls were white, which helped brighten things up, and the furniture was upholstered with emerald green and mustard yellow.

I sat beside Father, who almost always had his nose in some newspaper or book. He never seemed to care about these meetings like Mother did. I wished I could be reading, or really doing anything other than this.

At last, Mother sprung from her chair and stood in the window. "She's here! Alice is here! Hannah, bring out the tea!"

But to our surprise, it wasn't Alice whom Hannah led into our parlor moments later, but Lillian. She stood there in a long, unseasonably warm coat, her head held high.

"Lillian!" I blurted out, "Please, sit!" I motioned to a chair. My mind raced with ideas and questions. I glanced at the area where Lillian's stomach should have been, but her coat was much too bulky to reveal any shape at all.

Mother was clearly annoyed. "Lillian, we are expecting company at any moment. It is in no one's best interest for you to be here when they arrive."

"Oh, Mrs. Wellstone, this will only take a moment. I actually came here to speak with you."

Mother glided across the room to join Lillian on the settee adjacent to her, intrigued. "Do tell," she said, clasping her hands together.

Why would Lillian come here to speak with my mother?

Lillian fished around in a small velvet satchel she had brought with her. She retrieved a book and handed it to Mother.

"*Sense and Sensibility,*" Mother read aloud. The blood drained from my face. "You didn't come all this way just to bring me a novel, so I suggest you come right out and say whatever it is. I am a very busy woman, you know."

"Open it up and read the contents on the first page," Lillian said with a smirk. "I believe Estella knows exactly what this is." Sudden images of the barn dance flooded my mind. I hadn't brought the book home afterward.

Father still sat in his chair, listening intently to this conversation without speaking.

"It was found at some servant party," said Lillian. "To my suprise, my maid claimed to have seen Estella in attendance."

Mother read Henry's note to me on the first page and gasped. "Estella! Please tell me this is untrue! Running about with servants?" Her eyes were filled with accusation.

Lillian seemed pleased with herself. "Isn't that right, Estella? My maid saw you—and, dare I say, an Indian man—dancing last week at the McNerry's farm. I was so concerned for you. I thought perhaps you were in danger, or in some kind of trouble." She said all of this in an overly theatrical tone of distress.

"Why are you doing this?" I asked in disbelief.

"Well, in some way I feel like I owe it to you, you know, to look out for you and your family's reputation." She smiled and closed her satchel once more.

"Good heavens, oh my Lord." Mother stood and rested her hand on her forehead dramatically.

Father piped in. "If you could leave us alone with Estella, we'd like to speak with her."

I swallowed hard at Father's sudden participation.

"Yes, absolutely!" Lillian stood, tightened her coat, and prepared to take her leave.

"Thank you for coming all this way," said Mother, her voice strangled.

Lillian stopped beside me and rubbed my shoulders. "This is what's best for everyone," she said softly.

No words came to my dry, parted lips, and no breath passed between them either. I could do nothing but shake my head and wait for the end of the world.

The moment the door had closed and Lillian had gone, Father turned to me with a raging red face. "Now, listen here, young lady. You're making a fool of our family, and I will not have it! I am going to take care of this at once, I promise you that." I drew in a sharp breath and winced. Mother fanned herself as though she just could not bear the situation. "You are never to see this man again. Have you no respect for Henry and his family name?"

I stared at Mother in desperation. "But Bodaway told me about some complication between Henry and Lillian—"

"Who is Bodaway?" Father snapped.

My throat dried up. "Well... he's a friend."

Mother shook her head. "You're going to believe that *animal* over your closest, most trusted friend? I think not. Those kinds of men only want one thing, your money. And whatever else you give them." Her face twisted in disgust.

I tried holding back the scream that kept creeping up my throat, but finally it was too forceful to hold in. "Which is it, then? When Alice tells you to keep me from Lillian, she's a bad influence, but now, when she conspires to ruin me, I'm to consider her as a reliable source?"

Father cut in. "Either you marry Henry as soon as the end of the week, or I will send you back to Boston on the first train tomorrow. We won't be putting this off for *another* month!" Father spat when he became passionate, he sprayed us all with his anger. He threw up his hands in frustration. "God, Estella! It is like we don't even know you. Who are you, really?"

I had always felt that there was some soft place for me to rest with Father, that if anyone cared for my happiness, it was him. But now he looked at me with such wrath and disdain that I knew, without a doubt, that whatever soft place I might have found in the past existed no longer. I was to marry Henry by the end of the week, and that was final.

\*\*\*

That evening we prepared for my fitting—that is, my fitting for an expensive, extravagant wedding gown. Since the timeline of my wedding had been moved up, I would need the dress much sooner than originally planned. Perhaps my parents had planned all along to move up the date, and I had only given them a convenient excuse.

Hannah entered the parlor. "Ladies, the designer is here."

A man walked in behind her with a satchel of drawings and fabric and a measuring tape. He brought a young seamstress along with him.

"Welcome, Jean!" Mother said, gesturing for them to sit. "Would either of you care for some tea?"

"Yes please, both of us." The man smiled. He was handsome, his dark hair speckled with gray and combed into a side-part, and his brow puckered and creased with lines one only acquired from long hours of concentration. His young assistant seemed sweet natured, but had a timid presence about her. "This must be our lovely bride," said Jean, and waved his hand towards me.

"Yes." I managed a smile, but my insides still ached.

"Mr. Wellstone, he will not be joining us, I take it?"

I almost laughed at the thought of Father caring about my wedding clothes.

"Heavens no," said Mother, "he's much too busy with work and preparing his racehorse for the big race this weekend!" In fact, he'd stormed out of the house soon after Lillian left, completely missing our scheduled tea with Alice, and hadn't spoken a word to me since.

"Close to the wedding, yes?" Jean added.

Mother rolled her eyes. "He simply *must* race, but I assure you, he will be rested for the wedding festivities the next day."

Hannah entered with another maid, bringing tea.

After the young girl took my measurements, I was free to sit. The three of us sat around in a circle, with our short-legged table between us. It usually held Mother's hideous knickknacks and fragile antiques, but today it was covered with sketches and designs.

"I was thinking something like this," Jean said, and pulled out a small paper which showed an elaborate drawing of a wedding dress.

"It's beautiful," Mother gasped. She and I leaned in to admire the detail as Jean and his assistant sat back, seemingly pleased with their work.

Jean poured a cup of tea and handed it to me. "What are your thoughts? While Marie was taking your measurements, your mother informed me of how we have little time for alterations, but... If there is something you're inclined to change, by all means, speak now. Marie and I will work tirelessly, day and night, to have this dress finished for you."

The gown would be made of a stunning off-white silk. Its full skirt cascaded to the floor with embroidered golden rosettes that trailed along the hem. The neckline scooped from shoulder to shoulder where frilled lace layered over the bodice. The sleeves were made of the same lace and fell loosely to the elbow.

"Excellent work," said Mother. "Just exquisite. I can't imagine changing anything. Thank you for being so gracious about the sudden change. Estella, dear, tell Jean what you think."

"It *is* beautiful," I admitted, touching the drawing. I wasn't ashamed to enjoy such fine clothes, but the thought of my wedding snuffed any flicker of joy I tried to muster.

# CHAPTER TWENTY

*Thursday, July 27*

Bodaway

As Art and I walked into work returning from our lunch break Thursday afternoon, Henry Hamilton stopped me at the door. He grabbed my shoulder and shoved me aside so that the rest of the workers could walk by. "Just the man I was looking for," he started, but I brushed his arm away from me.

"What do you want?" I asked, my back against the wall.

Art stopped and watched me carefully.

"You can get to work," Henry ordered, but Art lingered.

"I'm fine," I mouthed, and Art finally backed away.

"Listen, Irving Wellstone would like to see you in his office, and he sent me to escort you." He smiled wryly.

"I can go of my own accord. I don't need you on my arm."

"I don't doubt that you can, but an order is an order, and who am I to disobey the boss?" He gave me another condescending pat on the back, then pushed me along towards the stairwell.

I could feel heads turning and eyes watching me as we moved among the workers. If the mill hadn't been so loud, I could probably have heard their snide remarks. Going to see the boss was never a good sign, and I had more of a reason to fear Irving Wellstone than any other man here.

Henry and I climbed the stairs and moved to Irving's office, one door down from Henry's. "This is where I drop you," said Henry. "Best of luck to you, then." With those last mocking words, he entered his office.

I stood alone at Irving's closed door, unamused, and prepared myself for whatever was to happen. I lifted my hand, gave the door a few solid knocks, and waited.

"Come in," I heard a moment later, and entered. Irving's office was almost identical to Henry's. Among the few differences were the portrait hanging over his desk and the way the room didn't smell so much of alcohol.

Irving rose from his desk at my arrival and walked to meet me. "Close the door behind you," he demanded, and I complied.

The man looked completely frazzled—exhausted, even. His under-eyes were dark through his spectacles, and his hair, though thinning, stuck up in several places. "I understand that you are the Indian boy running around with my daughter." He lifted his heavy lids to meet my eyes, but I didn't respond.

He stuffed a hand into his coat pocket and fished around for something. "You know, I could cause a lot of trouble for you, young man. However, I like to think of myself as a man of honor, and instead, I'm willing to offer you a deal."

Irving stepped out from around his desk and shoved a fold of cash into my hand. "You're through here at the mills, and this is a little something to ensure that you'll leave town before the wedding on Sunday. I can't have you sticking around, presenting a distraction to my daughter."

"Sunday?" I interrupted.

He ignored me. "Let me make myself abundantly clear. You are to stay away from Estella. If you do not, I'll be forced to act further, with more extreme means of action."

I thumbed through the cash, then scoffed at him. "You think you can buy me, that you can solve all your problems with money? Sure, you can fire me, but on what grounds do you believe you can send me out of town?" I tore the cap from my head and clutched it in my hand.

Heat rose from depths of my chest to the top of my scalp as I remembered how Henry had used the same tactics on Estella's friend Lillian. "You rich people are all the same." I shoved the money back into his chest. "You can't buy me off, and I don't need your money to get out of town. I'll be gone before the wedding on Sunday, you can be sure of that. I have some loose ends to tie up first."

"That's right, you will be," he spat in my direction before pushing his glasses up his nose. If he were anyone else, I would have ripped what little hair he had left right off his head.

I couldn't believe Estella was to marry so soon, and I wasn't going to stand by and watch it happen. After the races, I was as good as gone. My brother needed me, and I would be by his side for his operation—the place I was always meant to be.

\*\*\*

## *Friday, July 28th*

The wind ripped through my clothes and my hair as Grace cantered with unfaltering speed across our grassy haven. I pulled her to a trot, and then to a walk. Squinting, I looked to the sky. Dark clouds hung over us, hiding the afternoon sun, and the air smelled of rain.

I reached into my pocket and retrieved Art's watch. He'd been kind enough to lend it to me the night before. Though he tried to convince me to stay another night, I declined, and settled for the stables with Grace.

We trained for hours yesterday, and we had the rest of today to improve before the races tomorrow. Grace still hadn't beaten Black Magic's time yet, but with some more practice she was sure to get there. I grasped the watch firmly and leaned forward to pat her neck. "I know you've got it in you," I whispered.

I took the reins in one hand and kept the watch in the other, watching the second hand closely. I steadied myself with a deep breath. When I clicked my tongue, she took off, following closely along the perimeter of the clearing as if it were a track. *That a girl,* I thought, the whole world a mess of colors as she cantered.

When she raced across the end of the lap, I looked at the time: one minute and three seconds. "You were so close!" I shouted in frustration, then continued more softly. "Only a few seconds away from beating Black Magic."

I dismounted Grace and patted her nose with a sigh. "I know you're trying. Rest a minute, and then we'll run it again." A raindrop splashed across my hand. "Before we get rained out."

***

## Estella

"Shall I take your coat?" Henry asked as we arrived at Town Hall for our engagement party. It was pouring rain outside, but we were warm and safe inside. The wedding was only three days away. Soon, I would be this man's wife. "Yes," I said to Henry. "Thank you."

The hall was so beautifully decorated that one might think it was actually our wedding. Bouquets of expensive flower arrangements sat in each window lining every wall, and at least a dozen servants dressed in black dresses and suits served punch and wine, and took coats.

The floor gleamed, having been freshly polished for this event. The people of Pinebrook gave us their congratulations and well wishes, and I made so much small talk that my face began to ache from smiling.

Henry's arm slid through mine as he cleared his throat and announced a toast. "Ladies and gentlemen, thank you all for gathering here today to celebrate this blessed arrangement. In a few short days, I will have the great honor of being united in holy matrimony to Estella Coraline Wellstone. We are truly grateful to all of you. Without further ado…" Henry took a glass of wine from a passing servant and lifted it high. "To my beautiful fiancée. May she forever stay as lovely as she is in this special moment." The room full of ball gowns and suits followed his lead and drank to my beauty.

Everyone went back to their chattering and mingling.

A quartet began, reminding me that Henry and I were to lead our guests in the first dance of the evening.

He reached his gloved hand out to me and I took it. "You've grown distant from me," Henry whispered in my ear as we circled the dance floor. "I can feel it in your very breath. I know you better than you like to think I do." An assortment of colors swirled around us as the guests joined in.

"And I know *you* much better than I should like," I returned, leaning in closer to his ear. "But I do give you credit for being so very perceptive." Each word dripped with more sarcasm than the last. "I know about Lillian... about her child."

Henry's face went pale, but to my surprise, he danced on. "I don't suppose I know what you're talking about."

"Come now. You've never been one for idiocy, and I've grown tired of your games." The music stopped, and I pulled my hands from his with a sudden harshness.

As the quartet had come to the end of the song, I found my way to the refreshments. Taking another glass of wine, I tipped its contents into my mouth and observed my surroundings. Was this what my life was to amount to? Parties, dresses, and a scoundrel for a husband? Must I turn a blind eye to his indiscretions as though they never happened?

I watched Henry from a distance. He shook hands and smiled at our guests, all of whom were here to celebrate our impending marriage. Not a single person could resist his crooked smile or miss a chance to look upon his face that could've been sculpted by heavenly beings. It all turned my stomach.

Henry glanced out the window closest to him, and instantly his skin waxed in the candlelight of the ballroom. Recollecting his composure, he excused himself from his guests and, with a stealthy step, moved for the front doors.

Seamlessly, I glided across the ballroom floor, nodding to my guests until I reached a window at the front of the building. I peered through the glass, straining my eyes to see two warped figures outside through the heavy rain that drummed constantly against the gravel.

Lillian stood outside, next to Henry. She was drenched from head to toe and had a desperation in her face and posture that I'd never before seen so intense. I couldn't hear what she was saying from the window, but she was quite animated, her arms flying about as she shouted. Henry attempted to calm her, but she wouldn't be still.

My head felt light. I couldn't be sure if it was due to the overwhelming anxiety closing in on me, or all the wine I'd consumed. With one hand on the wall for balance, I moved from the window and finally reached the front doors. I pushed them open and the cool, damp air on my skin sobered me instantly.

I stepped out just in time to see Lillian throw a small satchel at Henry. It hit the ground, silver coins spilling out into the rain. "Money won't buy my innocence, nor will it buy a father for our child!" she screamed as though it came from the pit of her stomach.

Just then, someone spoke from behind me. "Oh, goodness! You poor girl, out in the rain." It was Alice. Her hair was pulled back tightly and she wore a gray silk gown, just as intimidating as usual.

A confused servant girl appeared next to her in the doorway. Alice turned to her. "Please, prepare my carriage at once." The girl nodded, then disappeared. Alice descended the stone steps, entering the night with us.

Henry whirled around in shock to meet my eyes, finally realizing I was there. The look of pure shame on his face nearly made my wine have a miraculous reappearance as I reconciled that everything Bodaway heard was true.

I rushed to Lillian's side as a sob tore through her. I wrapped my arms around her tightly, and could feel the size of her pregnant stomach resting on me. I hated Henry for what he did to her, and knew I could never forgive him for it.

Alice continued speaking. "Henry, why don't you take Estella back inside and enjoy the rest of the night. I will see Lillian home. The poor girl is clearly unwell." Her tone was hardly sympathetic.

Henry took my arm gently, pulling me along with him. "Come, Estella, you'll catch a cold."

I ripped my drenched arm away. "Did you think you could fool me? Keep me from the truth forever? You would live a lie so our lives could go on as usual?" The rain picked up harder. Our party clothes were ruined.

"That's what they do, Estella!" Lillian snapped. "Some of us have learned the hard way."

"That is enough from you!" Alice cut in. Her voice was blunt, but controlled. "Henry, you two will return to your party this instant, and I will see to it that Lillian is brought home safely." She took Lillian's arm in her own as she spoke.

"Is this what will be done to me?" I retorted. "In time, will I be silenced for questioning the ways and motives of the Hamilton family? Or will you simply dispose of me?"

"The rain may be taking a toll on your cognitive state, my dear. But Lillian must rest. Are you willing to argue that?"

Lillian nodded to me, defeated. "She's right. It's best for me to be at home in my condition. Go celebrate your engagement while you're still in the Hamiltons' good graces." She rested her hand on her stomach.

"Lillian, I *am* coming with you." I called out over the rain, with a firmness I didn't realize I possessed.

She turned and looked at me with the faintest glimmer of hope.

Alice sighed. "If you insist on abandoning your party, come along. Henry, give word to Estella's family of her whereabouts. The guests will be wondering where she is."

Henry's face in a twisted state of distress. His hair clung to his head in the rain, and water dripped from his nose and lips. "Estella, won't you come back with me?" he pleaded softly, knowing full well I would not unlink my arm from Lillian's.

"Henry, we have nothing to talk about!" I tightened my arm around Lillian, protectively.

"Do you think I want to be in this damned rain?" His breath hovered around him. "Don't you see? I did this all for you, for our families!"

"For goodness sake," Alice muttered.

I ignored Henry. "You're going to be alright." I whispered to Lillian while rubbing her shoulders, then looked to Alice. "We need to get her home." "Yes," said Alice, and wiped rainwater from her eyes. "I've already sent for the carriage."

Henry smoothed his hair back and said a few final words. "Well, you've got honesty now, Estella. Just remember that this is what you asked for." He cleared his throat. "Mother, ladies, if you will excuse me." He returned to his party in a completely ruined suit, with only his limited imagination to come up with an intriguing explanation regarding his appearance and my whereabouts.

At Henry's departure, Lillian's whole body seemed to relax—including a loss of the strength in her knees.

"We're going to get you home," I assured her as I wrapped my arms around her, holding her up as best I could.

Alice, tight-lipped, joined me in flanking her. After what seemed like an eternity, the Hamilton carriage pulled up in front of us, and Alice opened the sleek black door.

I helped Lillian climb onto the carriage's leather seat, then tucked myself in closely to her side.

Alice joined us, then closed the door firmly behind her. She knocked sharply on the roof, signaling the carriage to go. The horses promptly pulled us away from Town Hall, the carriage wheels sloshing in the mud and headed towards the Sterling residence.

As we rode a short way, I took notice of Alice's strange silence. It seemed to me that there was nothing tranquil about it.

I hardly felt sick anymore; I was much too angry. My teeth hurt from clenching so hard, but I clenched even tighter as Henry's words echoed again in my head. The most infuriating thing about all of this was that Henry truly seemed to believe he was a just man, that he was doing the right thing. *You did this,* I accused him in my head. *I confronted you, and you lied to me. You had a chance to be an honest man, but you'd rather live with these secrets.*

"Oh, goodness!" Lillian's groan brought me back to reality as she rested a hand on the underside of her stomach.

"What is it, Lillian? You'll be home soon!" I tried to reassure her. The ride from Town Hall to her home was but a moment by carriage. "Look! I can already see light from your house."

Lillian's head rolled back in delirium as we pulled up the long drive to her doorstep.

Alice excused herself from the carriage. "I can go ahead of you and alert Lillian's mother of her condition. We're going to need all the strength we can get."

I looked to Lillian, who collapsed into me from exhaustion. She certainly couldn't walk without support. "Fine, but hurry!"

I held onto poor Lillian as tightly as I could in hopes of comforting her. I smoothed the hair from her face and spoke soothingly, wondering if she could hear me. "You're safe now. Sweet Lillian, you're home now."

I could make out faint figures coming towards us through the rain. Alice had returned with Lillian's mother, Sarah, and their maid, Nellie.

"Lillian!" her mother called, running to the open carriage door as fast as her feet would take her. "Oh, Lillian! I should've been home! I should've known you weren't in bed!" She climbed up to reach us, cupping Lillian's clammy face in her hands as she cried with guilt.

"We need to get her inside, and warm!" I interjected.

Sarah nodded and wiped her eyes. "Yes, yes."

Lillian managed to slide herself towards the edge of her seat, allowing her mother and Nellie to scoop her up by her underarms. Together, they carried her from the carriage, across the lawn, and, finally, over the threshold.

I followed behind and closed the door firmly, shutting out the rain and the cold air.

The house was warm, and undisturbed by the rain. We stomped mud and water on its hardwood floors without a second thought.

"We need to get her to her bed!" Sarah cried, looking up the discouraging steepness of the house's stairwell.

"Wait!" Nellie cried out with a small voice as she fished around in her damp apron with one arm still wrapped tightly around Lillian's upper body. She retrieved a small glass bottle that fit within the palm of her hand. She uncorked it with her teeth and then waved its contents beneath Lillian's nostrils.

*Smelling salts!* I thought to myself. *Please, God, let this work!* My eyes were fixed upon Lillian's pale face in search of any movement.

First her dark eyelashes fluttered, then her eyes shot open as she gave a small gasp.

"Oh," her mother exclaimed, "thank goodness! Lillian, try and stand. We won't let you fall, but you need to try and walk up the stairs."

Lillian's hand went to her head. "Oh," she groaned. "My head is aching." Her voice had a little more strength now, and her cheeks turned pink, a much more life-like shade than it had been previously.

"I know, my darling, don't try to speak." Sarah and Nellie held Lillian up on either side, allowing her to keep her balance. "Let's get you to bed where you can rest." They walked her slowly up the stairs and out of sight.

The whole time, Lillian hadn't seemed to notice me or Alice in the room.

It wasn't until that moment I realized how weak my knees were. I let myself sink to the stairs with an exasperated sigh.

"Estella," said Alice, resting a cold and bony hand on my shoulder, "you really should go home. I'll make sure Lillian gets everything she needs."

"I won't leave her side, but *you* shouldn't feel obligated to stay." I met her gaze, not hiding my distrust.

Nellie came rushing down the stairwell and set some dry garments in my lap. "Here, miss, we don't want you catching sickness."

I hastily stood, clutching the garments to my chest. "Is there something I can do to help?"

"No, miss, you've already helped enough. I'm bringing some tea to my lady now. But she's asking for you, so you can change your clothes and go to her bedside."

Alice chimed in. "I should be glad to go along with you to Lillian's bedside. The poor girl's had an awful fright."

Nellie nodded to us, then started for the kitchen.

"How kind of you to worry about Lillian," I said dryly, then took my fresh set of clothes upstairs. The only thing louder than my doubt of Alice's good intentions was the sound of her footsteps echoing on the wood floors.

The halls were dark, but a soft light shone from Lillian's doorway. As I entered her room, Lillian was lying back with her eyes closed while her mother sat in a chair beside her, caressing her hair.

Sarah looked up as we lingered in the doorway, a small smile of gratitude on her lips.

Lillian's wet clothes had been hung over her folding screen to dry by the fireplace. I slipped behind the screen and peeled my soaked dress from my cool, damp skin. The fire's glow warmed me in an instant. I quickly put on the dry garment, a pale green, woolen housecoat lined with silk. I tied the robe around myself securely, then pulled my wet hair over my shoulder and wrung it out. Large droplets of water splashed on the brick hearth until my hair was merely damp and tangled.

I hung my wet party dress next to Lillian's just as a soft knock came from the doorway, and I peeked my head around the folding screen. It was Nellie with a tray of tea.

"Allow me, Nellie." Alice's white face moved through the dimness of the room like an apparition. She met the maid at the door and took the silver tray from her hands.

"Be careful," Nellie warned. "Don't burn yourself."

Alice carried the tray to Lillian's bedside and poured the steaming tea into a teacup.

Nellie looked at me and shook her head. "I'm terribly sorry that I didn't think to make tea for the rest of you. Lillian's medicinal herbal tea is no delicacy." Her nose crinkled at the thought.

"Tea won't be necessary," I said. I turned to observe Alice at Lillian's bedside with Mrs. Sterling. Alice wore a very concerned look on her face, and had even taken Lillian's hand in her own.

I tried to keep my doubt of her good intentions from showing on my face, but it was nearly impossible. "Thank you for the tea, Nellie," I said softly. "You've had an eventful evening. Why don't you rest a while, and we'll send for you if you're needed."

"Are you sure?" Nellie glanced to Lillian's mother, who didn't seem able to notice anything other than Lillian at that moment.

"Rest," I reassured her.

The tiny thing gave a great sigh. "Oh, thank you, miss." She nodded, then left us to ourselves.

I went to Mrs. Sterling and rested my hands on hers. "Sarah, your skin is cold to the touch, you must be freezing."

She rubbed her eyes, coming finally out of her daze. "Yes... I suppose I am." Her clothes were still wet, and she was shaking.

"Mrs. Sterling," I said gently, "you should change out of those wet clothes and rest a moment."

"We wouldn't want *two* Sterling women bedridden," Alice added.

Sarah rubbed Lillian's hand. "I shouldn't leave her."

"She's safe now," I replied, "and if you wish to clean up, *I* won't leave her side. Either way, she should drink her tea." I reached over to Lillian's nightstand where Alice had set the tea tray. The dainty porcelain cup was still too hot, burning my fingers at the touch.

Sarah stood and kissed Lillian's forehead. "As long as you're with her and she doesn't leave this bed." She frowned, probably thinking over the events that had led to this.

"I won't allow it," I assured her.

"Thank you, Estella. You've always been a sweet friend to this family." She hesitated. "I can't express my apologies enough for the way Lillian has acted of late. It's been very trying on this household, so thank you." She patted my arm, then left us.

I took her seat beside Lillian and carefully placed my friend's small hand in my own. Alice still hovered over Lillian's bed. "You know," I said, "you don't have to stay anymore. Lillian's safe with me, and I can't imagine those wet clothes to be very comfortable."

I added an edge to my voice. "Also, I don't want you to be here when Lillian comes to. Her heart can't handle much more, not tonight." I sighed and smoothed my sleeping friend's forehead.

Alice cleared her throat and clasped her hands at her waist. "Well, I've never been one to stay where I'm not wanted."

Somehow, I had a hard time believing that.

"Mind you, Estella, don't stay too long. As you said, Lillian is safe now. I can imagine how worried your mother must be after you ran off from your engagement party." Alice glanced down at Lillian one last time, then dragged her hand along my shoulders as she passed me by. "Don't let her tea sit too long; it will go cold." Her footsteps echoed down the hall as she left the room.

I rolled my neck and shoulders, trying to shake the itch Alice had left crawling over my skin.

Just then, Lillian stirred awake. Her eyes, child-like, focused on me. "Estella…" she said softly, then propped herself up slightly. She attempted to sit up further, her pink comforter resting loosely over her stomach, but couldn't manage it. "Estella, I don't know why you came." Despite her words, she sounded relieved.

"Don't you move," I said, putting my hands on her shoulders. "Lie back down and relax. I came because despite all that's happened, I still love you dearly."

The pale green of my house coat was almost the same color as Lillian's skin. She rested her hands on her pregnant stomach as she spoke. "I can't imagine why you would come. I've been so terrible to you." She spoke softly, without resentment. Her eyes teared up and the faintest traces of color spread across her face again. "I don't suppose you would grant me your forgiveness."

I tucked her into the comforter. "You have it," I smiled, pushing her hair off her forehead.

Lillian rested her head on the mountains of pillows behind her and stared at the cracks along the ceiling. "I am sure you know what ailment I suffer from now." A look of pain crossed her face. "I thought that if I were to stain your reputation, then Henry would have to take responsibility... but that only seemed to hasten your wedding plans. It was plain sinful of me, and I seem to have lost my head this evening."

"Don't fret another moment," I said. "We can never know how we would react in such a position until we're faced with it. I can't begin to understand what you've been going through, Lillian." I took her hand and caressed it.

"I don't deserve you," she whispered, her eyes wandering. "Do you remember when we used to play with our china dolls right here, pretending that we were never going to change, never going to grow old?" A small tear slid down the side of her face, and she smiled. "Those days seem so long ago, but at the same time, when you're sitting here with me, it's almost as if nothing has changed, as if it was just yesterday you were here."

How well Lillian had put to words exactly how I'd felt all summer. I'd been lamenting about our lost girlhood, about the children that did as they pleased and had no responsibility beyond eating the food placed before them and sitting still in church. They were inseparable and they loved each other very much.

Those children were not gone, only changed, but that love was as constant as it always would be. I crawled into Lillian's covers with her and held her close.

Her pink room, filled with childhood memories, no longer seemed to close in on us. The warm firelight created a nostalgic environment, a familiar embrace. "Lillian," I said, "it wasn't so long ago that we were girls. You're right about that." I tucked my head close to hers. "In fact, are you *certain* that it wasn't yesterday?" She smiled. We lay in silence for a while, listening to the fire crackle and the gentle tick of the clock above the mantle, but eventually, Lillian spoke up again. "Did Alice Hamilton stay awhile after bringing me home?"

"Not very long," I said quietly. "Why?"

"It's no secret to me how she feels about this baby. You can be sure she didn't come here to celebrate her grandchild." She rubbed her stomach tenderly. "After she learned about my condition, she told me my only options were to leave town or to give my baby up. There was no way to prove that my child is any relation to Henry… Which, sadly, is true."

I sat up on my elbows. "What are you going to do?"

She pressed her lips into a flat line and was quiet for a moment before answering. "You know, there was a time, early on, when I would have happily given away this baby. I felt like it was a reminder of my mistakes, and that it would ruin me. But now..." She shook her head. "I love this baby, Estella. This is my child, and I will not give it up for anyone else to raise. It's hard to describe the overwhelming love a mother feels the first time she realizes her baby is moving inside her."

"Alice won't care about that," I said grimly. "What if she doesn't leave you be, even after the child is born?"

"I'll raise the child as my own," she said firmly. "I will *not* be forced by anyone, even Alice Hamilton, to give up my child—that is for certain." She was working up a sweat. "But as you can imagine, she didn't take kindly to that answer."

"Alright, alright," I soothed, lying back down with her. "It isn't good to overwork yourself in this delicate condition. Just be calm. I never meant for you to bow down to Alice. She's not the Queen of England, though I'm certain she believes she's the Queen of Pinebrook." I raised my eyebrows and we both laughed. "Why don't you try and drink some tea," I said, patting Lillian's brown hair away from her glistening face. She still looked pale, and I feared it was my fault. I didn't want to bring up either Henry or my wedding; she was too fragile.

I reached over to Lillian's night stand and lifted the warm china cup. Its aroma was indeed as bitter as Nellie had warned, though it was also somehow familiar. I brought the cup to Lillian's small, dry lips, and held it there as she drank it.

"Do *you* love him?" she asked softly, her doe eyes batting in genuine curiosity.

"No," I said numbly. "I don't believe I could ever bring myself to fully love Henry Hamilton."

"And what of the Indian man Nellie saw you dancing with? Oh, that dreadful night." She wrinkled her nose and visibly cringed at her own mention of the barn dance.

"Bodaway?" I smiled and tucked myself into the covers again. "It doesn't matter what I feel. I can't give myself over to those feelings... I just can't."

"So you do care for him!" she whispered, her face wide with shock. "An Indian."

"I care, but what am I to do?" My heart sank. "I'm promised to another, and you know that my family would never allow such a scandal."

"Yes, and what a scandal indeed." Lillian giggled at the idea, then continued in a more serious tone. "As long as I've known you, your decisions have been made for you. But... you know in your heart what you want, I'm sure of it. You just need to believe in the decisions you make." She rubbed her pregnant stomach.

"That was a strangely mature observation," I said, surprised. It felt as though she had just lit a candle and illuminated all my insecurities and problems.

"I'm not *completely* daft, you know." Her brows crowded together and her lips curled in a tiny smile.

I threw the covers off and sat on the edge of Lillian's bed. She was right. I needed to believe in every decision I made. Bodaway had reminded me of that, too. "I really should be getting home, Lillian. Should I send for your mother?"

"Don't leave me." Her doe eyes pleaded with me.

I took her limp hand, sighing. "I'll stay for a while longer," I said, then slipped back into her covers and held her close.

She managed another smile before dozing off.

The warmth of the room and the quiet air could make anyone drowsy. My own eyelids became heavier and heavier until I drifted off into the night.

*\*\*\**

A *scream.*

A scream to triumph over all other screams.

The sound jerked me out of deep sleep, disorientated, into full-on panic. That scream had by now become a series of screams, each one striking me with a different, painful explosion.

Lillian's arms were wrapped tightly around her stomach. She writhed, pulling her knees as close to her chest as her body would allow.

"Lillian!" I shot upright in bed and ripped the blankets from us in one fluid motion, revealing the bright red puddle that soaked us both. The sweet, metallic smell of blood met my nose, and my hands instinctively covered my mouth to keep myself from retching.

My green housecoat was now stained crimson, and Lillian's thin nightgown could have, morbidly, matched it.

I swallowed the bile rising in my throat. "Lillian!" I cried, louder this time, praying that someone would hear me. I patted her face gently, willing her back to me, but her skin was waxy and once more discolored.

Before I could call a third time for help, the bedroom door swung open. "Oh Lord!" Lillian's mother shrieked and rushed to the bedside. Her eyes rolled back into her head at the sight of the blood. Her posture weakened and she collapsed into my arms.

My eyes burned and my heart pounded in my ears as I struggled to set Mrs. Sterling on the chair next to Lillian's bed without dropping her.

There was a sound at the doorway, and my eyes shot up to see Nellie and Hannah hurry in.

"Hannah!" I sighed, practically in hysterics. "Oh, Hannah, it's terrible!"

Lillian still cried out in pain, holding her stomach. I returned to her side and clasped her hand as Nellie pulled the blankets from the bed, completely exposing Lillian and the extent of the mess.

Hannah placed a trembling hand over her heart as she took in the scene. Me in my blood stained housecoat, Lillian's mother unconscious, slumped in a chair—and it was evident Hannah had no idea Lillian was with child until this moment. "She must be having a miscarriage," Hannah said, and covered her nose at the smell.

"You have to call for help!" I cried in desperation. "Hannah! Get the doctor!" I knelt by Lillian's side, repeating over and over, "It is going to be OK, everything is going to be alright."

I didn't know if a word of that was true.

"Nellie!" I screamed. "Use the smelling salts on Mrs. Sterling! We need her awake."

Hannah fled the room, and Nellie scurried to Mrs. Sterling's side with the smelling salts. A few minutes passed, but with Lillian in such pain, it felt like ages. Nellie was soon successful in waking Lillian's mother, who now sat among the bloody mess with her daughter.

Finally, Hannah rushed into the room with Doctor Leighton. He was a man of at least seventy, and had seen a lot in his lifetime as

Pinebrook's only doctor. He wore a long-sleeved white shirt with a black vest over it and carried a brown leather satchel.

The two crossed the room and joined the rest of us around Lillian.

"Thank God you're here, doctor," I sighed, and wiped sweat from my brow. I stood back with Hannah and let the doctor have his space.

His aged fingers fumbled over the buttons on his shirt as he rolled his sleeves up his arms. Finally prepared, he lifted Lillian's nightgown over her pregnant waist and bent to examine her. I had no idea how he could discern anything through all the blood, and with her writhing so.

Lillian's skin was turning new shades of green by the minute and her eyes fluttered, disconnected from reality.

Doctor Leighton rested the back of his hand on Lillian's forehead. "She's lost a lot of blood."

Lillian's mother looked desperately at me, knowing I had been with her in the moments before the terrible happenings. "I should have been there with my baby," she sobbed. "I came in to check on her, but she was sleeping so soundly that I didn't want to wake her." The woman began breathing deeply and rapidly. "But then I heard her screaming and screaming... and I came in to find her soaked in blood." She spoke as though to herself, and fanned her daughter with a rolled newspaper that had lain nearby.

The doctor let Nellie clean Lillian up a bit while he took the rest of us aside. "I'm afraid that Hannah's assumption was accurate. Lillian is having a miscarriage."

Lillian's mother almost collapsed to the floor, but this time Hannah was there to hold her as she cried.

I was shocked, hardly able to feel anything. "How did this happen, Doctor?"

"It's fairly common in young girls under these circumstances… in girls under such tremendous distress." He spoke softly enough that only I could hear. "We will need to deliver this child stillborn."

The weight of his words hung heavy in the air. "What can I do?" I asked.

"Lillian needs to be prepared for delivery, and I will need plenty of space to do my work." He observed the mess of the tea tray and the bloodied blankets.

Nellie, Hannah, and Mrs. Sterling hastened to perform the first task while I took the initiative to move the tea tray. I was carrying it across the room to Lillian's vanity when that bitter, yet familiar scent within the teacup stirred something inside me. Bringing the china cup to my nose, I breathed in the remaining aroma, then touched my finger to the spilled liquid and let it drip onto my lips.

To my horror, the familiar numbness of rue spread across my tongue.

"Doctor!" I called from across the room, and stood anxiously until he joined me privately. "What herb have you instructed Lillian to take in her tea?" I asked, a sort of dry shock catching in my throat.

"I instructed Lillian to drink dandelion leaf tea each day." His white, bushy eyebrows crowded together as he joined me beside the tray of spilled tea. He tasted the liquid as I'd done moments before, but the stern look that came into his eyes hardly confirmed my fears.

"Don't you see?" I prompted. " Lillian was clearly poisoned! I can distinctively taste traces of rue."

He looked at me with clear cynicism, then rubbed his eyes as though carefully considering what his next words should be. "If I were you, I would keep that assumption to myself."

"But why? Legal action should be taken against the person who did such a thing!" I imagined Alice pouring hot water over dried rue—the rue she kept in that horrid silk pouch— stirring it, letting it steep. My whole body grew hot as silent fury burned away at my insides.

Dr. Leighton gently took my shoulders in his huge hands. "That is *precisely* why you should never speak of this again. And I can't tell you for certain if there even *was* any rue in that tea. " He blinked a few times, waiting for me to understand him, but continued when I said nothing in response. "Lillian's position—an unwed young woman, miscarrying her child—looks very bad. People will be quick to think that Lillian purposely tried to get rid of the child."

My lips quivered and my eyes grew wider. "You can't seriously believe that!"

The doctor rubbed his tired eyelids with thumb and forefinger. "It doesn't matter what I believe. As of right now, Lillian needs attention."

As if on command, another cry came from the half-conscious Lillian, and both Dr. Leighton and I returned to her side.

Hannah looked up. "What can we do, Doctor? We've prepared plenty of water and clean linens."

"Very well. Now we must bring her back to consciousness." The doctor leaned over Lillian and rested the back of his hand over her cheek. He frowned, his face wrinkled hopelessly. "It is time for her to push."

Only a few candles lit the solemn room, along with the embers of the fire that no one was keeping up. Hannah sat at the foot of the bed to help deliver the baby, as she'd done with many women in Pinebrook. She'd even delivered Lillian, twenty years ago. She was so brave—braver than I, for certain. Hannah hadn't looked faint for a single second.

Lillian's mother patted her daughter's hair, trying with all her might to help Lillian stay awake and push while I stood a few paces behind Hannah and Doctor Leighton, ready to fetch anything at a moment's notice.

Lillian only pushed for a brief period of time before the baby's head emerged. Hannah took hold of it at once. "Another push," she instructed. Though weak, Lillian did as she was told. She whimpered, but the child stayed in place.

The doctor crouched beside Hannah. "This one's got broad shoulders," he said softly.

Hannah nodded, as though she already knew. "The poor thing might need a turn-around."

Without another thought, the doctor reached his hands into Lillian and carefully guided a limp baby boy out of her womb, into the world.

The room fell silent.

Doctor Leighton's face twisted in confusion, but then he sprung to silent action. He took the baby, laid it over his hand on its stomach, and vigorously rubbed its back.

Lillian watched through just the slivers of her eyes as its limbs bounced about with all the rubbing.

A small but prominent cry came from the tiny body in the doctor's hands.

"Oh, thank God!" Mrs. Sterling cried out, and fell upon the doctor's side, hanging onto him. "How can this be?"

He handed her the infant as though the child were a paper-thin work of china.

Hannah and I looked at each other and marveled. She wrapped her arms around me in an embrace of pure relief.

The doctor nodded to Lillian's mother. "God has worked something of a miracle for your family this evening. I can hardly believe it myself." He wiped his brow with his forearm. "The lad is just as healthy as any I've seen. Perhaps Lillian suffered from a significant uterine rupture, or she simply could have experienced premature labor." His head shook, baffled. "As for your daughter, she's lost a lot of blood, but the bleeding is slowing beautifully. She'll pull through, I've no doubt. Just let her rest."

Nellie and I began changing Lillian out of her ruined nightgown and into something fresh.

"Thank you, Doctor! Please, you must stay the night!" Mrs. Sterling begged. "Nellie, prepare the guest room at once!"

Doctor Leighton scrubbed his hands clean of Lillian's blood in the water basin Hannah had prepared, dried his hands, and packed his leather bag. "I should be very glad to stay the night in case Lillian were to need me." Then he left the room with Nellie.

Hannah and I watched as Mrs. Sterling handed the child to Lillian for the first time. Her arms were weak, but she was awake. She kissed the infant's pruney head, and her tears dropped onto its cheeks, causing it to let out a small, sweet cry.

"I'll bring up some hot tea." Lillian's mother kissed her head and left the room.

I opened the chest at the end of Lillian's bed, and found a small patchwork blanket that we'd often taken onto the lawn in summers past. "Here, so he doesn't get cold." I knelt by her side and helped swaddle her son in the blanket.

"Thank you," she whispered.

Hannah touched my shoulder. "Estella, you need to change out of this stained coat and put your other clothes back on. They're dry enough now." She frowned. "I'm surprised your parents haven't sent the whole town after you yet."

"I know," I said. "Allow me a few moments to say goodbye?" I widened my eyes in pleading.

"Don't take too long." Her voice was hoarse with exhaustion. "The carriage is waiting for us downstairs." With one last squeeze to my shoulder, she left.

Finally alone with Lillian, I sat at the edge of her bed and watched her with her son. Her eyes met mine, wide with panic, like she already knew I had something terrible to tell her.

"You've been so strong," I whispered, gently sliding my finger into the baby's palm. His fingers closed around mine.

"I don't want to think about what would have happened if you hadn't been with me." She rubbed her eye in exhaustion. "I've never felt so strange as I did tonight."

"Lillian…" I hesitated, remembering the doctor's words. "It *was* very strange what happened to you. So strange, in fact, that I'm almost certain it was intentional." I bit my lip, waiting for her reaction.

Her dark eyebrows raised. "Are you suggesting that I did this to *myself?*" Her voice rose almost to a shout.

"No! No, that's not what I am trying to say." I closed my eyes, mustering the courage to speak aloud what consumed my thoughts, then fixed my gaze upon Lillian again. "I believe Alice put rue in your tea this evening in hopes that you would miscarry." I spoke in the lowest voice possible, filled with the irrational fear that Alice could somehow hear me.

Lillian swallowed hard, her hand going to her throat. "You believe that she could be capable of such a horrible thing? There was so much blood." Her gaze drifted to the stains on my robe. "I feel it in my bones, I really do. I believe Alice Hamilton is capable of anything."

"If this is true... As long as my child is breathing, Alice will be a danger to my family." Lillian held her son closer to her chest, filled with a new burst of energy. "But nobody would ever believe me." She looked at the empty doorway to make sure we were alone, then back at me. "I know what I need to do. I'm going to take my child, and my mother, and we're going to leave this place just as soon as I'm well."

"Lillian, this feels so unjust! You can't just leave! Where would you even go?"

"I don't know." She sighed and rested her head close to her child. "It doesn't matter. The only thing that matters now is this." She looked at her baby with an abundance of love and protectiveness. "I'll do whatever it takes to keep my family safe. Besides, a fresh start in a new city wouldn't be so bad."

Lillian seemed so sure, and even optimistic. She'd just been poisoned and almost lost her child, but now she was smiling and dreaming about a new life. She was doing what she thought was right, and that was a luxury I'd only dreamt of.

Nellie appeared in the doorway. "Miss, Hannah sent me to hurry you."

"I'll be down in a moment," I sighed. I slipped behind the folding screen and began untying my crusty, stained housecoat. My party dress had dried quite nicely, and felt warm as I pulled my arms through. I draped my filthy robe over the screen and smoothed my own skirts before returning to Lillian's side.

"A fresh start does sound nice," I said matter-of-factly, as though we hadn't skipped a beat in our conversation. "But you're exhausted. There's no need to make a life-altering decision right this moment." I leaned over her and kissed her head, and then the child's.

"No," she said, looking up at me in all seriousness. "I've made up my mind."

I took Lillian's hand and gave it a squeeze. "Promise me you will *not* leave without a proper goodbye. Promise me that, or I won't leave your side."

"I promise," she whispered. "Now go on, Hannah's waiting for you." She waved me off, but caught my arm again at the last moment. "Thank you, Estella. For everything."

I turned and gave her a smile. "Always."

\*\*\*

Hannah met me at the front door and wrapped a cloak around my shoulders before leading me quietly outside. The rain had stopped, but I felt the air still damp on my face as we climbed into the carriage's seats. The doors shut us in and the coachman pulled away.

We rode in quiet thoughtfulness, accompanied only by the sounds of the horses' hooves stomping and the wheels spinning in the mud. I must have been asleep with Lillian for hours, because it was clearly now well into the night.

Hannah sighed and put her arm through mine. "You're a good friend, Estella. I mean it. Just seeing you tonight in those awful, blood stained clothes, willing to help Lillian without a second thought…" She trailed off.

I didn't respond right away, but eventually turned to face her. "Hannah."

She looked at me.

"That child was Henry's." We stared at each other. I said it again. "Lillian just gave birth to Henry's child, and he knew about it this entire time." I hesitated before making my boldest accusation. "And I believe Alice had something to do with the baby's premature birth. I believe she intended a miscarriage."

Hannah's face grew grim, and I hurried my words. "You were there! Nobody expected that baby to live, not even Dr. Leighton."

She began to speak slowly. "I always felt there was something not quite right about the Hamiltons. They have secrets, that's for certain—as does every family—but I've never been one to make grand accusations based off of feelings." She looked away. "I know that what I told you about your duty to marry Henry made sense in the moment, but you're going to have to wake up every day and be happy with the decisions you've made in your life." Her sure voice never wavered.

Our hanging lantern swung about as the coach rattled over a bit of uneven ground. The light settled again, illuminating the gray hair poking out from beneath her cloak's hood.

"Hannah," I said, "Tonight put some things in perspective for me. You've been like a mother to me. There's not a lot of goodness in this world, but you are exactly that. *Good.* You always do the right thing." I hesitated. "But me... I don't know what to do." I let out a sharp breath.

Hannah put her arms around me. "There's nothing I want more for you than a happy life with a man who treats you well. If you think that Henry is *not* that man, then you will know what to do." She gave me a sad smile and rubbed my shoulders, ignorant of how similar she sounded to Lillian with those words she had spoken to me.

*Lillian.* Flashes of blood and screaming rushed back into my head. "What's happened tonight must stay between us," I said.

"Cross my heart. You know I'll always protect you."

# CHAPTER TWENTY-ONE

## Saturday, July 29th

### Estella

My chest was heavy and there was an unpleasant numbness crawling over my skin. Mother had instructed me to ready myself, as we were to leave for the races after taking a light meal. I arrived in the dining room as ordered.

Her eyes met mine with approval as I sat beside her, fully dressed with the exception of my bonnet. I removed my white gloves and laid them in my lap.

Hannah filled my crystal glass with water. She placed a soft boiled egg in front of me, then set a bowl of strawberries between Mother and me.

I didn't touch them. The egg's smell had turned my already-fragile stomach.

When Mother noticed me slouched in my seat, mindlessly twisting Henry's pendant, she let out a long huff. "Estella, quit fidgeting. You need to eat. You are going to look like a *stick* for the wedding tomorrow... Not to mention those dreadful bags beneath your eyes! The Sterlings should have been more considerate than to keep you all evening. You certainly do not wish to be ill at the races, my dear." She pushed the bowl of strawberries closer to me.

I wasn't hungry in the least, and hearing Mother talk so mindlessly about Lillian made my fists clench in my lap. "Yes, how very inconsiderate of Lillian to be unwell."

Mother hardly seemed to notice. "You know, Sarah Sterling sent word to your father this morning that they intend to move! And of course your father is much too generous with them. He offered to *purchase* the home that he *gave* to them! Can you imagine!" She shook her head, her sandy curls moving with her in agreement.

"There is no shame in tending to widows," I said, my words sharp. "Even *you* wouldn't argue with that."

Mother finally picked up on my insolence. "Your father does enjoy tending to things, doesn't he? In fact, he 'tended to' your little problem earlier this week." Her hint at Bodaway was clearly an attempt to provoke me.

The small, familiar flame within me flared up, and I didn't try to snuff it out. "Then why can't he take care of my *real* problems? Henry and his family! I've seen what Alice is capable of, and I have no desire to be linked with her." I pushed the strawberries back towards her and crossed my arms.

Mother rose and smoothed the wrinkles from her dress. "Estella, you had better start changing your attitude. Your father does what he must for all of our benefit. Henry and his family are hardly the problem."

The flame grew within me as I stood in anger. I wanted to shout about Lillian and her child, but for their sakes, I held my tongue and spoke evenly. "Would you like to know my opinion on that, Mother? Where's my father?"

"He's in his study, worried sick about you." Her face twisted in annoyance as I stormed out of the dining room.

Yes, I was *sure* he was worried sick. Sick enough, no doubt, to keep him reading and smoking in his study.

I made my way to my father's study. The room was small and smoky, enclosed in mahogany paneling. Mother had discarded a pair of chairs from the main house—effectively out of her sight. One sat before his desk, the other against the wall where his stocked liquor cabinet stood. Sure enough, Father was sitting at his desk, cigar in hand, completely unbothered by the day's events.

"What exactly did you say to Bodaway?" I asked, raising my voice.

"Please calm down, Estella. Your voice is shrill." He removed his glasses and rubbed his eyes. "What on Earth are you talking about?"

"Bodaway, Father. Mother said you *tended to* him."

Father cleared his throat and adjusted his gray vest until it was straight. "Oh, that one. I simply had to let him go. We can't have any distractions lurking around, threatening to ruin our reputation. You know as well as I that this marriage is very important."

"What have I ever done for you to treat my future as your personal gain? You have no care as to what kind of man Henry is, or the character of his family—and I can assure you there's no goodness or honor in the Hamilton family name! Now, Bodaway, the most honorable person I know, must suffer the consequences of my misconduct? You cannot begin to understand what that means."

Mother walked into the study before I finished speaking. She waited for me to fall silent, then said, "I think it's time for us to talk." She floated towards the liquor cabinet against the wall, poured a small glass of whiskey for herself and Father, and tipped the glass down her throat.

"Talk about what?" Mother rarely drank, so this was sure to be a significant conversation.

She looked at me, and massaged her temple gingerly. "You are not our natural daughter." They fell out of her mouth so smoothly, but those words were like a train crashing into my ears. "Your father and I couldn't have any children." Her eyes welled and her cheeks flushed deeply. "You were raised well enough to know the shame in that." She poured herself more whiskey.

I backed away until I touched the wall, my knees threatening to give way. That wall was the only thing keeping me from crumbling to the ground.

This news shattered the very foundation I'd lived on all my life. Everything I thought I knew about myself was a farce. It was as though the tiny, flickering flame that had nagged at me my whole life finally had its way with me, consuming every part of my being. My mother's words revealed the truth of that flame. They melted me down to the bare minerals of my existence, until everything else was gone and only one thing demanded my attention.

"Why did you never tell me this?" I asked, my voice rising in fury. "You saw me struggle to find my place my whole life, always feeling unwanted, and it never occurred to you that I might want to *know* this?"

Mother transformed into a stranger as she glided across the room to the cushioned chair in front of Father's desk.

"Estella," Father said, "there is no need to raise your voice to your mother." He rubbed his eyes once more in frustration.

"My mother? You *apparently* are not my parents at all!"

Rachelle rolled her eyes. Rachelle—that's who she was. A wife, a respected woman in society. But not, in fact, my mother. "You always find a way to make it about you, Estella. For once, just listen."

I wanted to shout, but had no voice. I couldn't form the words.

Rachelle waved a hand to the unwanted, outdated chair against the wall. "Sit."

I obeyed mindlessly. "Who am I?" I whispered.

"Hannah!" She called. "Join us in the study, please."

A few moments passed before her footsteps approached the door. "Yes, Madam," Hannah said. When she saw me, my shaken state, her face paled.

Rachelle turned back to me. "When your father and I realized we couldn't have any children, Hannah came into our lives. A poor widow, with child, looking for a place to work."

Hannah brought one shaking hand to her lips.

"We offered her more than merely a position—a family and future for her child."

My stomach tied in a thousand knots, and my hands trembled. I looked to Hannah in desperation. "Is this true?"

She returned a sad, helpless gaze, but denied none of it.

I felt like I was about to be sick. "I don't know any of you anymore."

"Don't give me that insolence," Father reprimanded. "Nothing has changed, Estella. Your mother and I have given you everything. We've raised you in a beautiful home and presented you with every opportunity for the finer things in life. You've never seemed to object to any of those things."

"But this life and its responsibilities don't run in my blood, do they? Not in the way you've led me to believe for so long." I tried to speak firmly, but my voice wavered.

Rachelle scoffed. "Estella, we only ask that you be grateful. The least you can do is accept this marriage without causing us any further embarrassment."

I couldn't hear much more beyond the pounding in my ears. I pushed my way around Hannah, leaving the study behind me. If they called my name, I didn't know. I could hardly breathe until I was inside my bedroom.

Everything looked so foreign. I felt like an unwanted guest in my own home.

I had no family, Bodaway probably hated me, and I didn't know who I was anymore. I sat at my vanity, as I so often did, and looked at myself in the mirror. *Who am I?* I asked myself again. I looked the same as I always had, though there was a difference in my eyes. It was as though I was hollowed out on the inside.

My little yellow flower lay on the vanity, the only thing I had to remember Bodaway by. I touched it gently, so as not to crumble it.

If Bodaway left, I wouldn't even have Grace any more. Of course, I'd be glad for *him* to have her. She had always been his horse. That didn't change the fact that I'd miss them both dearly.

I stared at the flower for a while longer, then at Henry's family crest, which lay beside it. For the first time, I could admit to myself that I loved Bodaway. Maybe he and Lillian were right, that my decisions had always been made for me, that it was time I took my life into my own hands.

So much had changed with one conversation. I longed to tell Bodaway about my family, about how all the feelings I'd had about not quite finding my place all made sense now. About how the duty in my blood apparently never existed.

I finally knew who I was not, but I needed to know now who I was.

I closed Henry's pendant inside a small golden box on my vanity, the reminder of him disturbed me. I did indeed owe my family this marriage. They were not obligated to take care of me, but they had. I may be discontented, but I was not ungrateful.

Father's voice came from below. "Estella, we must be going half past the hour!"

His tone was normal, as though nothing had changed. We still had the races to attend. Perhaps they would give me one last chance to slip away and see Bodaway.

I looked at myself in the mirror and wiped my face. If my parents wanted to pretend nothing was wrong, then pretend I would. I pulled on my gloves, pinned a straw bonnet into my hair, and tied its silk ribbon beneath my chin.

I was ready.

\*\*\*

## Bodaway

It was Saturday. All anyone could talk about around town was the big wedding planned for the next day, and how Estella had been spending all her time with Henry and his family. She was helping at the orphanage, having big dinners, taking tea… all the things that wealthy people did.

I hadn't thought she'd be weak enough to give in so easily. Well, that was her problem now. I'd said my piece to her the other day, and it wasn't enough. I had to focus my attention on the race today. Everyone in town would be going. Even the mill workers were granted an extended lunch in order to attend.

I'd been intensely preparing Grace for this race, and though I had my doubts about her capabilities, now was not the time to falter in my decision. I hated that I was racing her, but I'd managed to convince myself it was all for my brother.

I led Grace into town, giving her a few last moments of exercise before the race. We walked through the dusty streets among a stampede of Pinebrook citizens, Grace's lead wrapped around my anxious hand.

"John! Wait up!"

I almost ignored the voice calling after me over the crowds, but I eventually turned to see Mary, with Art following closely at her heels. Taking Grace by the bit, I stopped and waited for them to catch up.

"John!" Mary ran faster to meet me. She took me in a quick embrace, then wiped her brow with a sleeve. "John, Art finally told me what happened!" The words fell out of her mouth like those of a concerned, breathless child. "I surely hope he's misinformed, that you *don't* plan to leave town after today."

"I'm afraid so." I looked to Art, who was just reaching us. "I was never meant to stay here for very long."

Mary squinted in the harsh sun. "But you would leave without saying goodbye?"

I reached into my trouser pocket and retrieved Art's watch. "Of course not," I said, half-smiling, "You've both been more than kind to me. I think I owe you the respect of a proper goodbye."

Her eyes relaxed, her face lifting once more.

I held out Art's watch in his direction, the golden piece shining between my fingers. "I believe this belongs to you."

Art snatched it and tucked it away. "No sense in saying our farewells now! You've got a race to win, which generally means you'll be *at* the track." He slapped my back and nudged us all on our way.

Mary continued talking as we walked. "It's hard to believe you've never been to the races here in Pinebrook! There's hardly anything better to do in these parts."

"These days, I'm not much for betting. Every penny counts."

"Well, just wait till you see Black Magic run! If you were to choose any horse, she'd be the one to bet on. At least, that's how it was last summer." She waved a few dollars in my face.

"If you're going to burn money," I said, "you should burn it on my lot, Grace. Art's seen what she can do with his own eyes." I patted the horse's side.

"It's true," said Art, "but I'm not so confident that Grace has what it takes to beat Black Magic." Then Art added quickly, "At least, not so soon! But I sure hope she does. For your sake."

Mary chimed in. "It's all about strategy. You see, if you've got a solid plan based on logic, sense, and a bit of luck, you can win some good money." She winked at me.

"Ladies *love* it when you have money," Art added.

That didn't make me feel better. I had nothing but a penny to my name. Meanwhile, Henry glove-wearing Hamilton had half of Pinebrook as his inheritance.

"If you don't mind," I said, "I'm going to walk ahead. I need to be in a good state of mind before the races."

Art laughed. "Sure, sure, go ahead. Mary and I will meet you there." He reached out a hand, which I shook firmly. "If we don't see you till after, I wish you the best of luck, John."

"I really hope you win the money you need." Mary said, smiling hopefully.

I nodded to them both, then continued on my way. I wanted to be alone, partly because I had no interest in discussing how I was about to gamble what little money I had at a chance of making more money. Art knew how harshly I judged the men we'd roomed with who did the same.

But I was gambling for a noble cause. God should understand that. I reached into my pocket and felt the note about Keme and my entree fee.

My grandfather would have disapproved of this whole thing, but I knew my mother would have been proud of me for taking care of Keme.

\*\*\*

The race track was a lot smaller than I expected, made of dirt, fenced in simply, and surrounded by a grassy field. The air smelled pleasantly of popcorn and roasting peanuts.

A bellowing voice called out over the crowd. "All bets are to be placed before one! All bets are to be placed before one!"

Many people mingled around me, all rubbing shoulders, all trying to claim standing room as close to the track as they could manage.

I paid my entry, then headed for the stables. Grace and I squeezed through a crowd that parted at the sight of her magnificence. Everyone dressed nicely for the occasion, except for me in my simple work shirt. Their eyes followed me, and I was happy to lose them as I entered the stables.

Stalls lined both walls—I counted ten—and many were already occupied by riders and their horses. I led Grace into the nearest one available. She tossed her head from side to side, seeming agitated in this unfamiliar confinement. "Easy, girl." I smoothed her neck with my hand, brushing away any pieces of dust or debris I could find.

Shortly after settling Grace, a hostile silence fell over the stables.

"Look who it is." A man in the stall next to me scoffed under his breath. I looked up to see Irving Wellstone, head held high. The other men looked at him with vexed faces, but he didn't meet anyone's gaze as he led his infamous, elite racehorse, Black Magic, to her stall.

\*\*\*

It was almost time for the races to begin. Each rider stood with their horse at its stall and received a number. Mine was four, as it happened.

The other owners shook hands with the jockeys racing their prized horses, but no one shook mine—which was probably for the best since my palms were sweating profusely. I was the only man riding his own horse. Men like Estella's father would watch from the sidelines, collecting their money without putting in any of the work.

Hardly anyone acknowledged me, but I didn't care. I was there to win. Once we had all taken our numbers, the owners returned to their families and friends while the jockeys and I led our horses to the track, now completely surrounded by folks from Pinebrook.

"Riders up! Riders up!" the same booming voice from earlier announced.

I breathed in deeply, then out. I mounted Grace. *God, give me speed. Help me win the money that I need.*

We lined up along the starting line by a red flag staked in the earth. The lively crowd cheered and waved white handkerchiefs while the horses stood at the line, anxious, flicking their tails. The horse next to me stomped, impatient, but its jockey quickly regained its composure.

I leaned down and whispered, "Godspeed, Grace. We can do this." I rubbed her neck to reassure her.

An older man in a vest and suit walked out to the dirt track and raised a pistol. "On your mark... get set..."

I tightened my grip on the reins, the leather cutting into my calloused flesh. "For Keme," I whispered.

"Go!"

The gun shot rang out, and the horses were off.

I had forgotten how much I loved racing. The feeling of invincibility was addictive. For that moment, nothing mattered except the wind whipping past me and the rhythmic cantering of the horses' hooves.

The sun beat down on us as we raced in wide circles. Black Magic was no doubt the fastest horse on the track, but Grace and I were on her tail. We gained on them with every second.

Black Magic's jockey peered over his shoulder. He seemed unnerved to see me so close. "Come on, old girl!" he yelled in frustration. "Come on!"

The other horses were an eternity behind us. It felt like we were racing one on one, black against white, light against darkness. I could tell Black Magic was winded by the slight change in her gait, but Grace was stronger than ever.

Slowly but surely, we started to pass Black Magic. In the mess of blurry images, I saw Irving's face by the side of the track. He was dumbfounded at the sight of me, at the idea that *my* horse, out of all the fine, well-bred horses present, had a chance to beat his prize horse.

We did it. *Grace* did it. She passed Black Magic.

Something strange happened. The whole crowd grew silent, so that the only sounds were those of the horses' hooves.

We'd circled almost the complete five laps by then. I leaned in closer to Grace's white mane and focused on the scarlet flag, the finish marker, waving in all of its glory. *Almost there!* I gripped the reins tighter and tighter.

If Estella was watching, she'd be in awe of us, but I couldn't let myself think of her any longer. *Focus*, I told myself. *Focus.*

The moment Grace raced past the red flag, Black Magic followed.

I'd won first place.

The silent crowd broke out in wild applause and cheering, but I didn't care what they thought. I'd won the race. I *knew* Grace had it in her the whole time.

The other horses finished and their riders jumped down, defeated.

The owners hopped the fence and met their horses, staring at me with expressions of intrigue and utter shock. I'd slipped in right under their noses, a perfect dark horse.

Estella's father looked at me with something else, something closer to disdain.

Before I knew it, a crowd surrounded me, congratulating me and admiring Grace. It felt so odd to be in the middle of a crowd that had nothing to do with me sparking a fight.

The same man who'd fired the gun approached and adjusted his gray mustache. "May I present the winners with their cash prizes?" First he gave an envelope to the third place winner, then to Estella's father, and finally to me.

I stared at the envelope in my hands. Could this be enough to pay for Keme's operation?

Before I could open it, Mary's arms were around my neck. "That was incredible!" she said.

Art appeared and hit me in the shoulder. "You done good after all!" he said, then raised his eyebrows. "What'd I tell you? Ladies love a guy with money." He laughed.

But the only girl I cared about was nowhere to be found. I scanned the crowd without shame. Why wasn't she here? Henry patted Estella's father on the back, attempting to console him, but where was *she*?

Irving finally seemed to notice me. His eyes grew baleful as he excused himself from Henry and made his way to me. "I thought I told you to get out of town," he said, and took hold of my shoulder.

I threw his hand off of me. "And I told *you* I had loose ends to tie up." I waved the envelope of cash.

The crowd grew even bigger, and to keep up appearances, Irving reached out his hand to shake mine. "Well then, congratulations are in order." His face muscles tightened; a single eye twitched.

"Thank you, sir." I sent a glare back with my words.

"See to it that you don't dally much longer, boy," he continued in a lower voice. "My patience is only so strong." Then he turned and walked away, brushing off his shoulders as he went. His jockey followed through the crowd, leading Black Magic.

After a few minutes, the people around us started to leave, I assumed to collect their winnings. I was almost alone with my thoughts and my envelope of cash.

I led Grace back to the stables to return her number four. When I went inside, I found it empty. The freshly hayed floor was now trodden down and in need of a good mucking. I saw a trough of water still full enough for Grace to drink and led her to it.

Finally alone, I opened the envelope. My fingers counted each bill until I reached the back of the envelope.

Twenty-five dollars. I let out an audible sigh of relief and rubbed my face hard. It was *more* than I needed. Keme could have his operation, and I had gotten the money for it all on my own, as promised.

An older man in a wide-brimmed hat entered the stables carrying a leather satchel. "Excuse me," he said, out of breath, "but are you Bodaway?"

My eyebrows crowded together. "I am."

The man reached into the satchel and pulled out a letter. "I was sent to deliver this urgent message to you in person. I arrived just before the races, but it wasn't possible to get to you until now. Just when I had you in my sights, you took off." He huffed as he handed the paper to me. "I pray it's good news," he said, then nodded once and left me.

My hands trembled as I held the letter. It sent chills through my veins. I carefully opened the envelope and pulled out its contents.

*Dear Bodaway,*

*We have no words to express just how sorry we are that it is necessary to send this letter. Earlier this week, your brother was taken ill with smallpox. He tried to fight off the disease, but he proved too weak, and passed suddenly in his sleep from the fever. Never forget you always have a family here. Rely on God for strength. We do not always understand His ways.*

*With our deepest condolences,*
*William and Margaret*

Bile quickly rose in my throat and I couldn't stop from vomiting. I didn't bother to wipe my lips, every fiber of my being burned. I shook my head, "This isn't real," I whispered to myself. "This isn't happening." But the letter was real and it was still in my hands. I crumpled its contents and threw it to the stable floor, among the vomit and horse dung.

Before I realized it, I was running. I didn't even know where I was running to. Everything around me was blurry and insignificant. I ran even though no amount of running could help me escape my new reality.

I didn't know how much time passed, but eventually I came to my senses in a place I knew well.

The old cabin in the forest.

I stared at my fists, then let out a cry that was more like a scream and punched the closest tree like it was the reason my brother was dead. "Why!" I screamed. "God! Here I am crying out to you, but where are you, huh?" I grabbed my hair and sunk to the dirt at my feet. "Where were you when my brother was sick? When he needed you most?" I waited, looking up. No reply. I was alone.

I'd never cried like this before. My mother had even used to talk about how I'd never cry as a child. Yet now I could hear myself grieving. I felt an ache so deep inside me that it couldn't be ignored. My fists were bloody and mangled, but they reminded me I wasn't dreaming.

"I should have been there," I whispered. "I should have been there!"

I screamed these words so loud that a few frightened birds flew off above my head.

\*\*\*

## Estella

Grace had won the races. She'd overcome all obstacles, and Bodaway had earned the money for his brother. I needed to see him, to tell him everything, but after his victory I watched him escape the crowd, heading for the stables as soon as he was able.

Henry had left the races by then, consoling my father, while my mother discussed final touches with Alice about my impending wedding.

The crowds shortly dispersed, leaving me a clear path to the stables. I passed between ladies in colorful dresses, every one seeming to be talking about Grace.

The stables were dark and empty. I hoped I hadn't missed my chance to speak with Bodaway. I held onto my hat as I passed through the doorway.

Yes, Grace stood in her stall… but Bodaway was nowhere to be found. "Where's Bodaway, Grace?" I looked around. "He must be fetching a treat for his prize horse."

I moved towards Grace's stall when the smell of stomach bile reached me. I was careful to step away from the mess, and a nearby crumpled paper caught my eye. Curious, I removed my gloves with my teeth, smoothed the paper, and read its contents.

A massive lump formed in my throat.

I knew I had to find Bodaway. He needed me. My hands fumbled with the stall latch, but finally I opened it. Throwing my arms around Grace, I whispered, out of breath, "Take me to Bodaway." She could understand me, she had to.

Using the edge of the water trough as a step, I mounted her in one swift, unlady-like movement, and she was off, running as fast as her tired feet could take her.

We dashed through the small crowd of people still left milling about from the races, including my own mother.

"Estella! What on Earth!"

I looked quite the sight, I'm sure, riding away on a horse that didn't belong to me in my expensive new clothes. My matching hat promptly flew from my head and disappeared behind me.

The sky clouded over as though it might rain, and the warm air suddenly felt cooler. Once we cut away from the main road, I recognized where we were headed. We rode faster than I'd ever ridden. Grace's canter was much smoother than any gallop could ever be, but still, I braced myself and kept a firm grip on the reins to stay put. Branches snagged my sleeves, and my hair tumbled out of its fastenings.

Finally, through the wooded trail, I saw the cabin in the distance, and, just beyond the wood pile and under a tree, Bodaway.

I slid off Grace before she even came to a complete stop, stumbling as I caught my balance.

I didn't say anything. I *couldn't*. Bodaway sat under the tree alone, bloodied fists and head resting on his knees. He seemed unaware of my presence.

Cautiously, I approached him. I felt as though I were sneaking up on a sleeping bear. When I was close enough, I reached my hand out gently and touched his shoulder. "Bodaway," I said softly.

He whipped his arm away and glared up at me. "Don't touch me!"

His eyes were so black and wild that I jumped back and struck the next tree. "I'm sorry!" I said, my words floundering in the air. "I just found the letter, and I know what happened. I know about your brother."

He didn't lift his head. "My brother is dead because of me. He died thinking I abandoned him." Bodaway looked up. "God abandoned him the *one time* he needed help."

I moved closer to him again and crouched down. "It's not your fault that your brother died." I swiped a strand of his hair from his swollen eyes. "You can't blame yourself."

"What are you even *talking* about? You don't know a thing about what I'm feeling. I can't even take a single breath without being reminded that I'm alive and Keme's dead. I could've stopped this if I'd only been there."

Tears pricked my eyes. I tried to hold them back. "I'm not trying to understand," I said. "I'm trying to comfort you with what I know to be true."

Bodaway's face twisted and he scoffed. "The truth is far from comforting." He stood and wiped his bloody fists on his clothes, then walked over to Grace. "I'm leaving this place. There's nothing keeping me here anymore." He watched me with empty eyes.

"What do you mean there's nothing keeping you here?" I looked away, down at the ground, almost too scared to ask. "What about… me?"

His expression grew angrier. "Look at me, Estella! Is this what you want? I don't have anything to offer you, no money, no home, no family. I can't be what you want, and I *won't* change for you! I won't change for anyone. You talk like you hate your life here, but you'll never leave it. You fit right in." He shook his head and laughed in disbelief. "Trust me, this is what's best for everyone." He leapt onto Grace and looked down at me with an expression that told me he was taking one last look.

"Stop it!" I screamed. "Stop this, you know I don't care about any of that!" I reached up, offering my hands.

He met my gaze. "Yeah? Then come with me." I pulled my hands away, hesitating.

"That's what I thought." His tone was cold, unsurprised.

"Things are even more complicated than I'd ever imagined," I whispered, trying not to provoke him further.

"Well, like I said before, there's nothing keeping *me* here."

"Where will you go?" I shouted, realizing my voice was frantic. "You're not thinking clearly, Bodaway. You're grieving!"

"No, this is the clearest I've thought in a long time. Don't you see? I'll go out West, away from everyone." He wrapped the reins around his hands.

"So you're just going to abandon me?"

He shook his head and scoffed again. "You can't spend your whole life waiting for someone to save you, least of all me. I couldn't save Keme, and I'm not going to save you."

Before I could respond, he commanded Grace to run.

She did.

I grasped at the hollow place within my chest as I struggled for air. It was as though Bodaway had left with the real me, leaving my shell behind. I stood there for a long time holding his letter. It was the ghost of what had been, and a reminder of what *could* have been.

A raindrop touched my face, then another, and another, until it was pouring.

It was just me alone with the rain and the trees.

# CHAPTER TWENTY-TWO

## Estella

I was restless that night. Every passing moment brought me closer to my wedding the next morning. Though I hadn't spoken of my true past since discovering the circumstances of my birth, the revelation had hardly left my thoughts for a moment.

Because of my absurd behavior in running off with Grace after the races, Hannah had been given strict instruction to stay with me all through the night. She had prepared a bed of blankets and pillows along my floor, and seemed to be sleeping just fine.

I sighed, crossed my arms, and willed my eyes to remain shut as I attempted to count sheep. It was no use when my thoughts inevitably turned to Bodaway.

After tossing about for quite some time, I realized I wouldn't sleep a single moment. Unrest gnawed too hungrily at my stomach. I peeled the blanket from me, rose, and stepped carefully over Hannah on my way to my wash stand.

I pressed the back of my hand to my damp forehead, then poured a glass of water. I took a greedy mouthful, its coolness sliding down my throat. My distress made me weak, susceptible to wandering thoughts. Each time I closed my eyes, Bodaway stood there with Grace, staring at me blankly. It was a most unsettling feeling.

Bodaway had made me feel like I could do anything, he made me feel safe. With him gone for good, I had no choice but to reconcile with the nothingness that was all I had left. I'd been concerned with everyone's expectations around me for so very long, but it took the revelation of my birth to realize *I* was the only one getting in my way.

My heart sank as I peered out my window. Our land was cloaked in darkness, but I imagined I could see all the way to the empty stable beyond the fields, where Grace had onced lived.

Bodaway hated me now, and I didn't know what to do—he certainly seemed to think there was nothing more to be done. My eyes drifted to the sliver of the moon above. It made me wonder if he was looking at the same moon tonight and thinking of me. I returned to my bed and sat on its edge.

A soft stirring sounded from the floor, then a breathy yawn.

Hannah sat up, rubbed her eyes, and noticed I was awake. "Can't sleep?" She seemed nervous as she stood in her long linen dressing gown and moved to my vanity, where she lit a single candle.

I'd had plenty of time to think since the truth came out, to try to imagine what I would have done in Hannah's position. I really had nothing to be angry about regarding Hannah's choice. She had done what she had to do to survive and to provide for me.

"I haven't slept a bit all night," I said softly. I patted the empty place on my bed, inviting her to join me.

Hannah came and sat beside me, the flicker of her candle danced on the wall. "I suppose this gives me an opportunity to explain myself, seeing as this may be our last time to speak privately."

I nodded, but said nothing.

"Estella, I don't know where to begin..." Hannah went silent for a moment. "First of all, I want you to know that this was *never* the life that I intended to lead with my own flesh and blood."

I stared into the candle's fragile flame.

"When your father died and left me a widow, with child, I had very few choices. I needed work, and the people employing pregnant, unmarried maids were few and far between. I love you, and I always wished life could've been different. I know you're angry with me—"

I cut her off. "I've just learned the startling news that I'm not who I thought I was. I'm not angry, not now. I *was*... What I mean to say is I understand why you did what you had to, but it's a lot to unravel right now."

"I've always thought of you as a mother. More so than... Rachelle." I forced myself to use her first name. It felt right. "What do I do?" I continued, staring at my true mother in desperation. "Hannah, I can't go through with this! I can't marry Henry." I pulled my nightgown off my shoulders and showed her the faded bruises left by Henry.

Hannah's eyes welled up. She took me into her arms, held me close. She caressed my hair and told me everything would work out for good. I didn't know if she was right, but I had no doubt Hannah loved me as her daughter.

I'd spent my whole life believing that it was my duty to become an exemplary lady of high society. I never believed I had any other option, so I accepted things as they were.

But now, the imagined family obligation had released its grip, and I felt oddly free—shaken and unstable, but free.

I had so many questions to ask Hannah, but no idea where to begin. How could I form a question around my entire life? How could she tell me about the person I would've been, the life I would've led? What about the people—the family—that I never knew?

She wiped a tear from her cheek and sniffled as she pulled something small and golden from her pocket.

"What's this?" I asked as she set the circle of gold in my hand.

An engraving on the back read "Delta," and she ran her fingers over it as she answered. "This was a gift meant for you from your father." She smiled with blue eyes twinkling, as though fondly remembering the past. "We had a feeling that you'd be a girl. I don't know how to explain it, but the good Lord revealed it to us. Before he passed, we'd settled on the name Delta. Where the river meets the ocean."

She looked me in the eyes and pressed her hand over mine, the golden piece inside both.

My true name was Delta. I liked it much better than Estella.

I pressed a golden notch on the object's side, expecting to see a ticking clock inside, but instead I found the face of a compass.

"Your father was a good man," said Hannah. "Very thoughtful. Seke was his name. He had dark, striking eyes, and the kindest face you ever saw. The look on my poor mother's face when I told her I was going to marry an Indian man... but nothing would stop us. We were in love." She shook her head and laughed, then turned serious again. "He was so excited for you to get here, so excited. He couldn't wait to be your father."

"What was he like, my father?"

Hannah's face lit up. "You remind me so much of him." She laughed again. "He spent so much time in the woods. Hunting, fishing, praying. He was a spirited soul, that one. He always knew *exactly* what he wanted, and would work at it until he got it. I admired that so much about him."

"How did he die?" I held the compass in both shaky hands.

"He was a wild one. Never could tell him to settle down. He had the biggest heart, and the strongest will." Hannah's tired eyes looked away as she lost herself in thought. "He died a very noble death.

"Back when we were young, we lived in the outskirts of Concord. Massachusetts, that is. That was where we met, too. I was working as a maid, and he'd been in town as a farm laborer. A few months after we married, he agreed to help build the new schoolhouse in town."

She cleared her throat. "I still remember the last time I saw him. The way his eyes lit up when he smiled back at me in the humble cabin he built for us. He told me he'd see me for supper, and I told him to be safe. But... that day there was a fire at the school they were building." The orange candlelight lit up Hannah's eyes. "The whole frame had caught fire before Seke even arrived."

I reached over and took her hands in mine. "There were two children trapped inside," she continued with apparent difficulty. "The other men were trying as best they could to put the fire out, but Seke didn't hesitate to burst through the doors himself and try to save the children. He... well, he never came back out." Hannah let out a small sob. "The flames took him. I didn't hear about it until the other men came to my doorstep that night with a body wrapped in blankets." She shook her head. "I'll never forget that pain."

I rubbed her hands with mine and pulled her close. "Thank you for sharing this with me," I whispered.

"It's important you know how much your father loved you. I had to move far, far away after his passing. That's when I came to Boston and met your family." She suddenly closed the compass in my hand.

"This is a lot to learn at once. I know you're confused and feel lost, but you can never *be* lost if you have a compass. You'll always be able to find your way." She raised my hands and kissed them.

Once she released me, I studied the compass, turning it over and over in my hands, tracing each detail of the engraving with my fingers.

Hannah pushed a strand of hair behind my ears. "You won't be marrying Henry Hamilton tomorrow, will you?"

I shook my head. "I need to do this. I need to leave Pinebrook, Hannah... Mother." I smiled. "Come with me, please."

Her look was so full of love. "I wish I could, my sweets, but this is my home. You need to discover who *you* are, Delta."

That was the first time anyone had called me by my true name. It felt natural to my ears.

She was right. I had to find out who I was on my own, who I was without the Wellstone name and fortune. I needed to beat my own path and make my own choices. "Thank you." A tear fell from my cheek.

Hannah wiped that tear away. "I suppose you should pack lightly. Time is of the essence." Her voice broke. "Just remember your compass, and you'll always find your way home." We shared one last, tight embrace, then she rose and went to the chest at the foot of my bed to fetch a satchel.

I filled it, taking only what I needed. A few dresses, some warm layers, and my compass. I recalled the moonstone hairpin that Hannah had given me—though not essential, I tucked it carefully inside the satchel.

"I'll never speak of this to anyone," said Hannah as she latched the bag for me. "I swear it. Go on now! You'll want to be gone before first light." Her eyes watered again. "I'm proud of you. Remember that."

"Thank you," I whispered. I looked around at my bedroom one last time, everything right where I had left it. In a peculiar way, it didn't feel as though I were leaving anything behind.

My father, Irving, and mother, Rachelle, had proven over and over that I couldn't measure up to their standards. I'm sure they hoped my marriage—only hours away, as far as they knew—would change that. My stomach knotted as I thought about Alice Hamilton. Had she truly poisoned her own grandchild to uphold her family name and influence?

Bodaway was all I had left in the world, and I might not even have *him* anymore.

I hooked my bag over my shoulder and gave Hannah one small nod before sneaking away from that house for the very last time.

\*\*\*

Sunrise was still a good hour away, and it was in my best interest to be on my way before then. I needed to find Bodaway, and the only person who would have an idea where to find him was that friend he'd been staying with all summer. Art, I thought I remembered. But there was still someone I had to see before I could accomplish anything else.

Lillian. I couldn't leave without seeing her one last time.

I took a path through the woods that would cut onto the main road. It was almost the same one I had followed to see Bodaway the night of my engagement, but I turned left instead of right at the fork. My dress caught in the trail brush now and again, but I carelessly pulled it free, unconcerned with tears or stains.

I hadn't the slightest desire for the finer things anymore. It wasn't in my blood, as had been ingrained into my mind for as long as I could remember. *Freedom* was in my blood, pulsing through my veins with every step further from the place I once called home. The beating in my chest and the coolness of night air against my ears made the half hour to town seem barely a moment.

Owls' calls haunted the forest as I approached the opening to the main road. Lillian would be fast asleep, but I imagined either Nellie or Sarah would be awake to keep a watchful eye on Lillian and the baby. My feet were quiet on the empty streets, but my breathing seemed to echo off the stone walls of the town buildings. I prayed that I might remain undetected.

*There.* I could see it. Lights in the windows, beckoning to me. Encouraged, I ran recklessly up the long drive, the gravel scratched beneath my steps. I held my few belongings tightly under one arm and rapped on the front door.

Silence followed, then the scuttle of tiny feet, and the door cracked open. Nellie's confused face appeared, and she ushered me in quickly. "Miss! What brings you here at this hour?" Her blond hair was tied back and she wore a loose-fitting nightcap.

"I can't explain it all right now, but I must see Lillian. I *must.*"

"Go on up then, she's awake with the lad. The poor child's a colicky one!"

I was already hurrying up the stairs. I had no time to lose, and I still needed to see Art.

Lillian's door was open. "Lillian?" I whispered, inviting myself inside.

She sat in a rocking chair by the empty hearth, her baby resting in her arms. "Estella!" she exclaimed. "What on earth?"

I rushed to her side and sat at her feet. "Listen, Lillian, I know it's late, but I had to see you one last time. You can't tell anyone that we've spoken or where I'm headed."

"You're leaving? Now? Goodness, Estella, where?"

I pulled away the hood of my cloak and let my hair fall about. "I'm not going to marry Henry. Instead, I plan to find Bodaway just as soon as I can leave."

Lillian's doe eyes grew two sizes. "The Indian man?" she whispered, turning away from the baby.

"Yes, the Indian man. There's… too much to explain, and not enough time. But I needed to see you one last time. We can write to each other, but I'm not quite sure where I will end up."

Lillian thought a moment before speaking. "I'm leaving too, you know, to England. Mother has family there, which means we'll have a place to stay, and a chance for a new life! Out of Alice's reach." She paused. "I'll miss you greatly, and I should be very happy to hear from you."

I took one of her hands and kissed it. "I'm glad for you, and I wish you every happiness in the world."

"Here." She pointed to her vanity. "There's a paper with my new English address on it. Take it, so that when you've settled you know where to reach me."

I found it, then folded it in half and tucked it into my belongings.

Lillian had a clock over her mantle. I had already stayed longer than I ought to have. "Lillian," I said softly, and went to her one last time. Her babe slept soundly, his little lips puckered peacefully. "I pray the Lord be with you in your travels, and that He keeps you and your family safe." I caressed the babe's head.

"Thomas." She looked up at me. "I named him Thomas, after my late father."

"Then, God bless Thomas." My lips spread into a smile, then I placed them in a kiss on Lillian's cheek. "Now, I really must go."

"Go," she said, "and find Bodaway. I swear I'll never give you up. God bless you both." She spoke in a whisper, clearly holding back a quiver in her voice.

I pulled my hood back over my head and departed.

\*\*\*

Once I was back in the street, it didn't take long to reach the mill housing. Instead of walking around the downtown green, as I had before, I passed straight through the middle of it. The experience was strangely liberating.

Lillian had given me the closure I'd needed. She was leaving too, and she was going to be very happy. Everything good about my life here would be gone in a matter of weeks, and then I would be alone, trapped as Henry's wife.

*I am leaving.* I reassured myself. *Even if Art won't help me, I'm leaving.*

As I rounded the corner shops, the mill housing came into view. Some men were still awake, judging by the lights, but other rooms were in complete darkness. To my relief and surprise, muted light came from Art's room, but I still felt uneasy. What if he wasn't there? What if he wouldn't help me?

Slowly, I approached the door and used my ungloved fist to give three hard knocks. There was some rustling before the door opened to Art's surprised face.

"I'm so sorry to burden you this early," I said, "but it is *very* urgent."

He must have seen the desperation in my eyes, for he stepped aside and let me in. "You'll have to be quiet, my roommates are still asleep." He looked over at the three other men passed out and snoring, then motioned to a chair at the room's dining table. "Would you like to sit?"

I smiled and took my seat.

"So," he said, sitting next to me, "it's no secret you're supposed to be getting married today." He glanced at the bag by my feet.

"I am not." I cleared my throat. "Art, I have to know exactly where Bodaway is."

Art studied me with a look of concern. "He went to be with his brother in Maine. At least, that's what he told me yesterday, before the races. I never did get to say a proper goodbye. The rotten, no-good elbow ran off right after the races." He smiled.

I shook my head. "Not anymore. He received news that his brother died and then told me he'd head west. I'd hoped you might have a more precise location for me."

"God rest his soul." Art rested his face in his hands. "Then your guess is as good as mine. Maybe better."

"But where could he be *heading* out West? Art, I need to find him." I reached over and grasped Art's hand. "I should have made this decision a long time ago. I've never been so sure of myself in all my life."

Art pulled away and rose from his chair. "I told you, I don't know where he'd run off to. He mentioned his father out West a couple times. Maybe he's headed out to join him." Art placed his hands on his hips. "If any smart human being's heading west, they're joining the wagon train."

"Wagon train? I thought the trails started in Missouri."

"He's probably with a group starting in the Northeast, traveling to Missouri together. Safer that way. But this whole scenario depends on *if* he's with the wagon train at all."

I laughed, relieved. "But that's it! You just have to be right!"

Art didn't mirror my enthusiasm. "I hope for your sake I'm right, Estella."

"He only left just yesterday! He can't be that far!"

At my raised voice, a man tossed over once in his bed, then continued snoring to himself.

I could hardly remember how to breathe right, let alone remember to be quiet. The only thing on my mind was finding Bodaway.

Art rolled his eyes at me. "There's no way I'm letting you wander about God's Earth on your own." He shook his head like he couldn't believe what he was about to say. "I'm going with you, Estella, and don't you try and stop me."

I jumped up from my seat, and threw my arms around him. "Oh thank you, Art, thank you! But… Delta. My real name is Delta."

He looked confused, but seemed to recognize the seriousness in my tone. "OK, then, Delta."

Art crossed the room to a small table by his bedside, then took something from a metal box on a table beside it. He returned to me and held out a silver coin. "Eventually, you might need it. I know it's not much, but Bodaway would want me to help you. You know, if he was thinking straight." He smiled crookedly.

I smiled. "Thank you so much, Art. You have no idea what this means to me." I grabbed my bag and stood. "Now let's hurry."

"Woah there, hold on." Art raised his hands. "How do you expect us to *get* anywhere?"

My heart dropped. We had no horse, and the sun was beginning to rise. My family would soon discover I was gone.

I could see Art's mind working. "I have a thought," he said at last. "Mary works at the McNerry farm, and I'll bet you she could loan us a horse."

My face twisted with concern. "You mean *steal* a horse?"

Art laughed. "Well, I'll bring it back."

At this point, what other options did we have? "Fine," I said.

Art put on his cap and a thin coat that hung by the door. "Let's go."

\*\*\*

We began our way down my usual trail through the woods, but veered to the right after a quarter mile.

Farm life started early, but Mary would probably still be asleep.

Art pointed through the woods. "Farm's just through those trees up there." He held onto his cap as a gust of wind brushed past us.

I wrapped my arms around my body, bracing myself against the sudden chill.

We approached the very same barn we'd danced in not long ago, but it seemed different now. The whole farm was at rest, asleep.

Art turned to me, his breathing short from our brisk walk. "You, my lady, are going to have to go in and wake Mary."

"Me? Why me?"

"She's fast asleep in the loft with two other girls. I can't very well barge in on a couple of ladies in their nighties—"

"Well, what am I supposed to say? She barely knows me!"

"Just the truth! We need a horse, and we need one now." Art opened one of the barn doors and gave me a small shove. "But you'd best hurry." he pointed at the sky streaked with traces of daylight.

I swallowed hard and headed inside the barn.

The animals were in their stalls, and I was met with the scents of fresh hay and manure. I let the recollection of my days spent with Bodaway tending to Grace embolden me, and made straight for the rickety wooden ladder at the back of the barn.

I climbed one loose, shifting rung at a time, telling myself not to look down, but to my dismay, my eyes wandered to the alarming distance between me and the barn's dirt floor. I tore my focus from the ground to the top of the loft. I was close. The wood was rough beneath my palms, digging into my skin.

"What on earth are *you* doing here?"

That surprising voice prompted a gasp from my lips.

Mary was peering over the edge of the loft, her orange braid dangling over her shoulder.

"Hello," I said, staring straight up at her.

"If you were trying to be stealthy, it isn't working. You're breathing louder than a sick cow."

"I'm sorry, I really am, but I have a favor to ask of you. Mary, I know that you don't know me well…" I took a breath, trying to keep my balance on the ladder. "But I need a horse."

She crossed her arms over her white slip nightgown. "Why would I hand over a horse that doesn't belong to me when I've got no idea what you intend to do with her?"

"Mary," Art called from the open barn doorway, "I'll bring' em back, I promise."

Mary looked past me and saw Art. She hesitated a moment, then said, "Keep your voices down, you'll wake the whole barn!" She turned, likely to check on the girls sleeping behind her, and then looked back at me. "Watch out," she warned. "I'm coming down." She began descending the ladder, forcing me to back down at an uncomfortable speed.

My hands trembled by the time we reached the bottom, and Mary couldn't contain a snicker at my inexperience.

With Mary awake, Art apparently felt comfortable enough to enter the barn. He pointed to a brown beauty of a horse, sturdy and tall. "How about this one? Looks fast."

Mary sighed and shook her head. "You come in here, to my place of work, and start making demands…" But she was already fastening a leather bridle to the horse of Art's choosing. "I'm not letting a saddle out of this barn, so you'd better get used to riding bareback. Mary muttered. I swallowed hard.

She led the horse outside and we followed close behind. Art shot me a triumphant smile, which Mary caught as she set the lead in his hand. "You bring him back, you hear?" She looked at me, then at Art. "My neck is at risk for whatever little plan you two thought up."

"It's for John," said Art. "We've got to try and catch him on the wagon train… if he *is* on the wagon train."

Mary rolled her eyes. "Well then, you should've started with that. What are you waiting for? Get on with it!"

Art hugged her tightly, then promptly helped me onto the massive brown horse.

"He's perfect," I said to Mary, full of gratitude.

"Take care of him, please." Mary ran her hand along the horse's flank, but somehow I knew she was talking about Bodaway.

"I will," I reassured her.

Art situated himself on the horse in front of me. "You sure you're ready?"

I took a deep breath, but this time without hesitation. "Go," I said, and wrapped my arms around him.

Then we were off through the field and away from the main roads. Every mile we moved away from Pinebrook felt like another burden lifted from my back.

I left Estella behind, but I took Delta with me to find a new life.

# CHAPTER TWENTY-THREE

## Bodaway

Every year around this time, Keme and I used to watch a group of optimistic travelers pack up their belongings and head for the Oregon Trail in Missouri. Even my father agreed it was always safest to travel in groups. The long journey west could prove difficult, and traveling together could mean the difference between life and death. It wasn't a journey for the faint of heart.

My hope was if I rode close to the Connecticut River, I might be able to catch this year's group of travelers and join them.

By the end of my first day, I'd traveled over forty miles, endured the heat of the summer day, and led Grace across the river before reaching their camp.

The travelers welcomed me with open arms, overflowing with generosity and hospitality like I'd never known. The summer evening set in, and all the travelers set up camp for the night, laughing, enjoying each other's company, and cooking a fine dinner.

The travelers' leader, Abraham, made it his mission to befriend me. He and his wife, Catherine, had traveled for weeks already. They began as far north as one could in the states, and intended on making it all the way to Oregon Country.

Being from Maine, I couldn't help but feel a small connection to them. Of course, these days, thinking of Maine only reminded me of my loss. A sharp pain tugged at an empty space within me.

"Now," laughed Abraham, "you look like you've started your fair share of fires." He dropped an armload of firewood between us.

"One or two, at least." I crouched to the ground where Abe had arranged stones into a fire pit. With a heavy stick beside the pit, I raked the coals that had been smoking throughout the day. New glowing embers surfaced and their heat radiated at once.

Abe picked through the firewood until he came across a few smaller, dry pieces to use as kindling. "Once you get those flames going again, maybe I can catch us a nice fat squirrel for supper." He said this to tease his young wife, who obviously didn't find his jokes amusing.

"I'm afraid stew and cornbread will have to do," she said as she hung a clothesline that ran from their wagon to the evergreen next to us where I'd tied Grace for the night.

Abraham smiled a huge, toothy grin. "That's right fine by me. I'm about starved to death."

By the wrinkles under Abraham's eyes and the gray streaks in his hair, I'd have placed him at about fifty years old, but his young bride couldn't have been older than twenty-five. They seemed happy, though, like two halves of a whole. They relied on each other. They had to in order to make their westward journey, and that kind of reliance was a foreign concept to me.

I picked some dried grass from around the firepit and tucked it carefully around the kindling. I crouched closer to the glowing coals and blew on them until promising flames consumed the dry grass and licked the edges of the firewood.

"That should get things going again," I said as I sat up, pleased I was able to contribute.

Abraham's massive hand closed over my shoulder. "I appreciate it, Bodaway." He sat down in the grass and sighed. "You'll never see a more beautiful sky and all its glory than when you're sleeping right out under it."

I sat next to him and looked up as a few fireflies blinked by. The stars were too many to number, silently illuminating, while the moon rose at its own slow pace.

Catherine returned from their wagon and set a small pot over the fire. "I've heard the sky in Wyoming is something incredible." She poured a pitcher of water into the pot, then uncovered a bowl of meat she'd probably cooked the night before and emptied it into the pot. She stirred in a bit of salt and some kind of ground spices. "When do you think we'll get there, to Wyoming?" Catherine asked her husband.

Abraham leaned back. "That's a good question. Not for many months, to be sure. Once we make it to Missouri, we'll stay there until about April. Timing is everything."

Abraham told me all about himself for the next hour or so, which thankfully allowed me to offer as little information about myself as possible. He told me his plan to build a great log home and work his own land.

He'd raised cattle before, and he'd do it again. Someone had told him about the wild horses—hundreds and hundreds of them, he said—out West that were ripe for the taking.

Catherine seemed to enjoy listening to her husband dream about their future. She mentioned, as she prepared the meal, how she and

Abraham wanted to start a family once they'd settled, a comment which sent Abraham on another tangent.

He wanted ten children—good working hands, he said—but Catherine only laughed. She told her husband to consider the long journey that was ahead of them before anything else.

Finally, the moon hanging high, Abe asked me a direct question. "So, what do you think? You in for the whole of it? All two thousand miles?"

"I'm looking to be as far from this place as possible," I said, then regretted it. I'd accidentally sparked their interest.

"Why's that?" Catherine asked, seeming genuinely concerned.

I cleared my throat and tried not to make eye contact. "Oh, the usual. Just looking for a fresh start."

Abraham's eyebrows crowded, one eye slightly droopier than the other. "Where'd you say you came from again?"

"Just now? I came from a small town in New Hampshire. Before that, Maine. I spent most of my life there." I stopped myself from opening up further. "What about you two? What's your story?"

Abraham took his wife's delicate hand. "Well, my first wife passed away about two years ago. She... passed during childbirth. The young one didn't pull through, neither." He cleared his throat, staring into the fire. "But, then I met this lovely lady here."

His wife smiled at him like he was her whole world.

"Well," Abe continued, "we got married about a month ago."

I couldn't help but notice that Catherine appeared to come from money while Abraham seemed like he came from an entirely different place. She held herself with poise and spoke cleanly even though she'd come from Maine. Abe's accent was thicker and he had a rougher-looking exterior. It was hard to imagine how their paths had crossed.

"I thought Abe was the most interesting and intriguing man I'd ever met," said Catherine. "When my family didn't approve of our courtship, we knew we'd have to elope."

Abraham nodded. "Yup, we just took off and got ourselves married before God in a tiny little church." He laughed. "I don't think she's got any regrets just yet!"

They smiled at each other, clearly in love. Why had it been so easy for Catherine to leave everything she knew for love, for the unknown?

"What about you?" asked Abraham. "You've got a woman?"

"No," I said too quickly. "It's just me."

Catherine portioned the stew and handed me a bowl. "A strong, capable man like you won't have any trouble settling down out West." She smiled knowingly.

I took the bowl gratefully, but ignored her comment.

"This here is why I married you in the first place." Abraham spoke through a mouth filled with stew. "Who else is your equal? I've never tasted a better meal."

"Honestly, Abe, I know this isn't exactly *fine dining*, but you have no manners." She laughed and threw a napkin at him.

Abraham took it and rubbed his hands and face clean. "Eat up, boy. We've an early start in the morning. A couple of my oxen broke away from camp. The darn things've been living off the land all day." He shook his head. "You, me, and a couple of men'll ride off in the morning and spend the day attempting to wrangle the little fellers."

"Won't we be packing up camp tomorrow?" I asked.

"Nah, I think we'll let the horses and cattle rest here another day or two. That'll give us time to gather more supplies—it's good practice. I don't have to tell you what could happen if we run out of water on the desert trails."

"Seems like a fair plan." I nodded to my new friends and lifted the bowl to my mouth, drinking down every bit of stew.

\*\*\*

Later that night, after everyone had retired to their wagons, I laid under the stars, alone with my thoughts. I'd have to buy myself a wagon, if I was going all the way out West. I'd be worlds away from everything here... from Estella.

Everything I'd left behind still felt so raw, and I could barely think of Keme without a sharp sting pricking at my throat. Maybe I'd been too severe with Estella when she was just trying to comfort me.

No. I did what *had* to be done. She was probably already married to that no-good, glove-wearing flapdoodle by now. I turned over on the grassy earth and forced my eyes shut for the rest of the night.

# CHAPTER TWENTY-FOUR

### Delta

Art and I had traveled almost a whole day, but I still hadn't had any second thoughts.

Though I didn't doubt my resolve, I still found myself quite anxious about what must be happening back in Pinebrook. I swallowed hard, thinking of the chaos that must have surely ensued when my parents discovered I had fled. What had happened that morning? I hoped I would never find out.

The woods around us were thick, thicker than those I'd known back in Pinebrook. Evergreens loomed above us, their webbed branches blocked the blue sky from view. The air was fresh and new in my lungs and pushed its way pleasantly through my unpinned hair.

"If I'm right," said Art from the front of the horse, "and I almost always am, we should be cutting onto some well-traveled trails very soon. They're called the Dusties."

We'd been riding across unmarked ground for hours. "How will we ever catch up with them?" I sighed, feeling hopeless.

"Wagon trains travel at a nice, slow pace all day. Even make camp for days at a time. You and I, now, we're traveling with constant speed and minimal stopping." He brought the horse from a trot to a walk. "With that said, the horse will still need some rest soon. Once we follow the Dusties for a good ways, there should be a river for us to stop and water the horse."

I was blessed to have someone like Art traveling with me, leading the way. I wouldn't know the first thing to do or the first place to go.

After another half-mile, we left the woods behind us and entered a clearing. The sun was high, and without the trees' protection, the heat beat oppressively upon our backs.

"Would you take a look at that!" Art pointed down to indents in the earth beneath us.

"What?" I asked, fanning myself. "What is it?"

"These marks were made by wagon wheels, and lots of 'em. Look!" He pointed further along, where the grassy field was parted by a small dirt road. "The Dusties." He smiled and gripped the reins tighter, with greater confidence than before, then coaxed the horse into a trot.

Berry bushes and great pines grew plentifully along the road's edges. A few miles on, the sound of a nearby river reached my ears, and the air felt cooler on my skin. The thought of water made my dry lips part in thirst, and I used my sleeve to wipe beads of sweat from my burning forehead.

We rounded a bend in the road and a cluster of mountains settled into view. Lustrous, white clouds hung closely around them.

A sweet-smelling river came up before us, cutting off the trail abruptly.

"The Connecticut River," Art said as he dismounted the horse. "She stretches a long ways. It's amazing, really." He reached his hand up to help me down, then led the horse towards the river.

The poor creature practically dropped from exhaustion as it lowered its face to the water to drink.

"Let's stop here for a while before we cross," Art called back to me.

"Cross!" I exclaimed. "Cross the river?" I walked to the water's edge, observing the rapid current and wondering at its depth.

"Well," said Art, "how else do you expect to get to the other side?" He looked confused.

"Isn't it dangerous? The water seems strong."

"Sure is, but we'll be real careful and cautious. My family did it once, and we lived to tell the tale." Art laughed and shook his head as he sprawled out on the grassy bank, the horse still taking its fill.

Even with Art's attempt at encouragement, I was still uneasy about crossing. But if I was ever to catch up with Bodaway, I couldn't just give up out of fear.

I sat in the grass with Art and looked up at the cerulean sky. Was Bodaway thinking about me? Would he be angry when he saw me?

*Well, if he sees me. If I ever find him.*

After we rested in the coolness of the river bank for about an hour, Art was ready to move on. The horse had replenished her strength. "I say we cross before the sun starts to set," said Art.

"Seems like a smart plan." I felt unnerved, but determined.

"The river shouldn't be deeper than your waist this time of year, but it's strong. I think it's best if you ride the horse and I lead."

I took another long, apprehensive look at the current as I mounted the horse. "I'm ready when you are."

"Alright," Art said, speaking to the horse. "Come on now." She had no desire to get into the water. Art removed his shirt and covered the horse's eyes. "Come on," he coaxed.

She finally took her first, hesitant steps into the water.

*This is really happening.*

We were moving across the river, slowly but surely.

"Good Lord!" called Art. "She's cold!"

I could feel the water splashing at my feet as we progressed. The far bank couldn't have been more than another twenty yards away by then. We were so close. The river was loud, making it difficult to hear Art, but he seemed to be only calming the horse.

If she spooked, I'd be subjected to the river's will, but there was no turning back by then. We'd already come so far that it would take just as long, if not longer, to turn around and cross back than to finish the stretch of water in front of us.

"Steady now," Art said, pulling us along.

I felt a swelling uncertainty in the horse's body. I'd been around horses long enough to decipher what they were feeling, and I knew what I was sensing now was not good. "Art!" I called, trying not to sound frantic. "She's getting anxious."

"You don't think I know that?" he called back to me in frustration.

The horse jumped a little, as though she'd lost her footing. Art's shirt fell from her head and was immediately swept away.

She kicked and jerked about, while I leaned forward and clasped my arms around her neck to steady myself.

"Whoa there, steady, whoa!" Art hauled with all his might to keep the horse from running wild. "You need to jump *now*!" Art screamed over the noise. "Jump!"

My heartbeat quickened and sounded in my eardrums. I didn't bother to look before I plunged into the waters.

A frigid embrace met me as I hit the bottom. Art was right, it didn't rise above my head, but the current was stronger than I had expected. I struggled to keep my head afloat, but the current pushed water into my mouth and up my nose. I grabbed at the rocks underwater with what little energy I had left, but they were slick with algae.

I caught a glimpse of our horse who had bolted to land, but there was no sign of Art.

Were my arms and legs still thrashing? I couldn't tell. I felt as though I were slipping away from reality and into some warm, distant place. It felt like a dream. I remembered when Bodaway and I took Grace in the river to wash her. Grace had been there for me to hold on to, to keep me steady. Now? I was alone, floundering. There was no horse; there was nothing.

*Fight.*

That's all my mind could think.

*Just fight a little longer.*

A strong arm wrapped around my waist and pulled me from the river.

Through my distorted view, I could see the man's familiar dark eyes. He clutched my face. "Come on," Bodaway's voice commanded. "Stay with me!"

My arms were too weak to wrap around him, my vision still clouded. *Was* I dreaming, or had I died in the river?

I felt even more distant than before, drifting further and further from reality until everything was dark.

# CHAPTER TWENTY-FIVE

### Bodaway

I carried Estella to the soft grass and set her down carefully.
Art had managed to pull himself and the horse out of the river and was coughing up water on the bank, but he wasn't my concern right now. Estella's face, once so full of color, was now a pale blue. It made my stomach sick.

I couldn't leave her. I'd never leave her again. She came for me, even though I'd abandoned her. I knelt by her delicate unconscious body and caressed her soaked hair.

"John!" Art called as he approached. "Is she alright?"

My stomach knotted again. "I don't know. She swallowed a lot of water." I stood. "Get some firewood, and tie Grace up before she makes a run for it. If you could."

I rubbed the fresh scrapes on the palms of my hands. I'd recklessly leapt from Grace's back at the sight of the commotion in the water, not worrying if she stayed or fled. Luckily, she seemed content enough to graze a while.

Art didn't protest. "Whatever I can do to help. You wouldn't mind lending me that coat you've got, would you?"

I realized for the first time that Art was shirtless. I shrugged the thin coat from my shoulders and tossed it to him.

"Thanks," He nodded and buttoned the coat over his chest.

"I'll stay here with Estella. She needs to dry out before night settles in."

Art wrung out his cap and set off to help.

"Bodaway!" came Abraham's voice. He rode quickly along the river's edge towards us. "What happened here?" he asked, pulling to a stop beside me.

"There's been a terrible accident." I shook my head. It was difficult to focus on anyone but Estella.

"It's a right good thing you were out here looking for my oxen. These folks might've drowned if it weren't for you."

"I know these people, actually. They're friends of mine." I still hovered over Estella's body, waiting for any sign of consciousness.

"You'd best bring her into camp. I'm sure Catherine can fix her up in no time."

"Camp is a good eight miles from here," I said. "She shouldn't travel in this condition. Not for that long." I rubbed my face. "I think it's best if I stay the night here with my friends. I'll meet you back at camp tomorrow. Sorry I wasn't able to recover your livestock."

"Don't worry about it. A couple of us'll keep on looking. You just keep an eye on the girl." Abraham turned his horse around. "God be with you, Bodaway."

The evening sun was still warm and dried us out quick enough.

I sat in the grass with Estella next to me when Art approached again. "I found this downstream a ways while I was gathering firewood," he said. Art slipped a brown satchel from his shoulder and tossed it to me: Estella's whole life packed into one bag.

He then dropped the small armload of wood beside me and offered a handful of berries. "Here, eat up."

"No thanks," I said. I took them, but set them aside for Estella, if she ever woke up.

Art watched me with a careful eye. "You really should eat something. You'll be no use to her if you're weak."

He might be right. I'd been functioning all day with nothing in me but a bit of stew from the night before. I could feel the sun making me weaker by the hour; eating some berries would hardly change anything. Still, I put a couple into my mouth.

Art smiled and took a seat next to me. "There you go." He slapped my back, then laughed and ate a few berries himself. "I've got a wise word now and again."

\*\*\*

It took only a few minutes for me to start a small fire.

Art sat across from me eating more berries.

I was thankful he'd accompanied Estella. I knew it wasn't an easy journey. "Thanks for coming all this way," I said, "despite the fact I never gave you a proper goodbye."

Art half-smiled. "I knew you would've wanted me to. And now I've stolen your coat, so consider us even." His look became sincere. "I'm awfully sorry about your brother, John. I know how hard it is to lose a loved one."

I nodded, feeling that empty pain again, but grateful for his words.

Hours passed and the moon shone above as the fire burned down to embers. Art finally dozed off into slumber, but I couldn't. Not with Estella still struggling to come to. She tossed a little and mumbled, but nothing more. I sat close to her and held her hands in mine.

Would God have me pull Estella from the river just for her to die? First Keme, and now Estella?

I looked up at the night sky and clenched my jaw. "God, please." I had to force myself to pray. "Please let her wake up. I can't lose another one. Not now, not ever. Thank you for allowing those stupid oxen to break loose, for allowing me to pull her from the river. But please, God, let it be Your will that she wakes up."

*I wasn't there for Keme,* I thought, *but I will be here for Estella. I will never abandon her.*

I sat back and sighed, the frustration weighing heavily on my chest.

Yet, I had a flicker of hope that God had heard my prayer.

# CHAPTER TWENTY-SIX

### Delta

What seemed like seconds must have been hours. My clothes were dry when I slowly gained sensation in my toes again. I wrinkled my nose and clenched my hands into fists. My mind was thick with some sort of haze, but I was coming out of it.

My eyelids fluttered but remained closed.

A warm hand took hold of mine and I heard a smooth voice I knew well.

"You know I'm not a sensitive person, and that I struggle to express how I'm feeling, but… I need you. I thought I could just leave you behind, that I could forget that you'd ever existed, but it would be impossible to forget someone like you. It wouldn't make a difference if I ran across the Earth and lived out my entire life alone. I'd never stop thinking of *you*. There hasn't been one *second* since I left that I stopped thinking of you."

My eyes opened. Bodaway was crouched beside me, watching me carefully. Firelight shone on him, illuminating bronze skin and the hair falling about his shoulders.

I tried to speak, but instead of my voice, water came rushing out.

I must have swallowed half of the river, because my clothes were wet again as I coughed up the last of what was in my stomach. I sat back up and stared into Bodaway's eyes. *This is not a dream,* I thought, my throat stinging.

"You don't have to say anything," said Bodaway. "You're safe now." He took me into his arms, disregarding my spit-up. His skin was warm on mine as he rested his face on my neck, caressing my hair. He was trembling.

I must have looked a terror, given the last day's events, but he didn't seem to notice. "I could've lost you completely," he said, voice distraught, but relieved. "You just rest now." His voice had become a whisper, and he pulled me close.

I felt whole and safe in his arms.

Then I remembered Art, and raised my head to search for him. Had he made it out of the river in time?

"Art's fine," Bodaway said softly, "and so is the horse. Try and take it easy. We can talk in the morning."

The warmth of security washed over me and I gave myself over to exhaustion.

I was with Bodaway. Nothing could separate us now.

\*\*\*

The sun woke me at first light, and I gasped with the fear that I had woken in my bed, that this had all been only a dream.

I sat up hastily. Coals from the fire slowly burned out while birds pecked the grass around me. I saw my satchel, dried out and in one piece.

It hadn't been a dream. Art was passed out across the fire from me, and Bodaway's figure walked along the river some distance away.

He hadn't been a dream either.

There was so much I wanted to share with Bodaway, so many things I needed to say. I stood up and nearly tumbled over, still weak and in dire need of some food. Carefully, I started again towards the river to meet him.

When I came upon him, I realized Bodaway was praying by the water. I couldn't help but see him as innocent and pure. His attitude resembled that of a child, hands clasped, eyebrows crowded together. It was as though he were praying for the first time.

Bodaway turned and noticed me. His stiff shoulders relaxed and he reached out his hand for me to join him.

A rush of anxiety coursed through me as I stared past him at the river. I could suddenly taste its bitter waters again.

But Bodaway was there, and I was safe with him.

I took his hand and he helped me down the river bank, where we sat side by side. He glanced at me. "I didn't want to wake you. I figured I'd let you rest and take some time to pray." He looked out at the water, but seemed as though he were seeing something more.

"Many things have passed these weeks." He raked a hand through his hair. "Things I could control, and things I couldn't. And I've been *so angry* at God for such a long time now. I didn't realize it until now, but I've been blaming God for everything that's gone awry in my life instead of taking responsibility.

"I'm my own man. I can be a *different* man than my father. And Keme..." His eyes glassed over. "Keme lives on in everything I do. I feel closest to him in the early mornings." He lifted his eyes to the sky. "He's in heaven now, I'm sure of it. God has shown me mercy and grace so many times, but I've never taken the time to acknowledge it... or even to want it, for that matter." He paused. "But you... I owe you an apology for leaving like I did. My judgment was misguided by grief, and anger, and I—"

I stopped him. "You do not need to apologize for anything. It was *my* fault. I should've trusted my own judgment long ago and called off the engagement."

"No," he said firmly. "No, it was wrong of me to demand that of you. I want you to know that you don't have to leave with me, even now. I'd never hold it against you if you chose your life at home over whatever I could offer you."

I studied Bodaway's face. He meant everything he said, though his eyes were still full of pain.

I leaned in and kissed him.

His arms wrapped tightly around me, a tender urgency behind his kiss. In that moment, I was his, and I hoped he would never let me go.

Bodaway pulled away and brushed a loose strand of hair behind my ear. He touched my face and stared into my eyes.

"I'll go anywhere you are," I said. "When I'm with you, I *am* home."

"What about your family?" He looked away and rubbed his neck. "Or Henry?"

"Things have changed since you left." I pulled my knees to my chest and listened to the birds singing around us. "My only family is Hannah. She's my natural mother. She gave birth to me."

Bodaway stared at me, evidently confused.

"It's a long story, but my true name is Delta. My father... He was an Indian."

"I wouldn't doubt it." He looked at me seriously, then smirked. "Delta. It feels right."

"It was always meant to be my name."

He hesitated. "But are you sure this is what *you* want?"

I shook my head. "For so long, I've never truly had a choice in anything. Everything was for the sake of family duty. Now I know that the idea of those duties being in my blood was always a deception. I had to leave, to get away from everything I thought I knew, and I've never felt more sure of myself in all my life.

"*I* chose to leave my family. *I* chose to leave my wedding and everything else behind, because I finally know who I'm not." I hesitated, scared to admit the full truth. "I'm... I'm not Delta without you."

Bodaway took my hands carefully in his. "You're sure you want this life?"

"I've placed all my bets on you," I said with a smile. "Where are we headed?"

He stood and lifted me into his arms, embracing me tightly. "Oregon Country," he whispered.

That was sure to be a long trip, but I didn't mind one bit. I could live anywhere with Bodaway.

His lips tightened suddenly into a flat line. "There's something else, actually..." He fumbled over his words but then spoke rapidly, pulling a hand away to rub his neck. "I was just thinking, given the new circumstances... I thought it would only be right if we were married."

I wrapped my arms around his neck. "Nothing would make me happier."

"I feel like I've loved you my whole life," he said softly, his mouth beside my ear.

That was the first time I'd heard those words from anyone.

He continued, caressing my hair. "You're my family now, and I'm going to take care of you. I'll work hard to give you the life you deserve."

This was my second engagement in one summer. It was how I'd always imagined my engagement would be. Well, perhaps not taking place on a river bank after nearly drowning, but it was *happy*. Bodaway might not have any money, but he made up for it with character.

Money didn't mean a thing to me anymore. Only Bodaway.

"I love you," I said, and meant it.

# CHAPTER TWENTY-SEVEN

## Bodaway

"We should head for camp," I said, "if we want to avoid traveling in the heat of the day."

"John," said Art, preparing their horse to ride again, "I reckon I won't be continuing on. I need to start back to Pinebrook and get this old girl back to Mary." He patted the horse's side.

"Oh Art, won't you come with us?" Delta asked. "We've come so far together, and you've been such a blessing to me."

Art squinted up at the sun and then back at us. "John's right. I'd best be headed out before the sun gets too high. I'm taking the long way around this time." He chuckled. "Not going to risk my life through that river again. I've got my sister to think about. We're all each other's got."

He smiled. "I wish you both nothing but happiness and a safe journey to Oregon Country." He took Delta's hands and kissed her cheek. "This is where my journey ends, but yours is just beginning."

Then he stepped aside, gave me a good slap on the back for old times' sake. He took my hand in his. "It's been a real pleasure knowing you," he said, mouth twitching into a smirk.

"You're a good man, Art. I'm glad to have known you."

He laughed and pulled away. "I'd better go before I get all soft." Then Art mounted his horse. The sun lit his red hair like fire.

Delta and I waved to our friend as he followed the river eastwards and out of sight. He was the last reminder of our old lives.

I held out my hand to help Delta mount Grace, knowing she'd still be weak from the incident, then mounted after her. "You strong enough to hold onto me?" I asked.

"I think so." She secured her arms around my waist, and then Grace was off. We followed the Dusties a ways, along an easy road that crossed mostly through fields with small streams passing through. The air smelled of sweet grass and damp earth. Free birds flew overhead in the morning sky.

Delta rested her cheek on my shoulder as we rode. When I had her, I felt like I had the entire world, like I was a rich man. I had nothing to offer her but myself, unlike Henry. He could've offered her all the jewels and finery that money could buy.

But she'd chosen me.

\*\*\*

An hour of comfortable silence later, we'd left the fields and entered the woods. The scenery reminded me of when I'd first realized how fast Grace could run in the old woods of Pinebrook.

I had no idea what Oregon Country would look like, but my mother and the families on the wagon train had talked about miles and miles of untouched land, free for any man to work. I wondered if there were woods in Oregon, or if it would look completely different from what we knew.

Then I wondered if I'd see my father there, and my jaw tightened. I had never forgiven him for leaving me and Keme to our own devices without a letter to be found. Did he know about Keme? Would I even recognize my own father if I saw him? It'd been years since he'd left.

"How far will the Dusties take us?" Delta asked, interrupting my train of thought.

I grunted. "I've heard they lead all the way to Missouri, where the wagon train departs. But the trail should lead us into camp very soon."

She rested her head on my shoulder, curls tumbling about, and her lips brushed against my neck.

It felt wrong to be alone with Delta, unmarried and all. Everything inside me wanted to hold her in my arms and never let her go. It was a very dangerous combination.

We continued through the woods for a few more miles, until the trees thinned out around the camp clearing.

"We're here," I said, full of relief. I hopped off the horse and helped Delta down, then passed through the cluster of covered wagons and campfires.

Children ran between us, playing games and yelling to one another. Women sat around us, baking, mending clothes, and packing up supplies for the next day's journey. The men spent the days hunting, fishing, and whatever else they needed to do in order to protect and provide for their growing, traveling families.

"Hey, it's Bodaway!" a friendly voice called from beside one campfire. It was Abraham, and he waved for us to join him. "The lady lives! Where's the boy?"

"Headed back home." I glanced at Delta and felt a smile on my lips. "But *she's* coming with us."

Catherine jumped up. "Oh, this is wonderful news! We were so worried about you last night I could barely sleep! I kept thinking about the poor girl." She advanced and took Delta's hands sweetly. "Abe told me about your trial at the river. I prayed for you something fierce."

Delta lowered her eyes. "God spared my life. I'm just grateful that Bodaway was there."

"A godsend, I know! Oh, you must both be starving!"

"Yes," I said, "it's been a long day." I cleared my throat. "Abraham, Catherine, this is Delta."

"Here you go, Delta." Catherine handed her a small bowl of stew, and then me. It definitely wouldn't be what Delta was used to, but you'd never know it from the way she ate.

Delta and Catherine talked a ways away, leaving Abraham and me to make our own conversation. I had a favor to ask, and hoped he could help me. "Look, Abraham, I intend to marry Delta, and I was wondering if she could stay with you two—for the next night or so—until we can find a preacher?"

Abraham smiled and gave me a rough pat on the back, nearly knocking the stew from my hands. "There you go! That's a right honorable request." He burped and then slopped some more stew into his bowl. "You know, there's a preacher on the wagon train. Old Pastor Daniel. He'd be willing to marry you, I'm sure of it. Why, just last week he married a couple that's traveling with us now."

"Really?" I was surprised. "Where can I find him?"

"Don't you worry about the details. Catherine and I will take care of all the nonsense. And we'd be happy to have Delta stay with us for a night or so."

It amazed me how I'd found so much kindness from this couple in such a short time. I'd never been a social person, but for the first time I looked forward to knowing these people better. Maybe we'd be neighbors in the future, once things were settled.

I stretched out my hand and firmly shook his. "Thank you, Abraham."

***

I spent the afternoon helping Abraham and a few other men hunt and gather enough food to feed the livestock for the next few days of traveling. When Abe and I returned to camp that night, I found Delta helping Catherine wash and pack away pots and pans. I watched her work in the orange firelight, sitting on a log and drying dishes with a rag.

Delta was focused. It hadn't taken her long to jump in and help where she was needed.

Abe walked past me, two fat rabbits slung over his shoulder. "I come bearing gifts!" he said with a smile at his wife. She looked equally as tired as he, but was clearly relieved to see dinner for the night.

Delta looked up from her work as I approached.

"I didn't mean to interrupt," I said, and sat beside her.

She tossed the rag aside and smoothed her hair, which had been loosely tied back with a light blue ribbon. "You're a most welcome distraction," she reassured me.

I looked away, picking at the calluses on my palms. Seeing Delta again overwhelmed me with the thought of losing her. Even letting her out of my sight for a moment made my heart race.

"What is it?" She reached out and took my hands in hers.

"I talked to Abe today. He agreed to let you stay with him and Catherine tonight, until the wedding, if that's alright with you. It shouldn't be much longer. There's a preacher here on the train." I squeezed her hand. "Abe said he'd take care of the details."

Firelight reflected in Delta's eyes as she stared back at me. It was hard to believe she wanted to marry me. "So the wedding will be tomorrow?"

"If the preacher can marry us tomorrow, yes. That is, if you still *want* to marry me." I smiled, but a part of me was terrified she'd changed her mind.

She grabbed my hand tighter. "Perfect, then, it's settled."

I'd always struggled to imagine myself taking a wife and having a family of my own, but now I couldn't picture my life, my future, without Delta. She completed it.

I leaned over and kissed her forehead. "Sleep well, then. I'll see you tomorrow."

She seemed confused. "What about dinner?"

"Don't worry about me," I said with a smile. "I've got to feed Grace and make my own camp for the night."

"Fine, but if you leave now, you can't come back. We absolutely *cannot* see each other until the wedding tomorrow." She laughed. "It's bad luck!"

I laughed. "Good night." It pained me to let her out of my sight. I wanted to be there for her, to protect her, but this choice was good and right. Delta would be fine for the night.

I made my way through hanging garments and smoldering campfires on my way towards the small brook where I'd tied Grace. As I pushed a linen shirt out of my way, I found an old woman hunched over a wide, hand-woven basket. The campfire lit up her wrinkles, making her face seem ancient.

The woman's hooded eyes narrowed. "Kwaï," she said, greeting me in my native tongue.

"Kwaï," I responded. "I didn't mean to trespass through your camp."

"It must have been meant to be." She smiled and motioned for me to sit. "Now, tell me, what is your name?"

"Bodaway," I said, and lowered myself to the ground. This woman had piqued my curiosity.

"Bodaway?" She squinted at me. "Where does that name come from?"

"My mother is Navajo. The name comes from her culture, but my father is Abanaki."

"Very interesting." She smiled again. "I knew you were Abanaki, but the name did not fit." She brought a decrepit finger to her temple. "You see, I have the gift of knowing."

She'd lived her life in the old ways, no doubt. "And your name?" I asked.

"They call me Chepi. It is not often that I come across others like us among the white folks here."

I smiled at her. In a way, I felt like I'd met her before. "Well, Chepi, I could say the same to you."

She chuckled. "What brings you here in these parts?"

"I'm following the wagon train out West. Ever since I was a child, my mother and father talked about the untouched land where the Navajo people are from. They talked of how we could live like we used to."

"It is true, what you've heard. You are meeting your mother and your father?"

"Not exactly." I paused. "You're also headed West?"

"No, I am visiting small towns in Vermont. Ascutney, Windsor, Weathersfield. All very kind to our folk. I do good business in those parts." Chepi motioned to her basket of skins, furs and what seemed to be wood carvings. "Then I head back North. The train doesn't stop in these little towns, but I know my way around." She wiped the moist corners of her mouth. "But you didn't really come here to listen to me yammering on and on. Are you a customer?"

"No, I was just passing through. I need to make camp for the night."

Chepi closed her heavy lids. "There are no accidents. You were brought here for a purpose." She opened her eyes. "You have a glow about your face, and it is not solely one of youth. I can feel love radiating from your being."

Was it really that obvious that love had turned me stupid?

"What is her name?" Chepi asked.

"Delta," I told her without hesitation.

"That is a good name." Chepi lifted her basket of mysterious things. "I believe I have something for you." She fished around in the basket and pulled out a tiny deerskin satchel, which she set gently in my hands.

I pulled open its tassels and found a golden band within, fashioned like a vine with beautiful turquoise glass in its center. It was perfect for Delta.

"This is beautiful," I said with wonder, tracing the ring with my finger. "Where did it come from?"

Chepi set her basket aside. "I made that one. There isn't much more an old woman like myself can do these days. You said her name—Delta!—and I knew what to choose." She pointed at the turquoise glass. "This stone came from the coast of Maine. Lost, broken glass, tumbling about on the seafloor. The sand refined and smoothed its imperfections and jagged edges until it washed up right where it belonged, new and beautiful. I found it along the shoals, gleaming in the sun. It was a chosen piece. It is special."

I studied the ring. It *was* something special. "How much?" I asked, certain I couldn't afford it.

Chepi reached out and closed my fingers over the ring. "It's Delta's," she said, and looked me in the eyes. "It has *always* been Delta's."

Tears pricked my eyes and I cleared my throat. "Wliwni," I said in our tongue, thanking her.

She smiled warmly as I stood. "I'm glad you stopped by," she said. "Do not forget your roots, Bodaway."

I nodded gratefully as I left. Chepi's kindness wouldn't be forgotten.

I began my way towards Grace once more and didn't stop until I reached her. She was tied to a tree with the other tired horses, right where I'd left her. "Socializing?" I asked.

Grace's tail flitted about as I petted her nose.

I rested against the huge pine she was tied to and looked up at the stars. My stomach turned as I thought of Keme.

I wished with all my heart that he could be there with me. I wished that I could have been there for *him* when he needed me.

*God, what was the purpose of his passing so soon?*

I clenched my teeth, then took the fullest breath of air I could manage. I knew I had to reconcile myself with the past. Even if I'd been there for Keme, there was nothing I could've done to save him.

I tried not to think about how our father hadn't been there, either.

I looked at the ring again. The thought of giving it to Delta made me nervous. It was, well, *unique*. I worried she wouldn't appreciate its simplicity, being used to finer things like amethyst and pearls.

Well, tomorrow was the beginning of a new journey. A fresh start where everyone we met would know us as one.

I shifted off the tree and onto the grassy floor, then tried to close my eyes. Dreams of new beginnings and happy endings—and maybe just plain exhaustion—drifted me off to sleep.

***

"Estella!"

My eyes shot open.

Someone was calling out, "Estella! Estella!" over and over.

I stood and attempted to regain my sense of direction. I had to find Delta before "they" did, whoever "they" were.

That screeching voice pierced the night just as it had the floor of the busy mill.

It was Henry, and he'd come for his runaway bride.

The camp was waking up around me in panic, and nobody had any idea what was happening. Lanterns lit the wagons and men appeared with drawn pistols while the women and children stayed safely inside.

All the while, I ran through camp, my eyes scanning every inch for Delta.

Henry stood beside his horse in the center of the wagon circle, and the men from the train surrounded him in a cluster. Seeing them, I joined the back of the crowd.

I couldn't see Delta, but that meant she was safe. I sighed with relief.

Henry sneered at the men surrounding him. "I'm looking for my fiancée, you see. I've been riding all day and night to find her." He brushed away a lock of blond hair that had fallen over his eyes. "Her family sent me to bring her home where she belongs! We've all been worried sick."

Henry raised a handful of cash. "Have any of you gentlemen seen her? Wild dark hair; beautiful, blue eyes." He fumbled in his coat pocket and retrieved a small photograph of Delta.

I noticed all the men's eyes shifting from one to another. No one spoke up. No one *gave* us up. Why? Why would these people protect us? I found Abraham and met his stare, silently pleading with him not to say a word. I was sure he wouldn't.

Henry seemed to grow anxious. "Come on, now. Anyone?" He stared into one man's eyes so harshly that I feared he might give us up.

Abraham pushed his way to the front of the crowd, lantern in hand. "Alright, that's enough! None of us here have seen your fiancée. I'm sorry."

The stillness of night closed in around us as Henry shifted his glare to Abraham. "A shame, really," he said at last. Henry tucked the cash back into his coat and ran his hands through his hair.

Abe stiffened. "Now, after all this commotion you've caused—" He gestured to the crowd and the flickering wagon lights. "—I think it's best you leave."

Henry smirked, nodding as he stared at the ground. "Yes, I plan to leave very soon. Only, I have it on good authority that my fiancée *was* headed here. I think it's time that one of you fine gentlemen start talking." He cleared his throat. "Before I resort to certain *undesirable* means of persuasion." He tapped his side, hinting at what was hidden beneath his coat.

The men raised their own guns in response, but otherwise, nobody moved.

"I see," Henry said with a sigh.

He shook his head, and pulled a gleaming pistol from his coat.

The men began to speak, but a high voice broke through it all. "Henry, stop it! For heaven's sake, stop threatening these kind people!"

The men parted, their faces shocked, to allow Delta through. She walked out to meet Henry in a white nightgown and her hair in a loose braid.

Henry's eyes doubled in size, as if he'd seen a ghost. He ran to meet her.

"Estella! Are you OK?" He placed his hands on her shoulders, and everything inside me screamed to tear his head off. But instead, I controlled myself and only watched as she removed his hands from her body.

"Delta," she corrected. "My name is Delta."

He seemed confused. "You really *have* gone mad, haven't you?" He stared at her even more intently.

Delta shook her head. "How did you find me?"

"The moment your family learned of your disappearance, they posted a reward to anyone with information on your whereabouts. Luckily, a mill worker overheard a conversation containing very, very valuable information."

I silently scoffed as I realized the truth. One of my former roommates must have overheard Art talking and betrayed me. I gritted my teeth together, wishing I could get my hands around the man's neck, but Delta and Henry quickly drew my attention back.

"Henry," said Delta, "you need to leave." She crossed her arms and glanced behind herself, as though to remind Henry of all the people from the wagon train.

"Listen!" snapped Henry. "Your family is completely distraught over you. They sent over thirty men, all under my charge, to find you. We made camp about two miles from here, but I've been restless since your disappearance. I just couldn't sit back and waste a single moment of precious time that could otherwise be spent searching for you." He reached out to touch her hand. "Just... come home. It's not too late."

Delta flinched again as he touched her.

My stomach knotted and the rage built further within my chest. How much longer would I stand here in the shadows? I was dangerously close to going wild on Henry. It wouldn't be the first time.

"There is nothing you can say," continued Delta, "to make me go back with you. My family doesn't care a bit about me. They're likely overcome with shame that their daughter's run away and broken off her grand engagement." She paused, seeming to think of something, then continued. "We would be miserable, you know. You can deceive yourself, but you've not proved yourself an honorable man to me—or to anyone for that matter, and I will not be deceived or convinced otherwise."

Henry looked away as though she'd wounded him. "I know I'm not the best of men, but I *do* love you, whether you can believe that or not. Look, I can take you back right now! We could forget all this nonsense if you had any respect for your family or for mine!"

I audibly scoffed, and I flexed my hands into fists. He had the nerve to put that burden on Delta. It hardly surprised me.

Henry continued. "You want adventure? Let's get out of here! I can take you anywhere you want to go. Just come away with me and leave this all behind." He ignored the way Delta pulled back and reached out to clutch her arms.

That was enough.

I pushed myself to the front of the crowd, revealing my presence in the lantern light. "I think you'd best be on your way," I said.

Henry's mouth fairly dropped open. *"You?"* He spat in disbelief. "The savage from the mills? The racehorse boy?" He looked to Delta—then shook his head. He tore his cravat loose, threw his jacket to the ground, and lunged at me.

I welcomed his punch, taking the blow right to my face, stumbling back.

The men from the wagon train raised their guns once more, but I shouted, "No! Leave him for me!"

Out of the corners of my eyes I noticed the men circling closer, but they respected my wishes.

Delta screamed, but the only thing on my mind was beating the stuffing out of Henry Hamilton. I swung a right hook that landed on his mouth, the force if it knocked him backwards. My heart raced at his warm blood dripping over my knuckles. Henry picked himself up from the grass and growled as he tackled me to the ground. We traded blows. It was hard to tell which of us was the main source of the fresh blood staining our hands.

"Stop this!" Delta screamed. "Stop fighting!"

I sat up, clutching Henry by the shirt, and locked eyes with Delta. "Please," she begged.

No. He'd gone too far. This would be the last time we'd cross paths; I'd make sure of it.

I threw Henry to the dirt with all my might and picked myself up from the ground, only barely realizing I was covered in blood.

The wagon train men didn't seem fazed in the slightest.

Delta and Abe rushed to my side. "Are you alright?" asked Delta, taking me by the shoulders. "That was a stupid thing to do." "You should take a rest," said Abe.

By now, Henry had managed to pull himself up with the help of his horse. He straightened his collar and pointed a bloody finger at

Delta. "You're making a huge mistake! I hope you know that. You're an imbecile if you believe this will make you happy."

Delta seemed as if she wanted to say something more, but remained silent.

Henry wiped his mouth and tried to mount his horse.

"Wait!" Delta blurted at last and then *approached* him. "Henry, I want to speak with you alone."

I stepped close to her and snatched her wrist. "Are you *stupid?*"

She shot me a strained look. "I'll be fine."

"You don't owe him a thing."

"Bodaway, I need to do this." She pulled her wrist from my grasp and I let her go. Henry seemed pleased.

I was trying to protect her. Didn't she know that? My jaw clenched and I stood firmly in my place. I wasn't letting her out of my sight.

\*\*\*

### Delta

Abe motioned for most folks to return to their wagons, but kept a few of the men awake to stand guard. I was mortified, my cheeks burning at the commotion. This was all my fault.

"Unless you've come to your senses," said Henry, "what more could you possibly have to say to me, Estella?" He shook his head.

"That's just it. My name's not Estella."

Crickets filled the empty air while Henry looked at me like I was a lunatic. "What are you talking about?"

"My name was always meant to be Delta. Hannah, our family's house maid... She's my natural mother. Delta's the name she picked out for me from the beginning."

"What? Honestly, Estella, of all the silly excuses you could make not to marry me—"

"I'm being perfectly serious."

He squinted. "But... that would mean that you aren't a blood Wellstone at all."

I crossed my arms over my white nightgown. It was spotted with blood from when I had run to Bodaway. "No. I'm not."

Henry rubbed his face and laughed. There wasn't any humor to it. "My mother would never allow the marriage if she knew this. Of course, nobody has to find out."

"What about the things I know about *you* and *your* family? Henry, I know you're the father to Lillian's baby. I know how you refused to make her an honest woman. I *know* that your mother poisoned Lillian in hopes your child would die. I'll never forget that, not ever."

He seemed... pained. For a moment, Henry looked into my eyes with true and rare sincerity. For a moment, aside from all the blood on his clothes, Henry looked completely normal and rational. He looked so exhausted, and the sight reminded me I wasn't completely guiltless regarding the shame I'd caused our families.

I actually *pitied* Henry Hamilton. He didn't have an escape like I did. Henry belonged to that world, and it to him. He'd been sucked in so deeply by the responsibilities, the money, the pressure, and the prestige, that it had turned him mad. Perhaps the same could be said about me.

But in the end, he'd crossed a line by showing up here and starting a fight in the middle of the night. Moreover, facing the truth of his decisions, he couldn't bring himself to address them. "Look," he said at last, "your father... Irving... he made it very clear I was to bring you home. I should take you against your will if I have to."

I looked at Henry without anger. "Go home," I said. "For the first time in my life, I feel like there is some place I belong. A place where I can fully be myself."

I shifted my gaze to Bodaway and met his unflinching eyes. "I'm not going back with you," I continued to Henry. "I really am sorry that I could never love you the way you wanted me to. It's time we forget about all this. There must be something good in your heart, something that wants the same things *I* want. To be loved, to belong. There's no shame in that. I've made my decision, and you've made yours."

Henry seemed somber, as though he was, for the first time, truly taking in the weight of my words.

Bodaway still watched our every move.

Finally, Henry sighed and picked up his coat from the ground. He dusted it off and slipped his arms through. "What should I tell our folks," he asked, "when I show up without you? Even if I don't present you to them, they may still come for you."

I smiled. "This is your chance to do right by me, Henry. Tell them you never found me. That will give me enough of a head start to find my new life."

Henry shook his head. "I sure hope you never wake up one day to regret this."

I reached out and touched his arm. "Go home. Don't compromise yourself to be a man who makes your family proud anymore. Be a man who can stand confidently before God one day."

He gave me a half smile. "I'll do you this one favor, but then it's out of my hands. This is goodbye."

"I am grateful to you, Henry," I said softly. "Indeed, goodbye."

Henry gave one last glare to Bodaway before snapping his reins. I stood silently in my nightgown and watched him ride out of sight.

# CHAPTER TWENTY-EIGHT

### Bodaway

My whole body rippled with anger. I imagined my skin hot to the touch as Henry rode away. Why would Delta put herself in such danger after I specifically told her *not* to go near him? That poor excuse for a man wasn't to be trusted. I knew Delta was impulsive, but this felt like blatant disrespect.

I stared at Delta as she stood and watched Henry leave, doubt filled my head. Maybe we were rushing into things. Was Delta just being impulsive with me? Would she grow bored of me in time?

She seemed subdued as she stood there, arms wrapped around herself. Her dark hair was completely awry, and her eyes drooped from exhaustion.

Abe still stood close to me, and rested a hand on my shoulder. "Hey there, you don't look so good." I looked down at my shirt, the red speckles of Henry and my blood covering its front.

Delta finally rejoined us. "You're a mess," she agreed, then lifted the hem of her skirts and tore a piece of fabric.

I took it, wiped my hands, and then pressed the cloth to my split lip. "Why would you do that?" I asked.

"What are you talking about?"

I winced in pain, pressing the cloth to another tender cut. "You left with Henry after I told you not to."

"I needed a clear conscience."

I shook my head. "It doesn't matter. Henry wasn't in his right mind, Delta. He's dangerous." I gestured toward the wagons aglow in the middle of the night.

Delta's blue eyes seemed sincere. "I left everything I knew behind for a chance at a new beginning with you. That's something we'll never truly have if the ghosts of my past keep haunting me."

"No, Delta, what *you* need to understand is that I told you not to go for *your* protection, not to keep you from happiness or a clean conscience or whatever reason you justified talking with that ratbag." I wiped my face in frustration.

"You always tell me to make decisions for myself, that I'm my own person!"

"You *should* make decisions. All I am saying is, when I tell you something, it's for your own good. It's a far cry from you being a puppet on a string."

Abe put his hands in the air. "I should probably leave you both to it. Lovers' quarrels are not my strong suit." He chuckled and tried to back away.

Delta shot him a frustrated look. "Forgive me, Abraham. This whole thing is my fault. We're finished arguing, right? Nothing happened with Henry."

"You're *lucky* nothing happened," I muttered, then reached out and took her hands. "I couldn't live with myself if something happened to you that I could've stopped."

She looked into my eyes. "Nothing will happen to me. I know I'm safe with you."

I nodded with a sigh, trying to at least keep up the illusion of safety and security.

I knew in my heart that life is uncontrollable, but the one thing I could control was the path ahead of me, the steps I would take along that path.

Delta and I would have each other throughout all of life's uncertainty. We would face those unknowns with strength, with determination. We'd face them hand in hand.

\*\*\*

## *Tuesday, August 1st*

The morning finally came. I'd hardly slept since the night's disruption, but the sun shone bright and promising.

Today was my wedding day, and everything seemed to be working out for our good. Yet, there was a part of me that feared what might happen when Henry returned to Pinebrook empty-handed.

Delta and I had each other. That was the most important thing. We could face any obstacle, any trial, side by side.

I leaned against an oak near the horses and reached into my pocket for the ring.

My fingers stumbled over something I'd forgotten about completely. I pulled it free to look at it in the sunlight.

Keme's stone.

I'd never had the chance to give it to him.

Its flecks of minerals sparkled in the sun; its surface felt cool beneath my fingers.

Something special happened then.

I didn't feel guilt, and I didnt feel anger. I only felt love, and loss. I loved Keme. Losing him was the hardest thing I'd ever experienced.

Yet, I smiled.

I looked out over the land before me, across the green grass and the morning haze. It made me optimistic for the future, for the life God had set before Delta and me.

My gaze, still scanning the surroundings, noticed movement just upon the horizon.

I squinted to focus on the silhouette of a majestic horse and rider swiftly approaching.

I took a few paces from the tree, ready to stand my ground. Could this be another attempt to bring Delta back home and "to her senses?" The rider came closer and closer, but the early morning haze made it hard to discern details.

Then sunbeams pierced the haze, lighting up a familiar face.

"It can't be," I whispered, my knees weakening.

It wasn't Henry, nor any other member of Delta's family.

My lips parted as my eyes tried to make sense of the man approaching me. Broad shoulders and long raven hair, identical to my own.

It was my father.

Made in the USA
Middletown, DE
03 July 2024

56771562R00222